KID BEOWULF

and the Blood-Bound Oath
the

story and art by
Alexis E. Fajardo

Portland, OR

Kid Beowulf © 2008 Alexis E. Fajardo

ISBN: 978-0-9801419-1-7

Bowler Hat Comics is an imprint of
Ink & Paper Group, LLC.

First Edition
July 2008
10 9 8 7 6 5 4 3 2 1

A BOWLER HAT GRAPHIC NOVEL

STORY & ART by ALEXIS E. FAJARDO
COVER & PROLOGUE COLORS by BRIAN KOLM

EDITOR IN CHIEF	Linda Meyer
ASSOCIATE EDITOR	Garrett Howard
DIRECTOR OF MARKETING	Allison Collins
PUBLICIST	Emily Reis
MANAGER OF MISC. WONDERS	Jen Weaver-Neist
PUBLISHER	Bo Björn Johnson
CEO	Cameron Marschall
SPECIAL THANKS	Cassie Richoux
	Chris Huff
	Betsy Strobel
	John Peetz

Book design by Alan Dubinsky

Printed in Canada

Bowler Hat Comics
1825 SE 7th Ave
Portland, OR 97214
www.bowlerhatcomics.com
www.kidbeowulf.com

for my Grandfather

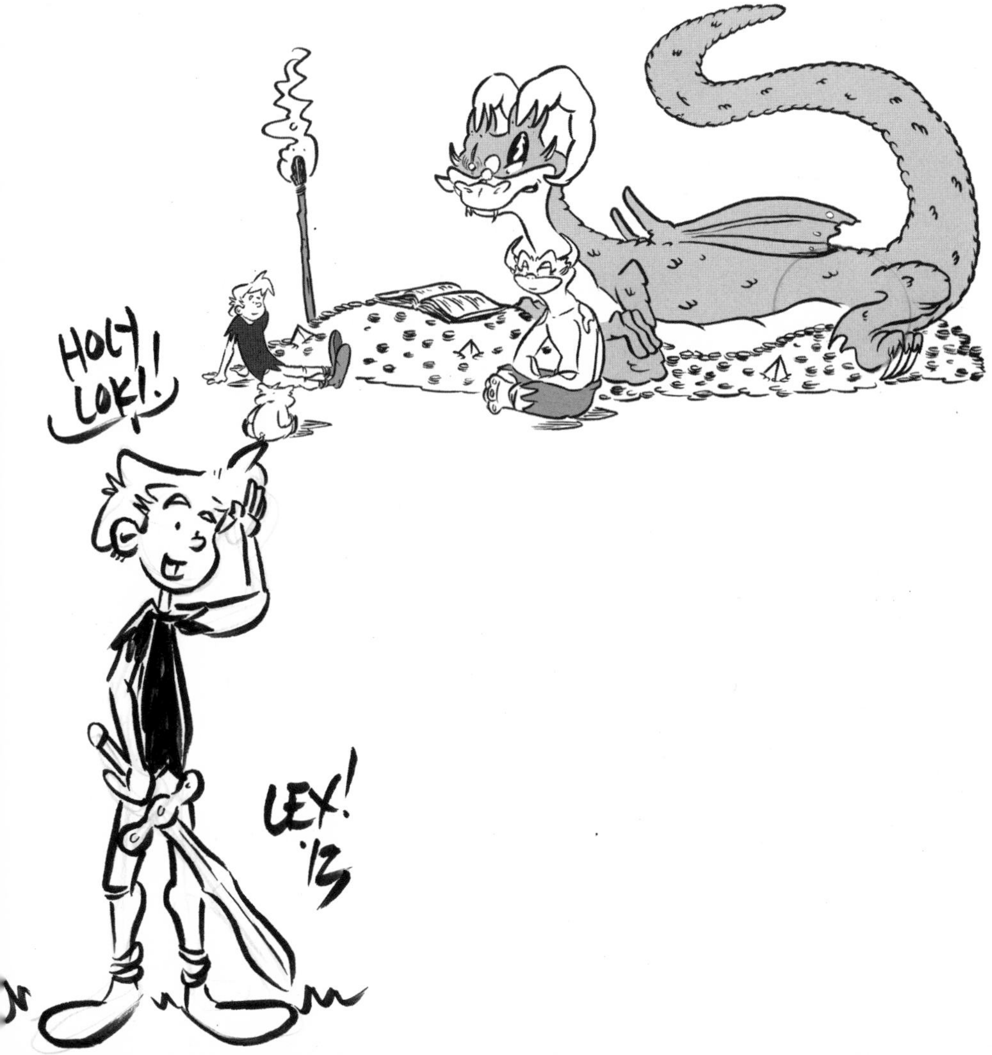
HOLY LOKI!
LEX! '13

Dramatis Personae

Pronunciation and spelling of names can vary widely with each translation. The names used here are either the most common or the most easily pronounced. For accurate and definitive name usage, I suggest a degree in Olde English.

The **Danes** are the indigenous people of **Daneland** and its ruling clan. Their home, ruled by **King Shild,** is nestled between tall cliffs off the sea-coast. Shild's sons **Hrothgar** and **Ogier** are often found exploring their homeland with their Great Dane **Wulf.**

Shild

Hrothgar
(roth-gar)

Ogier
(oh-jee-ay)

Dagref
(day-grif)

Froda
(froh-da)

Yrs
(yers)

Wulf

Ingeld

Hrethel
(reth-el)

Higlac
(hig-lak)

Edgetho
(ej-thoh)

The **Heathobards** are a migratory people from **Germania.** Led by **Dagref,** they have fought many battles in order to call Daneland their home. Dagref's son **Froda** will one day be their chief. **Yrs** and her father **Ingeld** are the newest Heathobard immigrants to settle in Daneland.

The **Geats** are a northern tribe from across the sea in **Geatland.** Longtime friends and allies of the Danes, they are led by **Hrethel. Higlac** is Hrethel's birth son. Higlac's best friend **Edgetho** was adopted at an early age by Hrethel when Edgetho's parents were killed in a sea-raid.

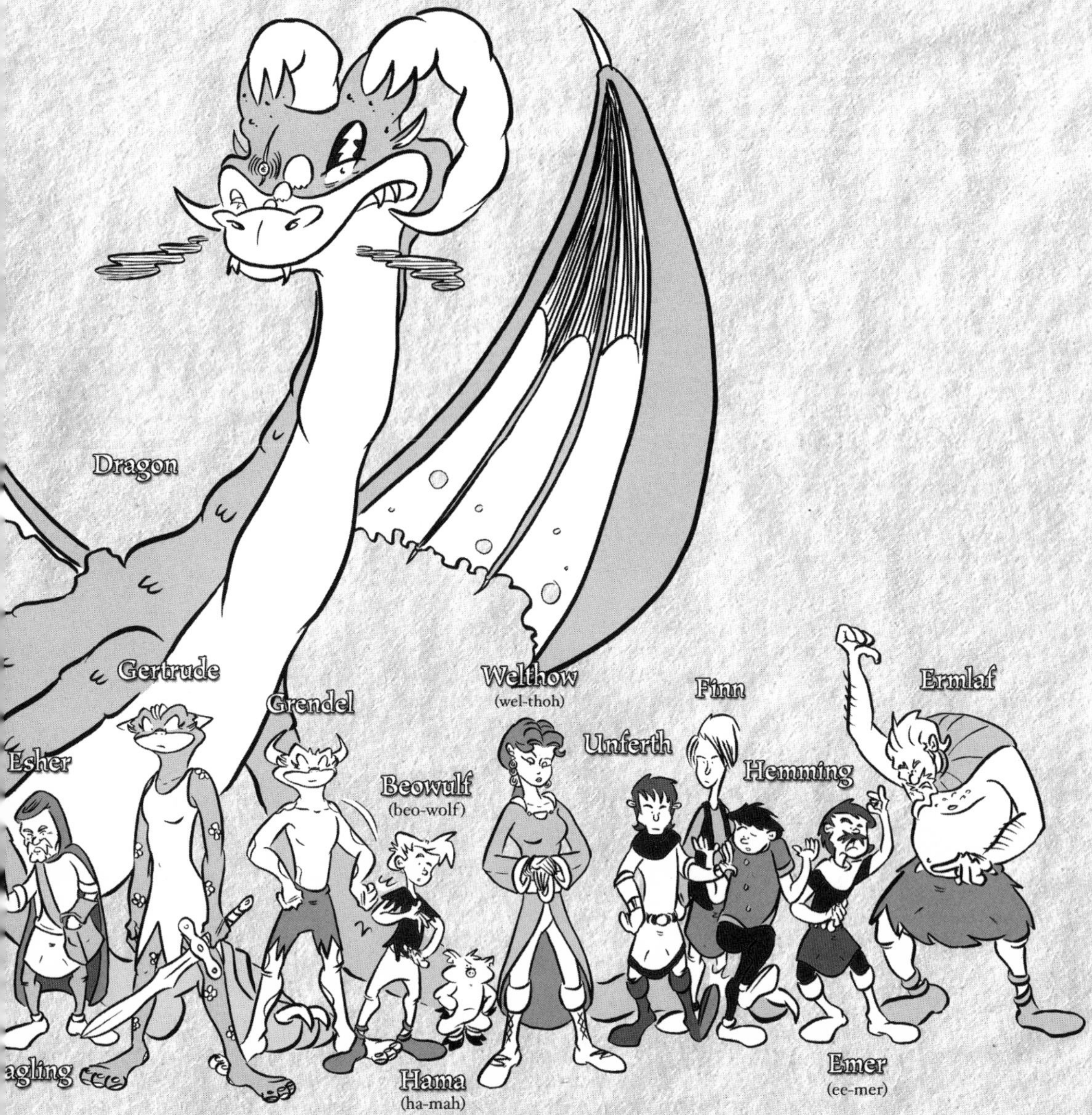
Dragon
Gertrude
Grendel
Esher
Beowulf
(beo-wolf)
Welthow
(wel-thoh)
Unferth
Finn
Hemming
Ermlaf
agling
Hama
(ha-mah)
Emer
(ee-mer)

The **Dragon** is the oldest living creature in all of Daneland. He resides deep below the **mere,** but knows of everything that happens above ground. The Dragon's only companions are a hoard of gold and the ancient speaking sword, **Nagling.**

Neither Dane nor Geat, but friend to both, **Esher** was present at **Gertrude's** birth. He was also present at the birth of twin brothers, **Grendel** and **Beowulf; Hama** the pig, was not.

Welthow is Hrothgar's future wife and queen of Daneland. Among her subjects are the wily boys **Unferth, Finn,** and **Hemming.**

Emer and **Ermlaf** are Heathobards; they are neither boys nor wily.

prologue

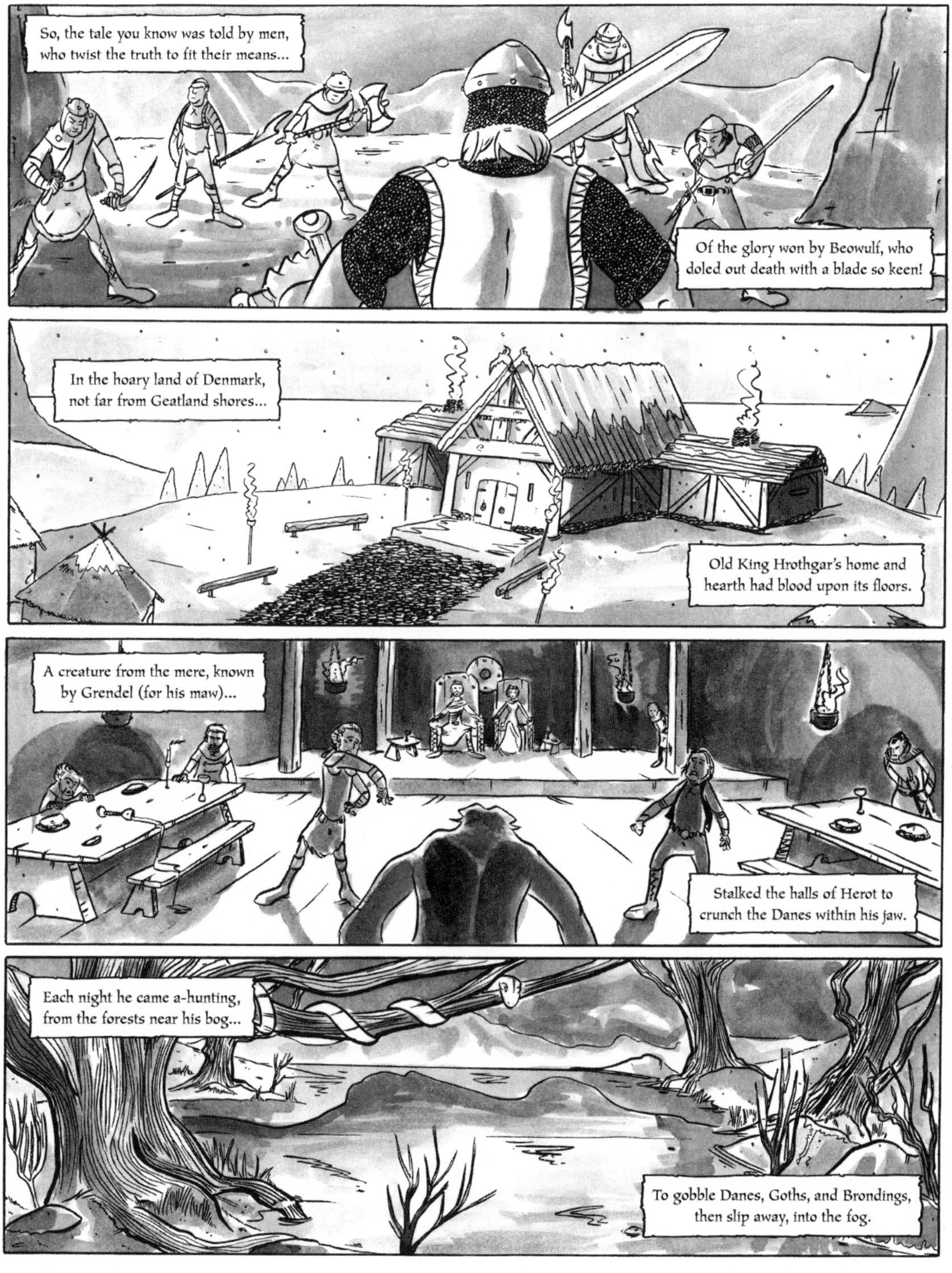
So, the tale you know was told by men, who twist the truth to fit their means...
Of the glory won by Beowulf, who doled out death with a blade so keen!
In the hoary land of Denmark, not far from Geatland shores...
Old King Hrothgar's home and hearth had blood upon its floors.
A creature from the mere, known by Grendel (for his maw)...
Stalked the halls of Herot to crunch the Danes within his jaw.
Each night he came a-hunting, from the forests near his bog...
To gobble Danes, Goths, and Brondings, then slip away, into the fog.

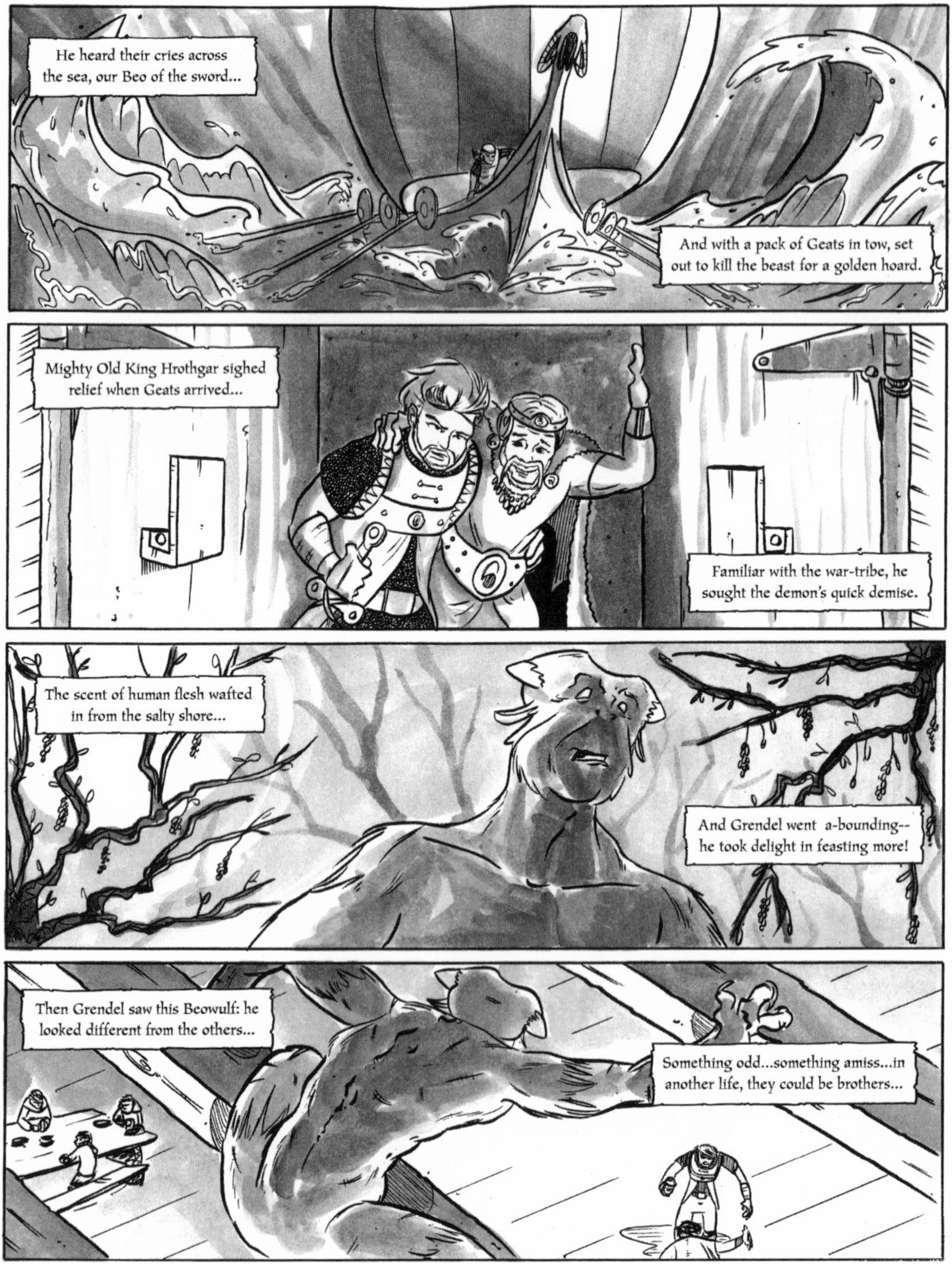
He heard their cries across the sea, our Beo of the sword...
And with a pack of Geats in tow, set out to kill the beast for a golden hoard.
Mighty Old King Hrothgar sighed relief when Geats arrived...
Familiar with the war-tribe, he sought the demon's quick demise.
The scent of human flesh wafted in from the salty shore...
And Grendel went a-bounding-- he took delight in feasting more!
Then Grendel saw this Beowulf: he looked different from the others...
Something odd...something amiss...in another life, they could be brothers...

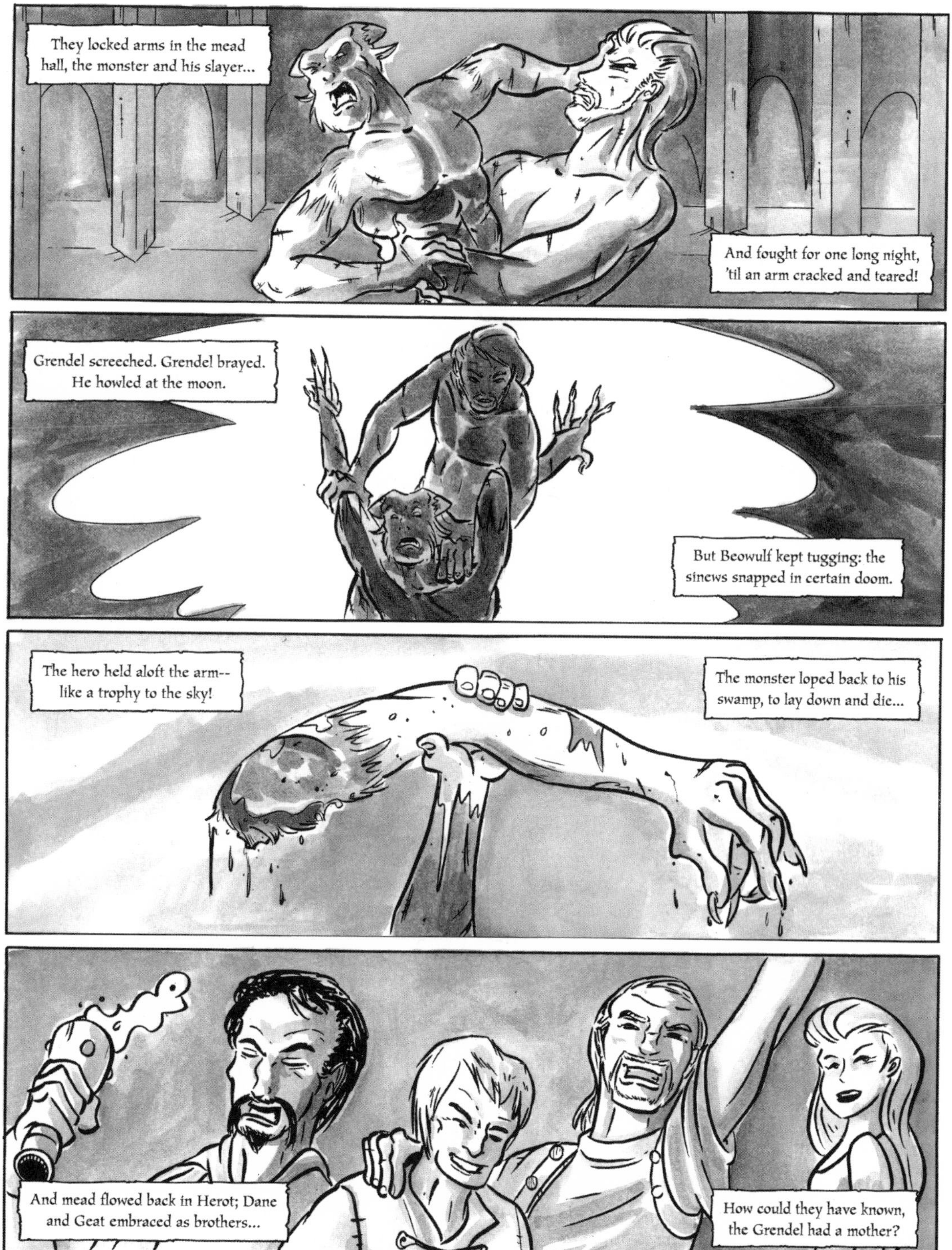
They locked arms in the mead hall, the monster and his slayer...
And fought for one long night, 'til an arm cracked and teared!
Grendel screeched. Grendel brayed. He howled at the moon.
But Beowulf kept tugging: the sinews snapped in certain doom.
The hero held aloft the arm-- like a trophy to the sky!
The monster loped back to his swamp, to lay down and die...
And mead flowed back in Herot; Dane and Geat embraced as brothers...
How could they have known, the Grendel had a mother?

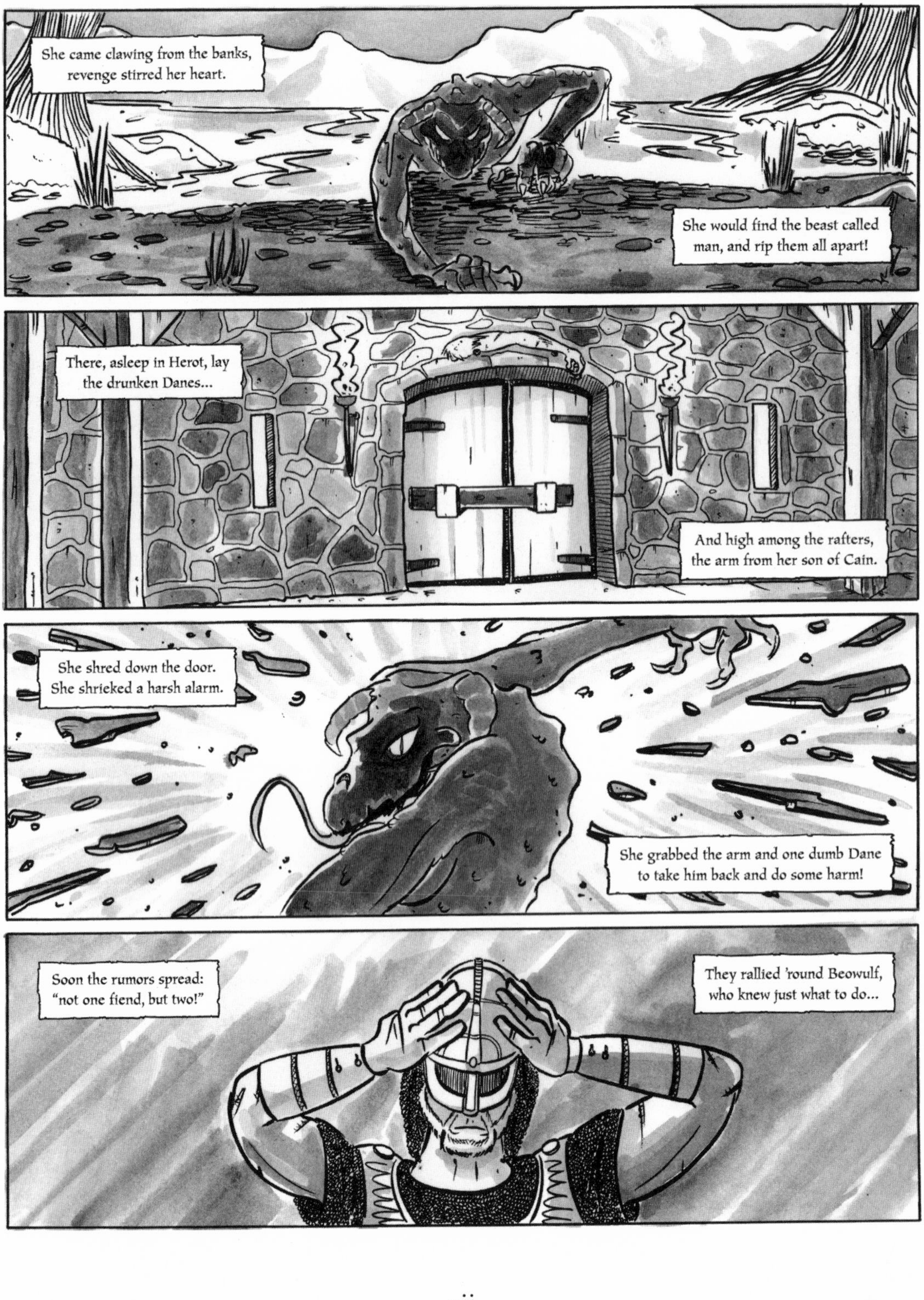
She came clawing from the banks,
revenge stirred her heart.
She would find the beast called
man, and rip them all apart!
There, asleep in Herot, lay
the drunken Danes...
And high among the rafters,
the arm from her son of Cain.
She shred down the door.
She shrieked a harsh alarm.
She grabbed the arm and one dumb Dane
to take him back and do some harm!
Soon the rumors spread:
"not one fiend, but two!"
They rallied 'round Beowulf,
who knew just what to do...

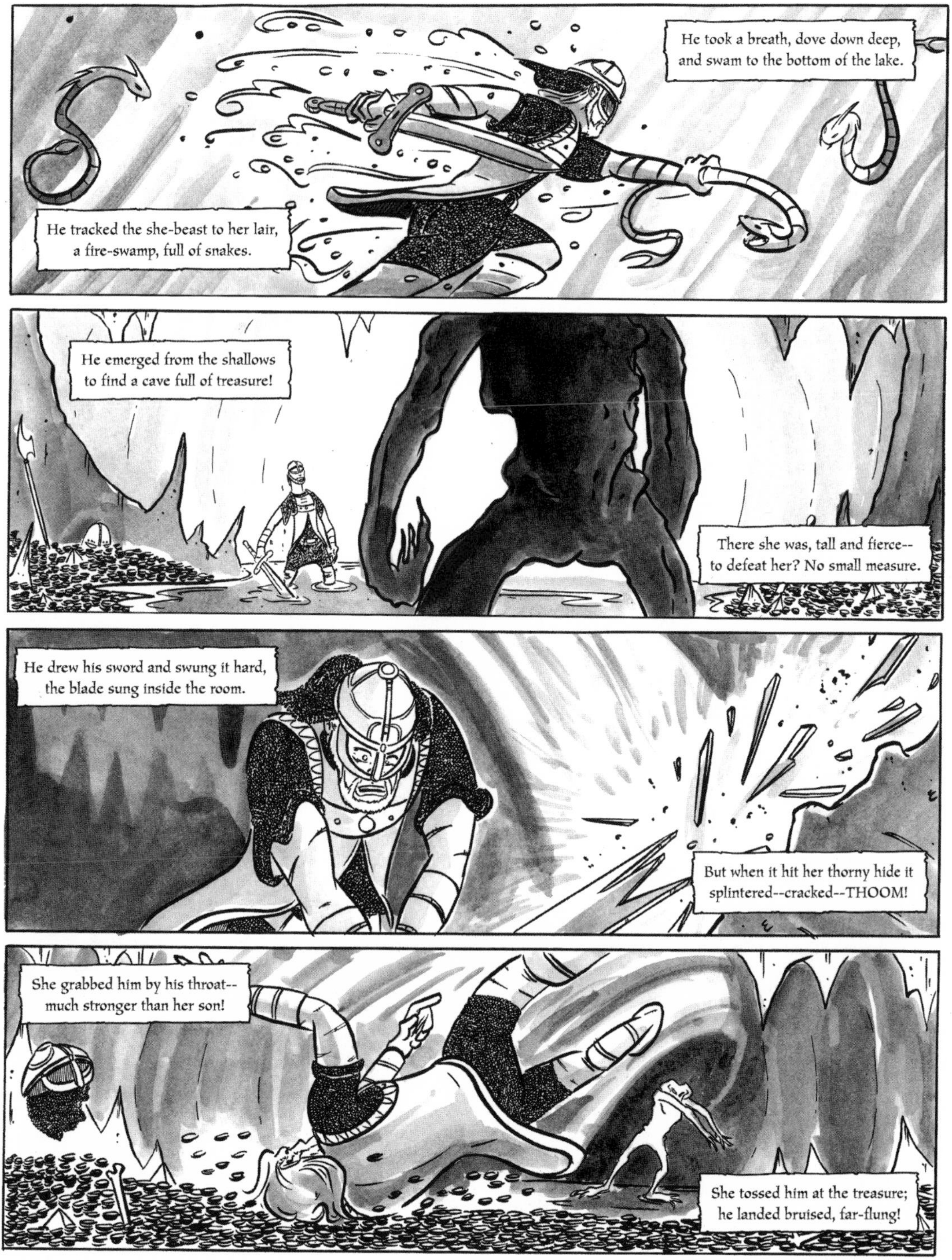
He took a breath, dove down deep, and swam to the bottom of the lake.
He tracked the she-beast to her lair, a fire-swamp, full of snakes.
He emerged from the shallows to find a cave full of treasure!
There she was, tall and fierce-- to defeat her? No small measure.
He drew his sword and swung it hard, the blade sung inside the room.
But when it hit her thorny hide it splintered--cracked--THOOM!
She grabbed him by his throat-- much stronger than her son!
She tossed him at the treasure; he landed bruised, far-flung!

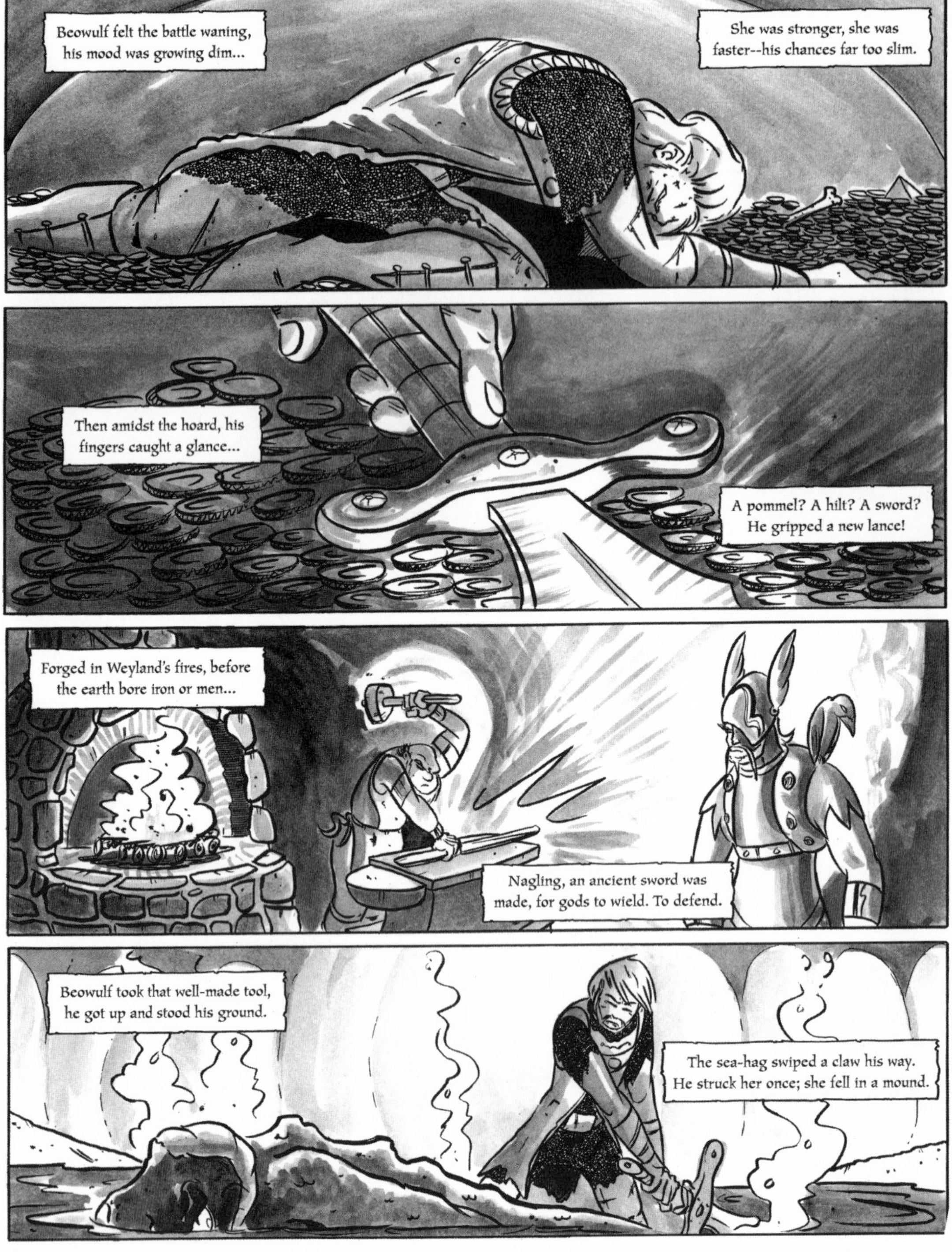

Beowulf felt the battle waning, his mood was growing dim...
She was stronger, she was faster--his chances far too slim.
Then amidst the hoard, his fingers caught a glance...
A pommel? A hilt? A sword? He gripped a new lance!
Forged in Weyland's fires, before the earth bore iron or men...
Nagling, an ancient sword was made, for gods to wield. To defend.
Beowulf took that well-made tool, he got up and stood his ground.
The sea-hag swiped a claw his way. He struck her once; she fell in a mound.

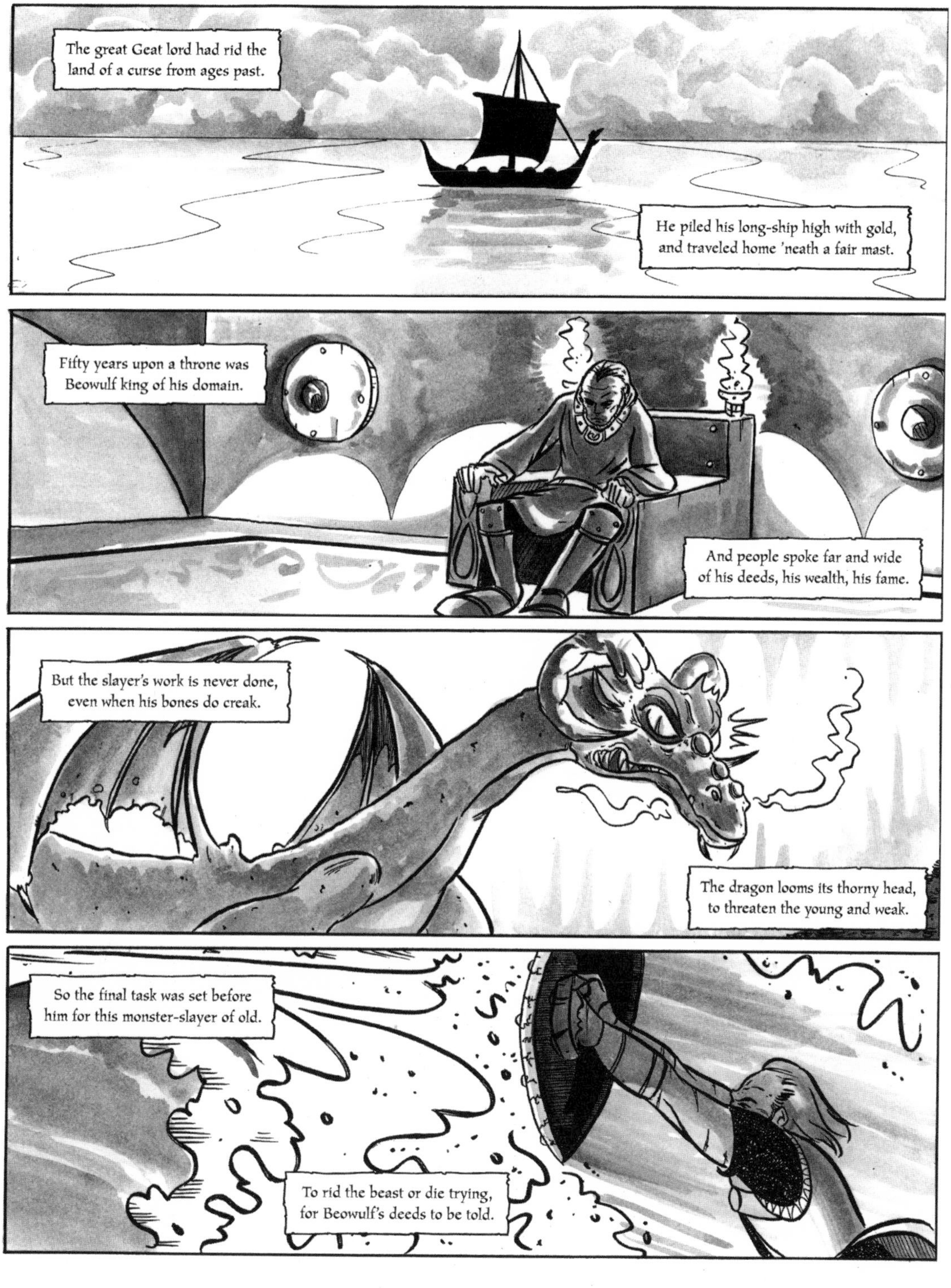
The great Geat lord had rid the land of a curse from ages past.
He piled his long-ship high with gold, and traveled home 'neath a fair mast.
Fifty years upon a throne was Beowulf king of his domain.
And people spoke far and wide of his deeds, his wealth, his fame.
But the slayer's work is never done, even when his bones do creak.
The dragon looms its thorny head, to threaten the young and weak.
So the final task was set before him for this monster-slayer of old.
To rid the beast or die trying, for Beowulf's deeds to be told.

At least, that's as men have told it--
as I said, they twist the truth.
Too blind to know the proper tale
of a king's run-rampant youth...

Part One

the past

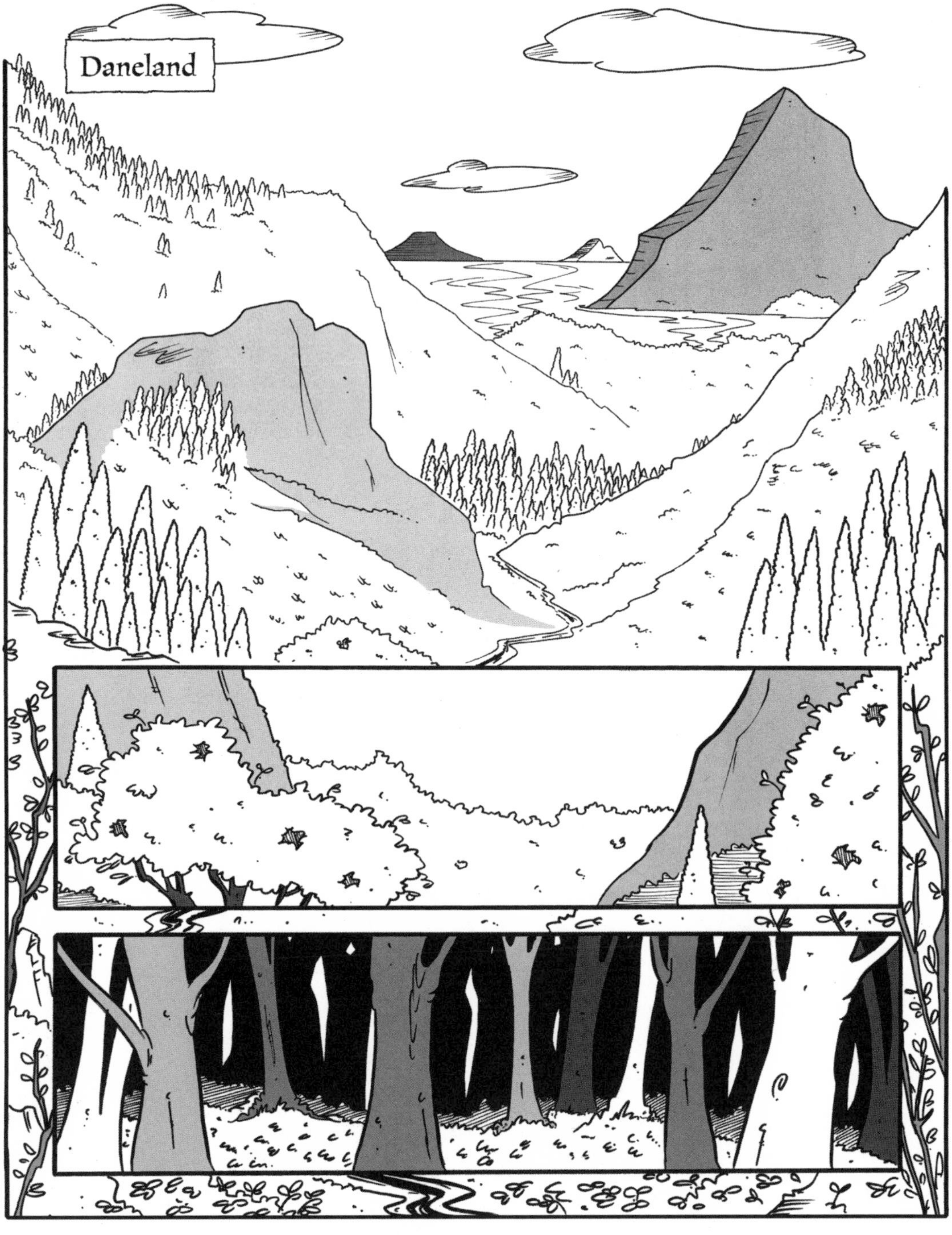
Daneland

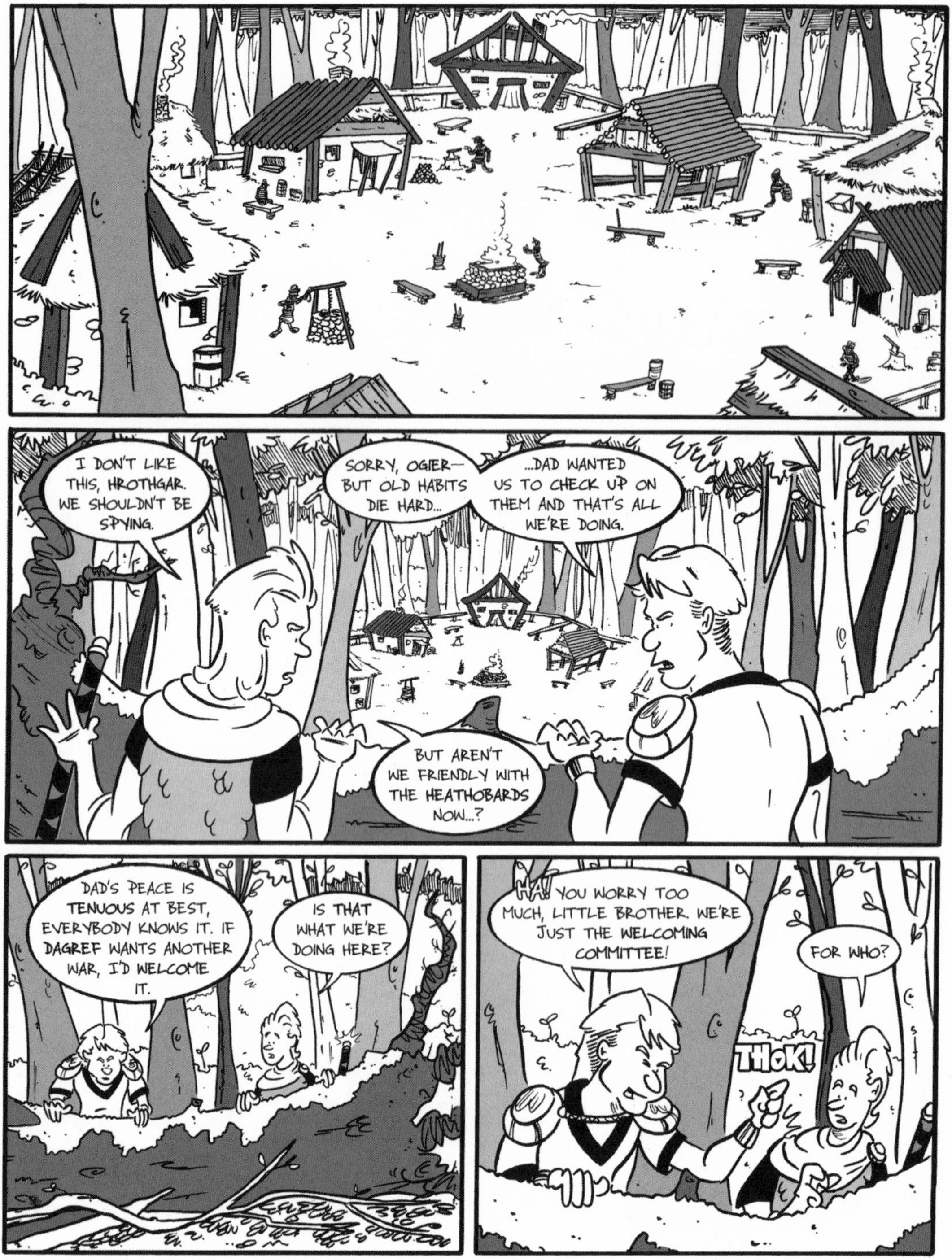

I DON'T LIKE THIS, HROTHGAR. WE SHOULDN'T BE SPYING.
SORRY, OGIER— BUT OLD HABITS DIE HARD...
...DAD WANTED US TO CHECK UP ON THEM AND THAT'S ALL WE'RE DOING.
BUT AREN'T WE FRIENDLY WITH THE HEATHOBARDS NOW...?
DAD'S PEACE IS TENUOUS AT BEST, EVERYBODY KNOWS IT. IF DAGREF WANTS ANOTHER WAR, I'D WELCOME IT.
IS THAT WHAT WE'RE DOING HERE?
HA! YOU WORRY TOO MUCH, LITTLE BROTHER. WE'RE JUST THE WELCOMING COMMITTEE!
FOR WHO?
THOK!

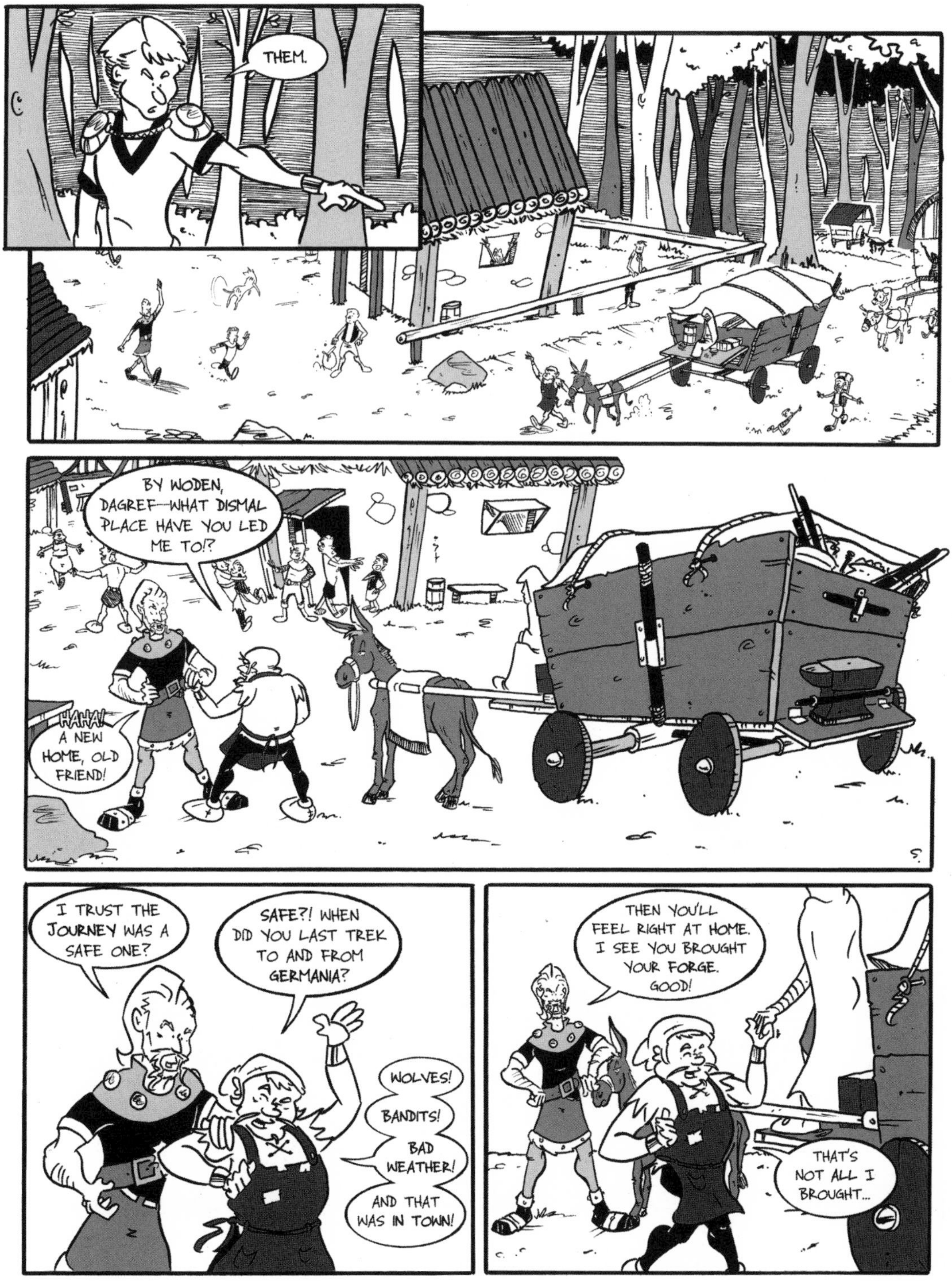
THEM.
BY WODEN, DAGREF--WHAT DISMAL PLACE HAVE YOU LED ME TO!?
HAHA! A NEW HOME, OLD FRIEND!
I TRUST THE JOURNEY WAS A SAFE ONE?
SAFE?! WHEN DID YOU LAST TREK TO AND FROM GERMANIA?
WOLVES!
BANDITS!
BAD WEATHER!
AND THAT WAS IN TOWN!
THEN YOU'LL FEEL RIGHT AT HOME. I SEE YOU BROUGHT YOUR FORGE. GOOD!
THAT'S NOT ALL I BROUGHT...

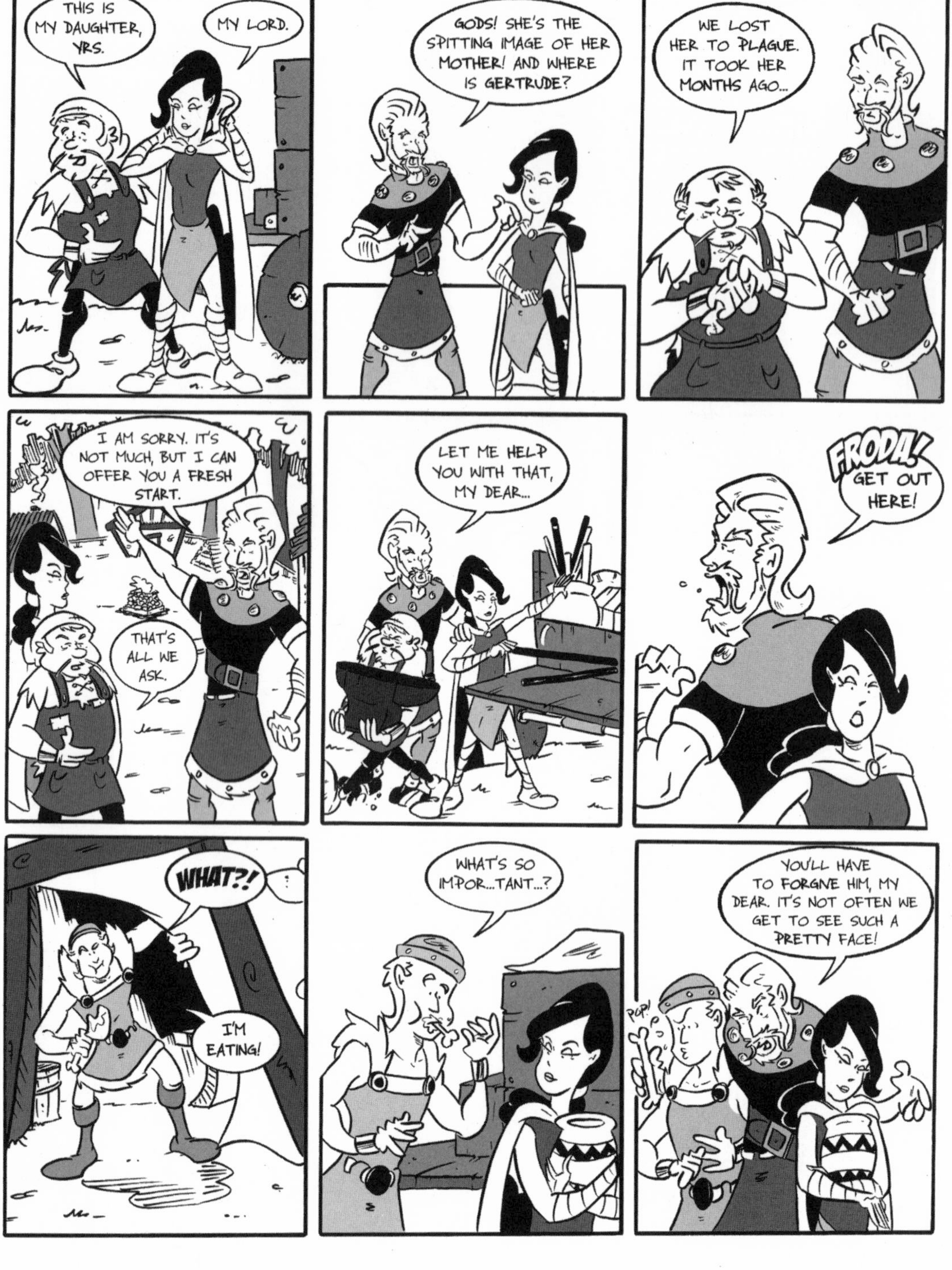
THIS IS MY DAUGHTER, YRS.
MY LORD.
GODS! SHE'S THE SPITTING IMAGE OF HER MOTHER! AND WHERE IS GERTRUDE?
WE LOST HER TO PLAGUE. IT TOOK HER MONTHS AGO...
I AM SORRY. IT'S NOT MUCH, BUT I CAN OFFER YOU A FRESH START.
THAT'S ALL WE ASK.
LET ME HELP YOU WITH THAT, MY DEAR...
FRODA! GET OUT HERE!
WHAT?!
I'M EATING!
WHAT'S SO IMPOR...TANT...?
POP!
YOU'LL HAVE TO FORGIVE HIM, MY DEAR. IT'S NOT OFTEN WE GET TO SEE SUCH A PRETTY FACE!

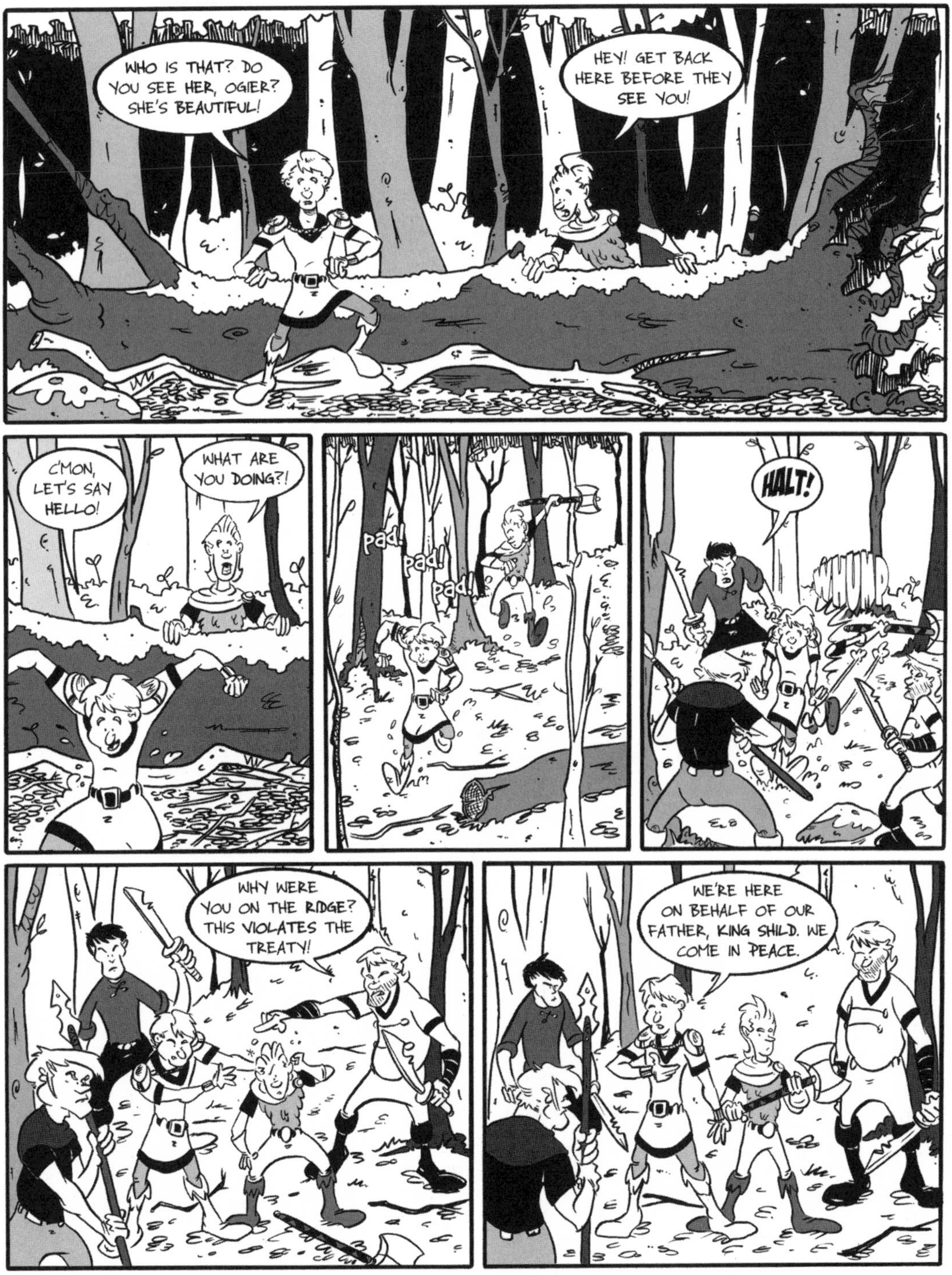
WHO IS THAT? DO YOU SEE HER, OGIER? SHE'S BEAUTIFUL!
HEY! GET BACK HERE BEFORE THEY SEE YOU!
C'MON, LET'S SAY HELLO!
WHAT ARE YOU DOING?!
pad! pad! pad!
HALT!
WHUMP
WHY WERE YOU ON THE RIDGE? THIS VIOLATES THE TREATY!
WE'RE HERE ON BEHALF OF OUR FATHER, KING SHILD. WE COME IN PEACE.

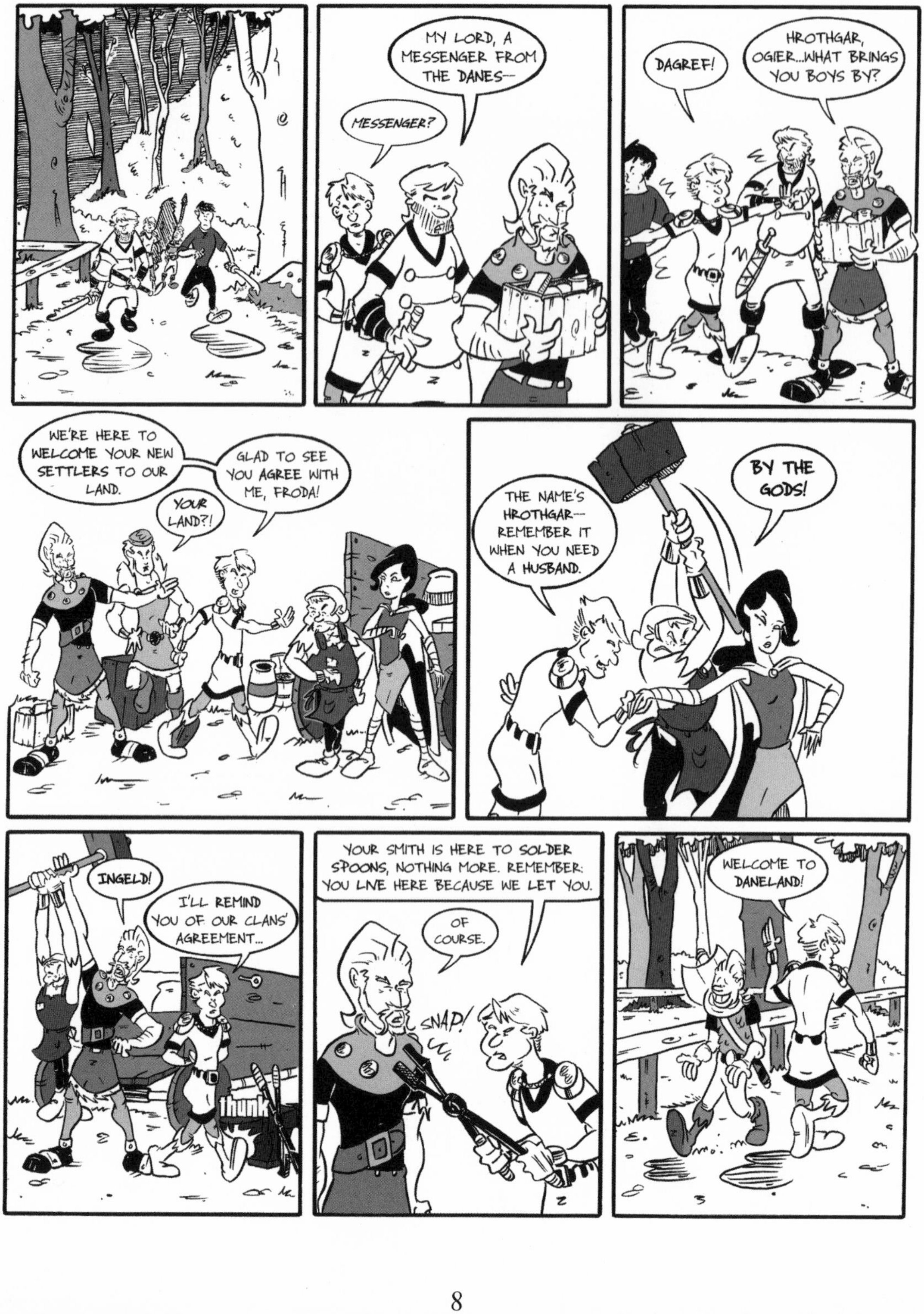
MY LORD, A MESSENGER FROM THE DANES--
MESSENGER?
DAGREF!
HROTHGAR, OGIER...WHAT BRINGS YOU BOYS BY?
WE'RE HERE TO WELCOME YOUR NEW SETTLERS TO OUR LAND.
YOUR LAND?!
GLAD TO SEE YOU AGREE WITH ME, FRODA!
THE NAME'S HROTHGAR-- REMEMBER IT WHEN YOU NEED A HUSBAND.
BY THE GODS!
INGELD!
I'LL REMIND YOU OF OUR CLANS' AGREEMENT...
thunk
YOUR SMITH IS HERE TO SOLDER SPOONS, NOTHING MORE. REMEMBER: YOU LIVE HERE BECAUSE WE LET YOU.
OF COURSE.
SNAP!
WELCOME TO DANELAND!

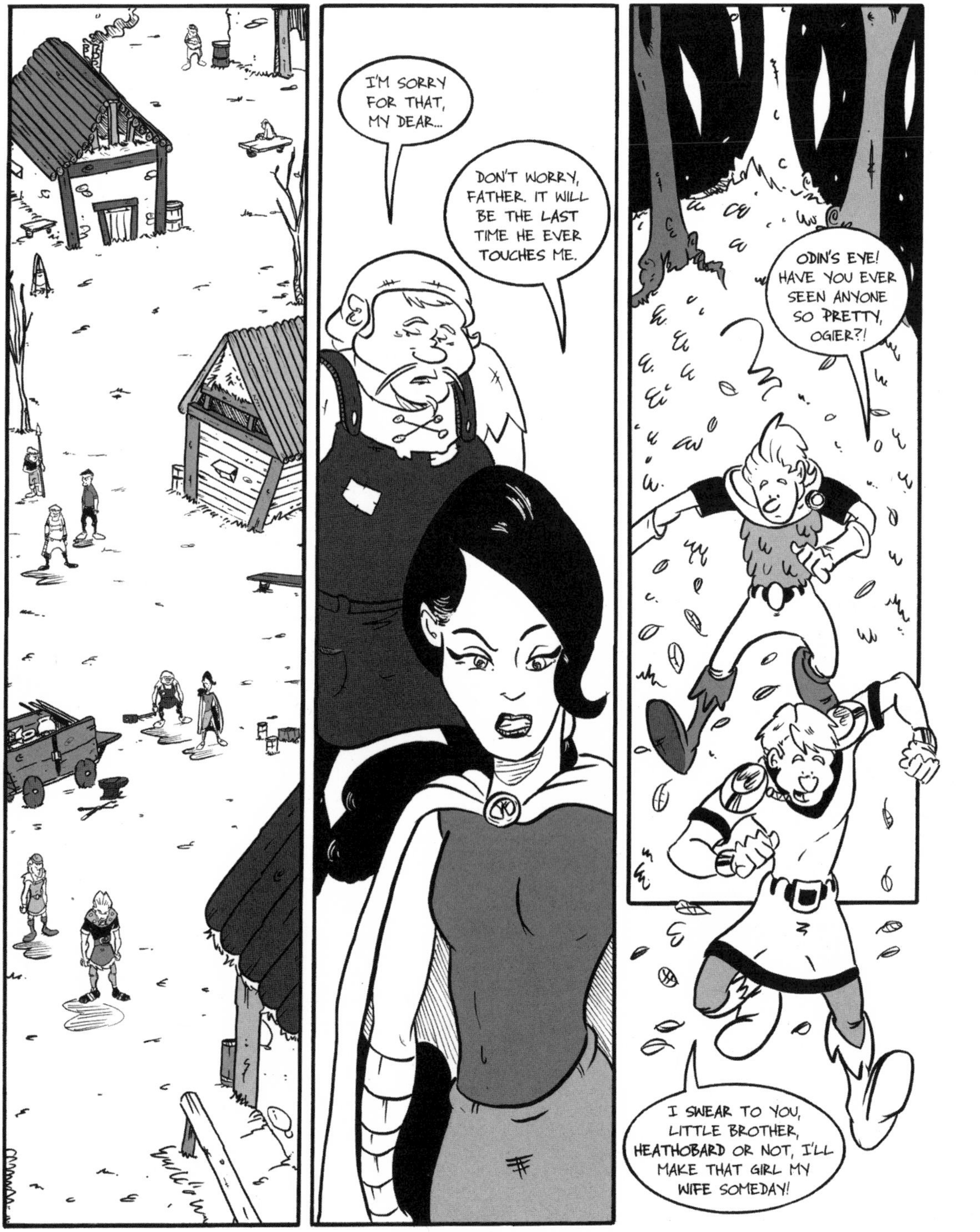
I'M SORRY FOR THAT, MY DEAR...
DON'T WORRY, FATHER. IT WILL BE THE LAST TIME HE EVER TOUCHES ME.
ODIN'S EYE! HAVE YOU EVER SEEN ANYONE SO PRETTY, OGIER?!
I SWEAR TO YOU, LITTLE BROTHER, HEATHOBARD OR NOT, I'LL MAKE THAT GIRL MY WIFE SOMEDAY!

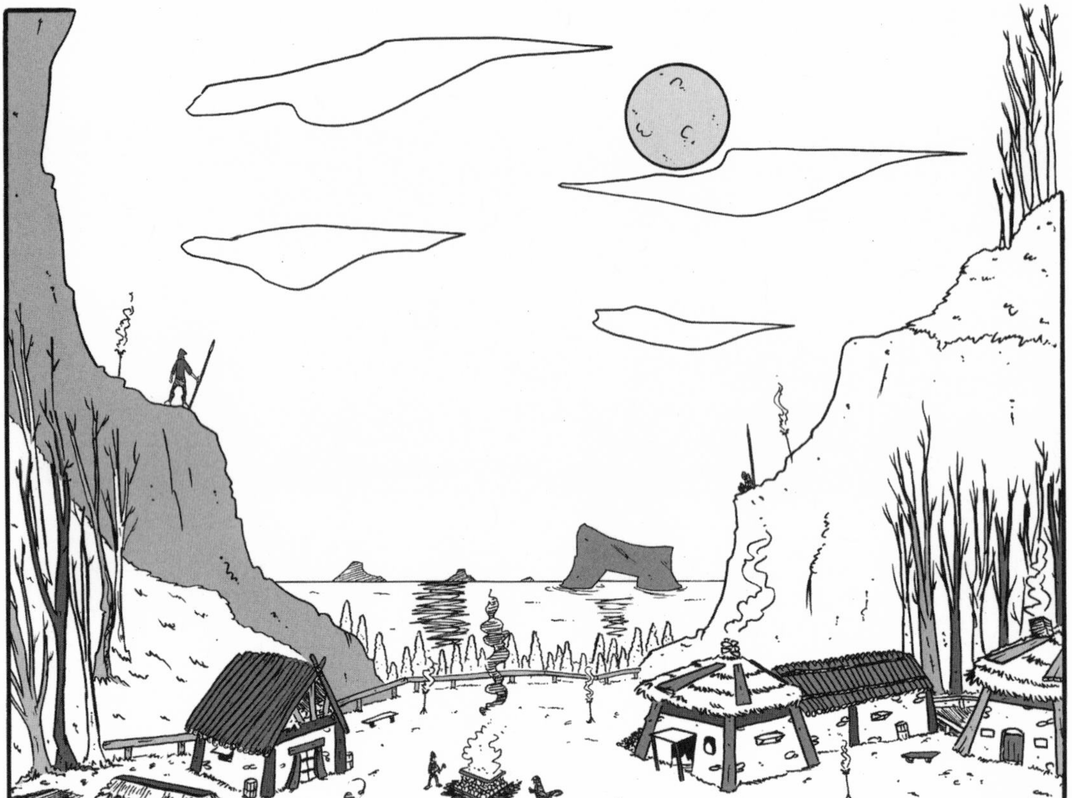

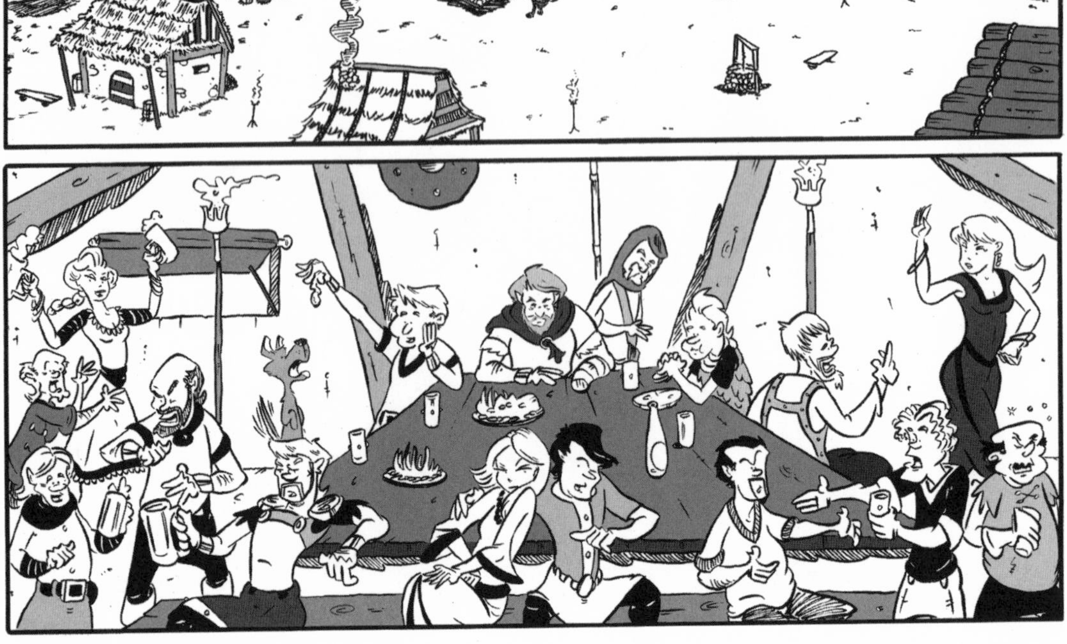

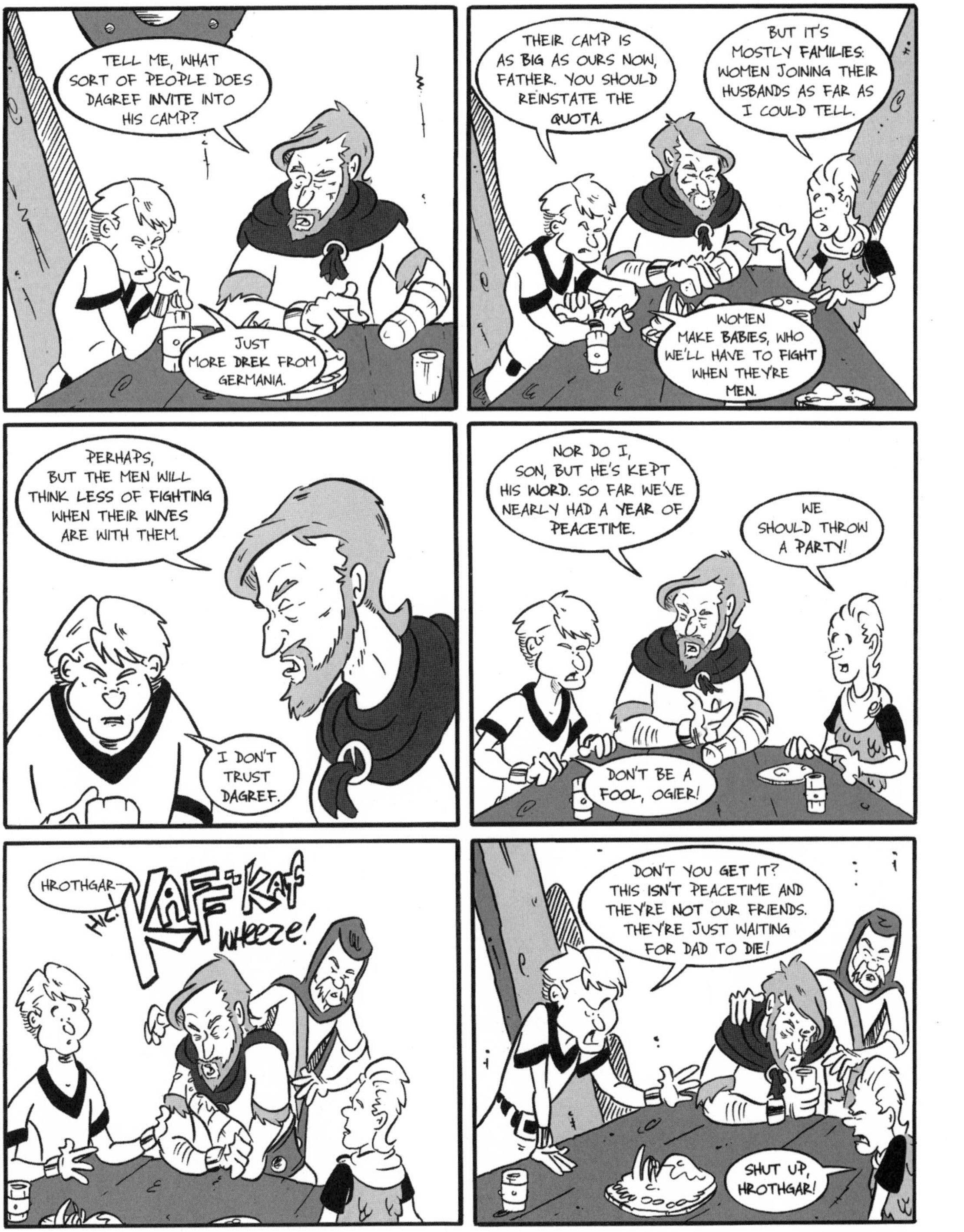
TELL ME, WHAT SORT OF PEOPLE DOES DAGREF INVITE INTO HIS CAMP?
JUST MORE DREK FROM GERMANIA.
THEIR CAMP IS AS BIG AS OURS NOW, FATHER. YOU SHOULD REINSTATE THE QUOTA.
BUT IT'S MOSTLY FAMILIES: WOMEN JOINING THEIR HUSBANDS AS FAR AS I COULD TELL.
WOMEN MAKE BABIES, WHO WE'LL HAVE TO FIGHT WHEN THEY'RE MEN.
PERHAPS, BUT THE MEN WILL THINK LESS OF FIGHTING WHEN THEIR WIVES ARE WITH THEM.
I DON'T TRUST DAGREF.
NOR DO I, SON, BUT HE'S KEPT HIS WORD. SO FAR WE'VE NEARLY HAD A YEAR OF PEACETIME.
WE SHOULD THROW A PARTY!
DON'T BE A FOOL, OGIER!
HROTHGAR—
HIC. KAF-KAF WHEEZE!
DON'T YOU GET IT? THIS ISN'T PEACETIME AND THEY'RE NOT OUR FRIENDS. THEY'RE JUST WAITING FOR DAD TO DIE!
SHUT UP, HROTHGAR!

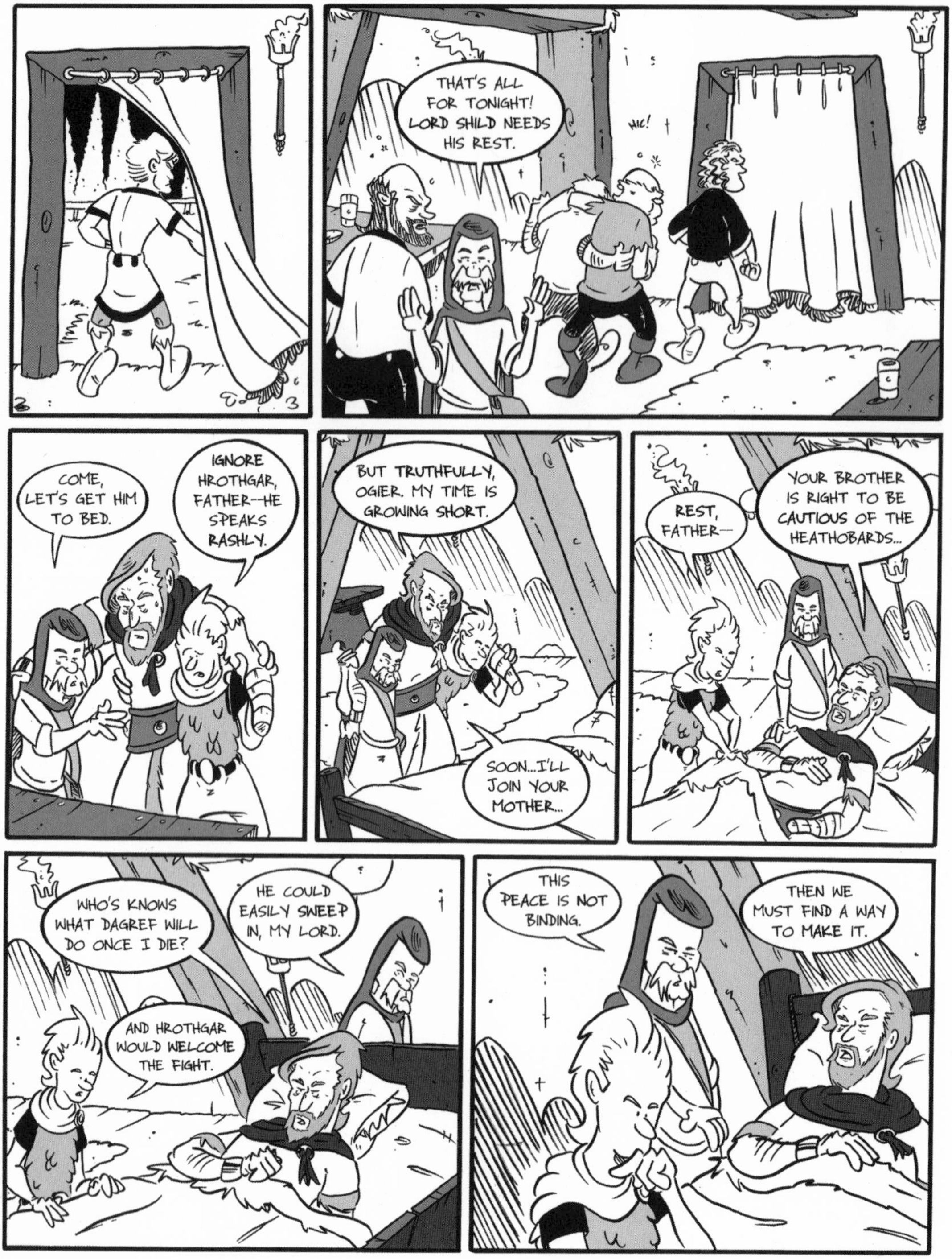
THAT'S ALL FOR TONIGHT! LORD SHILD NEEDS HIS REST.
HIC!
COME, LET'S GET HIM TO BED.
IGNORE HROTHGAR, FATHER--HE SPEAKS RASHLY.
BUT TRUTHFULLY, OGIER. MY TIME IS GROWING SHORT.
SOON...I'LL JOIN YOUR MOTHER...
REST, FATHER--
YOUR BROTHER IS RIGHT TO BE CAUTIOUS OF THE HEATHOBARDS...
WHO'S KNOWS WHAT DAGREF WILL DO ONCE I DIE?
HE COULD EASILY SWEEP IN, MY LORD.
AND HROTHGAR WOULD WELCOME THE FIGHT.
THIS PEACE IS NOT BINDING.
THEN WE MUST FIND A WAY TO MAKE IT.

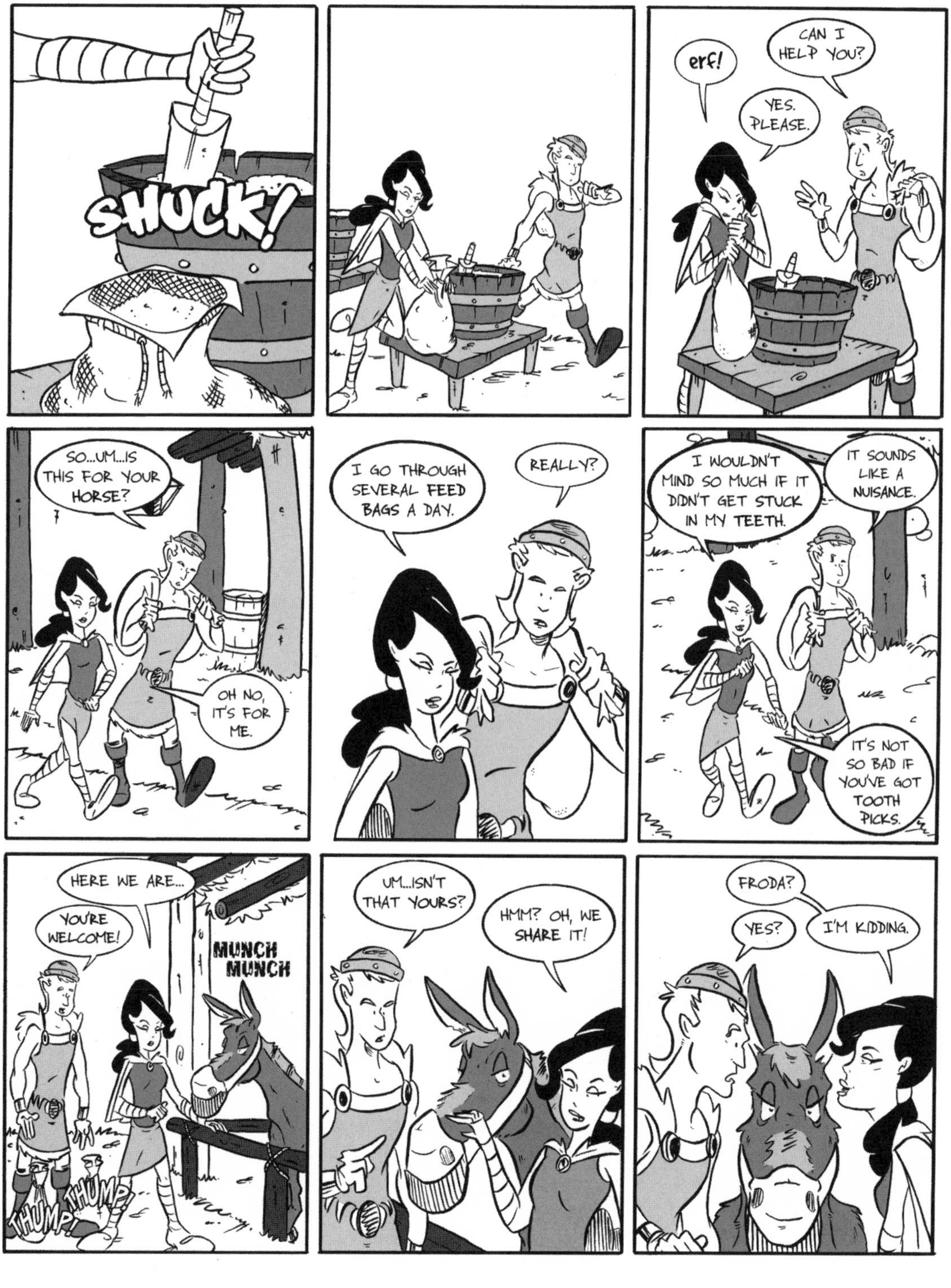
SHUCK!
erf!
CAN I HELP YOU?
YES. PLEASE.
SO...UM...IS THIS FOR YOUR HORSE?
OH NO, IT'S FOR ME.
I GO THROUGH SEVERAL FEED BAGS A DAY.
REALLY?
I WOULDN'T MIND SO MUCH IF IT DIDN'T GET STUCK IN MY TEETH.
IT SOUNDS LIKE A NUISANCE.
IT'S NOT SO BAD IF YOU'VE GOT TOOTH PICKS.
HERE WE ARE...
YOU'RE WELCOME!
MUNCH MUNCH
THUMP! THUMP!
UM...ISN'T THAT YOURS?
HMM? OH, WE SHARE IT!
FRODA?
YES?
I'M KIDDING.

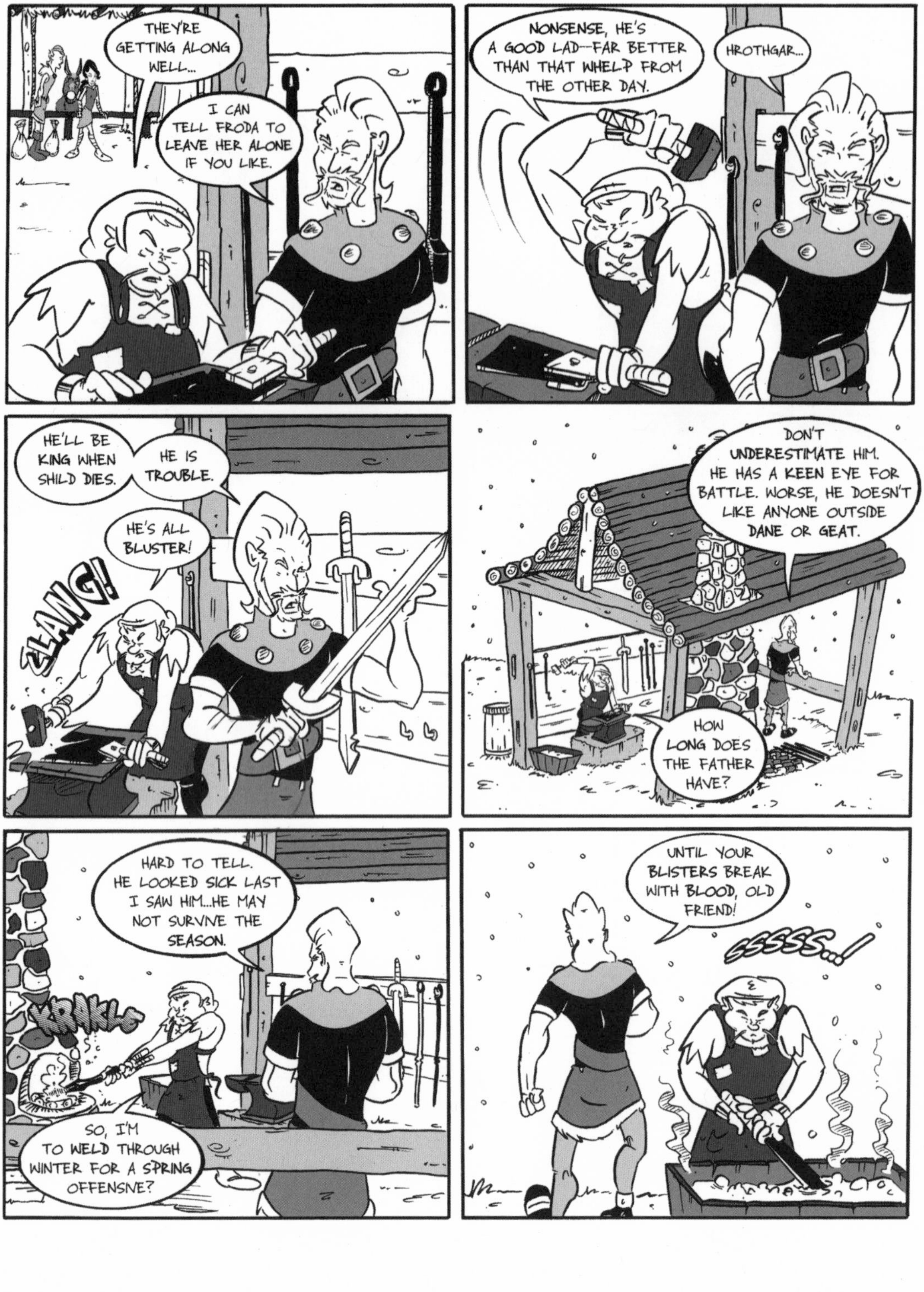

THEY'RE GETTING ALONG WELL...
I CAN TELL FRODA TO LEAVE HER ALONE IF YOU LIKE.
NONSENSE, HE'S A GOOD LAD--FAR BETTER THAN THAT WHELP FROM THE OTHER DAY.
HROTHGAR...
HE'LL BE KING WHEN SHILD DIES.
HE IS TROUBLE.
HE'S ALL BLUSTER!
CLANG!
DON'T UNDERESTIMATE HIM. HE HAS A KEEN EYE FOR BATTLE. WORSE, HE DOESN'T LIKE ANYONE OUTSIDE DANE OR GEAT.
HOW LONG DOES THE FATHER HAVE?
HARD TO TELL. HE LOOKED SICK LAST I SAW HIM...HE MAY NOT SURVIVE THE SEASON.
KRAKLE
SO, I'M TO WELD THROUGH WINTER FOR A SPRING OFFENSIVE?
UNTIL YOUR BLISTERS BREAK WITH BLOOD, OLD FRIEND!
SSSSS...!

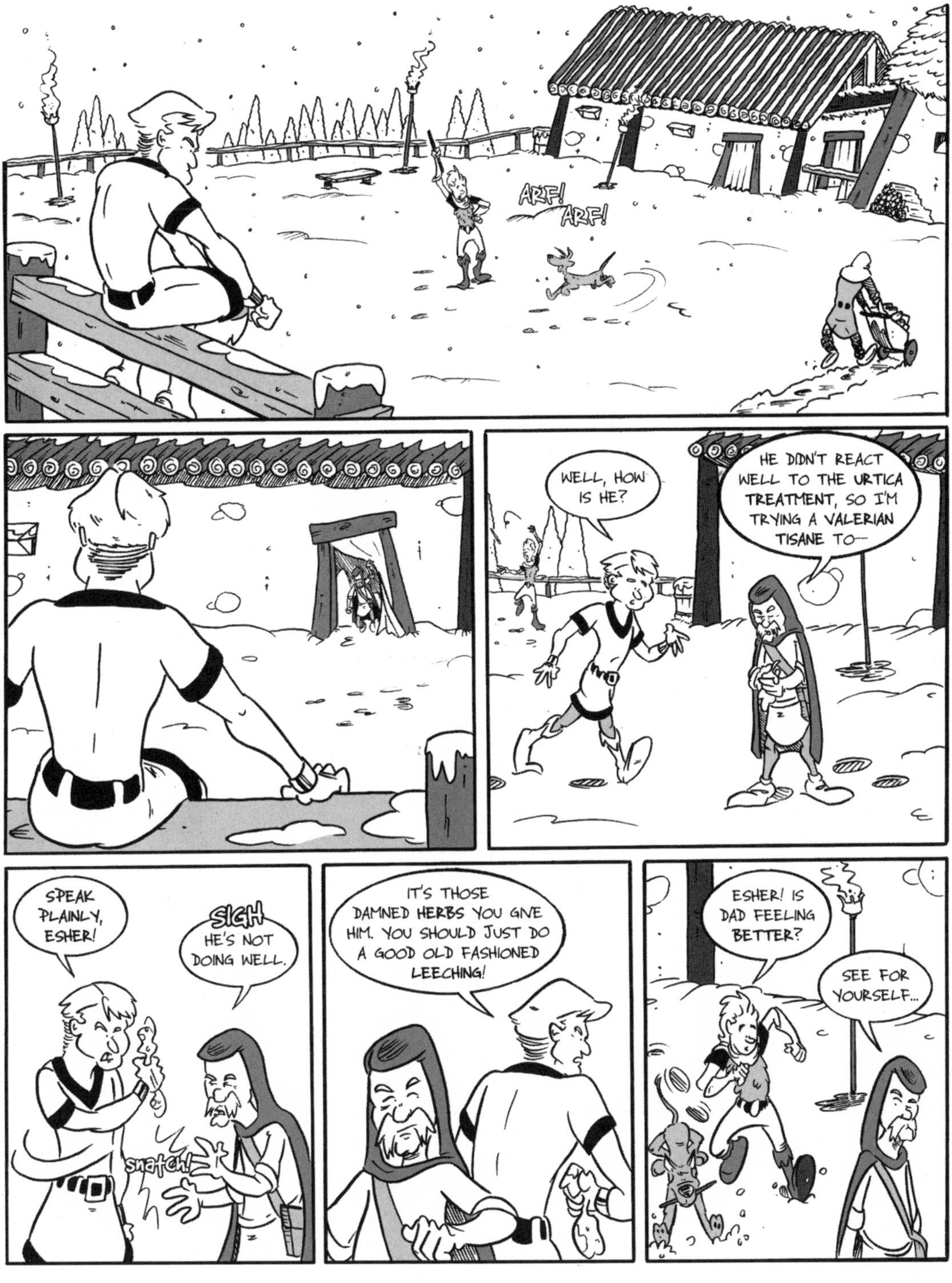
ARF! ARF!
WELL, HOW IS HE?
HE DIDN'T REACT WELL TO THE URTICA TREATMENT, SO I'M TRYING A VALERIAN TISANE TO--
SPEAK PLAINLY, ESHER!
SIGH
HE'S NOT DOING WELL.
SNATCH!
IT'S THOSE DAMNED HERBS YOU GIVE HIM. YOU SHOULD JUST DO A GOOD OLD FASHIONED LEECHING!
ESHER! IS DAD FEELING BETTER?
SEE FOR YOURSELF...

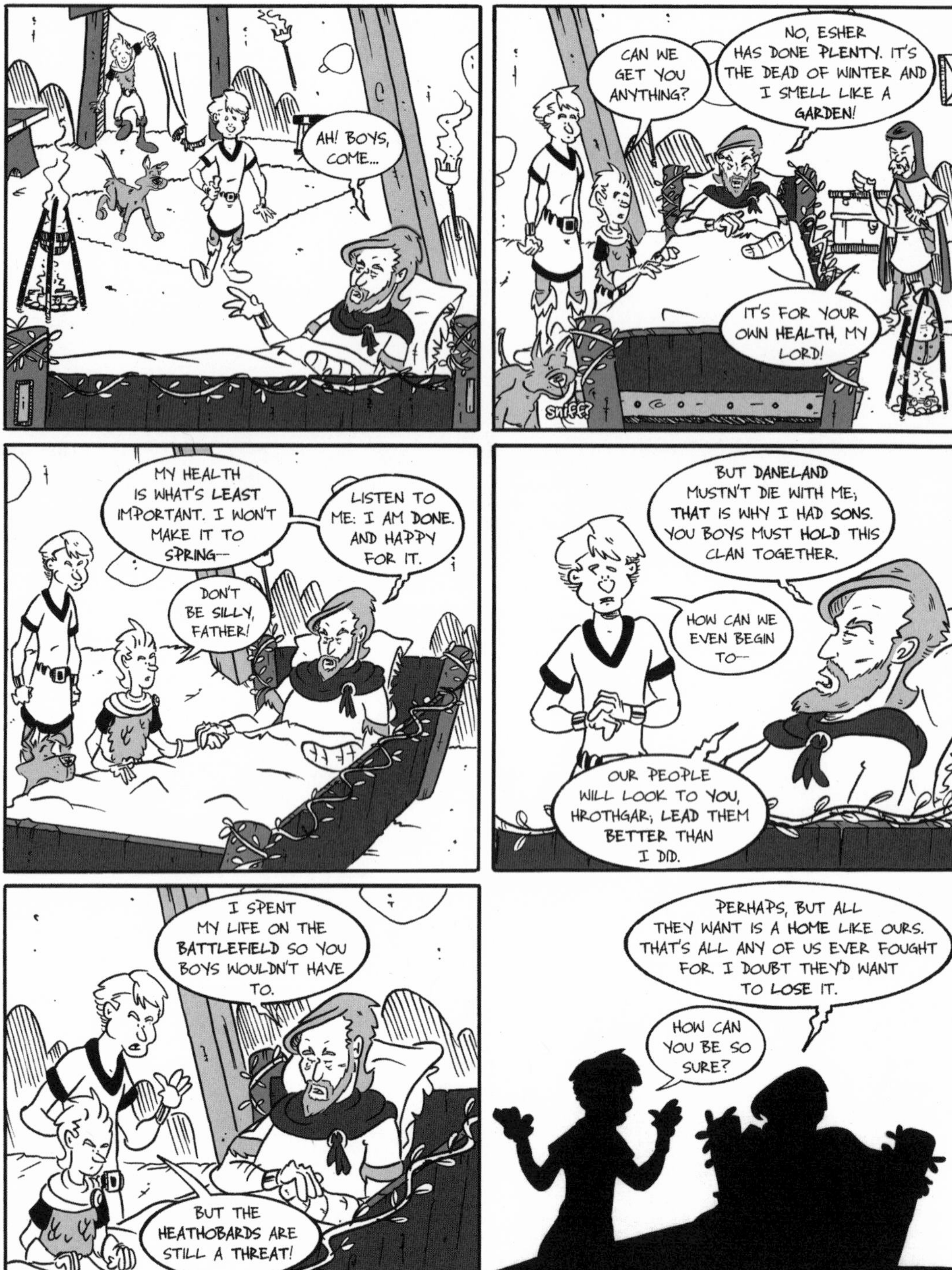
AH! BOYS, COME...
CAN WE GET YOU ANYTHING?
NO, ESHER HAS DONE PLENTY. IT'S THE DEAD OF WINTER AND I SMELL LIKE A GARDEN!
IT'S FOR YOUR OWN HEALTH, MY LORD!
SNIFF?
MY HEALTH IS WHAT'S LEAST IMPORTANT. I WON'T MAKE IT TO SPRING--
LISTEN TO ME: I AM DONE. AND HAPPY FOR IT.
DON'T BE SILLY, FATHER!
BUT DANELAND MUSTN'T DIE WITH ME; THAT IS WHY I HAD SONS. YOU BOYS MUST HOLD THIS CLAN TOGETHER.
HOW CAN WE EVEN BEGIN TO--
OUR PEOPLE WILL LOOK TO YOU, HROTHGAR; LEAD THEM BETTER THAN I DID.
I SPENT MY LIFE ON THE BATTLEFIELD SO YOU BOYS WOULDN'T HAVE TO.
BUT THE HEATHOBARDS ARE STILL A THREAT!
PERHAPS, BUT ALL THEY WANT IS A HOME LIKE OURS. THAT'S ALL ANY OF US EVER FOUGHT FOR. I DOUBT THEY'D WANT TO LOSE IT.
HOW CAN YOU BE SO SURE?

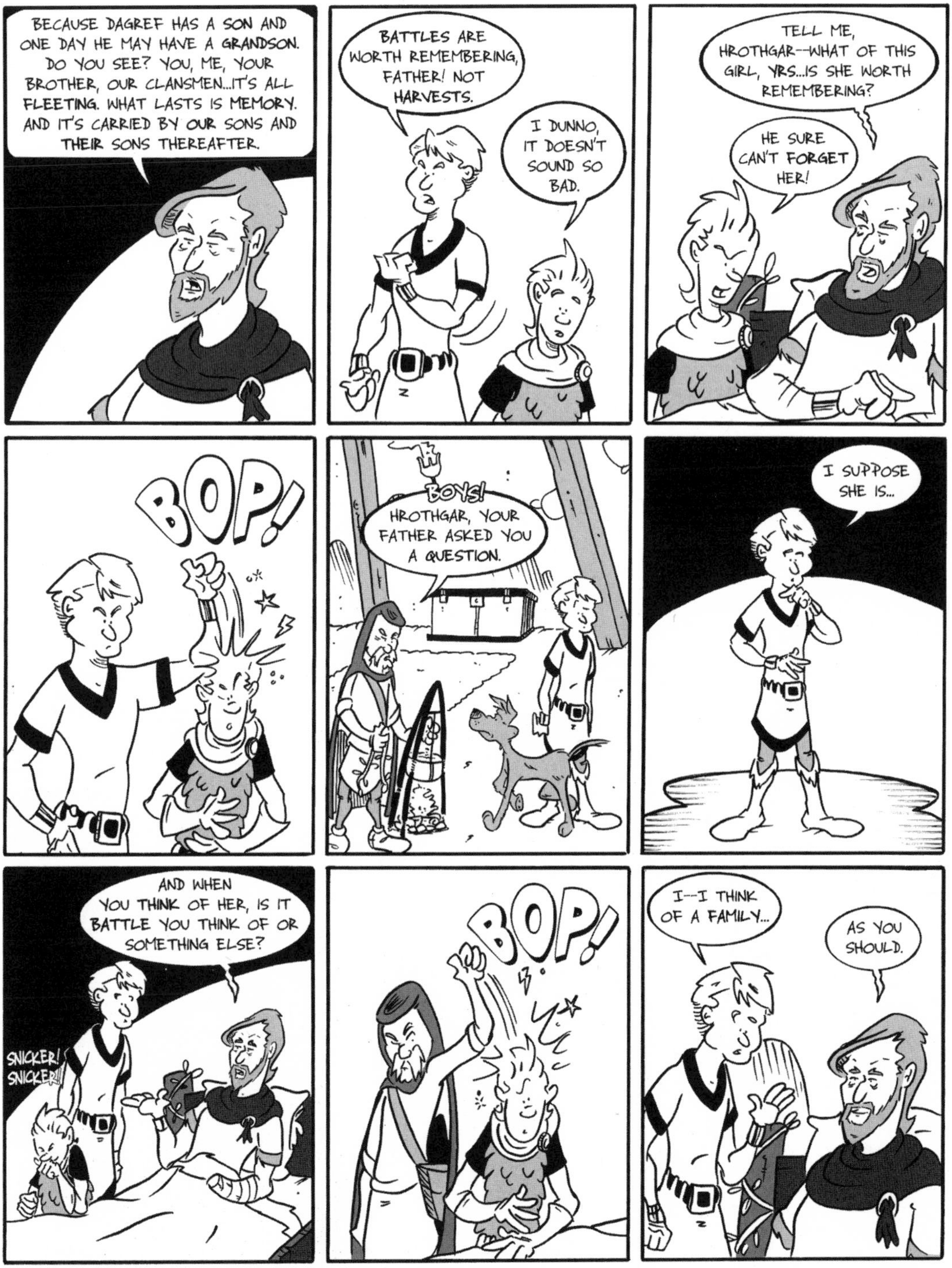
BECAUSE DAGREF HAS A SON AND ONE DAY HE MAY HAVE A GRANDSON. DO YOU SEE? YOU, ME, YOUR BROTHER, OUR CLANSMEN...IT'S ALL FLEETING. WHAT LASTS IS MEMORY. AND IT'S CARRIED BY OUR SONS AND THEIR SONS THEREAFTER.
BATTLES ARE WORTH REMEMBERING, FATHER! NOT HARVESTS.
I DUNNO, IT DOESN'T SOUND SO BAD.
TELL ME, HROTHGAR--WHAT OF THIS GIRL, YRS...IS SHE WORTH REMEMBERING?
HE SURE CAN'T FORGET HER!
BOP!
BOYS! HROTHGAR, YOUR FATHER ASKED YOU A QUESTION.
I SUPPOSE SHE IS...
AND WHEN YOU THINK OF HER, IS IT BATTLE YOU THINK OF OR SOMETHING ELSE?
SNICKER! SNICKER!
BOP!
I--I THINK OF A FAMILY...
AS YOU SHOULD.

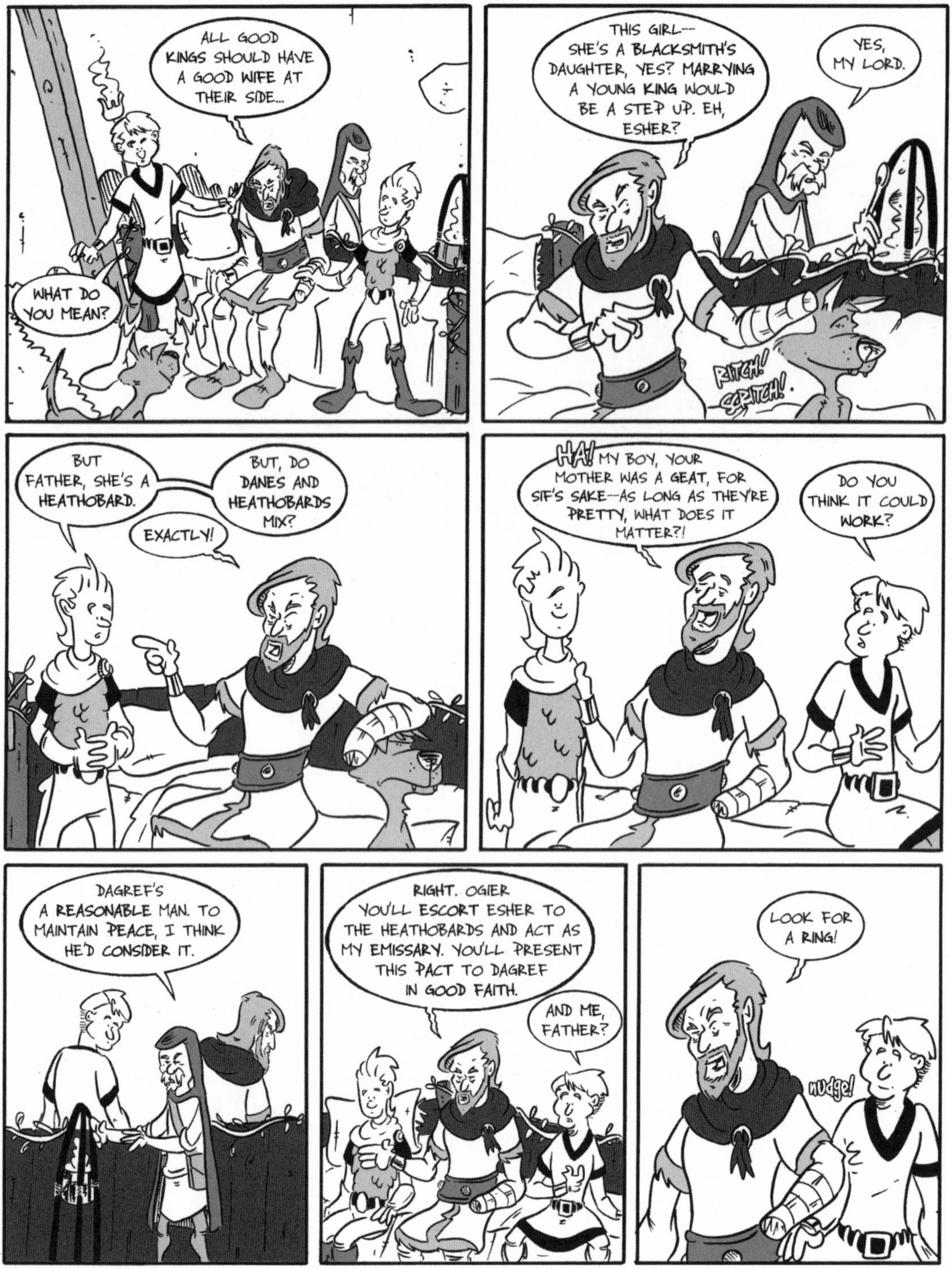
ALL GOOD KINGS SHOULD HAVE A GOOD WIFE AT THEIR SIDE...
WHAT DO YOU MEAN?
THIS GIRL-- SHE'S A BLACKSMITH'S DAUGHTER, YES? MARRYING A YOUNG KING WOULD BE A STEP UP. EH, ESHER?
YES, MY LORD.
RITCH! SCRITCH!
BUT FATHER, SHE'S A HEATHOBARD.
BUT, DO DANES AND HEATHOBARDS MIX?
EXACTLY!
HA! MY BOY, YOUR MOTHER WAS A GEAT, FOR SIF'S SAKE--AS LONG AS THEY'RE PRETTY, WHAT DOES IT MATTER?!
DO YOU THINK IT COULD WORK?
DAGREF'S A REASONABLE MAN. TO MAINTAIN PEACE, I THINK HE'D CONSIDER IT.
RIGHT. OGIER YOU'LL ESCORT ESHER TO THE HEATHOBARDS AND ACT AS MY EMISSARY. YOU'LL PRESENT THIS PACT TO DAGREF IN GOOD FAITH.
AND ME, FATHER?
LOOK FOR A RING!
nudge!

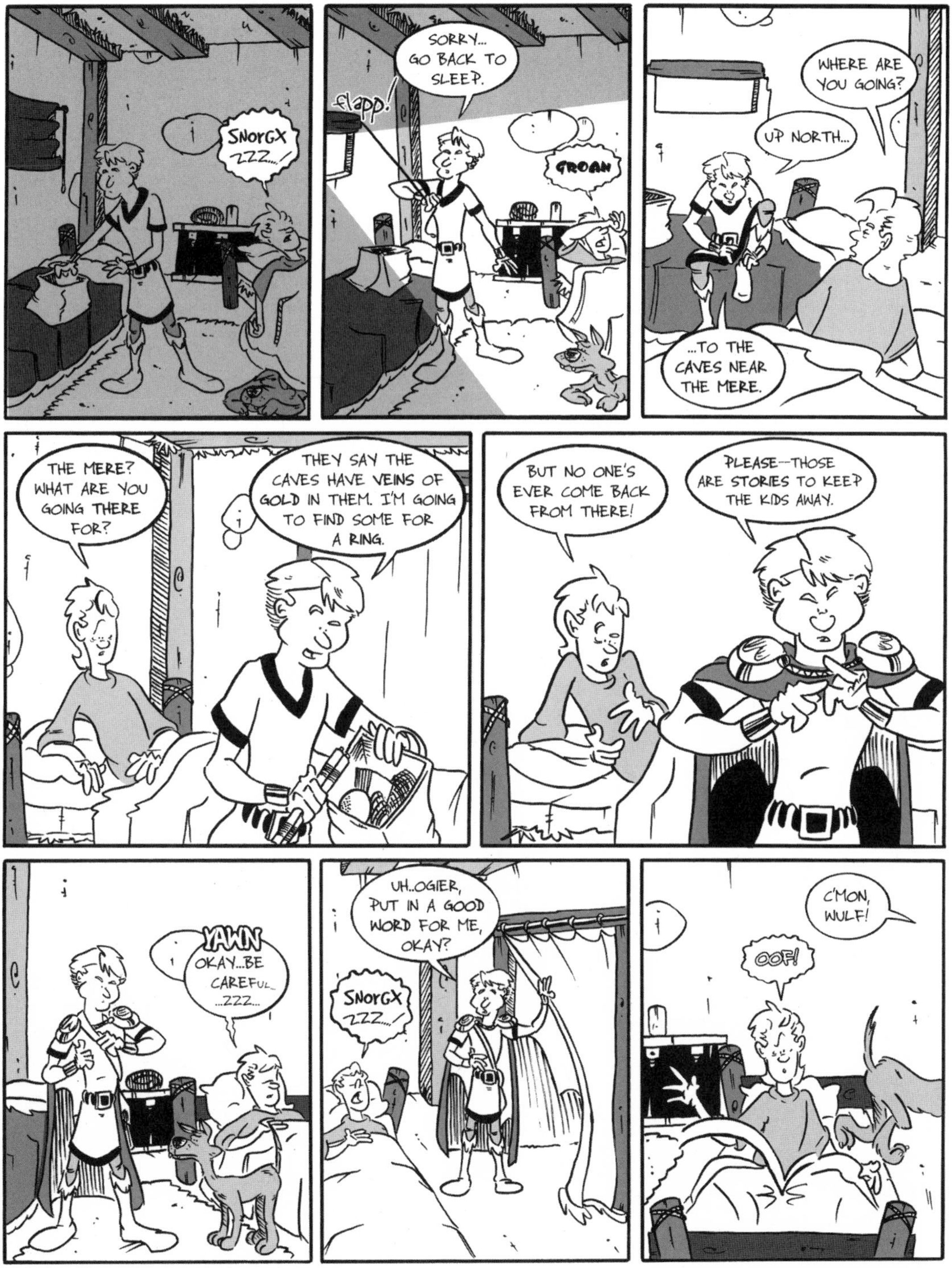
SNorGX
ZZZ...!
SORRY...
GO BACK TO
SLEEP.
flapp!
GROAN
WHERE ARE
YOU GOING?
UP NORTH...
...TO THE
CAVES NEAR
THE MERE.
THE MERE?
WHAT ARE YOU
GOING THERE
FOR?
THEY SAY THE
CAVES HAVE VEINS OF
GOLD IN THEM. I'M GOING
TO FIND SOME FOR
A RING.
BUT NO ONE'S
EVER COME BACK
FROM THERE!
PLEASE--THOSE
ARE STORIES TO KEEP
THE KIDS AWAY.
YAWN
OKAY...BE
CAREFUL...
...ZZZ...
UH...OGIER,
PUT IN A GOOD
WORD FOR ME,
OKAY?
SNorGX
ZZZ...!
C'MON,
WULF!
OOF!

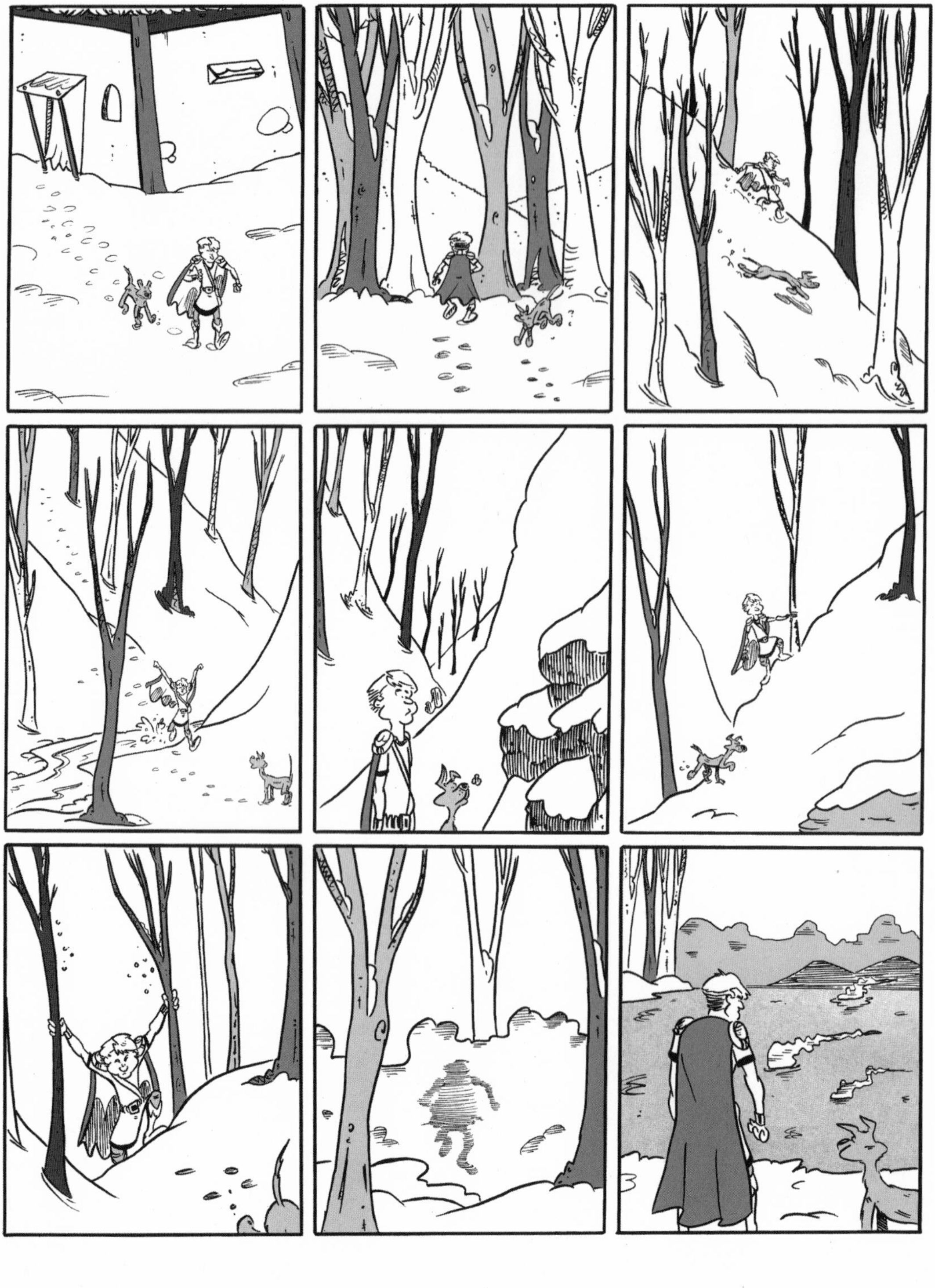

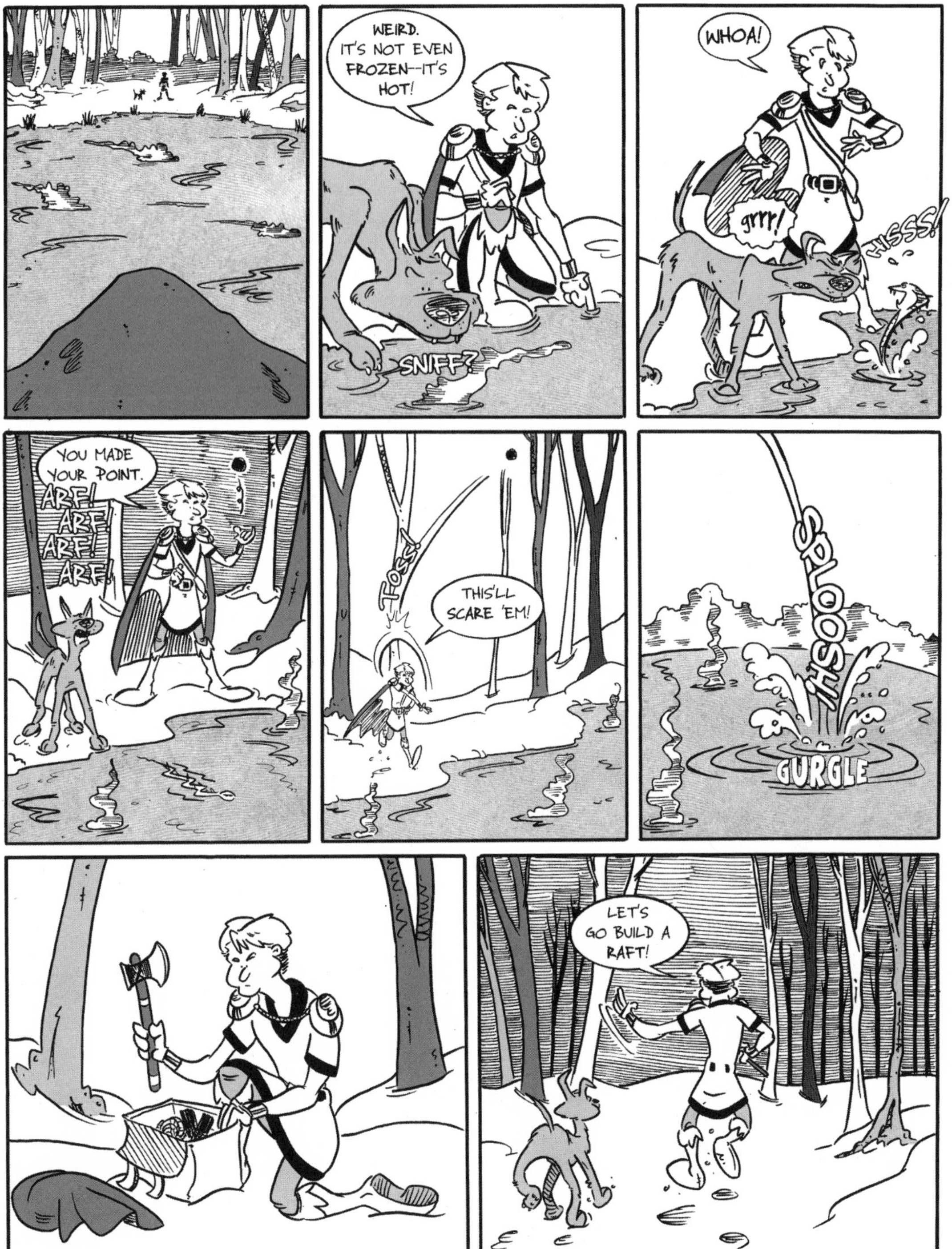
WEIRD. IT'S NOT EVEN FROZEN--IT'S HOT!
SNIFF?
WHOA!
grrr!
HISSSS!
YOU MADE YOUR POINT.
ARF! ARF! ARF! ARF!
TOSS!
THIS'LL SCARE 'EM!
SPLOOSH!
GURGLE
LET'S GO BUILD A RAFT!

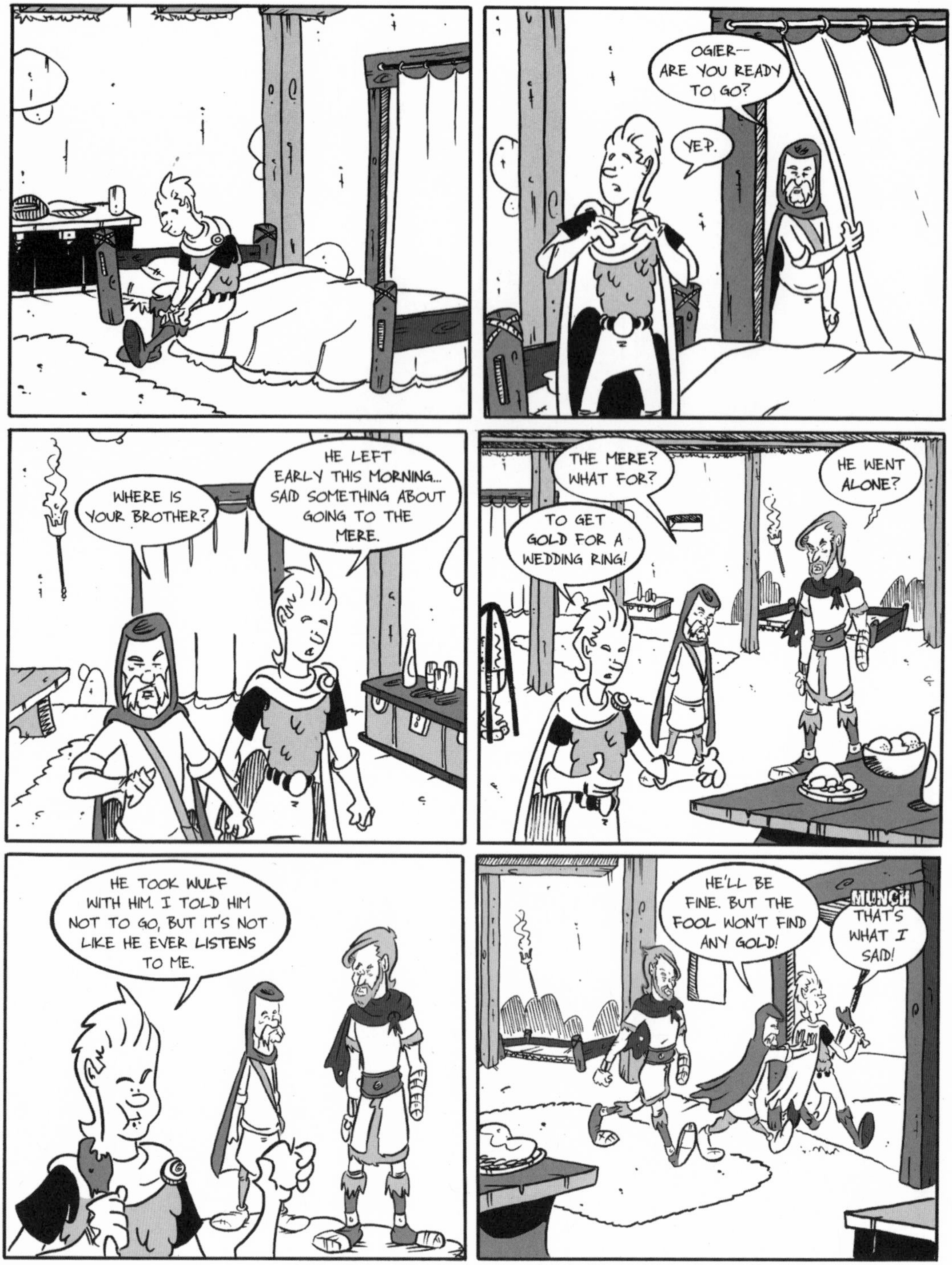
OGIER-- ARE YOU READY TO GO?
YEP.
WHERE IS YOUR BROTHER?
HE LEFT EARLY THIS MORNING... SAID SOMETHING ABOUT GOING TO THE MERE.
THE MERE? WHAT FOR?
TO GET GOLD FOR A WEDDING RING!
HE WENT ALONE?
HE TOOK WULF WITH HIM. I TOLD HIM NOT TO GO, BUT IT'S NOT LIKE HE EVER LISTENS TO ME.
HE'LL BE FINE. BUT THE FOOL WON'T FIND ANY GOLD!
MUNCH
THAT'S WHAT I SAID!

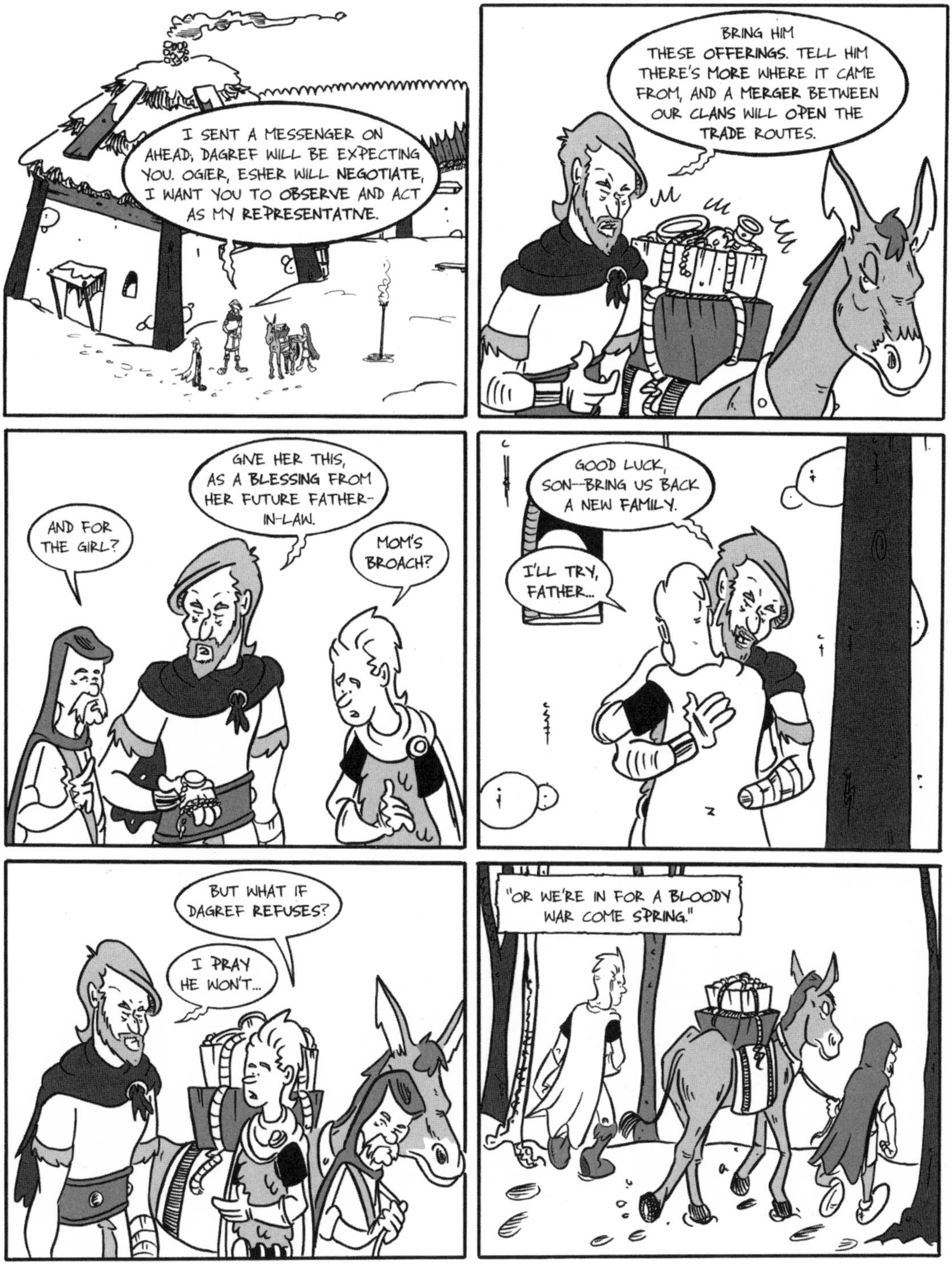
I SENT A MESSENGER ON AHEAD; DAGREF WILL BE EXPECTING YOU. OGIER, ESHER WILL NEGOTIATE, I WANT YOU TO OBSERVE AND ACT AS MY REPRESENTATIVE.
BRING HIM THESE OFFERINGS. TELL HIM THERE'S MORE WHERE IT CAME FROM, AND A MERGER BETWEEN OUR CLANS WILL OPEN THE TRADE ROUTES.
AND FOR THE GIRL?
GIVE HER THIS, AS A BLESSING FROM HER FUTURE FATHER-IN-LAW.
MOM'S BROACH?
GOOD LUCK, SON--BRING US BACK A NEW FAMILY.
I'LL TRY, FATHER...
BUT WHAT IF DAGREF REFUSES?
I PRAY HE WON'T...
"OR WE'RE IN FOR A BLOODY WAR COME SPRING."

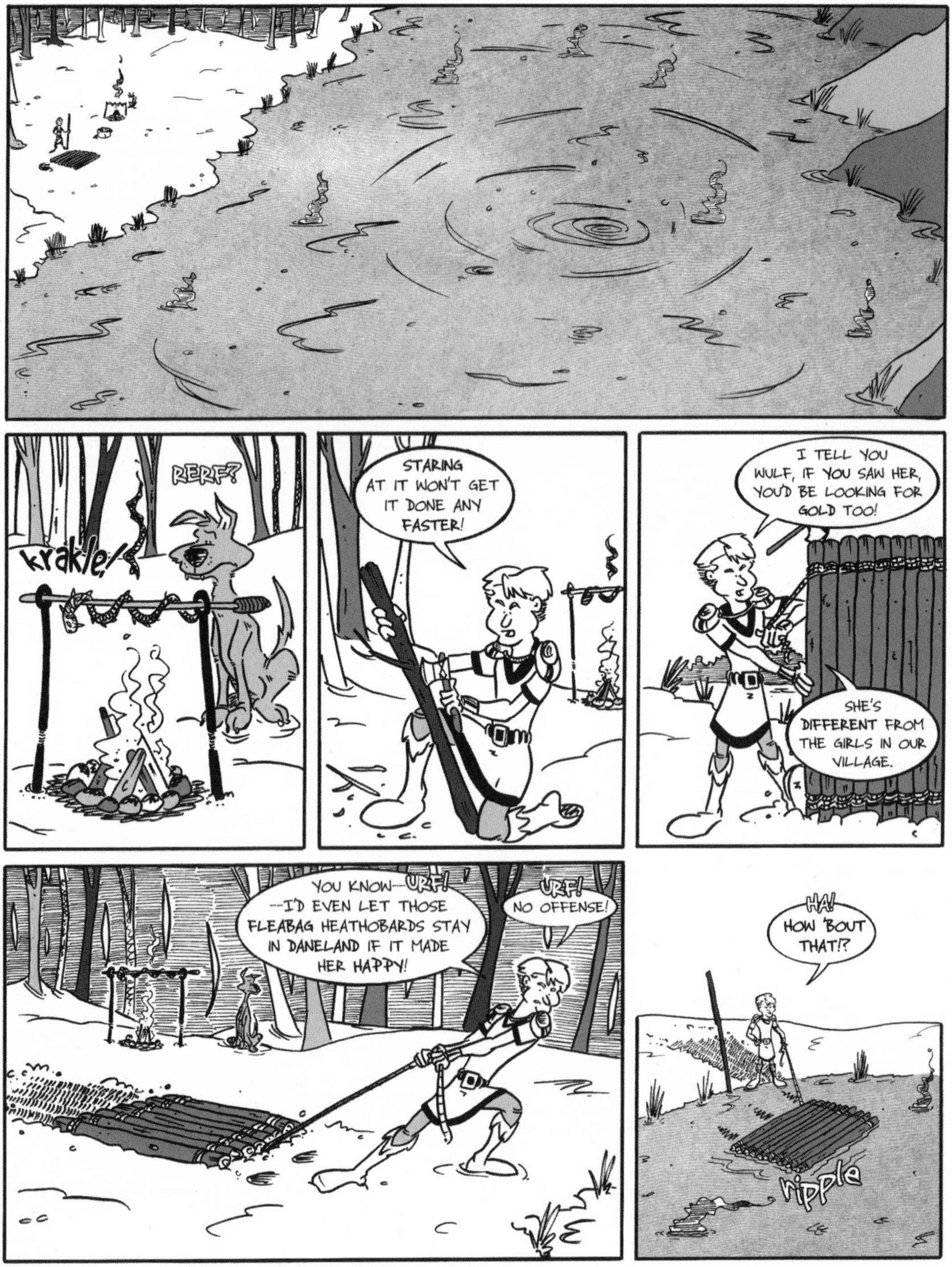

RERF?
krakle!
STARING AT IT WON'T GET IT DONE ANY FASTER!
I TELL YOU WULF, IF YOU SAW HER, YOU'D BE LOOKING FOR GOLD TOO!
SHE'S DIFFERENT FROM THE GIRLS IN OUR VILLAGE.
YOU KNOW--URF! --I'D EVEN LET THOSE FLEABAG HEATHOBARDS STAY IN DANELAND IF IT MADE HER HAPPY!
URF! NO OFFENSE!
HA! HOW 'BOUT THAT!?
ripple

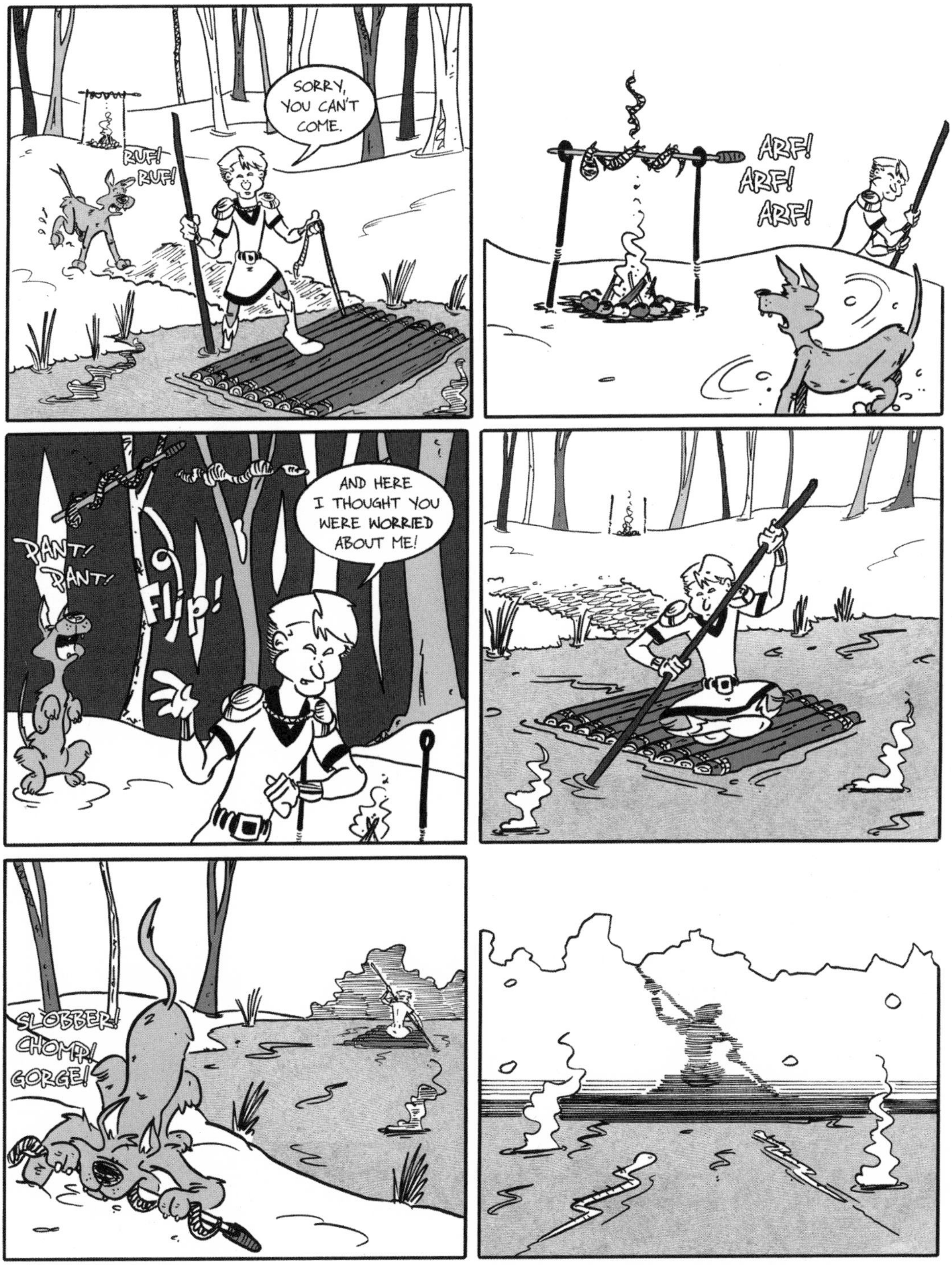

SORRY, YOU CAN'T COME.
RUF! RUF!
ARF! ARF! ARF!
PANT! PANT!
Flip!
AND HERE I THOUGHT YOU WERE WORRIED ABOUT ME!
SLOBBER! CHOMP! GORGE!

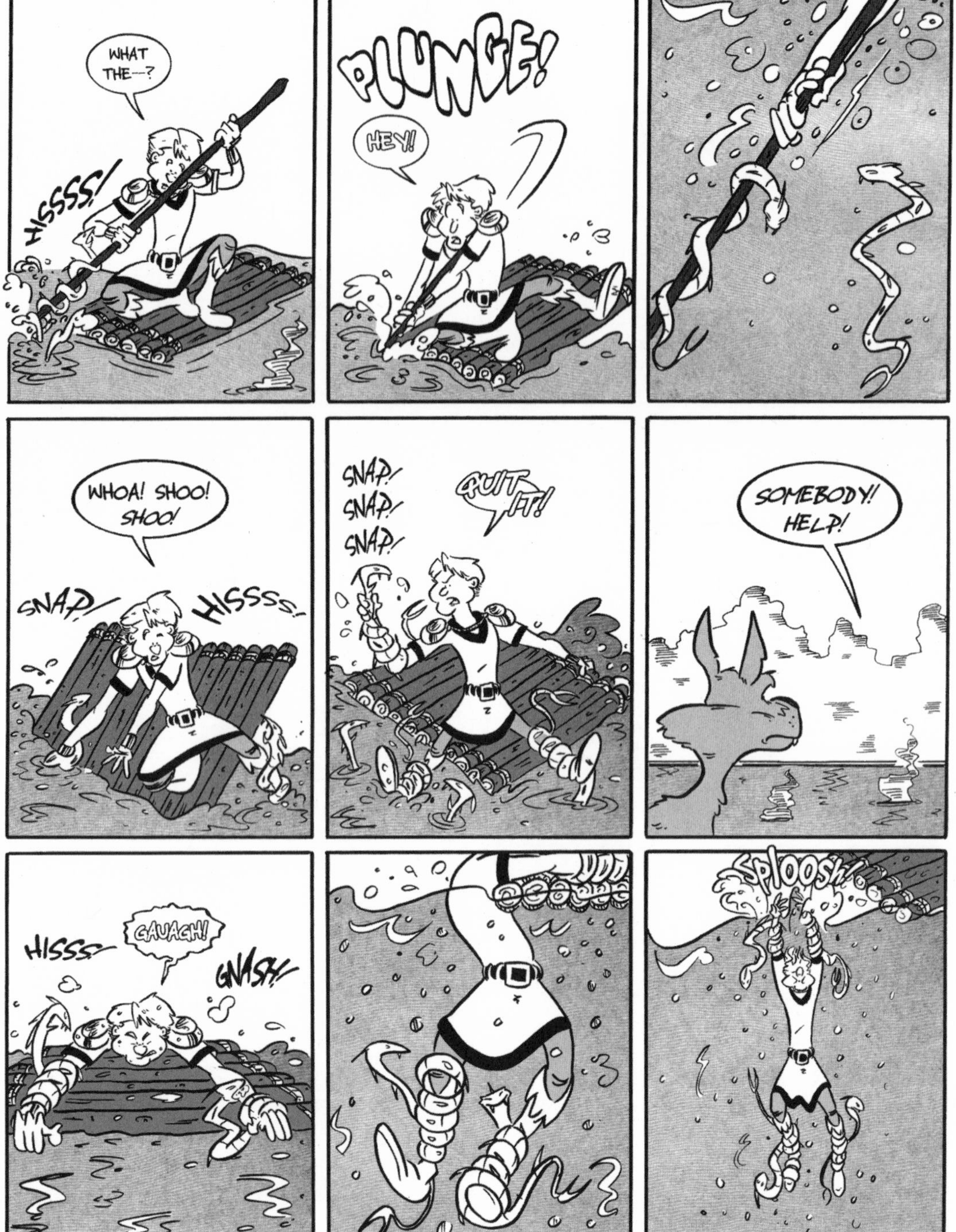
WHAT THE--?
HISSSS!
PLUNGE!
HEY!
WHOA! SHOO! SHOO!
SNAP!
HISSSS!
SNAP!
SNAP!
SNAP!
QUIT IT!
SOMEBODY! HELP!
HISSS-
GAUAGH!
GNASH!
SPLOOSH!

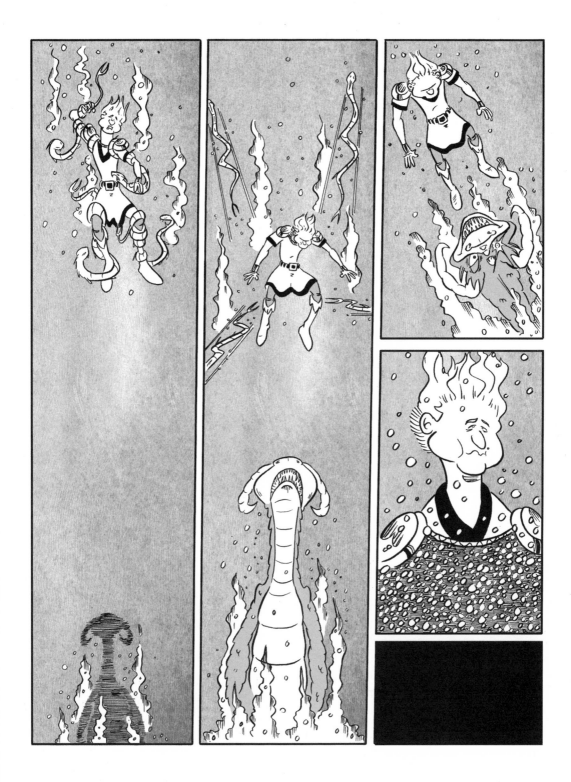

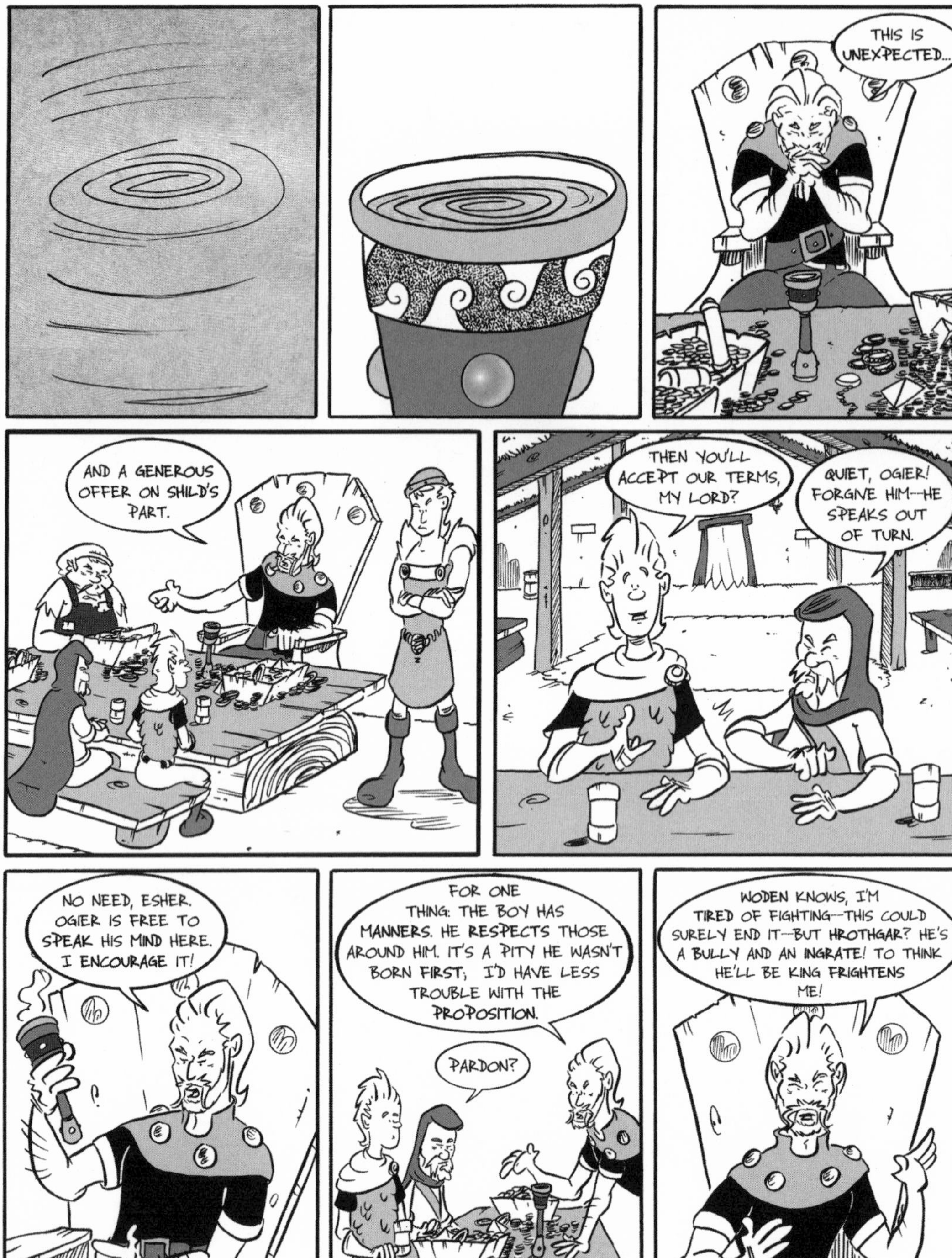
THIS IS UNEXPECTED...
AND A GENEROUS OFFER ON SHILD'S PART.
THEN YOU'LL ACCEPT OUR TERMS, MY LORD?
QUIET, OGIER! FORGIVE HIM--HE SPEAKS OUT OF TURN.
NO NEED, ESHER. OGIER IS FREE TO SPEAK HIS MIND HERE. I ENCOURAGE IT!
FOR ONE THING: THE BOY HAS MANNERS. HE RESPECTS THOSE AROUND HIM. IT'S A PITY HE WASN'T BORN FIRST; I'D HAVE LESS TROUBLE WITH THE PROPOSITION.
PARDON?
WODEN KNOWS, I'M TIRED OF FIGHTING--THIS COULD SURELY END IT--BUT HROTHGAR? HE'S A BULLY AND AN INGRATE! TO THINK HE'LL BE KING FRIGHTENS ME!

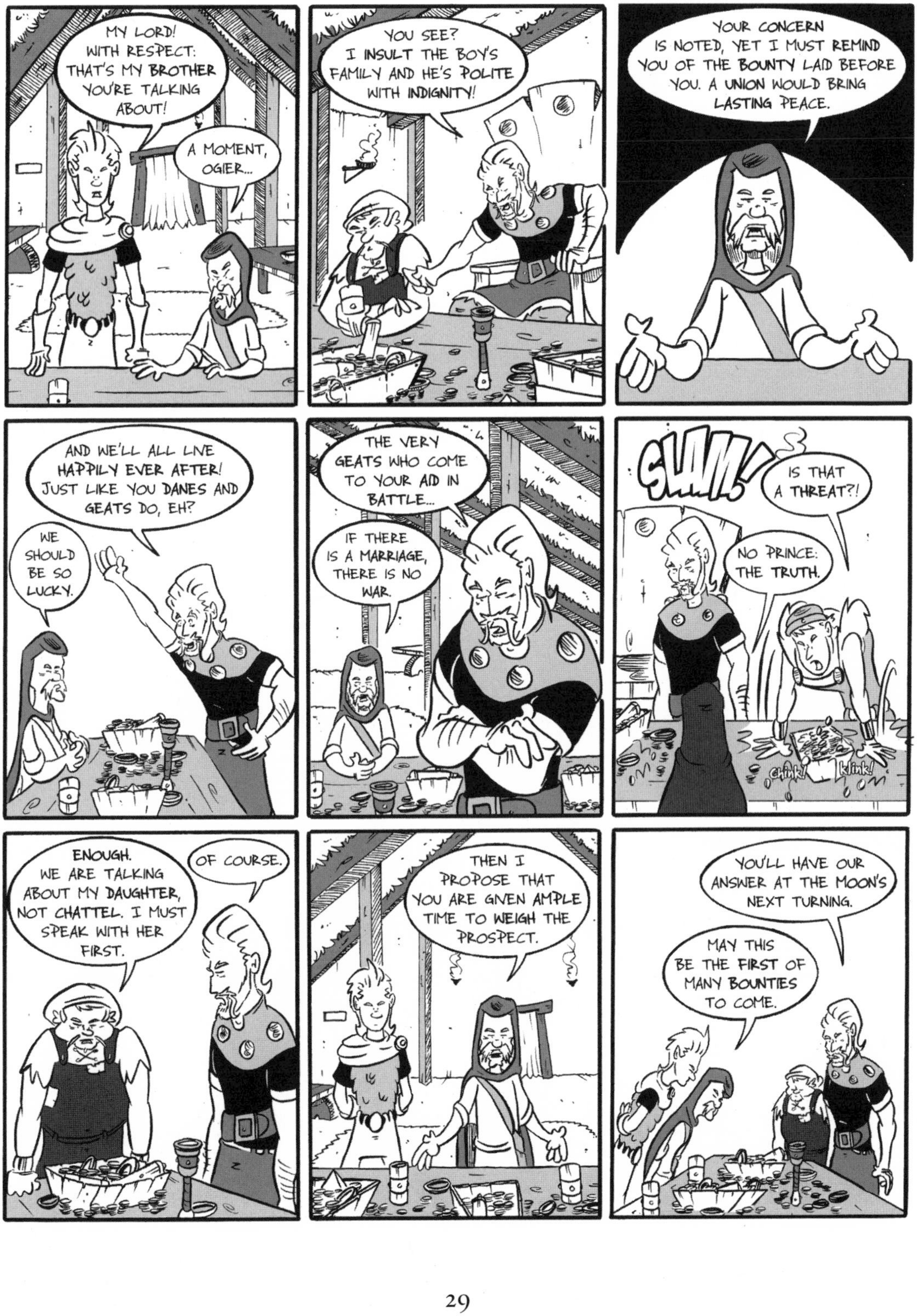
MY LORD! WITH RESPECT: THAT'S MY BROTHER YOU'RE TALKING ABOUT!
A MOMENT, OGIER...
YOU SEE? I INSULT THE BOY'S FAMILY AND HE'S POLITE WITH INDIGNITY!
YOUR CONCERN IS NOTED, YET I MUST REMIND YOU OF THE BOUNTY LAID BEFORE YOU. A UNION WOULD BRING LASTING PEACE.
AND WE'LL ALL LIVE HAPPILY EVER AFTER! JUST LIKE YOU DANES AND GEATS DO, EH?
WE SHOULD BE SO LUCKY.
THE VERY GEATS WHO COME TO YOUR AID IN BATTLE...
IF THERE IS A MARRIAGE, THERE IS NO WAR.
SLAM!
IS THAT A THREAT?!
NO PRINCE: THE TRUTH.
chink! klink!
ENOUGH. WE ARE TALKING ABOUT MY DAUGHTER, NOT CHATTEL. I MUST SPEAK WITH HER FIRST.
OF COURSE.
THEN I PROPOSE THAT YOU ARE GIVEN AMPLE TIME TO WEIGH THE PROSPECT.
YOU'LL HAVE OUR ANSWER AT THE MOON'S NEXT TURNING.
MAY THIS BE THE FIRST OF MANY BOUNTIES TO COME.

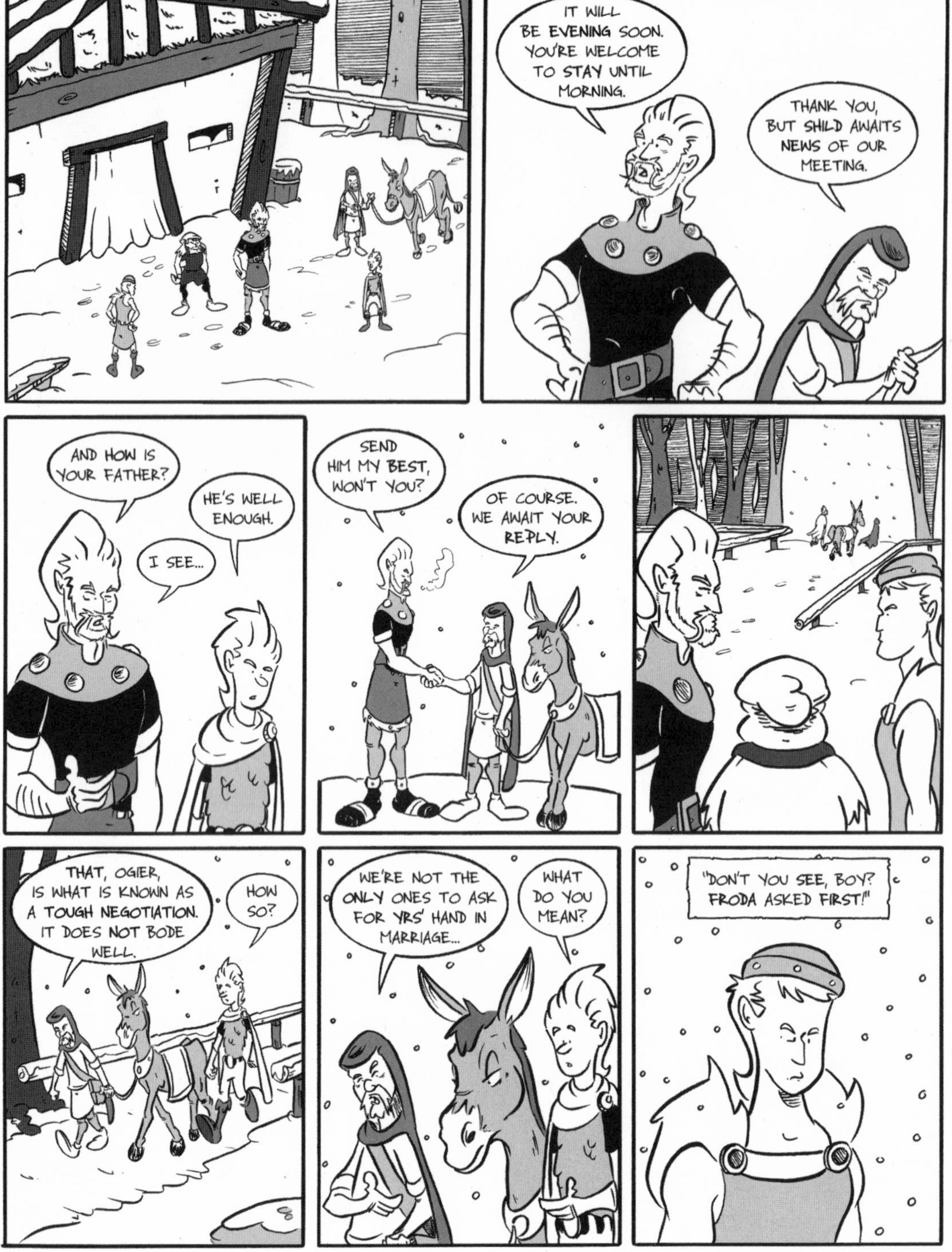
IT WILL BE EVENING SOON. YOU'RE WELCOME TO STAY UNTIL MORNING.
THANK YOU, BUT SHILD AWAITS NEWS OF OUR MEETING.
AND HOW IS YOUR FATHER?
HE'S WELL ENOUGH.
I SEE...
SEND HIM MY BEST, WON'T YOU?
OF COURSE. WE AWAIT YOUR REPLY.
THAT, OGIER, IS WHAT IS KNOWN AS A TOUGH NEGOTIATION. IT DOES NOT BODE WELL.
HOW SO?
WE'RE NOT THE ONLY ONES TO ASK FOR YRS' HAND IN MARRIAGE...
WHAT DO YOU MEAN?
"DON'T YOU SEE, BOY? FRODA ASKED FIRST!"

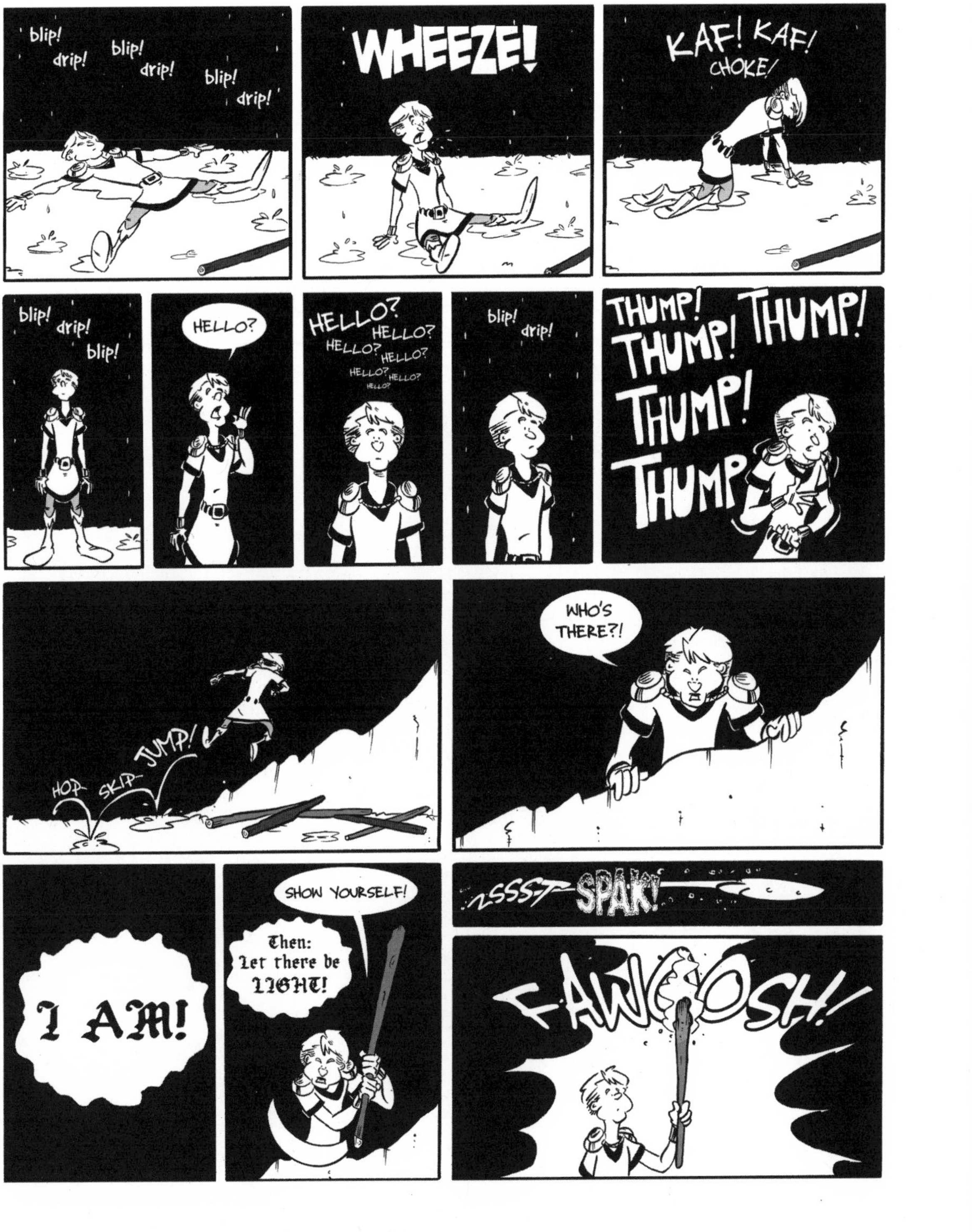
blip! drip! blip! drip! blip! drip!
WHEEZE!
KAF! KAF! CHOKE!
blip! drip! blip!
HELLO?
HELLO? HELLO? HELLO? HELLO? HELLO? HELLO?
blip! drip!
THUMP! THUMP! THUMP! THUMP! THUMP
HOP SKIP JUMP!
WHO'S THERE?!
I AM!
SHOW YOURSELF!
Then: Let there be LIGHT!
ZSSST SPAK!
FAWOOSH!

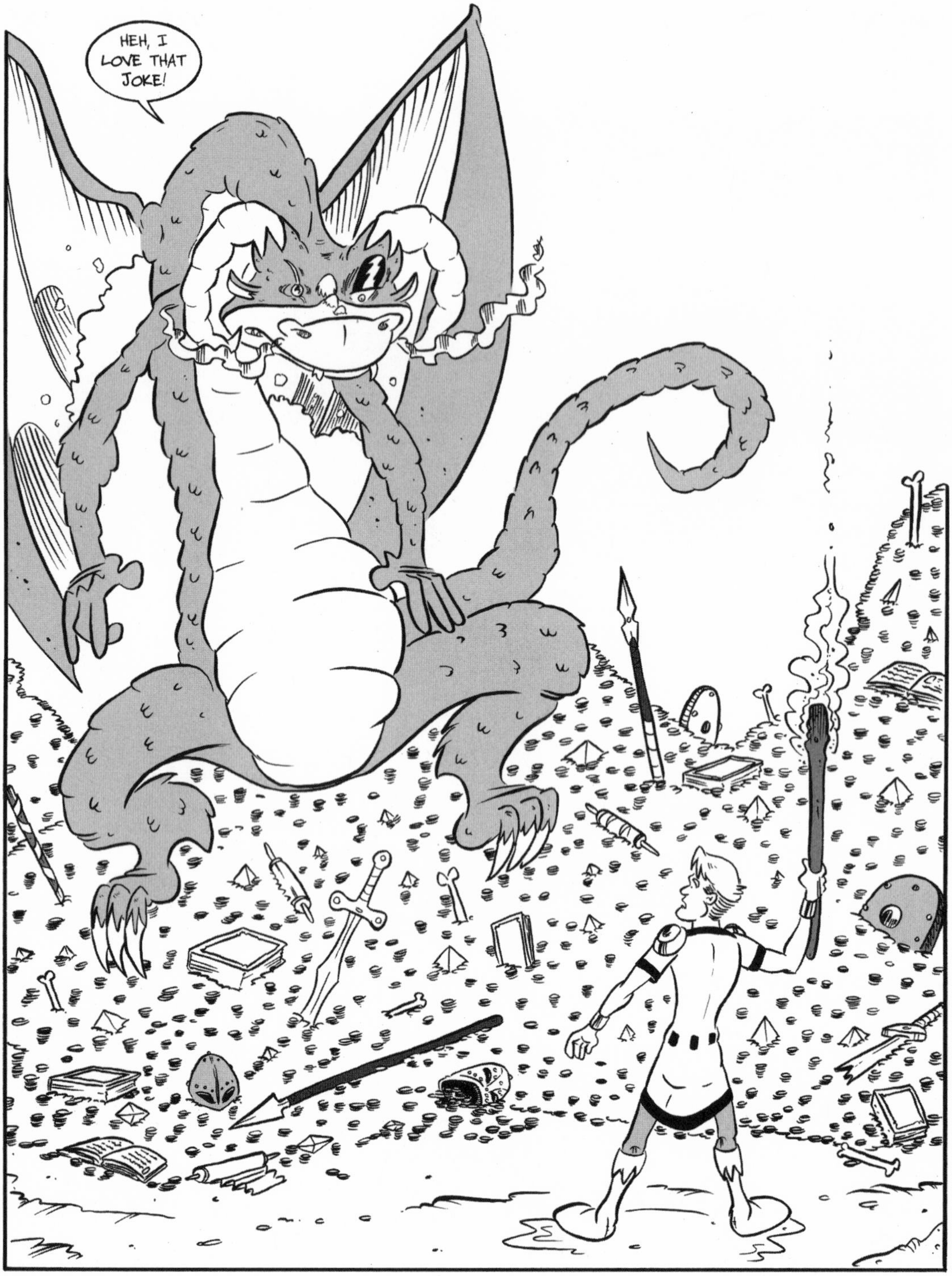
HEH, I LOVE THAT JOKE!

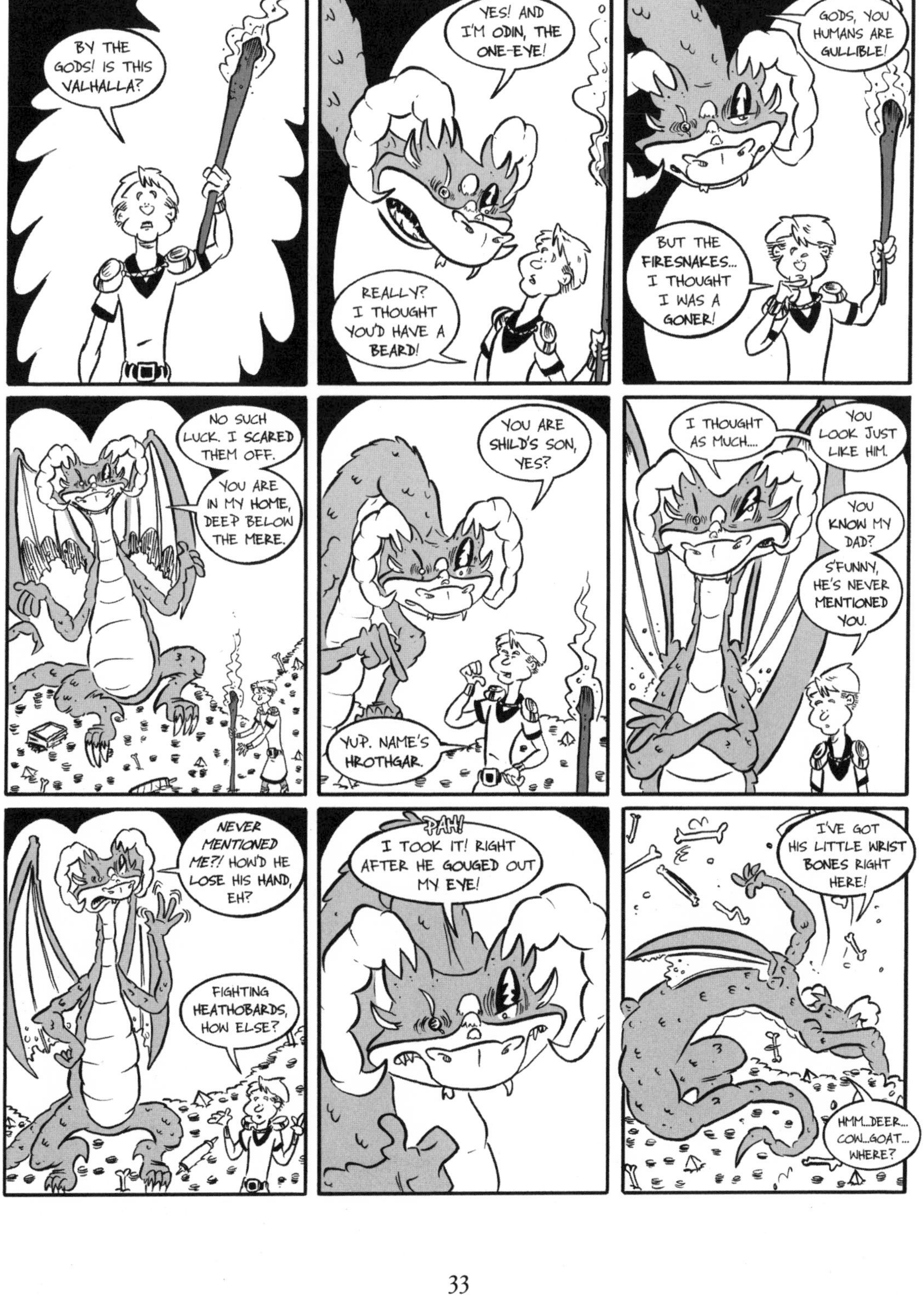
BY THE GODS! IS THIS VALHALLA?
YES! AND I'M ODIN, THE ONE-EYE!
REALLY? I THOUGHT YOU'D HAVE A BEARD!
GODS, YOU HUMANS ARE GULLIBLE!
BUT THE FIRESNAKES... I THOUGHT I WAS A GONER!
NO SUCH LUCK. I SCARED THEM OFF.
YOU ARE IN MY HOME, DEEP BELOW THE MERE.
YOU ARE SHILD'S SON, YES?
YUP. NAME'S HROTHGAR.
I THOUGHT AS MUCH....
YOU LOOK JUST LIKE HIM.
YOU KNOW MY DAD?
S'FUNNY, HE'S NEVER MENTIONED YOU.
NEVER MENTIONED ME?! HOW'D HE LOSE HIS HAND, EH?
FIGHTING HEATHOBARDS, HOW ELSE?
PAH!
I TOOK IT! RIGHT AFTER HE GOUGED OUT MY EYE!
I'VE GOT HIS LITTLE WRIST BONES RIGHT HERE!
HMM...DEER... COW...GOAT... WHERE?

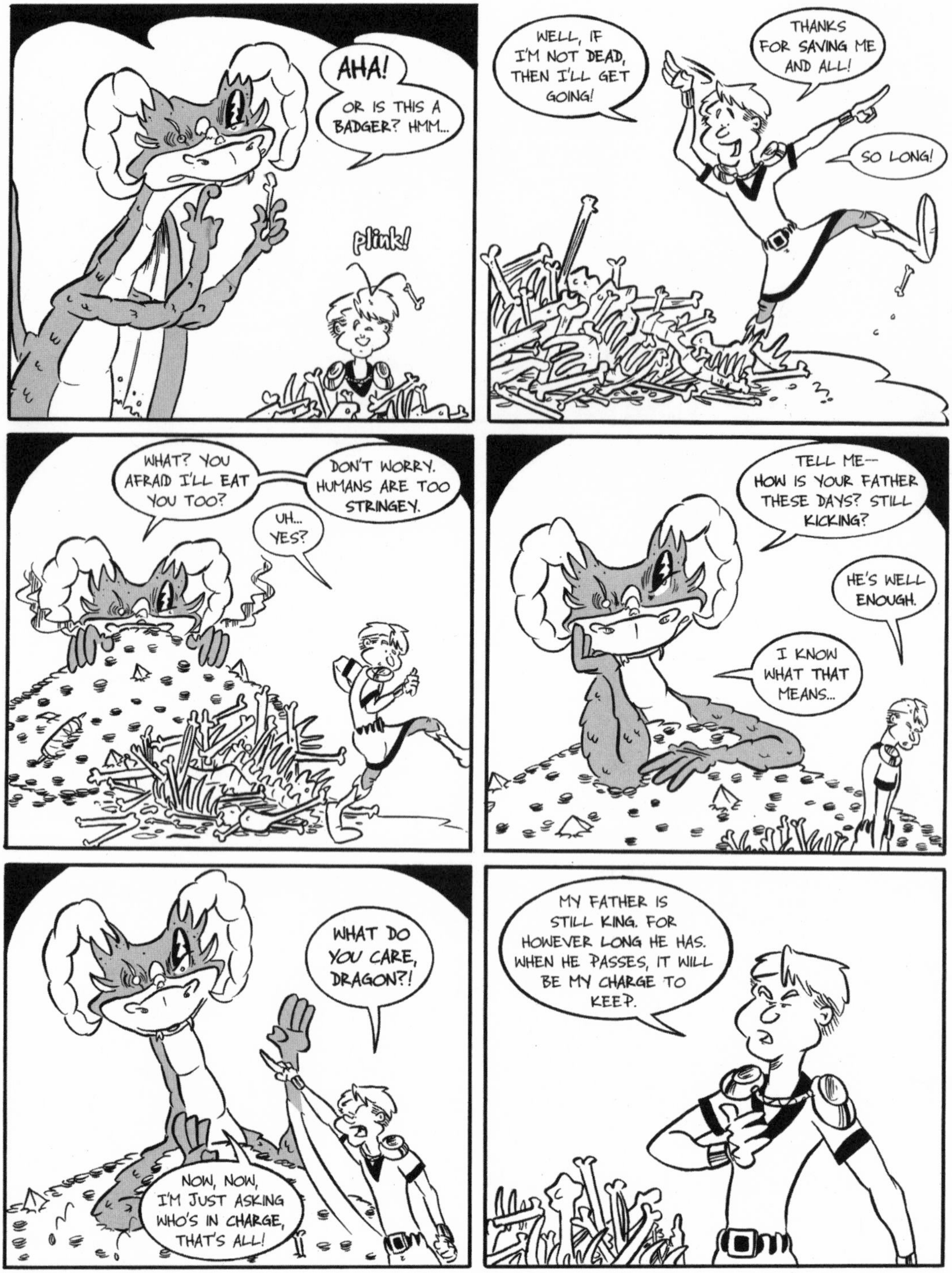
AHA!
OR IS THIS A BADGER? HMM...
plink!
WELL, IF I'M NOT DEAD, THEN I'LL GET GOING!
THANKS FOR SAVING ME AND ALL!
SO LONG!
WHAT? YOU AFRAID I'LL EAT YOU TOO?
DON'T WORRY. HUMANS ARE TOO STRINGEY.
UH... YES?
TELL ME— HOW IS YOUR FATHER THESE DAYS? STILL KICKING?
HE'S WELL ENOUGH.
I KNOW WHAT THAT MEANS...
WHAT DO YOU CARE, DRAGON?!
NOW, NOW, I'M JUST ASKING WHO'S IN CHARGE, THAT'S ALL!
MY FATHER IS STILL KING. FOR HOWEVER LONG HE HAS. WHEN HE PASSES, IT WILL BE MY CHARGE TO KEEP.

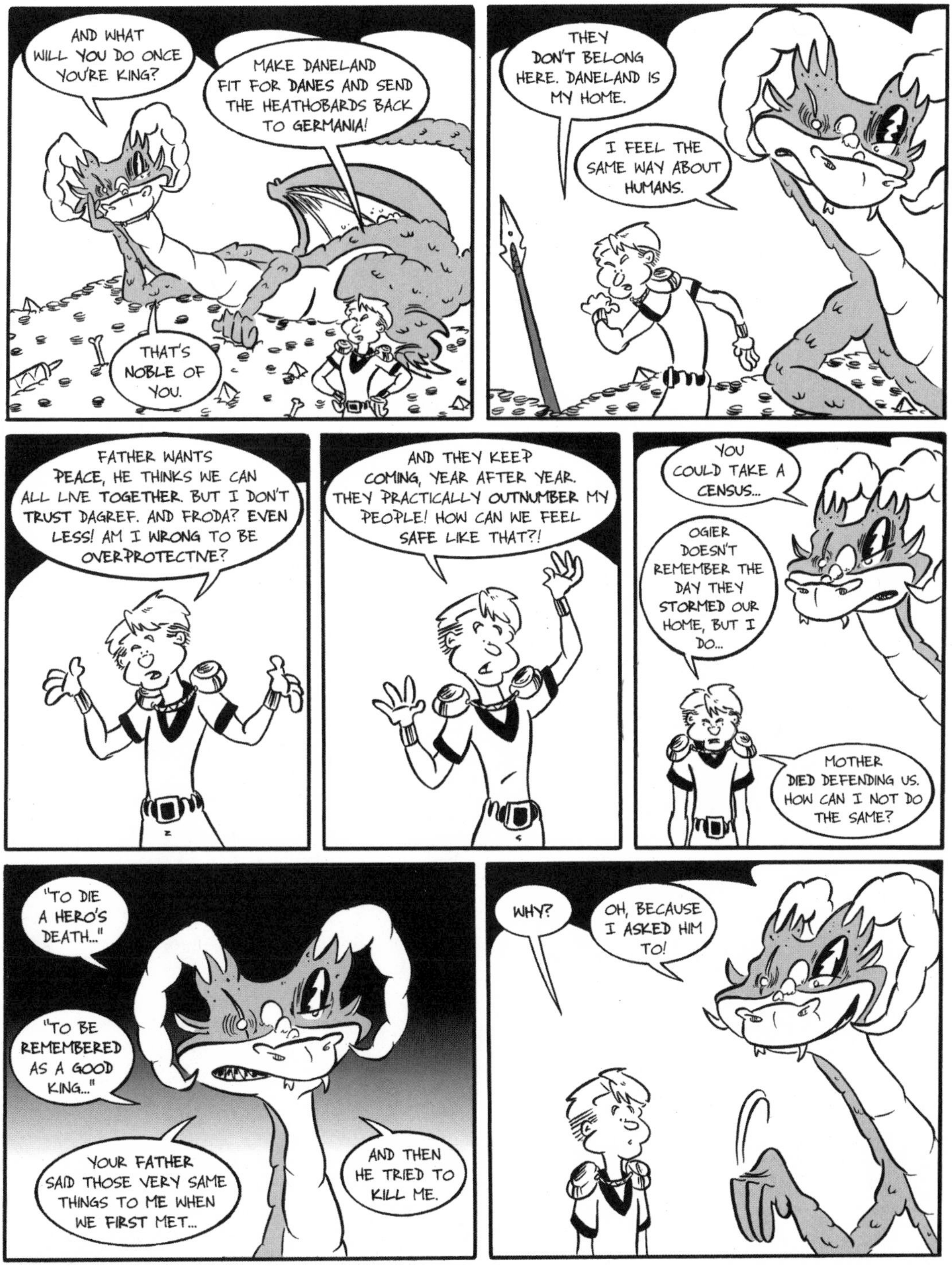
AND WHAT WILL YOU DO ONCE YOU'RE KING?
MAKE DANELAND FIT FOR DANES AND SEND THE HEATHOBARDS BACK TO GERMANIA!
THAT'S NOBLE OF YOU.
THEY DON'T BELONG HERE. DANELAND IS MY HOME.
I FEEL THE SAME WAY ABOUT HUMANS.
FATHER WANTS PEACE, HE THINKS WE CAN ALL LIVE TOGETHER. BUT I DON'T TRUST DAGREF. AND FRODA? EVEN LESS! AM I WRONG TO BE OVERPROTECTIVE?
AND THEY KEEP COMING, YEAR AFTER YEAR. THEY PRACTICALLY OUTNUMBER MY PEOPLE! HOW CAN WE FEEL SAFE LIKE THAT?!
YOU COULD TAKE A CENSUS...
OGIER DOESN'T REMEMBER THE DAY THEY STORMED OUR HOME, BUT I DO...
MOTHER DIED DEFENDING US. HOW CAN I NOT DO THE SAME?
"TO DIE A HERO'S DEATH..."
"TO BE REMEMBERED AS A GOOD KING..."
YOUR FATHER SAID THOSE VERY SAME THINGS TO ME WHEN WE FIRST MET...
AND THEN HE TRIED TO KILL ME.
WHY?
OH, BECAUSE I ASKED HIM TO!

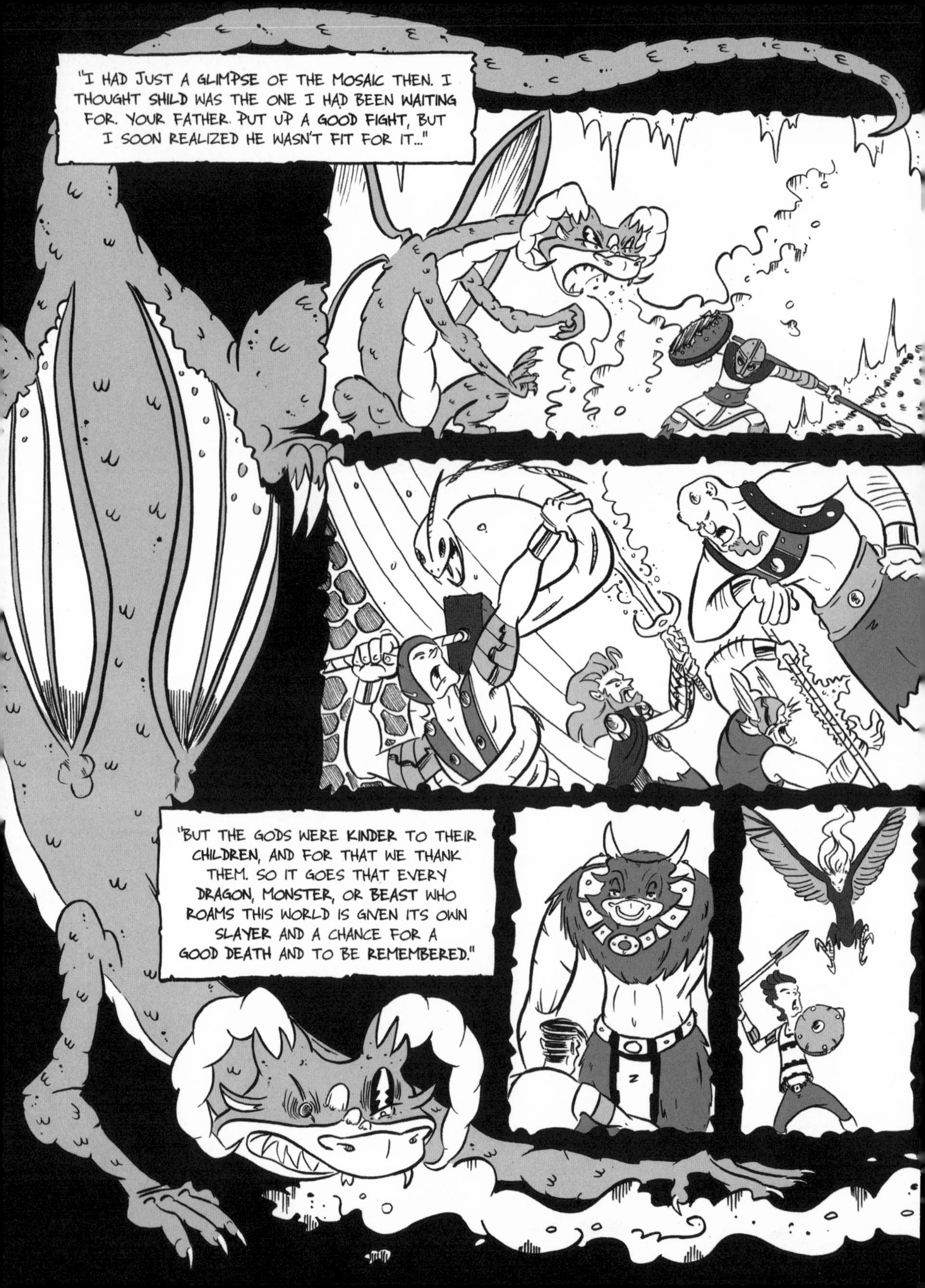
"I HAD JUST A GLIMPSE OF THE MOSAIC THEN. I THOUGHT SHILD WAS THE ONE I HAD BEEN WAITING FOR. YOUR FATHER PUT UP A GOOD FIGHT, BUT I SOON REALIZED HE WASN'T FIT FOR IT..."
"BUT THE GODS WERE KINDER TO THEIR CHILDREN, AND FOR THAT WE THANK THEM. SO IT GOES THAT EVERY DRAGON, MONSTER, OR BEAST WHO ROAMS THIS WORLD IS GIVEN ITS OWN SLAYER AND A CHANCE FOR A GOOD DEATH AND TO BE REMEMBERED."

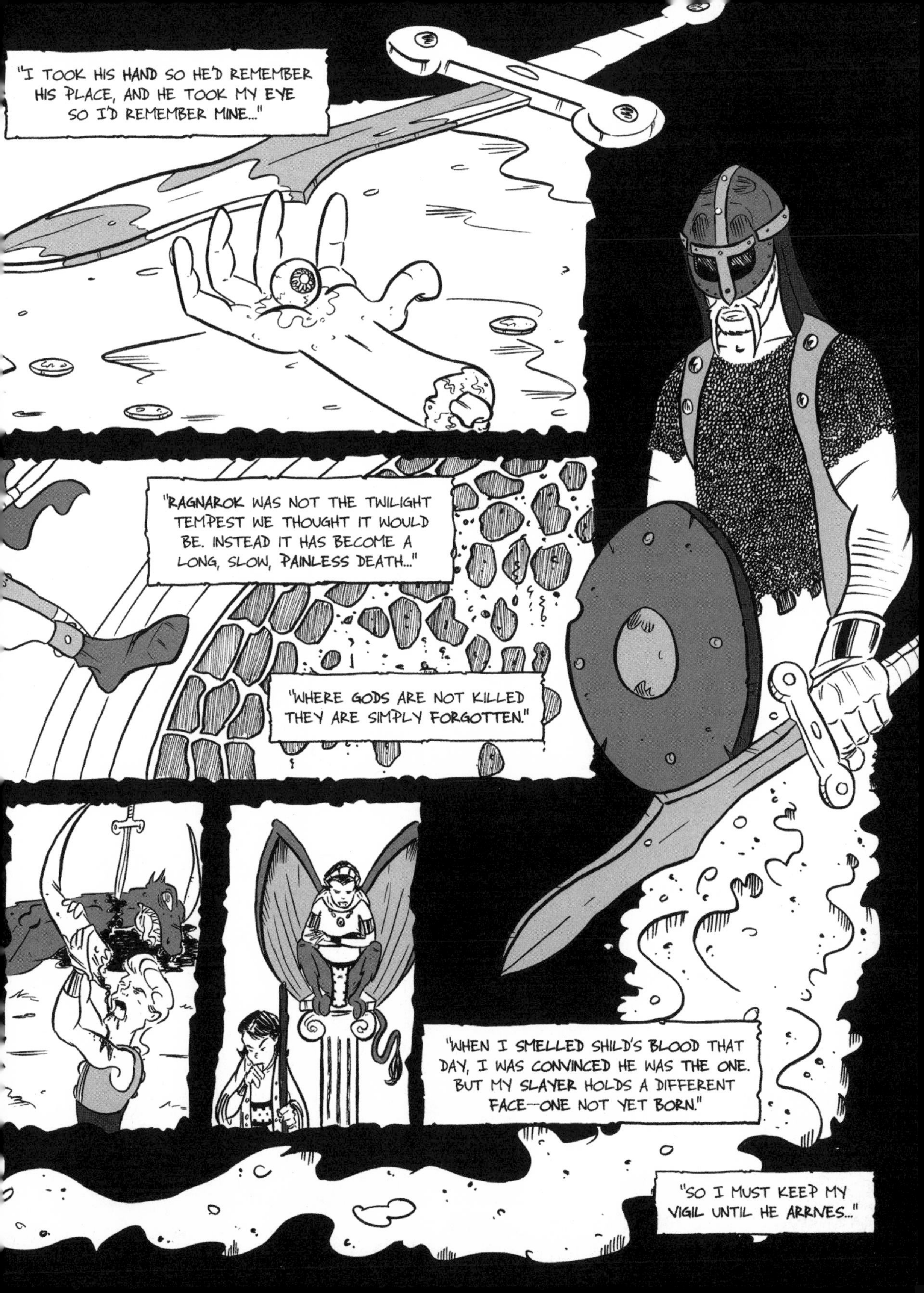
"I TOOK HIS HAND SO HE'D REMEMBER HIS PLACE, AND HE TOOK MY EYE SO I'D REMEMBER MINE..."
"RAGNAROK WAS NOT THE TWILIGHT TEMPEST WE THOUGHT IT WOULD BE. INSTEAD IT HAS BECOME A LONG, SLOW, PAINLESS DEATH..."
"WHERE GODS ARE NOT KILLED THEY ARE SIMPLY FORGOTTEN."
"WHEN I SMELLED SHILD'S BLOOD THAT DAY, I WAS CONVINCED HE WAS THE ONE. BUT MY SLAYER HOLDS A DIFFERENT FACE--ONE NOT YET BORN."
"SO I MUST KEEP MY VIGIL UNTIL HE ARRIVES..."

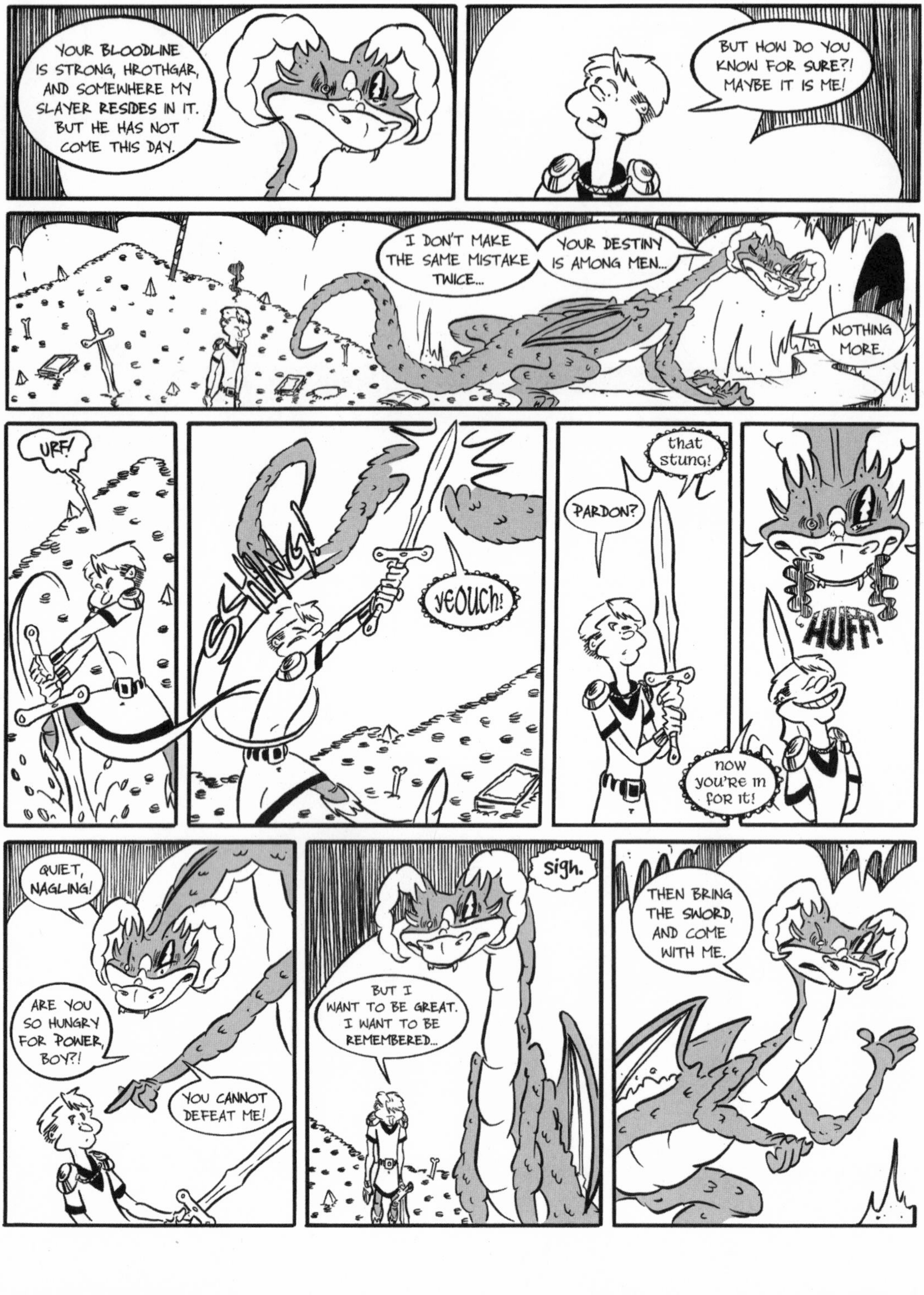
YOUR BLOODLINE IS STRONG, HROTHGAR, AND SOMEWHERE MY SLAYER RESIDES IN IT. BUT HE HAS NOT COME THIS DAY.
BUT HOW DO YOU KNOW FOR SURE?! MAYBE IT IS ME!
I DON'T MAKE THE SAME MISTAKE TWICE...
YOUR DESTINY IS AMONG MEN...
NOTHING MORE.
URF!
SSHING!
yeOUCH!
that stung!
PARDON?
HUFF!
now you're in for it!
QUIET, NAGLING!
ARE YOU SO HUNGRY FOR POWER, BOY?!
YOU CANNOT DEFEAT ME!
sigh.
BUT I WANT TO BE GREAT. I WANT TO BE REMEMBERED...
THEN BRING THE SWORD, AND COME WITH ME.

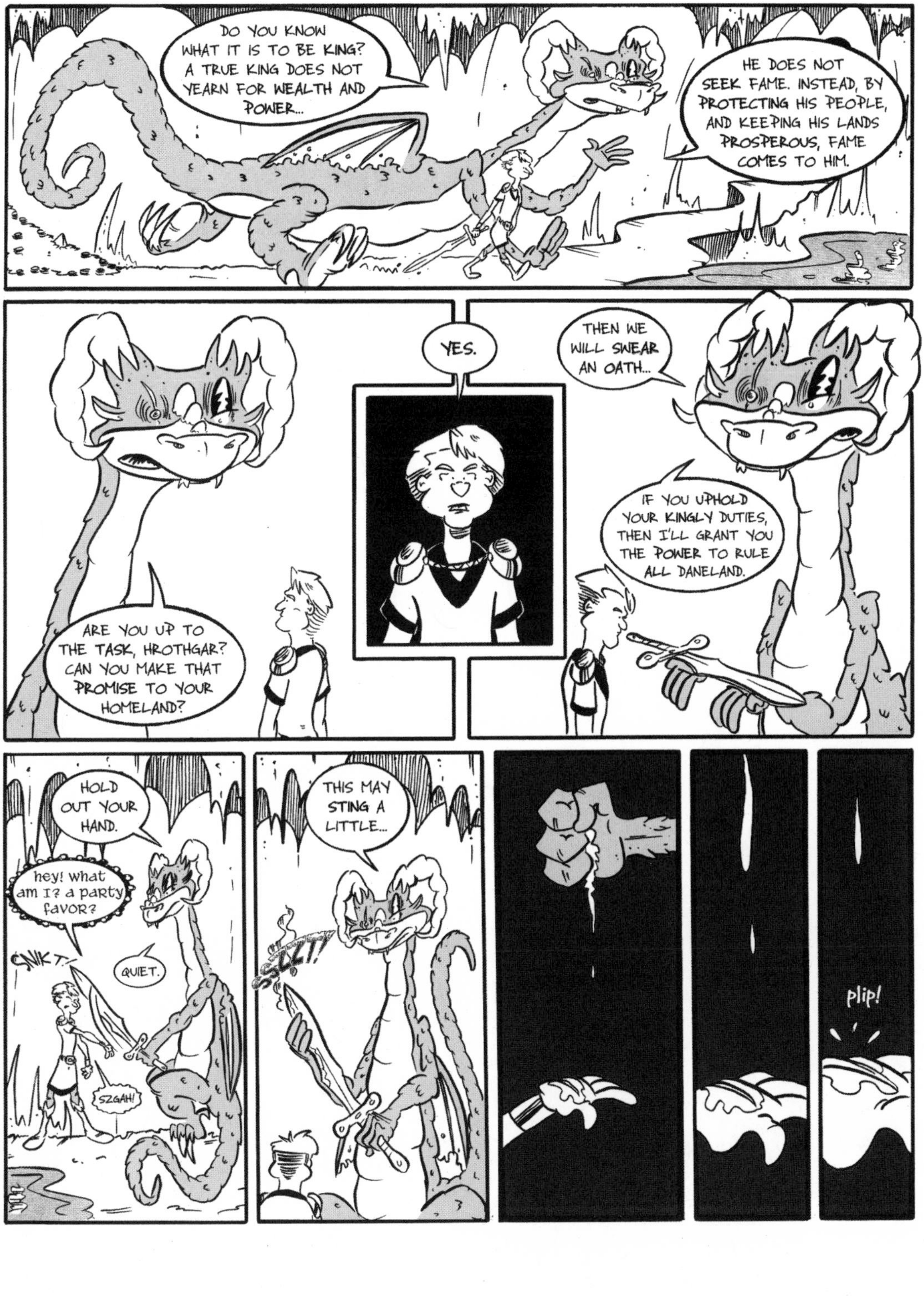
DO YOU KNOW WHAT IT IS TO BE KING? A TRUE KING DOES NOT YEARN FOR WEALTH AND POWER...
HE DOES NOT SEEK FAME. INSTEAD, BY PROTECTING HIS PEOPLE, AND KEEPING HIS LANDS PROSPEROUS, FAME COMES TO HIM.
ARE YOU UP TO THE TASK, HROTHGAR? CAN YOU MAKE THAT PROMISE TO YOUR HOMELAND?
YES.
THEN WE WILL SWEAR AN OATH...
IF YOU UPHOLD YOUR KINGLY DUTIES, THEN I'LL GRANT YOU THE POWER TO RULE ALL DANELAND.
HOLD OUT YOUR HAND.
hey! what am I? a party favor?
SNIKT
QUIET.
SZGAH!
THIS MAY STING A LITTLE...
SSZZT!
plip!

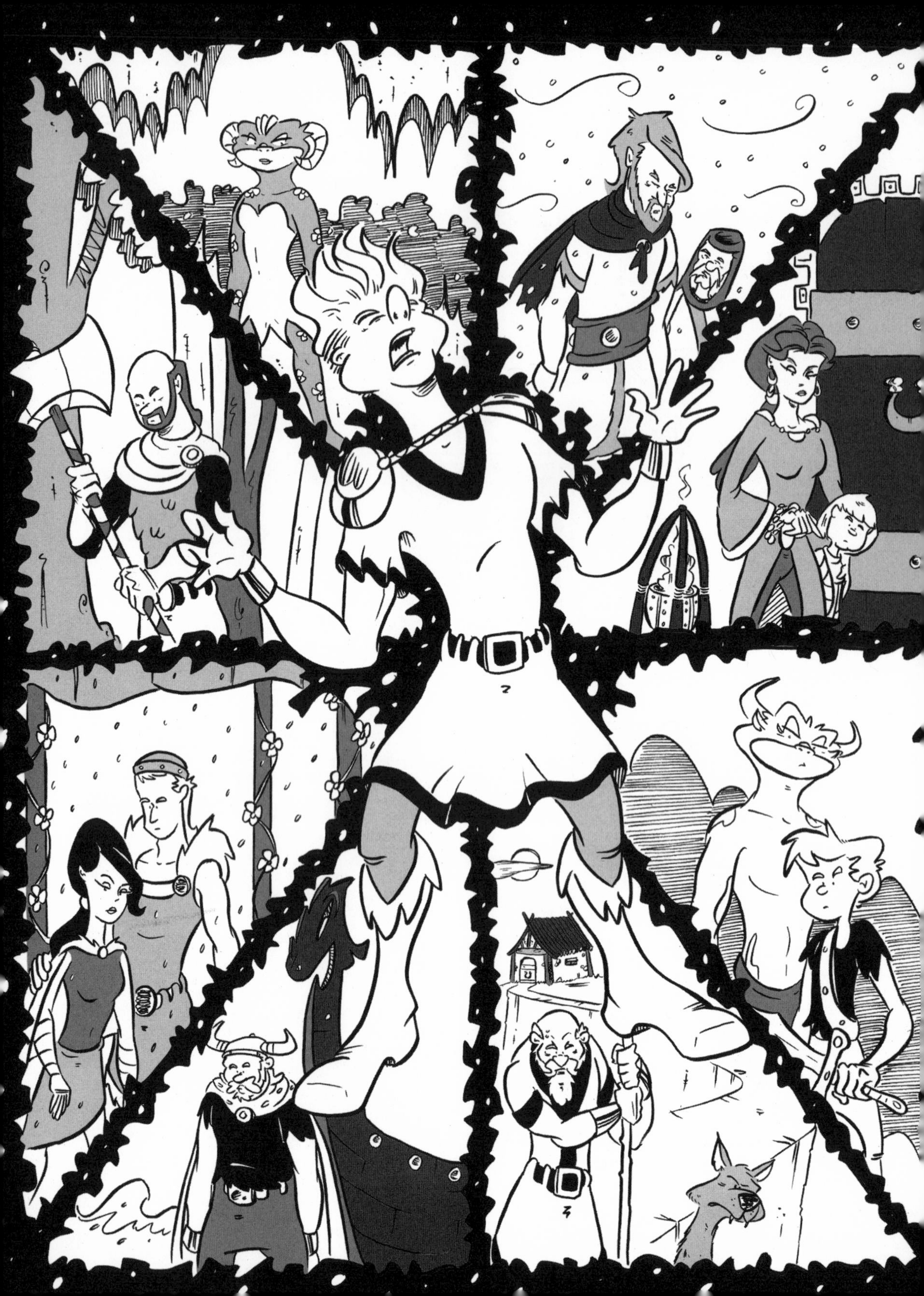

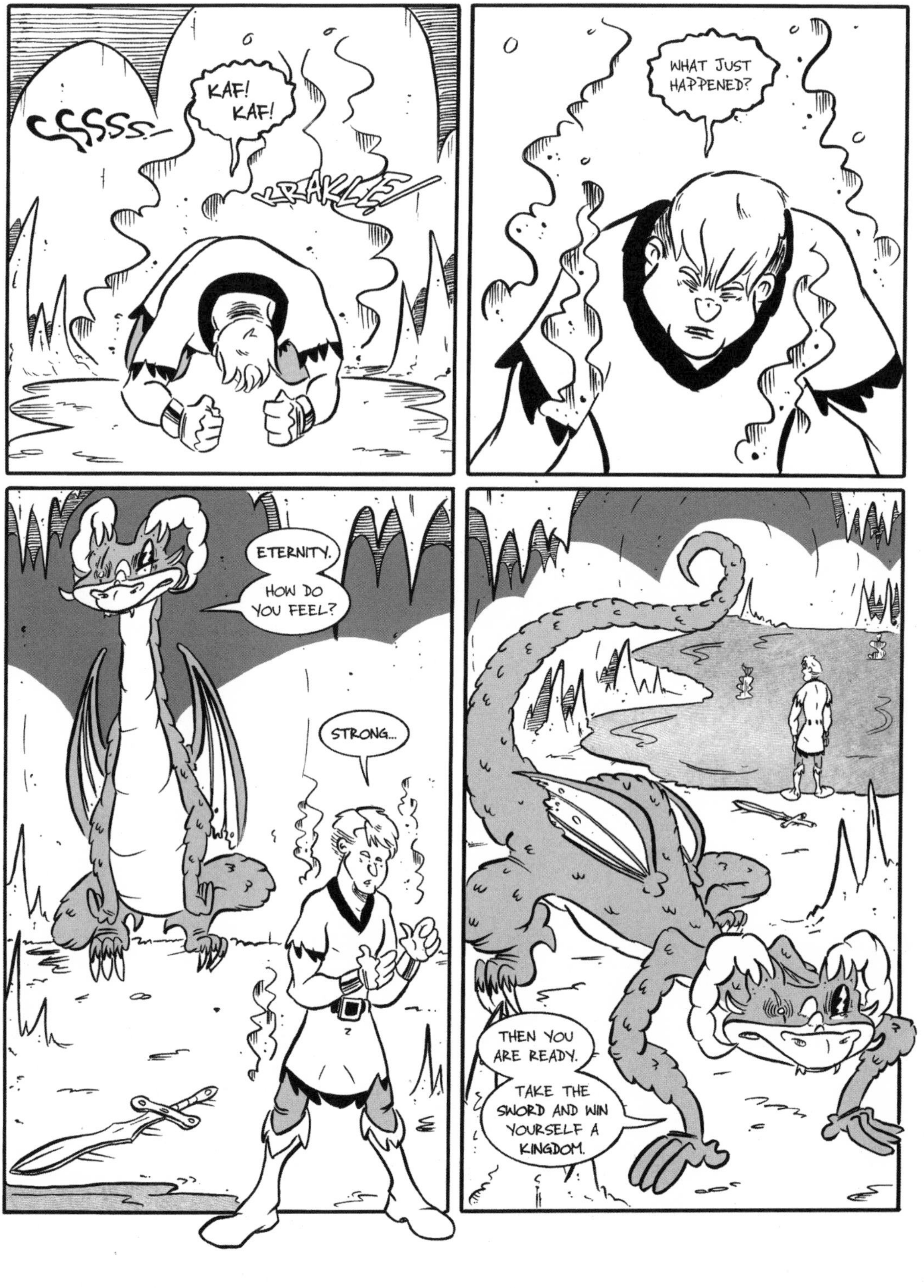
CSSSS
KAF! KAF!
KRAKLE!
WHAT JUST HAPPENED?
ETERNITY.
HOW DO YOU FEEL?
STRONG...
THEN YOU ARE READY.
TAKE THE SWORD AND WIN YOURSELF A KINGDOM.

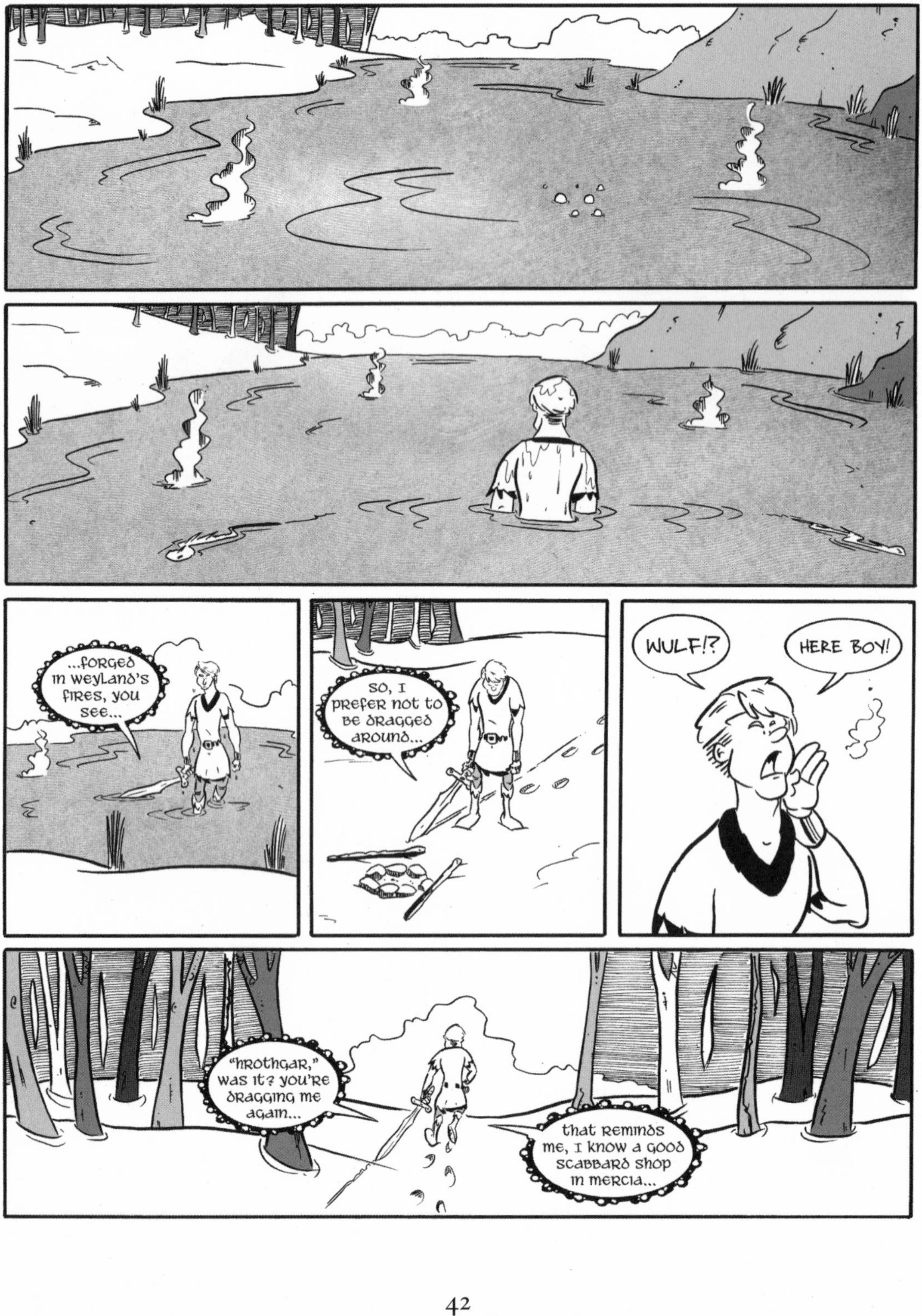
...forged in weyland's fires, you see...
so, I prefer not to be dragged around...
WULF!?
HERE BOY!
"hrothgar," was it? you're dragging me again...
that reminds me, I know a good scabbard shop in mercia...

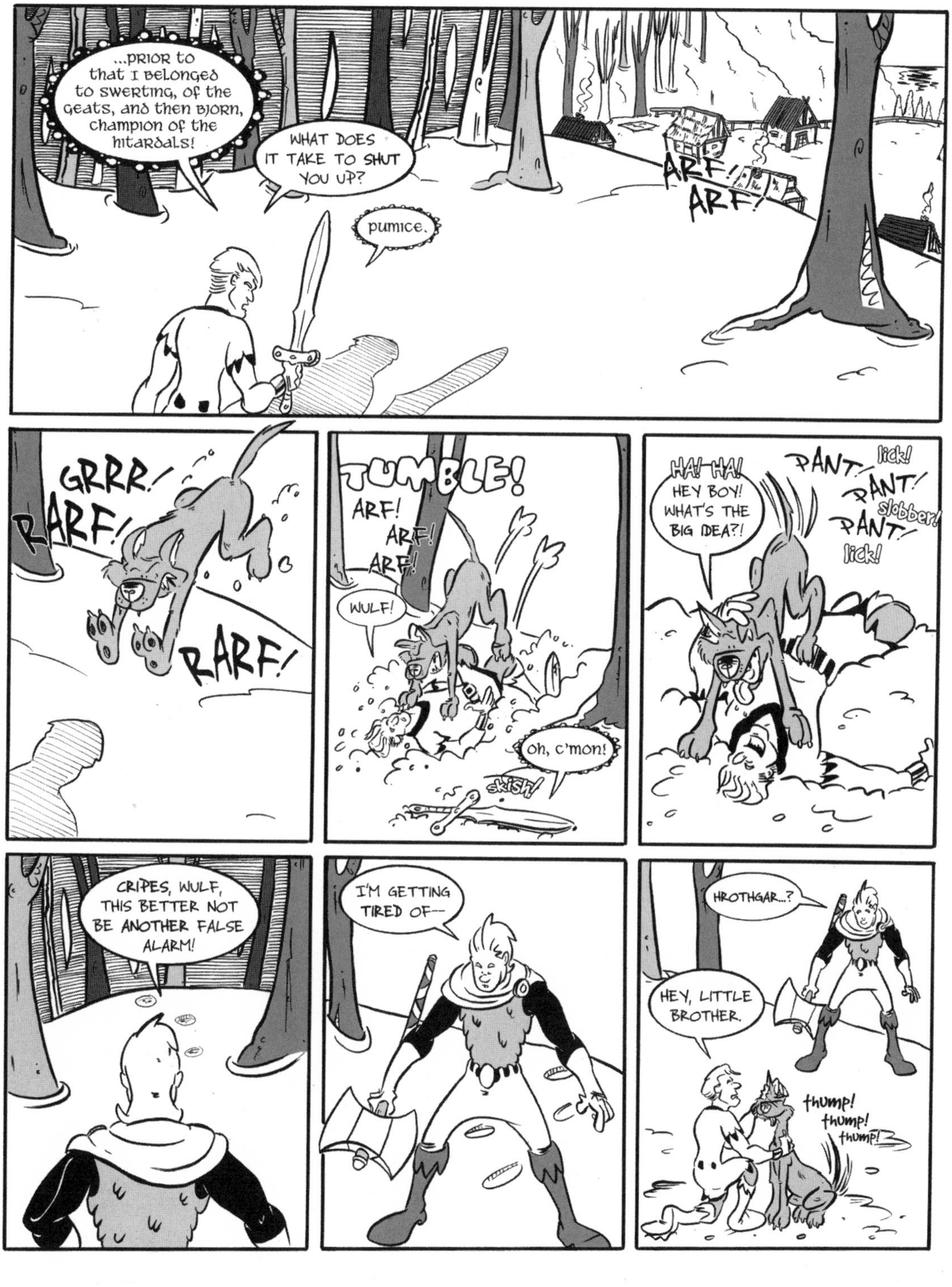
...PRIOR to that I BELONGED to SWERTING, OF the GEATS, and then BJORN, champion of the hitardals!
WHAT DOES IT TAKE TO SHUT YOU UP?
pumice.
ARF! ARF!
GRRR!
RARF!
RARF!
TUMBLE!
ARF! ARF! ARF!
WULF!
oh, c'mon!
SKISH!
HA! HA!
HEY BOY! WHAT'S THE BIG IDEA?!
PANT! lick! PANT! slobber! PANT! lick!
CRIPES, WULF, THIS BETTER NOT BE ANOTHER FALSE ALARM!
I'M GETTING TIRED OF--
HROTHGAR...?
HEY, LITTLE BROTHER.
thump! thump! thump!

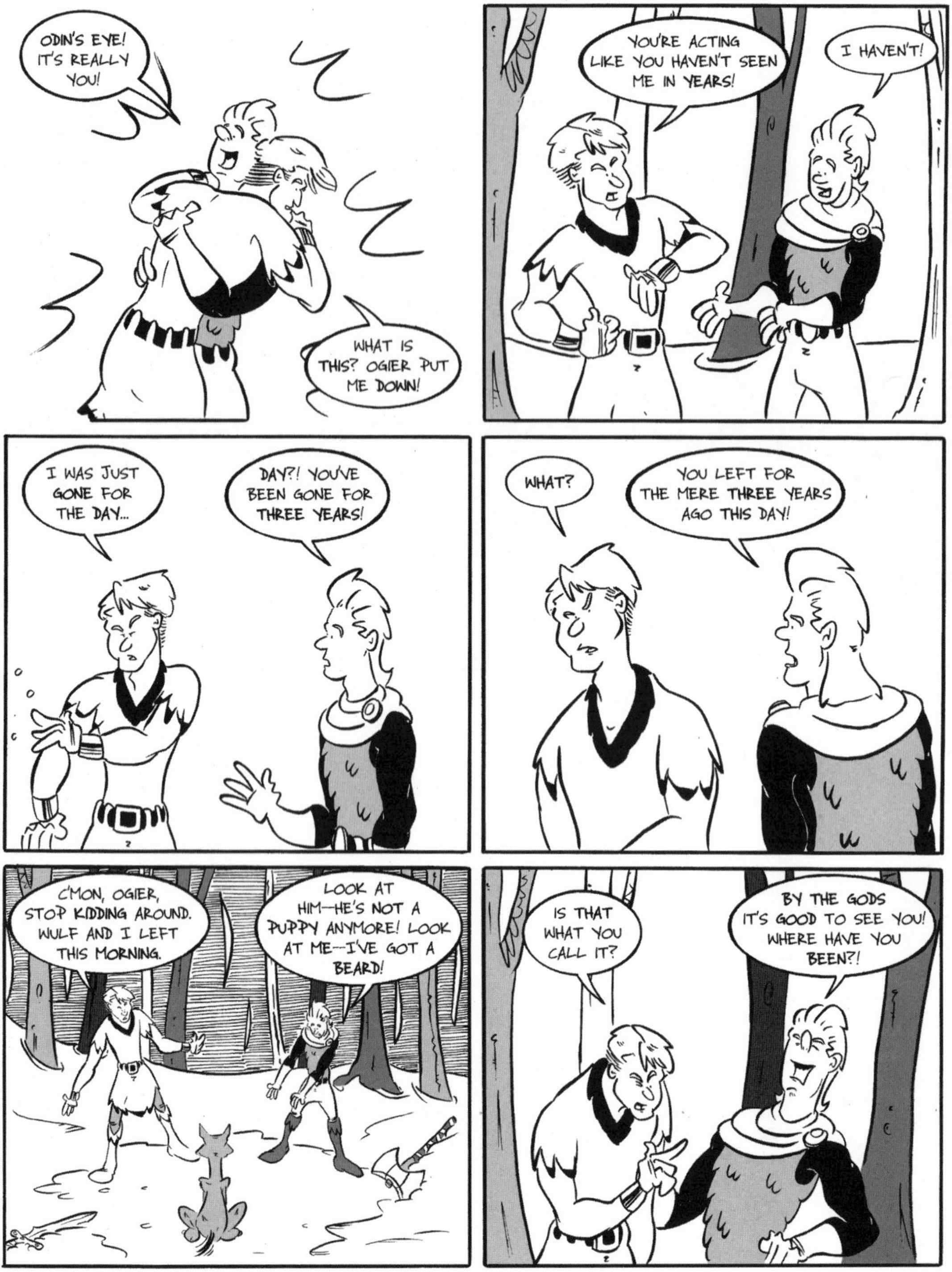
ODIN'S EYE! IT'S REALLY YOU!
WHAT IS THIS? OGIER PUT ME DOWN!
YOU'RE ACTING LIKE YOU HAVEN'T SEEN ME IN YEARS!
I HAVEN'T!
I WAS JUST GONE FOR THE DAY...
DAY?! YOU'VE BEEN GONE FOR THREE YEARS!
WHAT?
YOU LEFT FOR THE MERE THREE YEARS AGO THIS DAY!
C'MON, OGIER, STOP KIDDING AROUND. WULF AND I LEFT THIS MORNING.
LOOK AT HIM--HE'S NOT A PUPPY ANYMORE! LOOK AT ME--I'VE GOT A BEARD!
IS THAT WHAT YOU CALL IT?
BY THE GODS IT'S GOOD TO SEE YOU! WHERE HAVE YOU BEEN?!

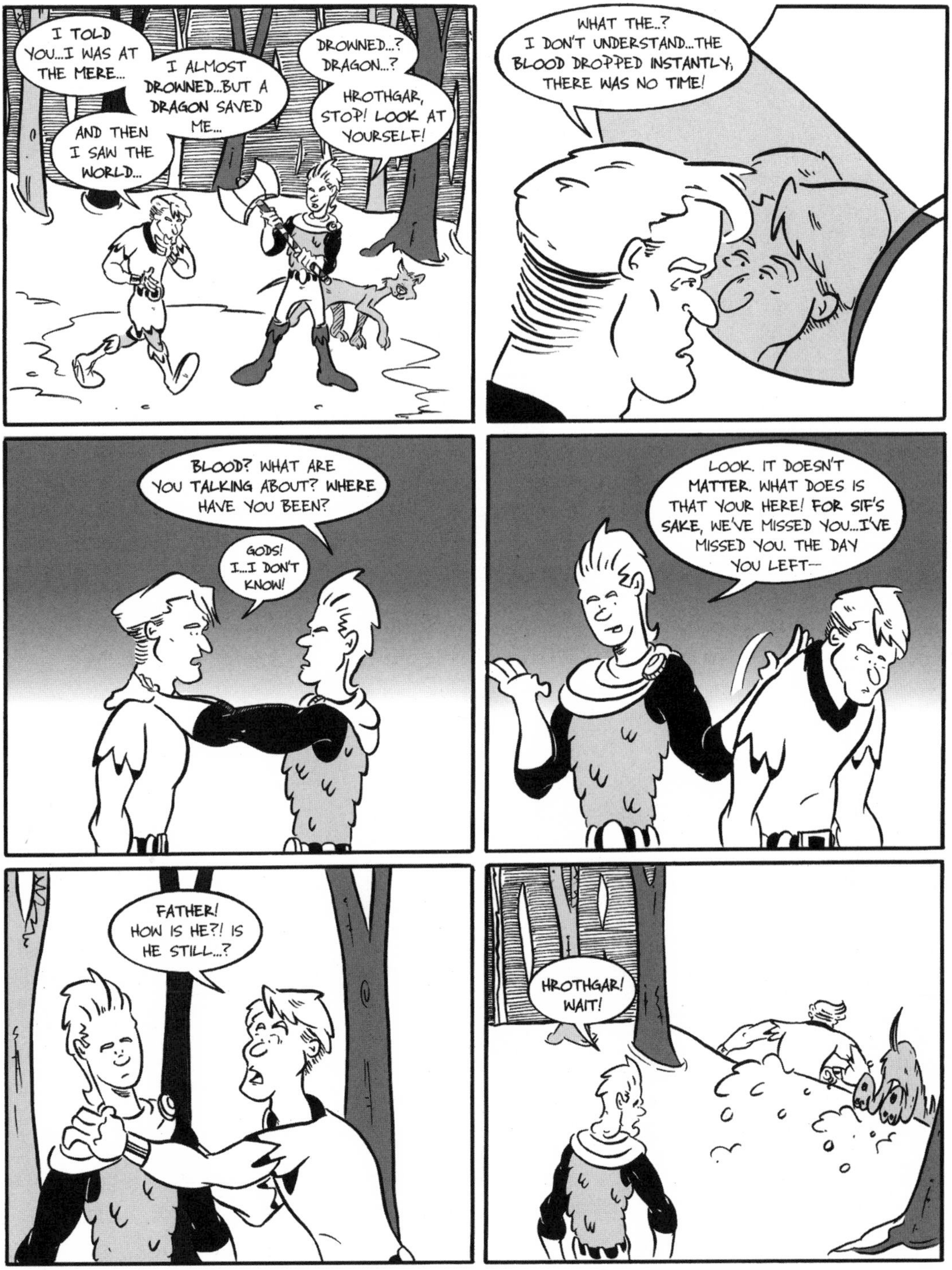
I TOLD YOU...I WAS AT THE MERE...
I ALMOST DROWNED...BUT A DRAGON SAVED ME...
AND THEN I SAW THE WORLD...
DROWNED...? DRAGON...?
HROTHGAR, STOP! LOOK AT YOURSELF!
WHAT THE..? I DON'T UNDERSTAND...THE BLOOD DROPPED INSTANTLY; THERE WAS NO TIME!
BLOOD? WHAT ARE YOU TALKING ABOUT? WHERE HAVE YOU BEEN?
GODS! I...I DON'T KNOW!
LOOK. IT DOESN'T MATTER. WHAT DOES IS THAT YOUR HERE! FOR SIF'S SAKE, WE'VE MISSED YOU...I'VE MISSED YOU. THE DAY YOU LEFT—
FATHER! HOW IS HE?! IS HE STILL...?
HROTHGAR! WAIT!

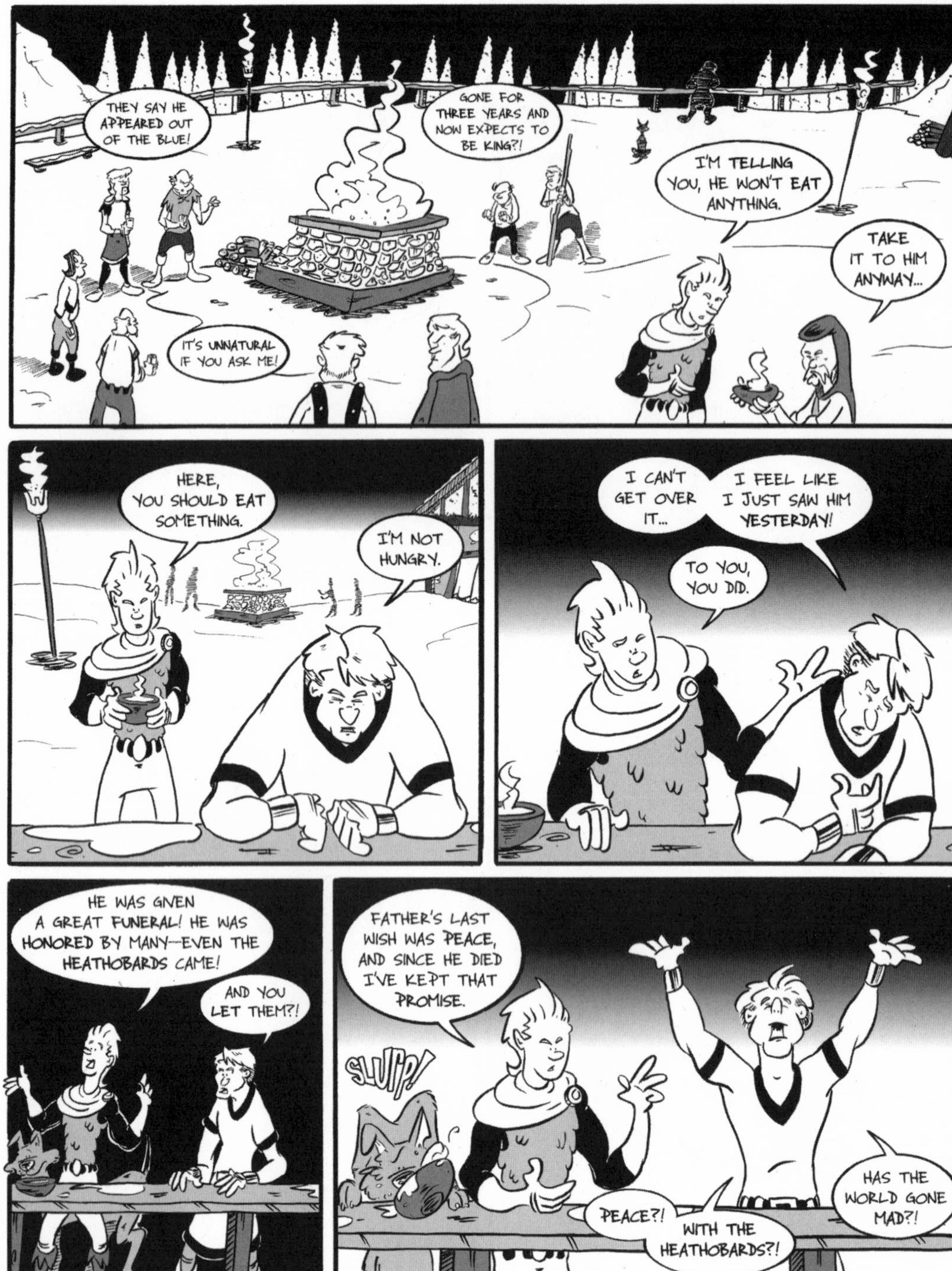
THEY SAY HE APPEARED OUT OF THE BLUE!
GONE FOR THREE YEARS AND NOW EXPECTS TO BE KING?!
I'M TELLING YOU, HE WON'T EAT ANYTHING.
TAKE IT TO HIM ANYWAY...
IT'S UNNATURAL IF YOU ASK ME!
HERE, YOU SHOULD EAT SOMETHING.
I'M NOT HUNGRY.
I CAN'T GET OVER IT...
I FEEL LIKE I JUST SAW HIM YESTERDAY!
TO YOU, YOU DID.
HE WAS GIVEN A GREAT FUNERAL! HE WAS HONORED BY MANY--EVEN THE HEATHOBARDS CAME!
AND YOU LET THEM?!
FATHER'S LAST WISH WAS PEACE, AND SINCE HE DIED I'VE KEPT THAT PROMISE.
SLURP!
PEACE?!
WITH THE HEATHOBARDS?!
HAS THE WORLD GONE MAD?!

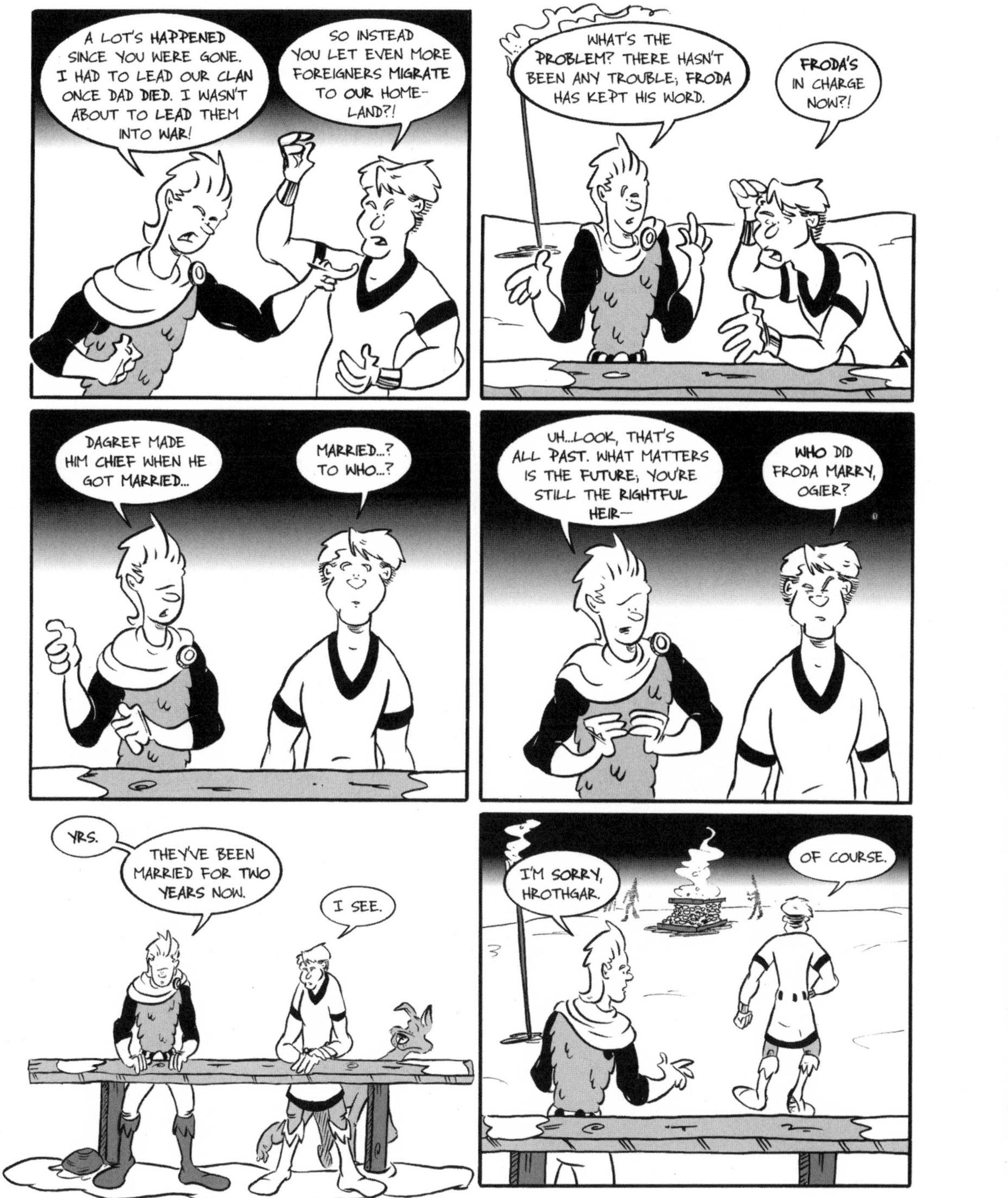
A LOT'S HAPPENED SINCE YOU WERE GONE. I HAD TO LEAD OUR CLAN ONCE DAD DIED. I WASN'T ABOUT TO LEAD THEM INTO WAR!
SO INSTEAD YOU LET EVEN MORE FOREIGNERS MIGRATE TO OUR HOME-LAND?!
WHAT'S THE PROBLEM? THERE HASN'T BEEN ANY TROUBLE; FRODA HAS KEPT HIS WORD.
FRODA'S IN CHARGE NOW?!
DAGREF MADE HIM CHIEF WHEN HE GOT MARRIED...
MARRIED...? TO WHO...?
UH...LOOK, THAT'S ALL PAST. WHAT MATTERS IS THE FUTURE; YOU'RE STILL THE RIGHTFUL HEIR—
WHO DID FRODA MARRY, OGIER?
YRS.
THEY'VE BEEN MARRIED FOR TWO YEARS NOW.
I SEE.
I'M SORRY, HROTHGAR.
OF COURSE.

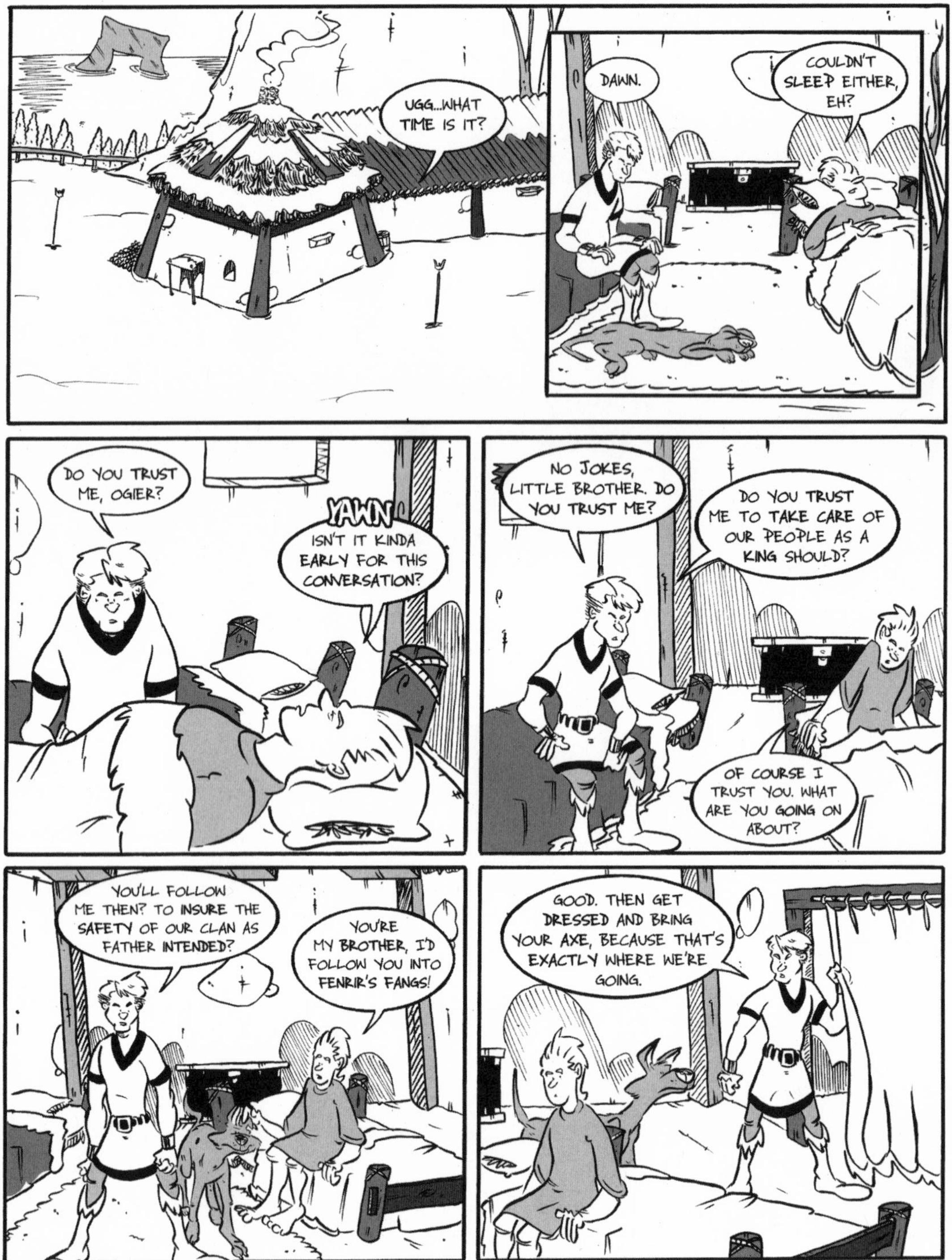
UGG...WHAT TIME IS IT?
DAWN.
COULDN'T SLEEP EITHER, EH?
DO YOU TRUST ME, OGIER?
YAWN
ISN'T IT KINDA EARLY FOR THIS CONVERSATION?
NO JOKES, LITTLE BROTHER. DO YOU TRUST ME?
DO YOU TRUST ME TO TAKE CARE OF OUR PEOPLE AS A KING SHOULD?
OF COURSE I TRUST YOU. WHAT ARE YOU GOING ON ABOUT?
YOU'LL FOLLOW ME THEN? TO INSURE THE SAFETY OF OUR CLAN AS FATHER INTENDED?
YOU'RE MY BROTHER, I'D FOLLOW YOU INTO FENRIR'S FANGS!
GOOD. THEN GET DRESSED AND BRING YOUR AXE, BECAUSE THAT'S EXACTLY WHERE WE'RE GOING.

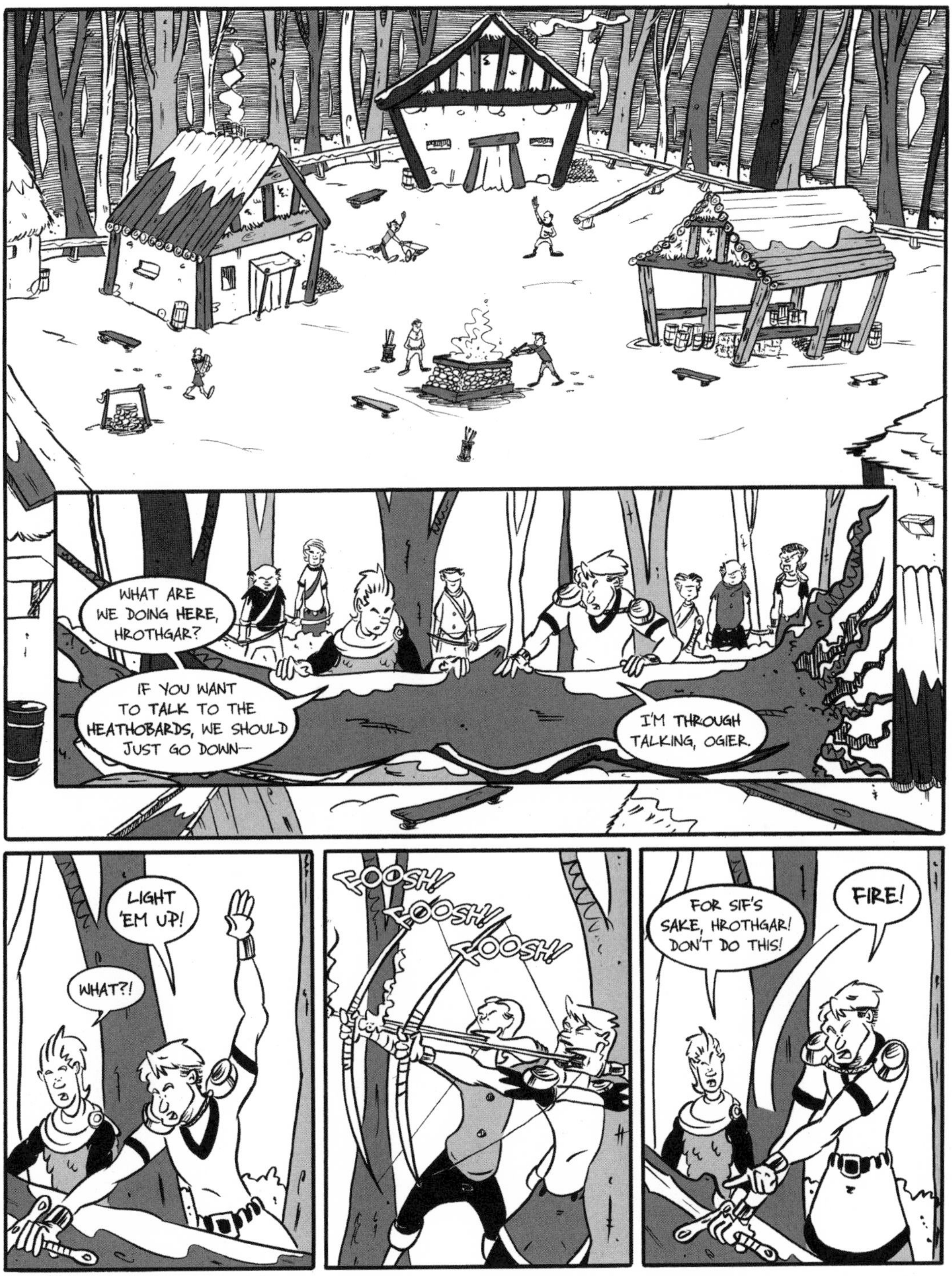
WHAT ARE WE DOING HERE, HROTHGAR?
IF YOU WANT TO TALK TO THE HEATHOBARDS, WE SHOULD JUST GO DOWN—
I'M THROUGH TALKING, OGIER.
LIGHT 'EM UP!
WHAT?!
FOOSH!
FOOSH!
FOOSH!
FOR SIF'S SAKE, HROTHGAR! DON'T DO THIS!
FIRE!

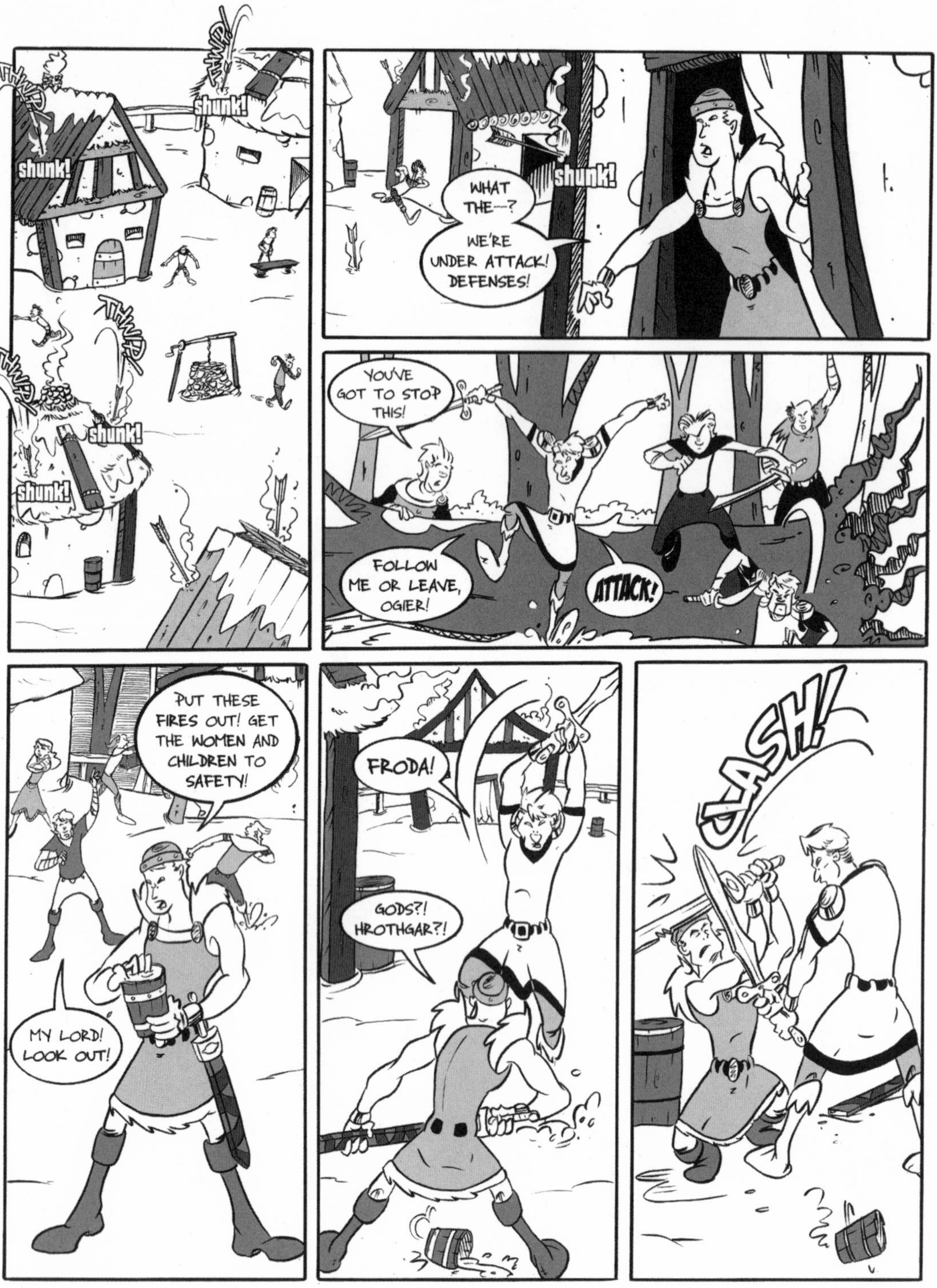
THWIP!
THWIP!
shunk!
shunk!
THWIP!
THWIP!
shunk!
shunk!
WHAT THE--?
WE'RE UNDER ATTACK! DEFENSES!
shunk!
YOU'VE GOT TO STOP THIS!
FOLLOW ME OR LEAVE, OGIER!
ATTACK!
PUT THESE FIRES OUT! GET THE WOMEN AND CHILDREN TO SAFETY!
MY LORD! LOOK OUT!
FRODA!
GODS?! HROTHGAR?!
CLASH!

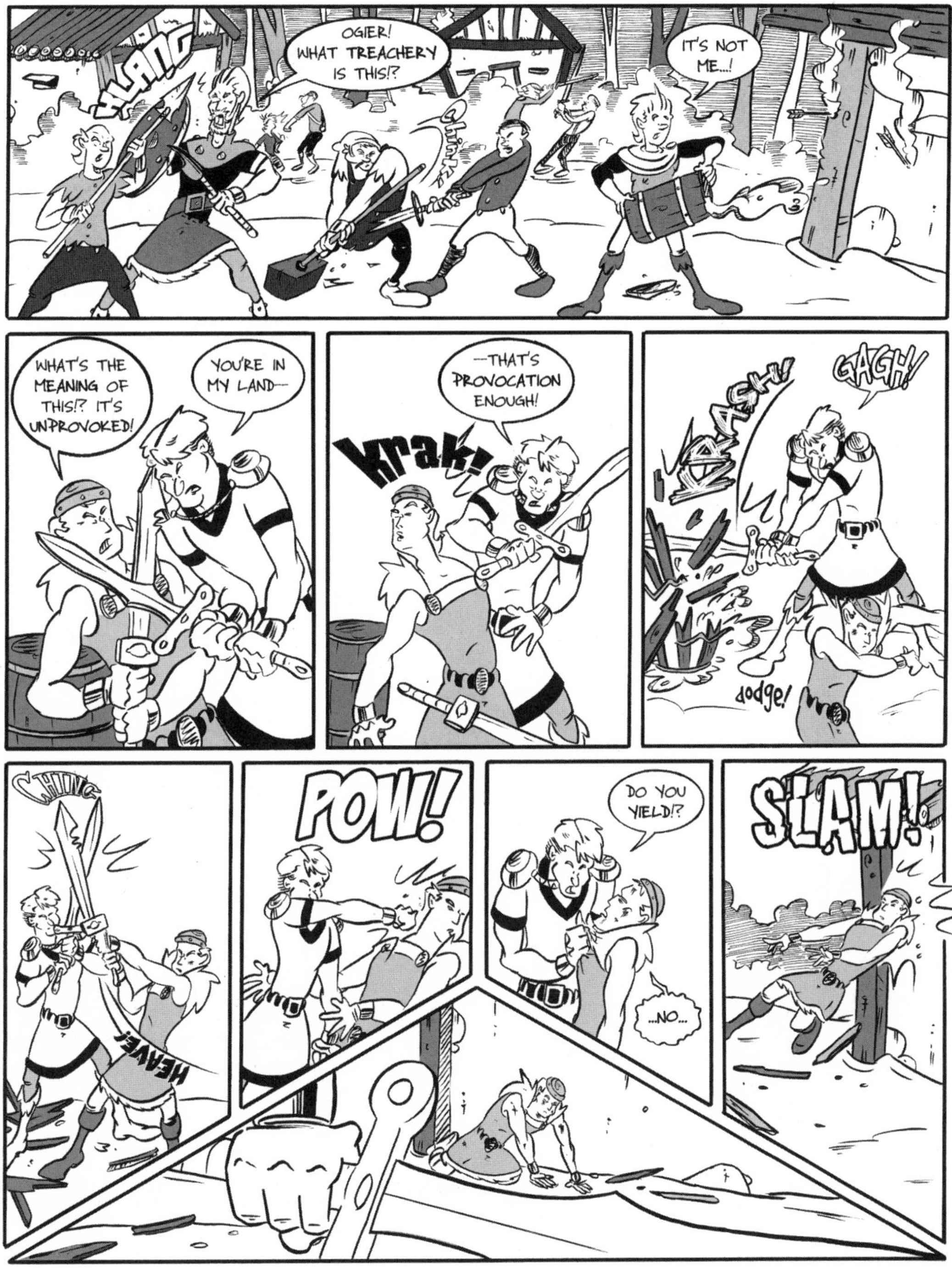
KLANG
OGIER! WHAT TREACHERY IS THIS!?
CHINK
IT'S NOT ME...!
WHAT'S THE MEANING OF THIS!? IT'S UNPROVOKED!
YOU'RE IN MY LAND—
—THAT'S PROVOCATION ENOUGH!
KRAK!
KRASH!
GAGH!
dodge!
CHING
HEAVE!
POW!
DO YOU YIELD!?
...NO...
SLAM!

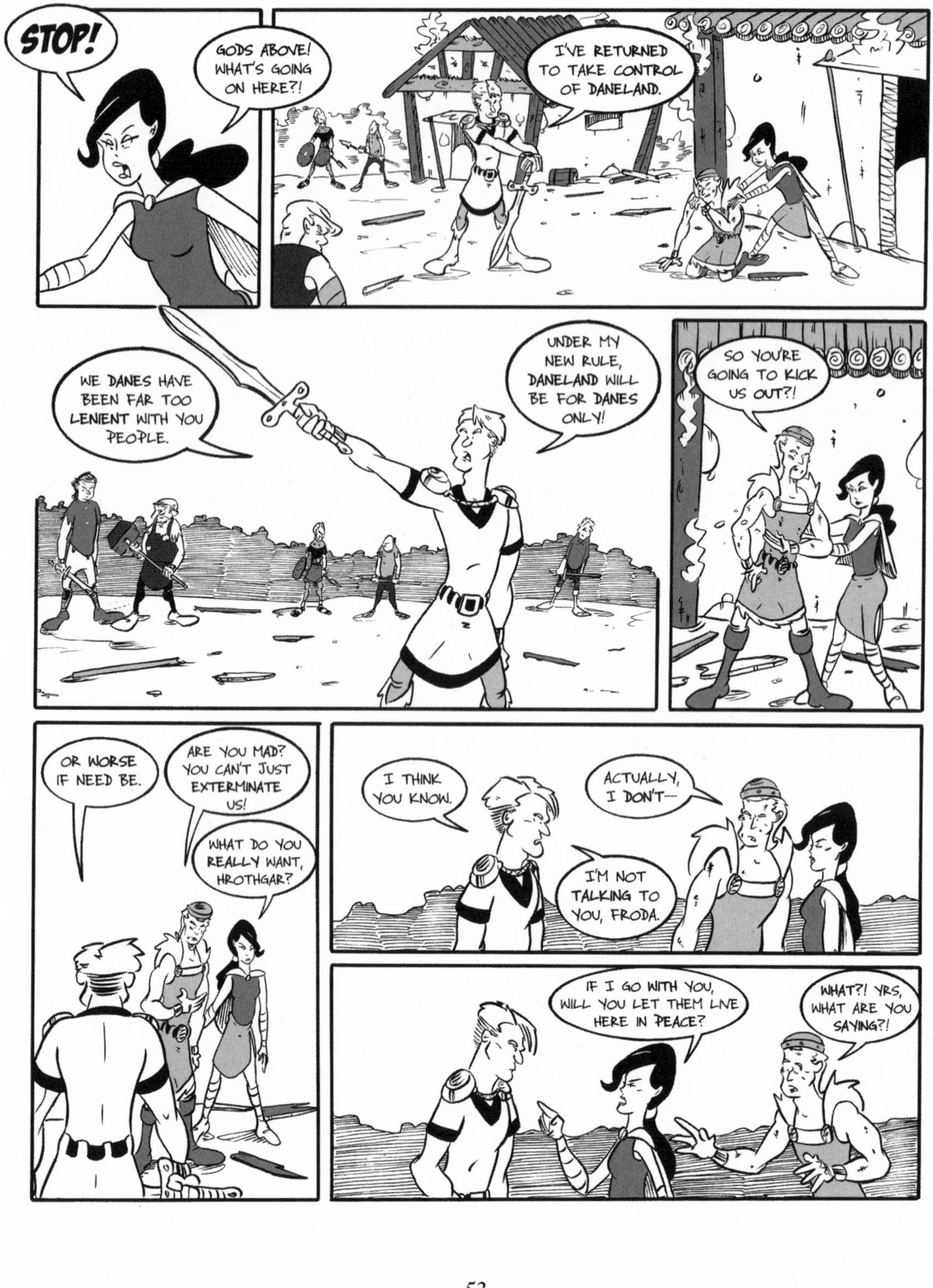
STOP!
GODS ABOVE! WHAT'S GOING ON HERE?!
I'VE RETURNED TO TAKE CONTROL OF DANELAND.
WE DANES HAVE BEEN FAR TOO LENIENT WITH YOU PEOPLE.
UNDER MY NEW RULE, DANELAND WILL BE FOR DANES ONLY!
SO YOU'RE GOING TO KICK US OUT?!
OR WORSE IF NEED BE.
ARE YOU MAD? YOU CAN'T JUST EXTERMINATE US!
WHAT DO YOU REALLY WANT, HROTHGAR?
I THINK YOU KNOW.
ACTUALLY, I DON'T--
I'M NOT TALKING TO YOU, FRODA.
IF I GO WITH YOU, WILL YOU LET THEM LIVE HERE IN PEACE?
WHAT?! YRS, WHAT ARE YOU SAYING?!

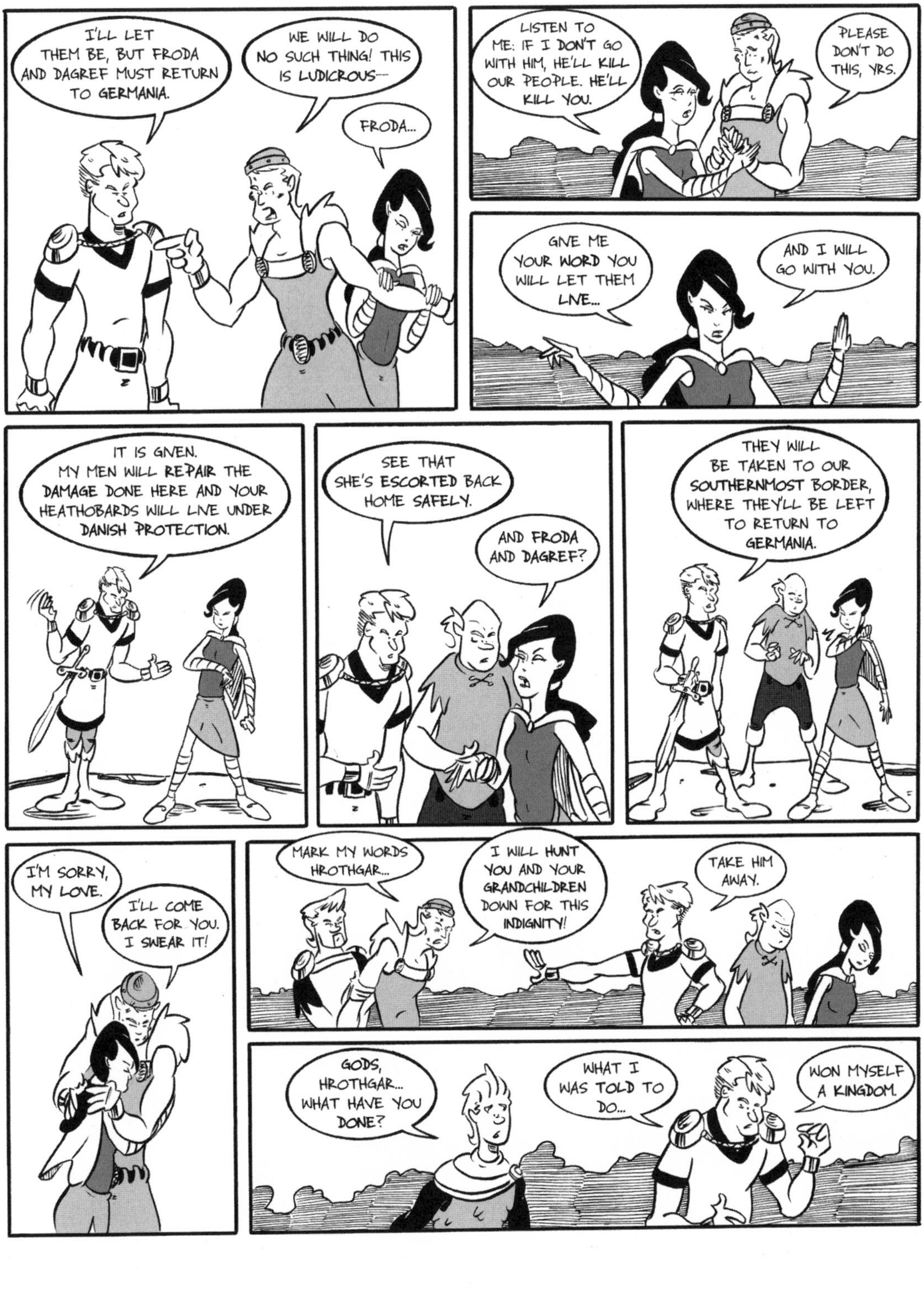

I'LL LET THEM BE, BUT FRODA AND DAGREF MUST RETURN TO GERMANIA.
WE WILL DO NO SUCH THING! THIS IS LUDICROUS--
FRODA...
LISTEN TO ME: IF I DON'T GO WITH HIM, HE'LL KILL OUR PEOPLE. HE'LL KILL YOU.
PLEASE DON'T DO THIS, YRS.
GIVE ME YOUR WORD YOU WILL LET THEM LIVE...
AND I WILL GO WITH YOU.
IT IS GIVEN. MY MEN WILL REPAIR THE DAMAGE DONE HERE AND YOUR HEATHOBARDS WILL LIVE UNDER DANISH PROTECTION.
SEE THAT SHE'S ESCORTED BACK HOME SAFELY.
AND FRODA AND DAGREF?
THEY WILL BE TAKEN TO OUR SOUTHERNMOST BORDER, WHERE THEY'LL BE LEFT TO RETURN TO GERMANIA.
I'M SORRY, MY LOVE.
I'LL COME BACK FOR YOU. I SWEAR IT!
MARK MY WORDS HROTHGAR...
I WILL HUNT YOU AND YOUR GRANDCHILDREN DOWN FOR THIS INDIGNITY!
TAKE HIM AWAY.
GODS, HROTHGAR... WHAT HAVE YOU DONE?
WHAT I WAS TOLD TO DO...
WON MYSELF A KINGDOM.

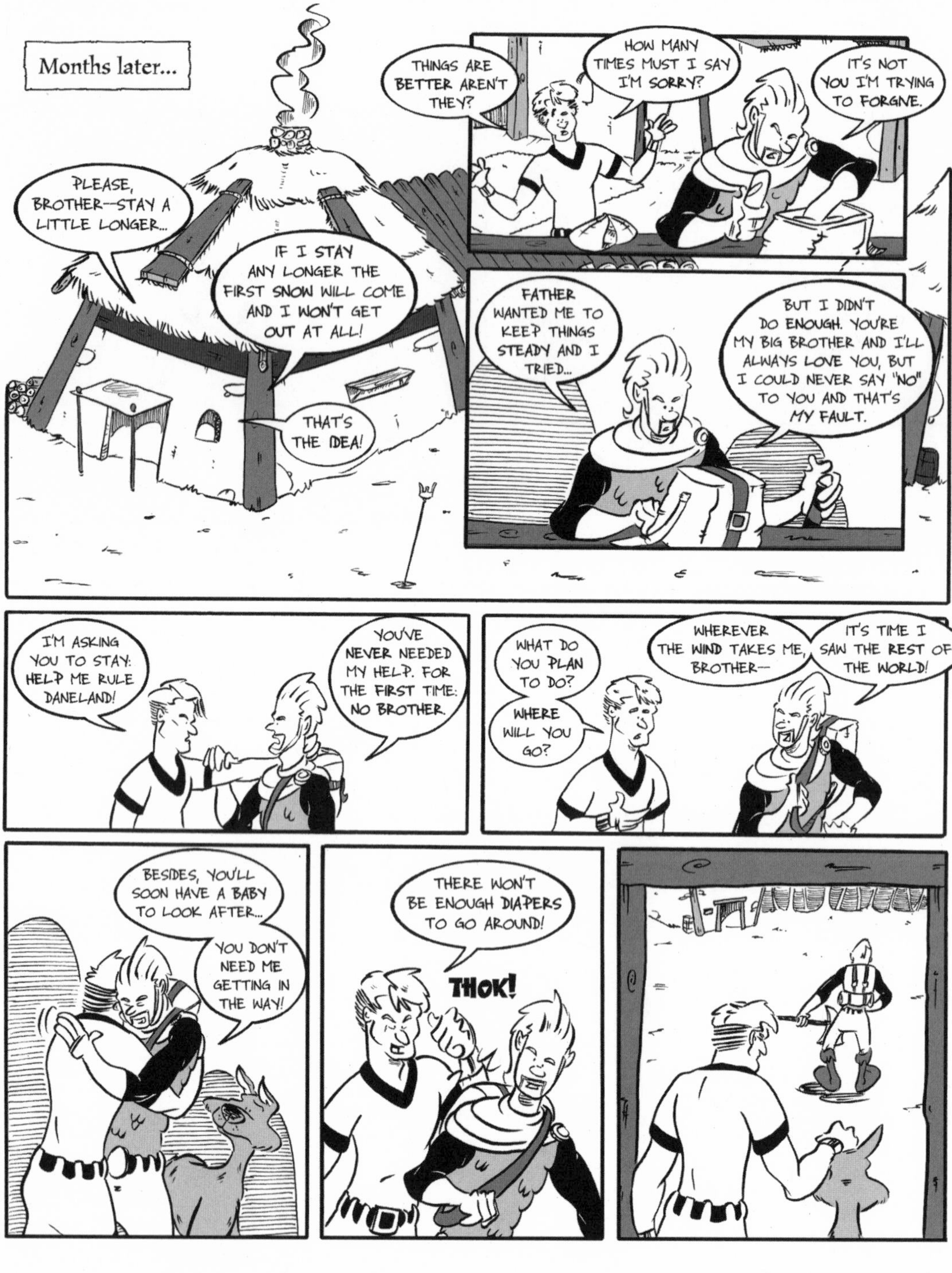
Months later...
PLEASE, BROTHER--STAY A LITTLE LONGER...
IF I STAY ANY LONGER THE FIRST SNOW WILL COME AND I WON'T GET OUT AT ALL!
THAT'S THE IDEA!
THINGS ARE BETTER AREN'T THEY?
HOW MANY TIMES MUST I SAY I'M SORRY?
IT'S NOT YOU I'M TRYING TO FORGIVE.
FATHER WANTED ME TO KEEP THINGS STEADY AND I TRIED...
BUT I DIDN'T DO ENOUGH. YOU'RE MY BIG BROTHER AND I'LL ALWAYS LOVE YOU, BUT I COULD NEVER SAY "NO" TO YOU AND THAT'S MY FAULT.
I'M ASKING YOU TO STAY: HELP ME RULE DANELAND!
YOU'VE NEVER NEEDED MY HELP. FOR THE FIRST TIME: NO BROTHER.
WHAT DO YOU PLAN TO DO?
WHERE WILL YOU GO?
WHEREVER THE WIND TAKES ME, BROTHER--
IT'S TIME I SAW THE REST OF THE WORLD!
BESIDES, YOU'LL SOON HAVE A BABY TO LOOK AFTER...
YOU DON'T NEED ME GETTING IN THE WAY!
THERE WON'T BE ENOUGH DIAPERS TO GO AROUND!
THOK!

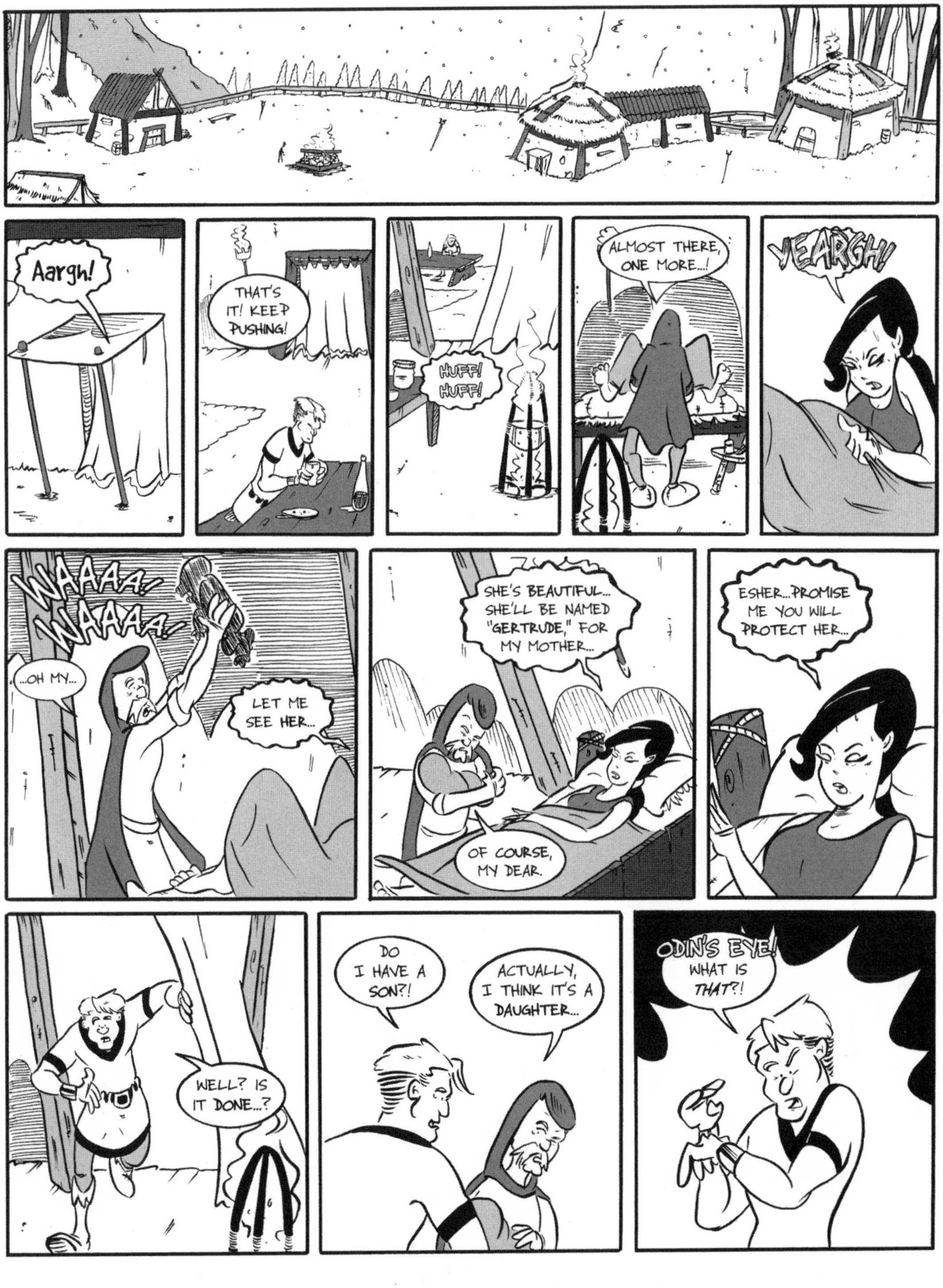
Aargh!
THAT'S IT! KEEP PUSHING!
HUFF! HUFF!
ALMOST THERE, ONE MORE...!
YEARGH!
WAAAA! WAAAA!
...OH MY...
LET ME SEE HER...
SHE'S BEAUTIFUL... SHE'LL BE NAMED "GERTRUDE," FOR MY MOTHER...
OF COURSE, MY DEAR.
ESHER...PROMISE ME YOU WILL PROTECT HER...
WELL? IS IT DONE...?
DO I HAVE A SON?!
ACTUALLY, I THINK IT'S A DAUGHTER...
ODIN'S EYE! WHAT IS THAT?!

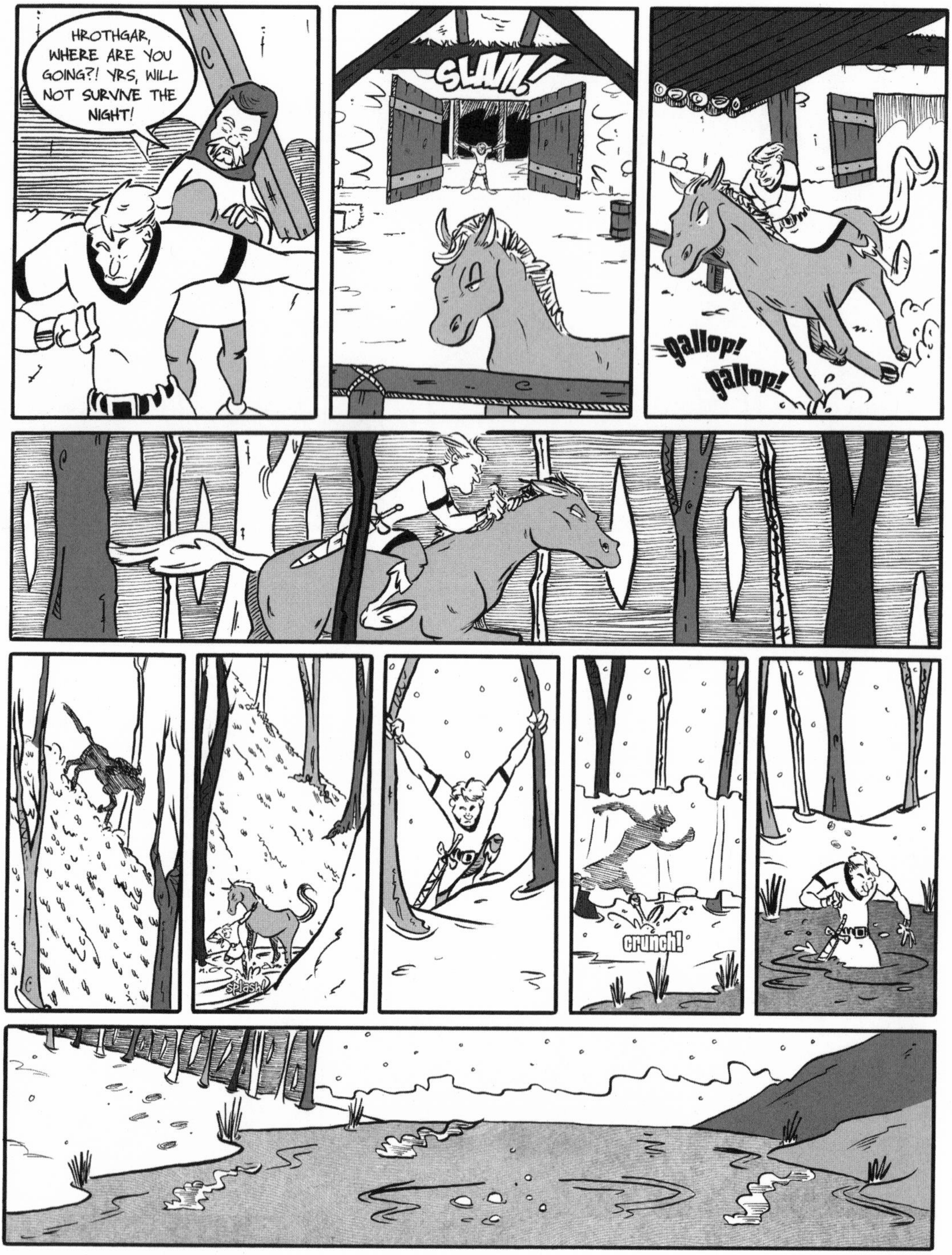
HROTHGAR, WHERE ARE YOU GOING?! YRS, WILL NOT SURVIVE THE NIGHT!
SLAM!
gallop! gallop!
splash!
crunch!

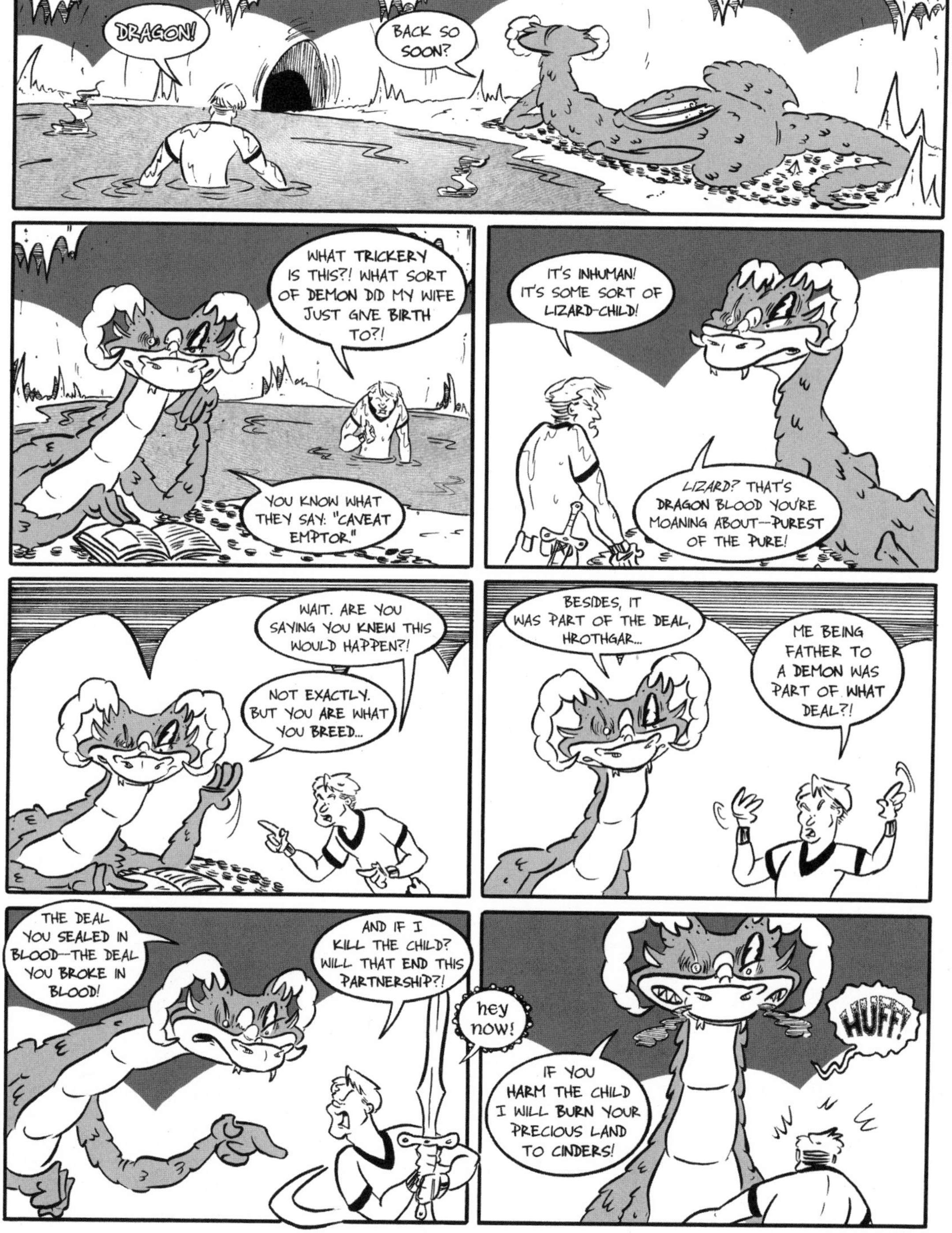
DRAGON!
BACK SO SOON?
WHAT TRICKERY IS THIS?! WHAT SORT OF DEMON DID MY WIFE JUST GIVE BIRTH TO?!
YOU KNOW WHAT THEY SAY: "CAVEAT EMPTOR."
IT'S INHUMAN! IT'S SOME SORT OF LIZARD-CHILD!
LIZARD? THAT'S DRAGON BLOOD YOU'RE MOANING ABOUT--PUREST OF THE PURE!
WAIT. ARE YOU SAYING YOU KNEW THIS WOULD HAPPEN?!
NOT EXACTLY. BUT YOU ARE WHAT YOU BREED...
BESIDES, IT WAS PART OF THE DEAL, HROTHGAR...
ME BEING FATHER TO A DEMON WAS PART OF WHAT DEAL?!
THE DEAL YOU SEALED IN BLOOD--THE DEAL YOU BROKE IN BLOOD!
AND IF I KILL THE CHILD? WILL THAT END THIS PARTNERSHIP?!
hey now!
IF YOU HARM THE CHILD I WILL BURN YOUR PRECIOUS LAND TO CINDERS!
HUFF!

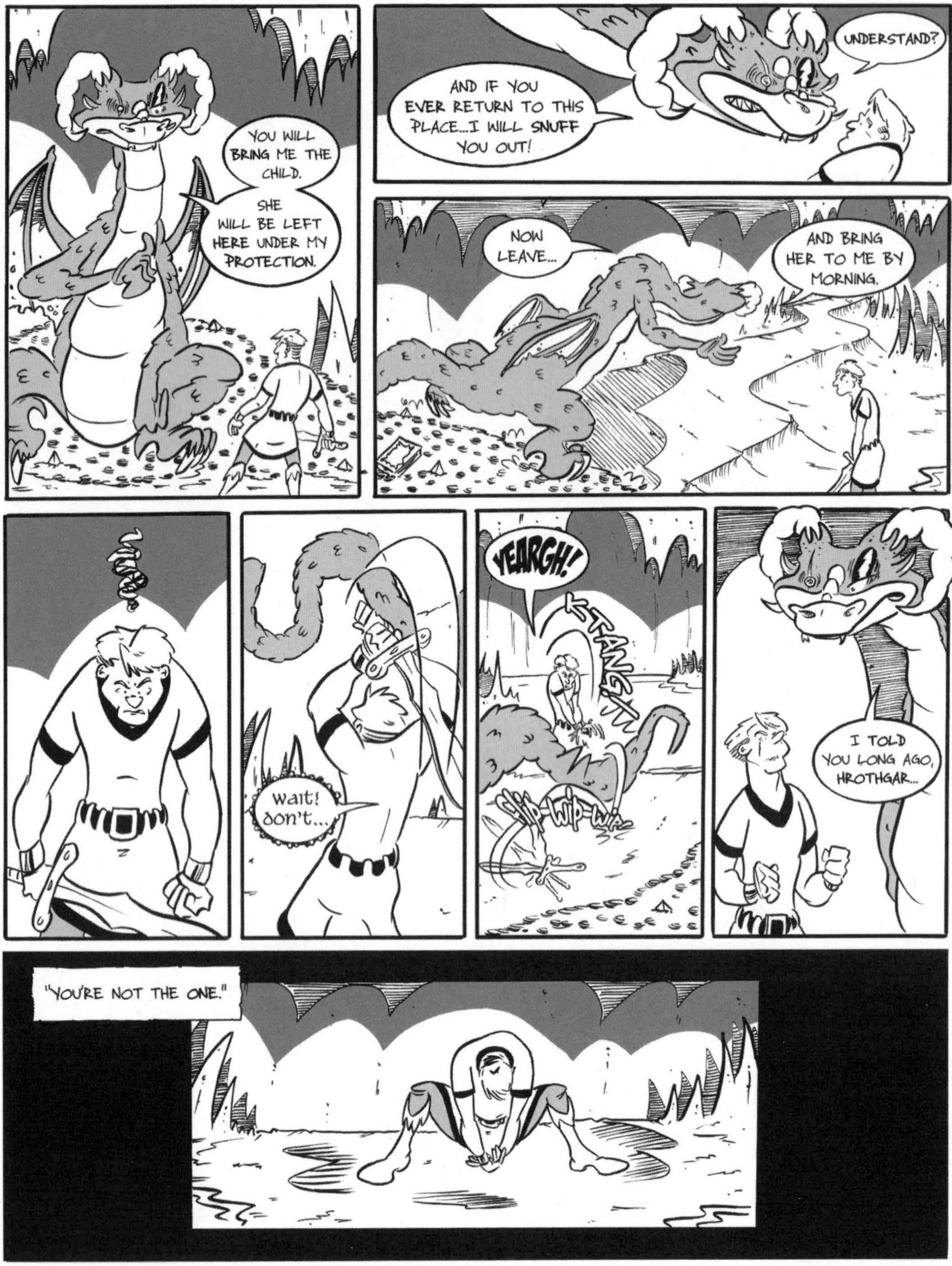
YOU WILL BRING ME THE CHILD.
SHE WILL BE LEFT HERE UNDER MY PROTECTION.
AND IF YOU EVER RETURN TO THIS PLACE...I WILL SNUFF YOU OUT!
UNDERSTAND?
NOW LEAVE...
AND BRING HER TO ME BY MORNING.
wait! don't...
YEARGH!
K-TANG!
I TOLD YOU LONG AGO, HROTHGAR...
"YOU'RE NOT THE ONE."

Part Two

the present

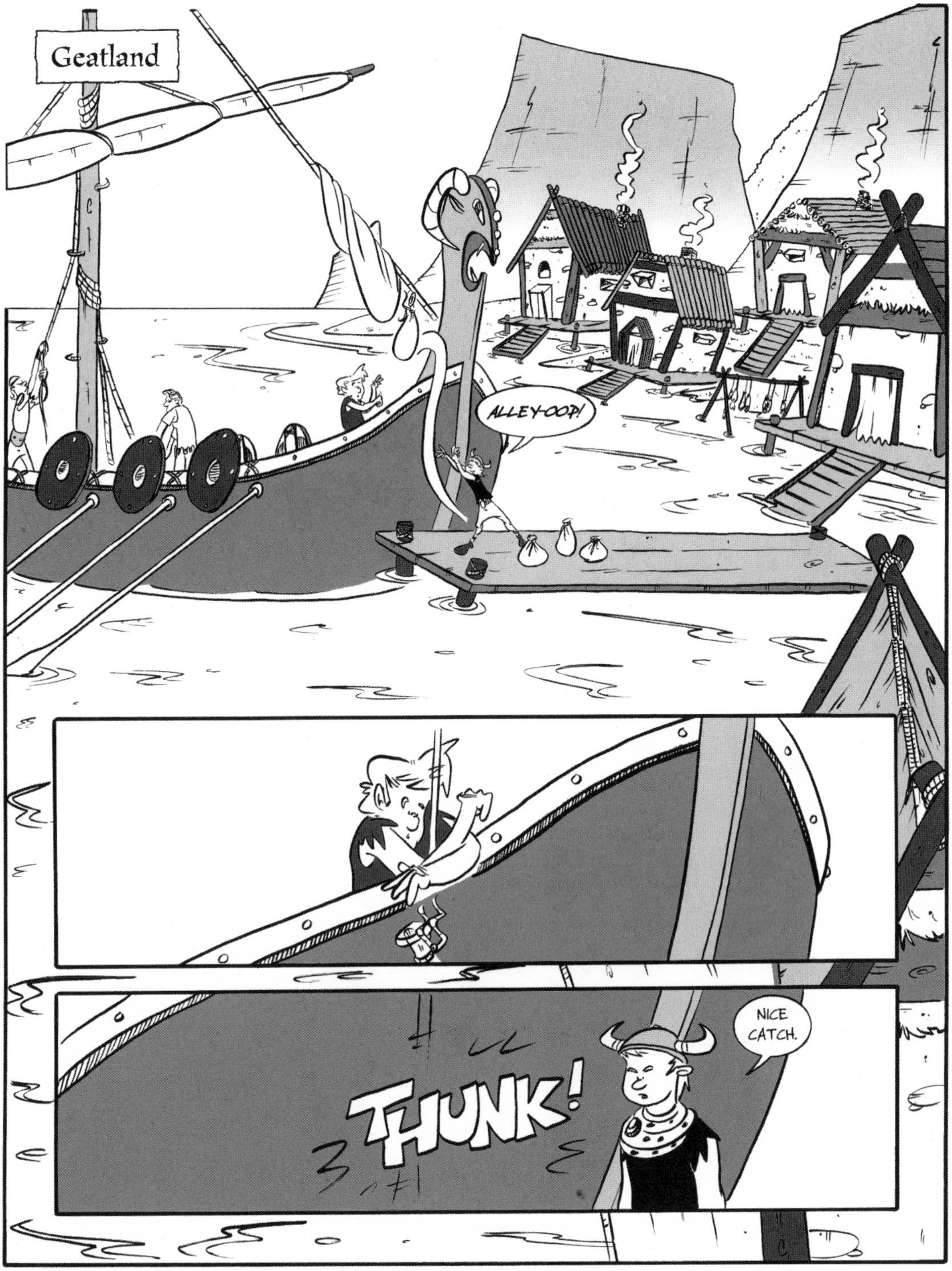
Geatland
ALLEY-OOP!
NICE CATCH.
THUNK!

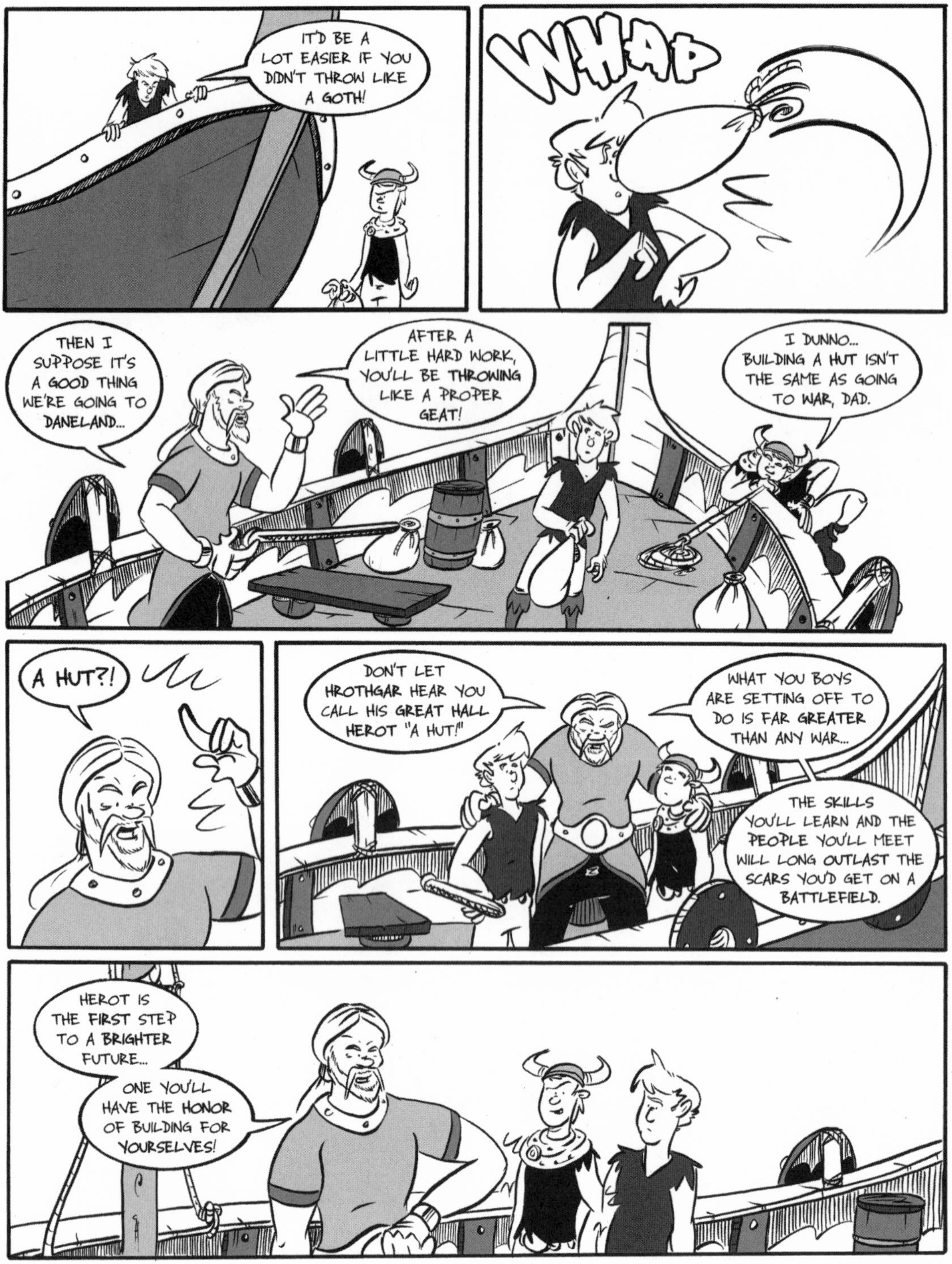
IT'D BE A LOT EASIER IF YOU DIDN'T THROW LIKE A GOTH!
WHAP
THEN I SUPPOSE IT'S A GOOD THING WE'RE GOING TO DANELAND...
AFTER A LITTLE HARD WORK, YOU'LL BE THROWING LIKE A PROPER GEAT!
I DUNNO... BUILDING A HUT ISN'T THE SAME AS GOING TO WAR, DAD.
A HUT?!
DON'T LET HROTHGAR HEAR YOU CALL HIS GREAT HALL HEROT "A HUT!"
WHAT YOU BOYS ARE SETTING OFF TO DO IS FAR GREATER THAN ANY WAR...
THE SKILLS YOU'LL LEARN AND THE PEOPLE YOU'LL MEET WILL LONG OUTLAST THE SCARS YOU'D GET ON A BATTLEFIELD.
HEROT IS THE FIRST STEP TO A BRIGHTER FUTURE...
ONE YOU'LL HAVE THE HONOR OF BUILDING FOR YOURSELVES!

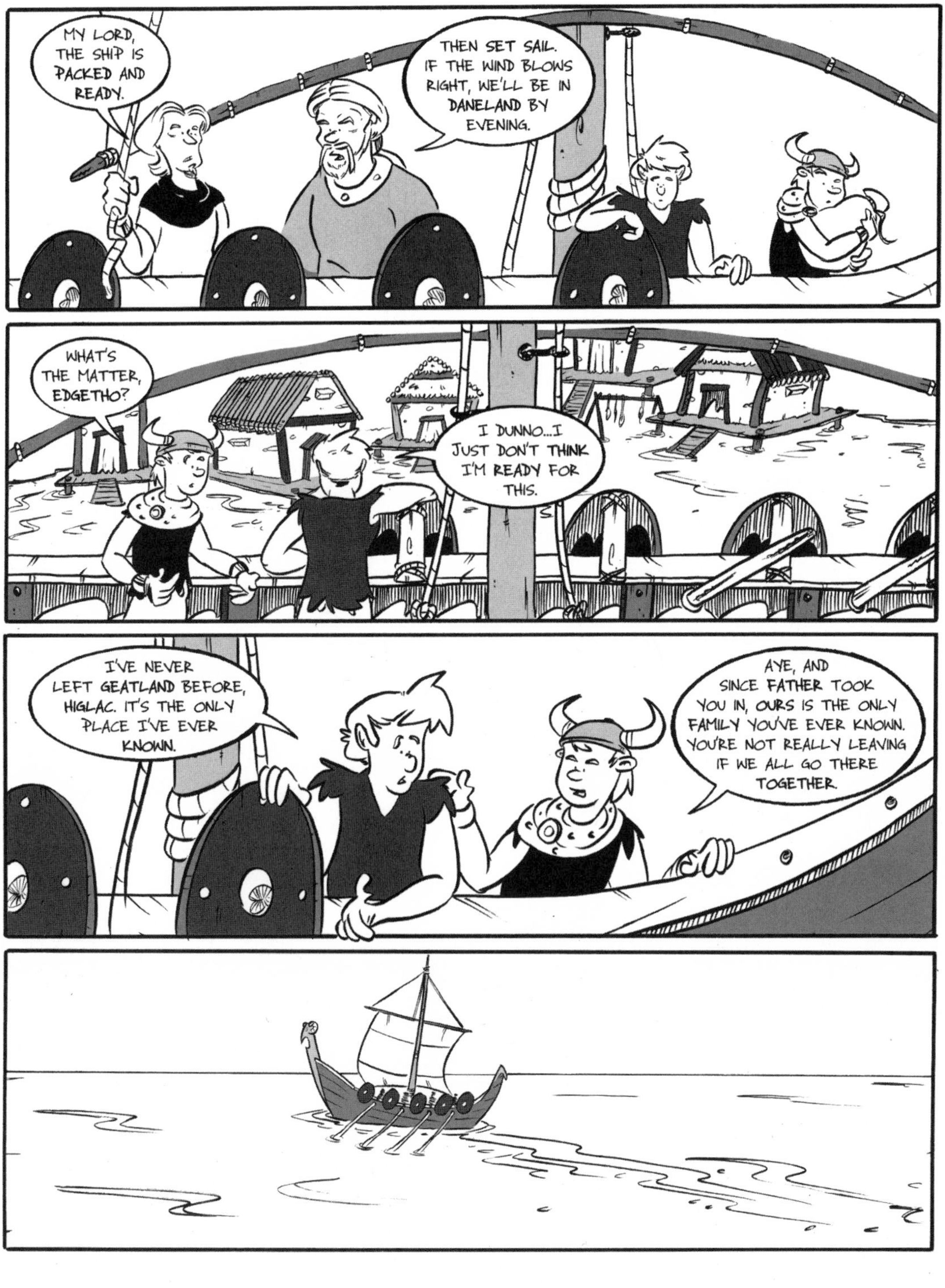
MY LORD, THE SHIP IS PACKED AND READY.
THEN SET SAIL. IF THE WIND BLOWS RIGHT, WE'LL BE IN DANELAND BY EVENING.
WHAT'S THE MATTER, EDGETHO?
I DUNNO...I JUST DON'T THINK I'M READY FOR THIS.
I'VE NEVER LEFT GEATLAND BEFORE, HIGLAC. IT'S THE ONLY PLACE I'VE EVER KNOWN.
AYE, AND SINCE FATHER TOOK YOU IN, OURS IS THE ONLY FAMILY YOU'VE EVER KNOWN. YOU'RE NOT REALLY LEAVING IF WE ALL GO THERE TOGETHER.

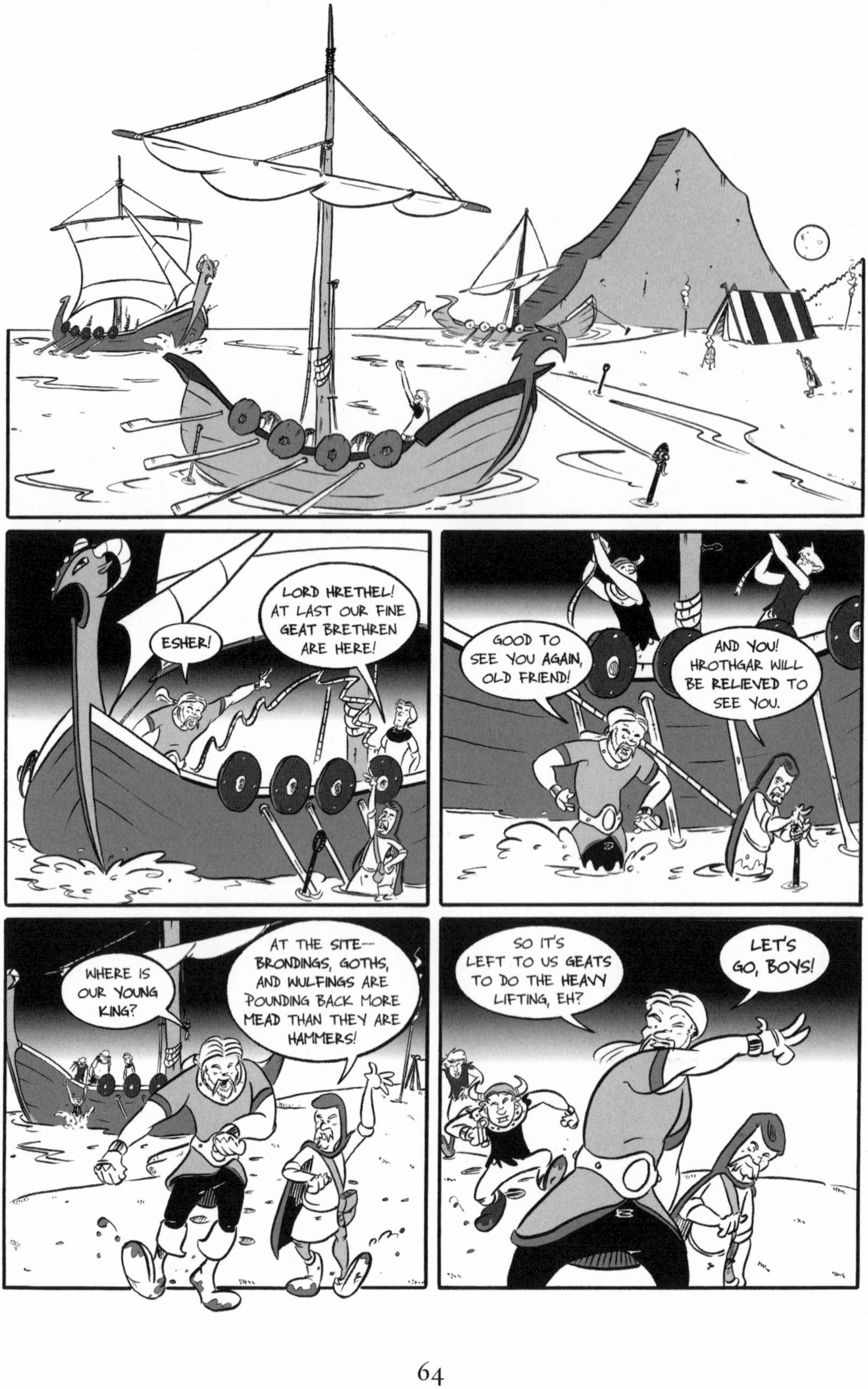
ESHER!
LORD HRETHEL! AT LAST OUR FINE GEAT BRETHREN ARE HERE!
GOOD TO SEE YOU AGAIN, OLD FRIEND!
AND YOU! HROTHGAR WILL BE RELIEVED TO SEE YOU.
WHERE IS OUR YOUNG KING?
AT THE SITE-- BRONDINGS, GOTHS, AND WULFINGS ARE POUNDING BACK MORE MEAD THAN THEY ARE HAMMERS!
SO IT'S LEFT TO US GEATS TO DO THE HEAVY LIFTING, EH?
LET'S GO, BOYS!

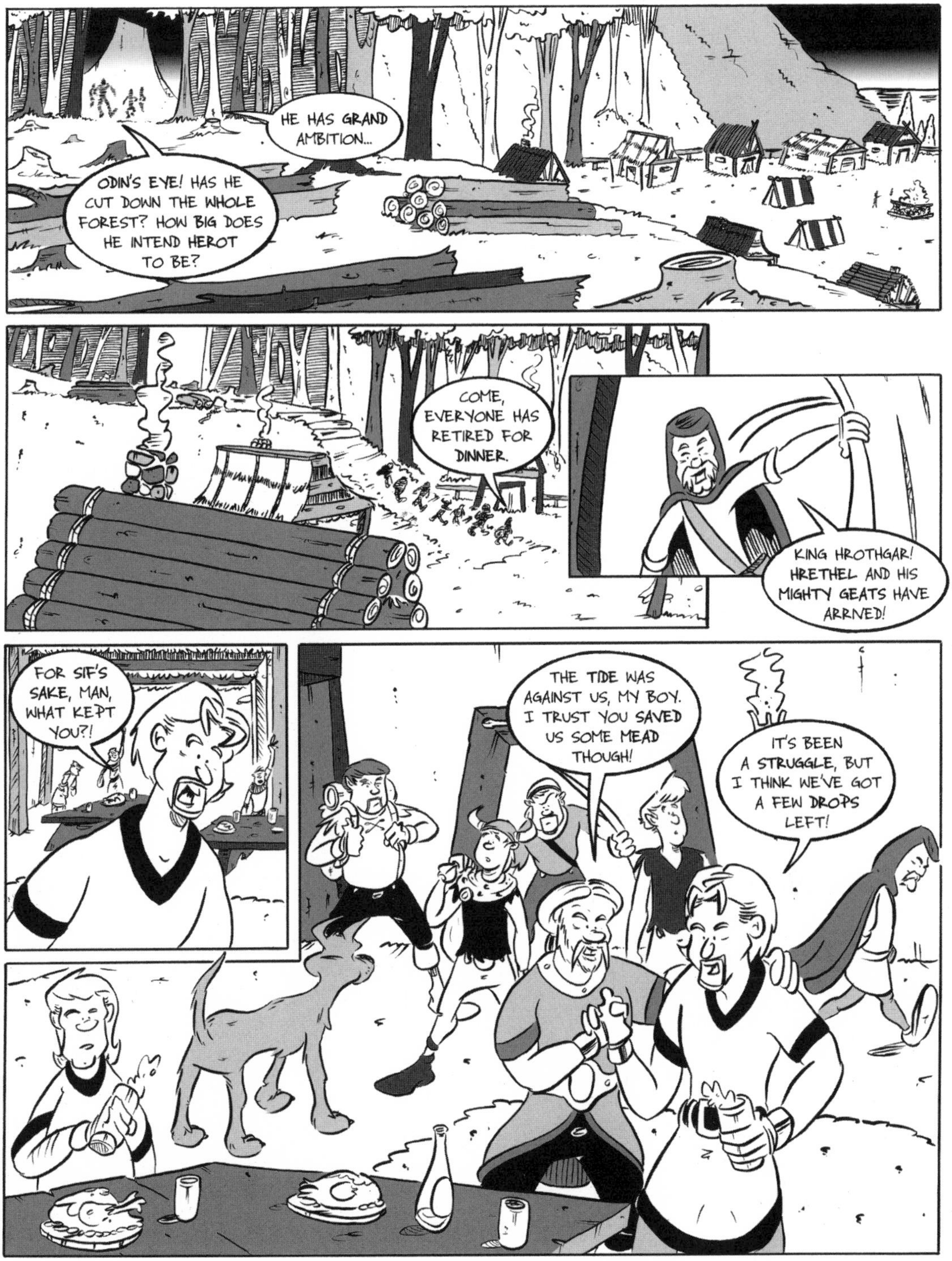
HE HAS GRAND AMBITION...
ODIN'S EYE! HAS HE CUT DOWN THE WHOLE FOREST? HOW BIG DOES HE INTEND HEROT TO BE?
COME, EVERYONE HAS RETIRED FOR DINNER.
KING HROTHGAR! HRETHEL AND HIS MIGHTY GEATS HAVE ARRIVED!
FOR SIF'S SAKE, MAN, WHAT KEPT YOU?!
THE TIDE WAS AGAINST US, MY BOY. I TRUST YOU SAVED US SOME MEAD THOUGH!
IT'S BEEN A STRUGGLE, BUT I THINK WE'VE GOT A FEW DROPS LEFT!

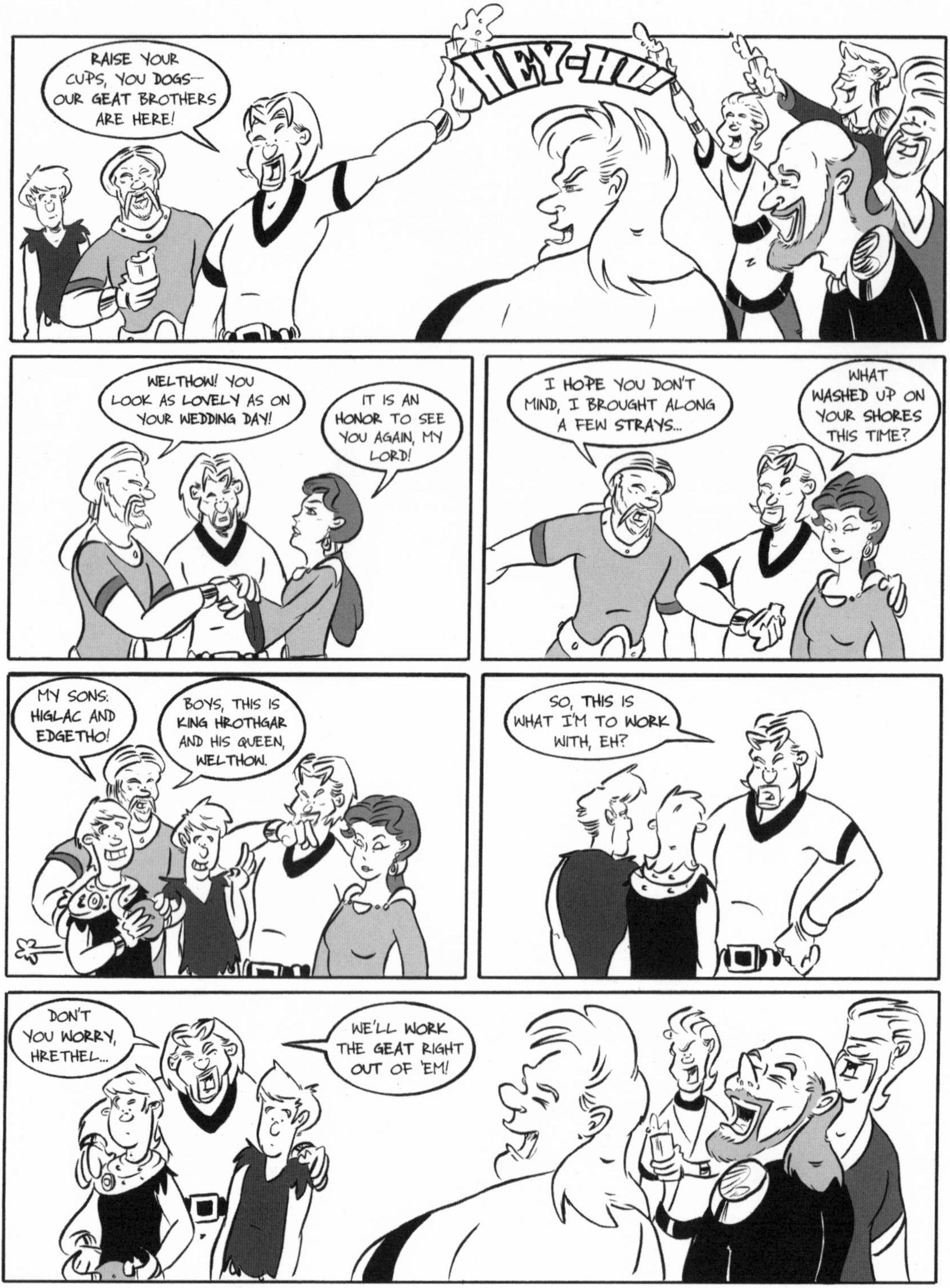
RAISE YOUR CUPS, YOU DOGS— OUR GEAT BROTHERS ARE HERE!
HEY-HO!
WELTHOW! YOU LOOK AS LOVELY AS ON YOUR WEDDING DAY!
IT IS AN HONOR TO SEE YOU AGAIN, MY LORD!
I HOPE YOU DON'T MIND, I BROUGHT ALONG A FEW STRAYS...
WHAT WASHED UP ON YOUR SHORES THIS TIME?
MY SONS: HIGLAC AND EDGETHO!
BOYS, THIS IS KING HROTHGAR AND HIS QUEEN, WELTHOW.
SO, THIS IS WHAT I'M TO WORK WITH, EH?
DON'T YOU WORRY, HRETHEL...
WE'LL WORK THE GEAT RIGHT OUT OF 'EM!

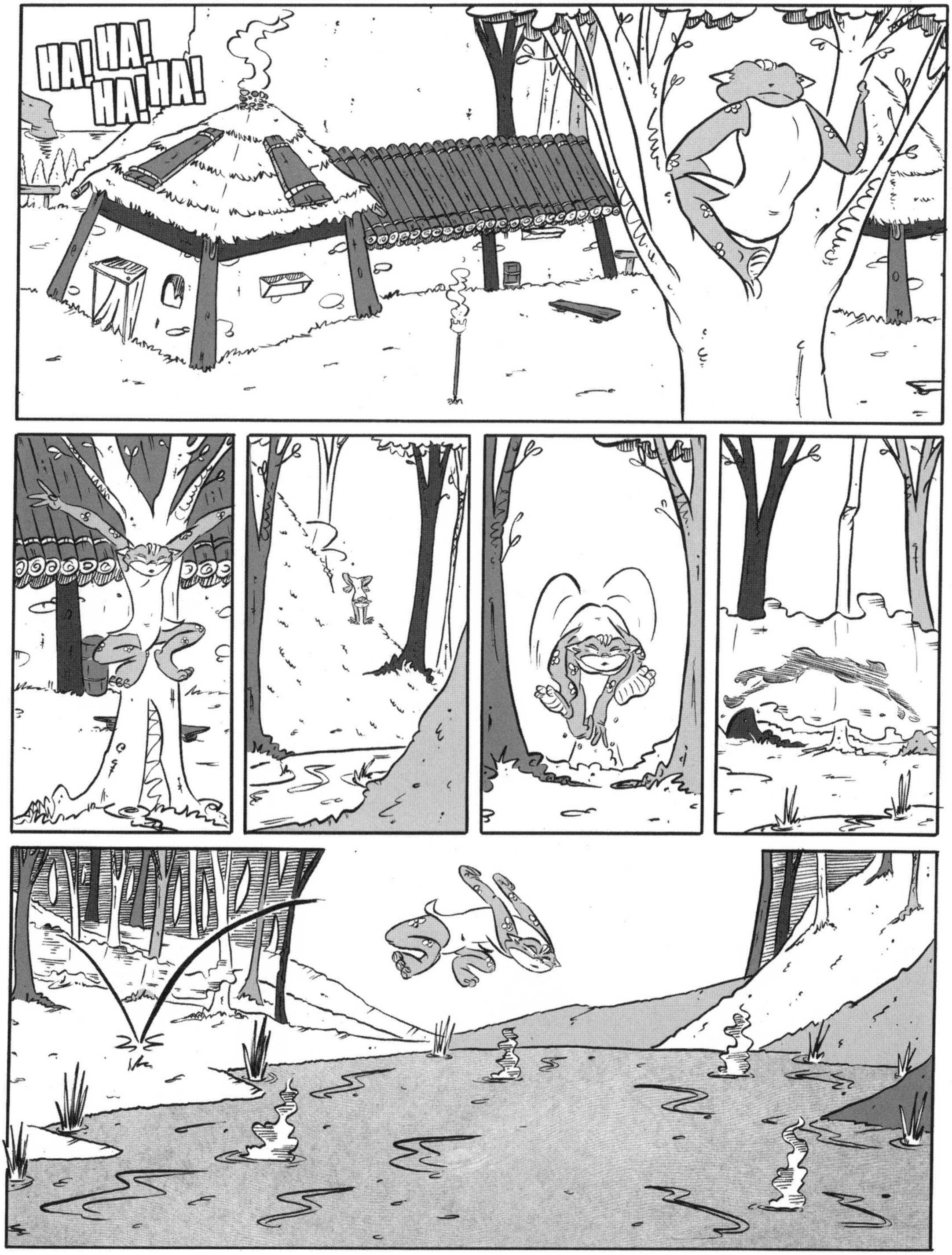
HA! HA! HA! HA!

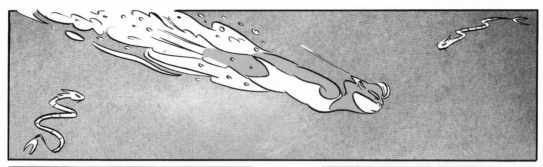

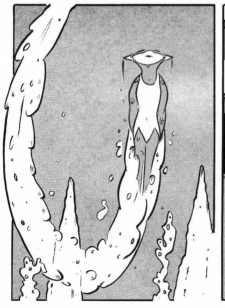

YOU'RE LATE.

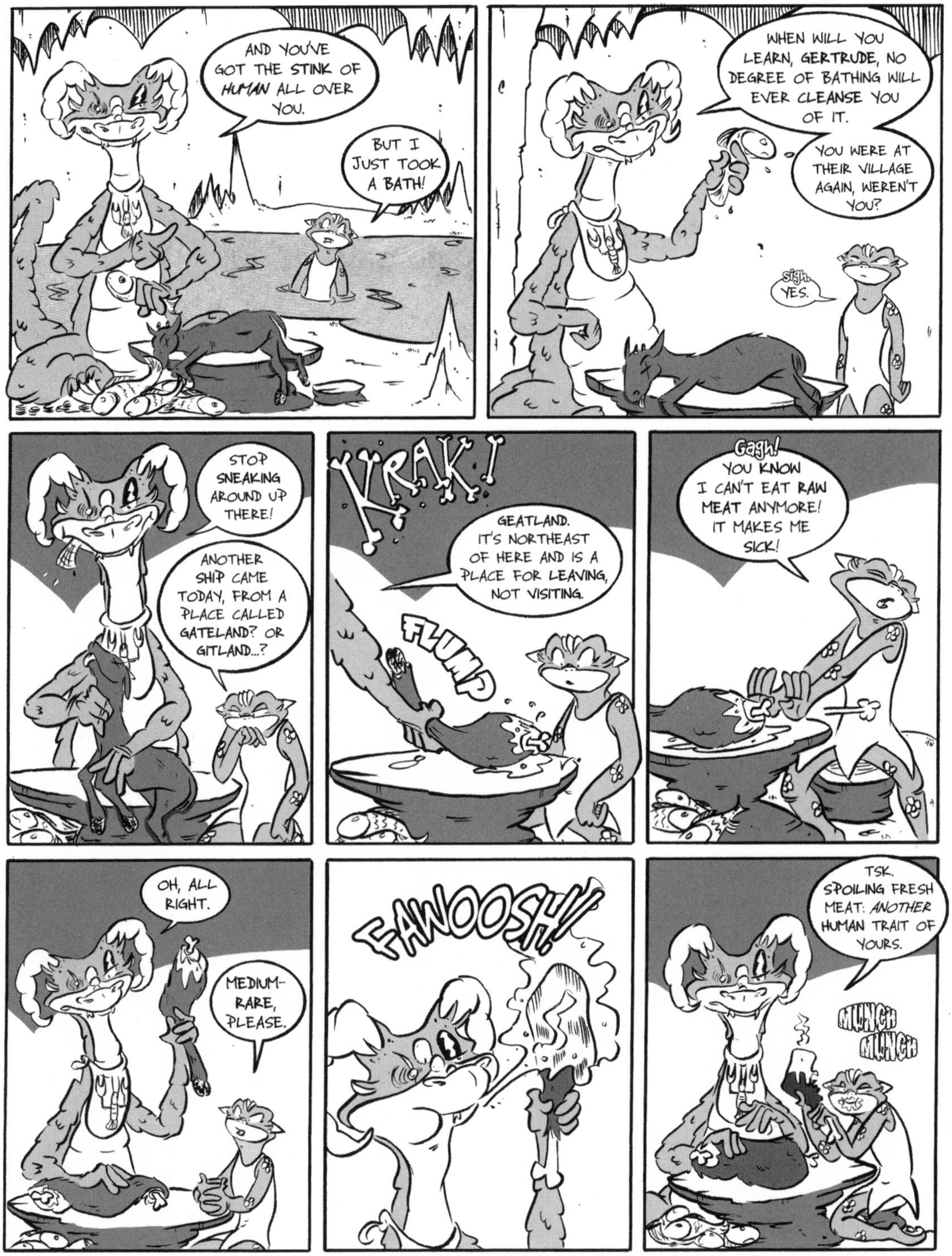
AND YOU'VE GOT THE STINK OF HUMAN ALL OVER YOU.
BUT I JUST TOOK A BATH!
WHEN WILL YOU LEARN, GERTRUDE, NO DEGREE OF BATHING WILL EVER CLEANSE YOU OF IT.
YOU WERE AT THEIR VILLAGE AGAIN, WEREN'T YOU?
Sigh. YES.
STOP SNEAKING AROUND UP THERE!
ANOTHER SHIP CAME TODAY, FROM A PLACE CALLED GATELAND? OR GITLAND...?
KRAK!
GEATLAND. IT'S NORTHEAST OF HERE AND IS A PLACE FOR LEAVING, NOT VISITING.
FLUMP
Gagh! YOU KNOW I CAN'T EAT RAW MEAT ANYMORE! IT MAKES ME SICK!
OH, ALL RIGHT.
MEDIUM-RARE, PLEASE.
FAWOOSH!!
TSK. SPOILING FRESH MEAT: ANOTHER HUMAN TRAIT OF YOURS.
MUNCH MUNCH

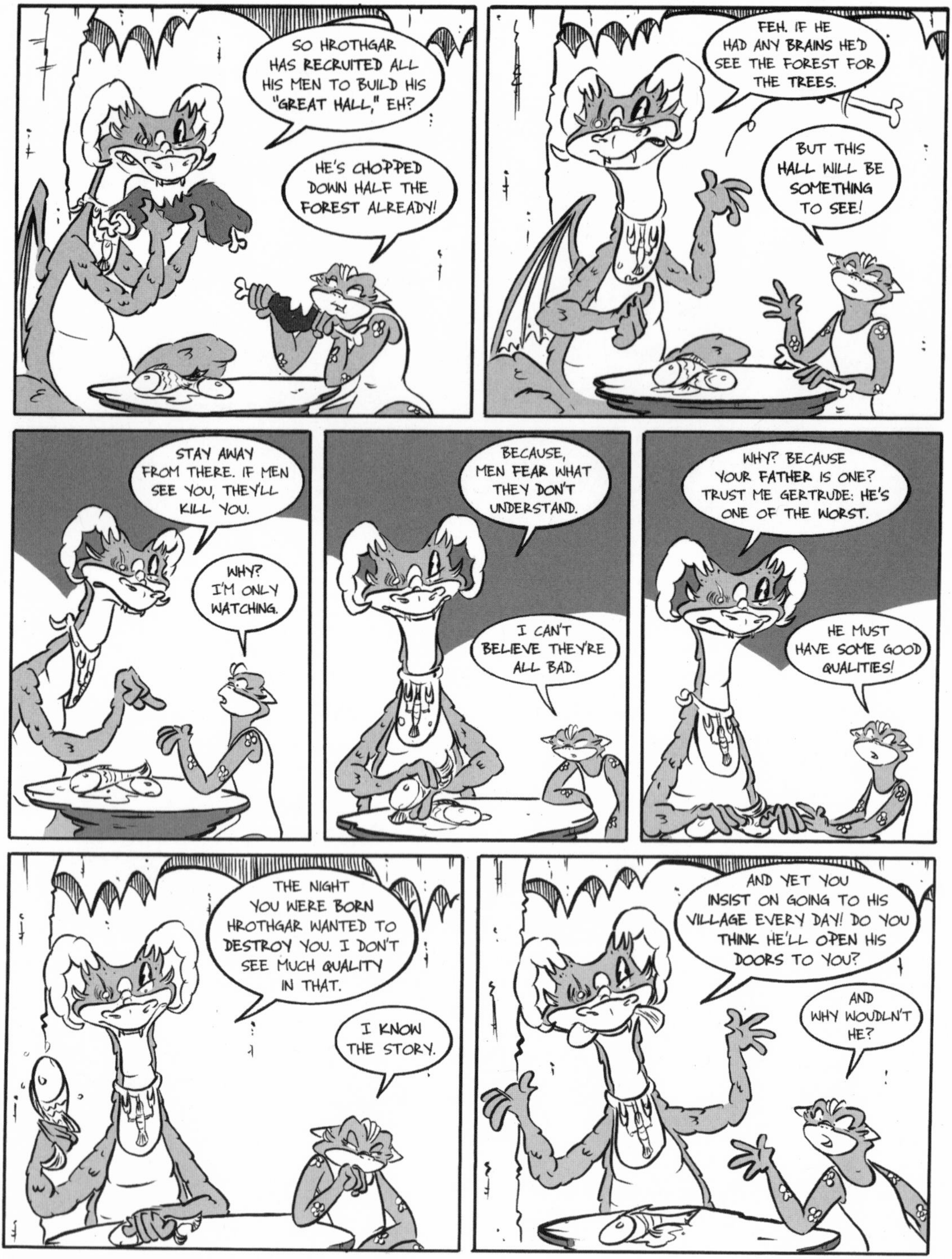
SO HROTHGAR HAS RECRUITED ALL HIS MEN TO BUILD HIS "GREAT HALL," EH?
HE'S CHOPPED DOWN HALF THE FOREST ALREADY!
FEH. IF HE HAD ANY BRAINS HE'D SEE THE FOREST FOR THE TREES.
BUT THIS HALL WILL BE SOMETHING TO SEE!
STAY AWAY FROM THERE. IF MEN SEE YOU, THEY'LL KILL YOU.
WHY? I'M ONLY WATCHING.
BECAUSE, MEN FEAR WHAT THEY DON'T UNDERSTAND.
I CAN'T BELIEVE THEY'RE ALL BAD.
WHY? BECAUSE YOUR FATHER IS ONE? TRUST ME GERTRUDE: HE'S ONE OF THE WORST.
HE MUST HAVE SOME GOOD QUALITIES!
THE NIGHT YOU WERE BORN HROTHGAR WANTED TO DESTROY YOU. I DON'T SEE MUCH QUALITY IN THAT.
I KNOW THE STORY.
AND YET YOU INSIST ON GOING TO HIS VILLAGE EVERY DAY! DO YOU THINK HE'LL OPEN HIS DOORS TO YOU?
AND WHY WOUDLN'T HE?

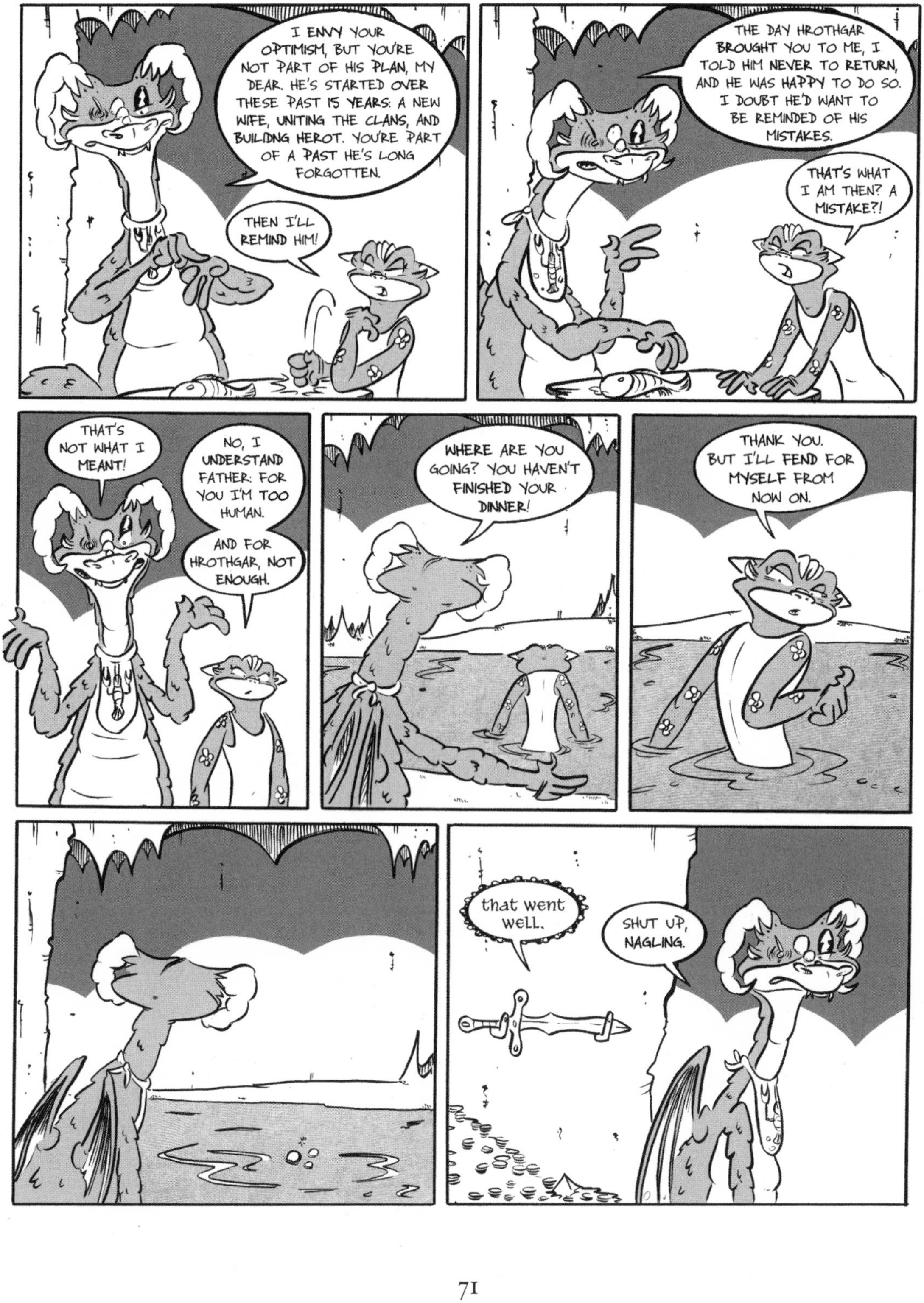

I ENVY YOUR OPTIMISM, BUT YOU'RE NOT PART OF HIS PLAN, MY DEAR. HE'S STARTED OVER THESE PAST 15 YEARS: A NEW WIFE, UNITING THE CLANS, AND BUILDING HEROT. YOU'RE PART OF A PAST HE'S LONG FORGOTTEN.
THEN I'LL REMIND HIM!
THE DAY HROTHGAR BROUGHT YOU TO ME, I TOLD HIM NEVER TO RETURN, AND HE WAS HAPPY TO DO SO. I DOUBT HE'D WANT TO BE REMINDED OF HIS MISTAKES.
THAT'S WHAT I AM THEN? A MISTAKE?!
THAT'S NOT WHAT I MEANT!
NO, I UNDERSTAND FATHER: FOR YOU I'M TOO HUMAN.
AND FOR HROTHGAR, NOT ENOUGH.
WHERE ARE YOU GOING? YOU HAVEN'T FINISHED YOUR DINNER!
THANK YOU. BUT I'LL FEND FOR MYSELF FROM NOW ON.
that went well.
SHUT UP, NAGLING.

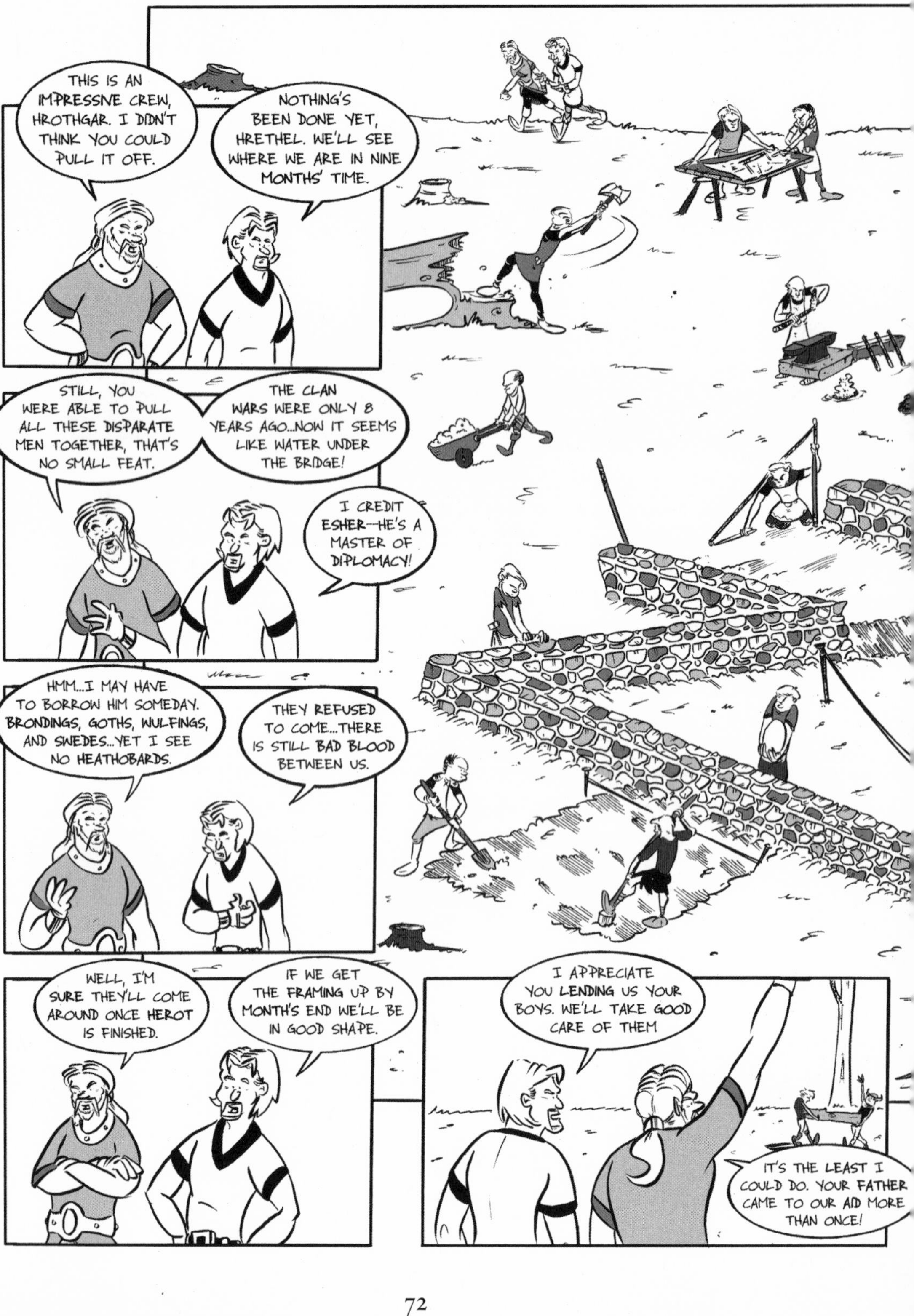
THIS IS AN IMPRESSIVE CREW, HROTHGAR. I DIDN'T THINK YOU COULD PULL IT OFF.
NOTHING'S BEEN DONE YET, HRETHEL. WE'LL SEE WHERE WE ARE IN NINE MONTHS' TIME.
STILL, YOU WERE ABLE TO PULL ALL THESE DISPARATE MEN TOGETHER, THAT'S NO SMALL FEAT.
THE CLAN WARS WERE ONLY 8 YEARS AGO...NOW IT SEEMS LIKE WATER UNDER THE BRIDGE!
I CREDIT ESHER—HE'S A MASTER OF DIPLOMACY!
HMM...I MAY HAVE TO BORROW HIM SOMEDAY. BRONDINGS, GOTHS, WULFINGS, AND SWEDES...YET I SEE NO HEATHOBARDS.
THEY REFUSED TO COME...THERE IS STILL BAD BLOOD BETWEEN US.
WELL, I'M SURE THEY'LL COME AROUND ONCE HEROT IS FINISHED.
IF WE GET THE FRAMING UP BY MONTH'S END WE'LL BE IN GOOD SHAPE.
I APPRECIATE YOU LENDING US YOUR BOYS. WE'LL TAKE GOOD CARE OF THEM
IT'S THE LEAST I COULD DO. YOUR FATHER CAME TO OUR AID MORE THAN ONCE!

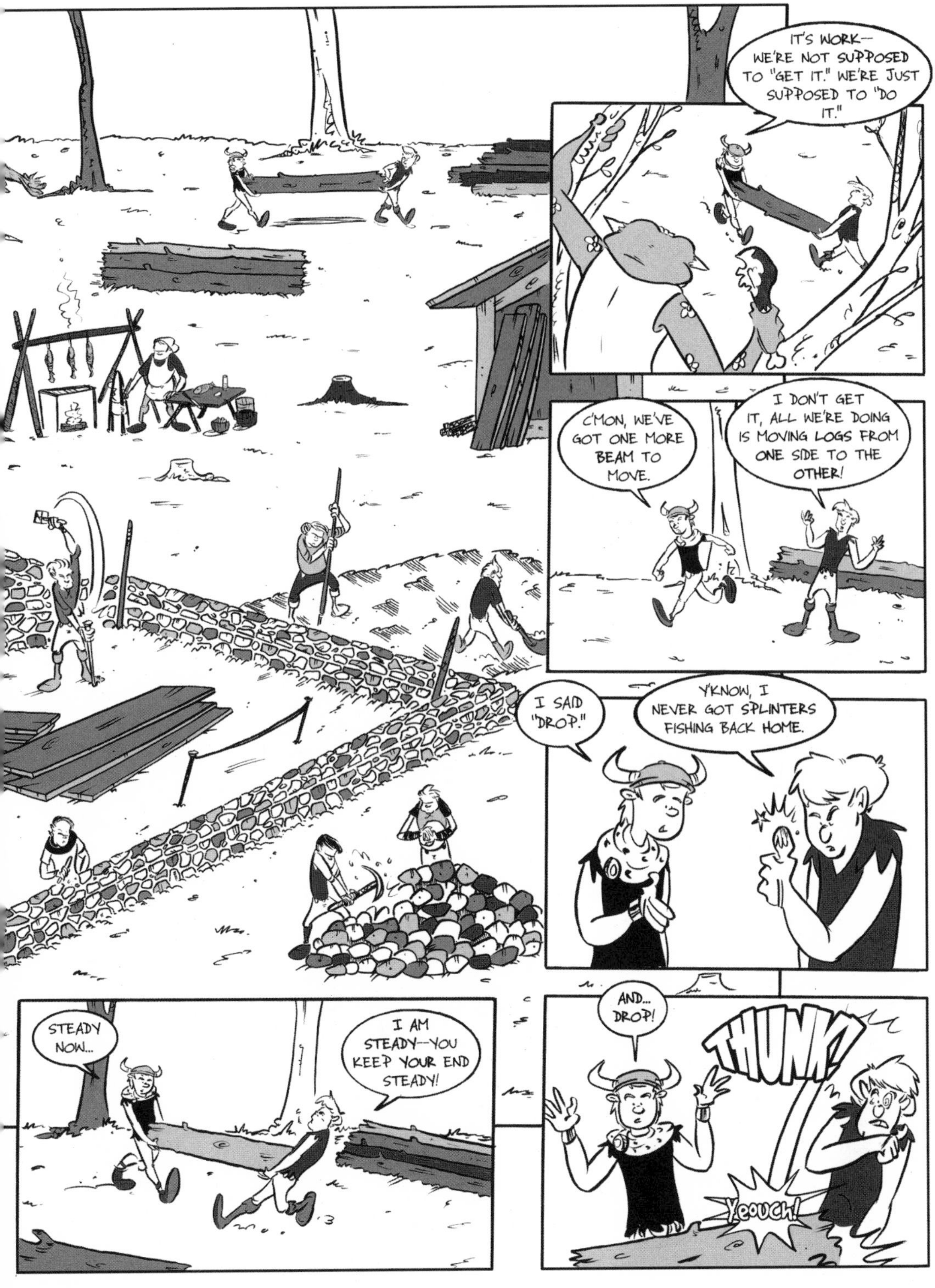
IT'S WORK-- WE'RE NOT SUPPOSED TO "GET IT." WE'RE JUST SUPPOSED TO "DO IT."
C'MON, WE'VE GOT ONE MORE BEAM TO MOVE.
I DON'T GET IT, ALL WE'RE DOING IS MOVING LOGS FROM ONE SIDE TO THE OTHER!
I SAID "DROP."
Y'KNOW, I NEVER GOT SPLINTERS FISHING BACK HOME.
STEADY NOW...
I AM STEADY--YOU KEEP YOUR END STEADY!
AND... DROP!
THUNK!
YEOUCH!

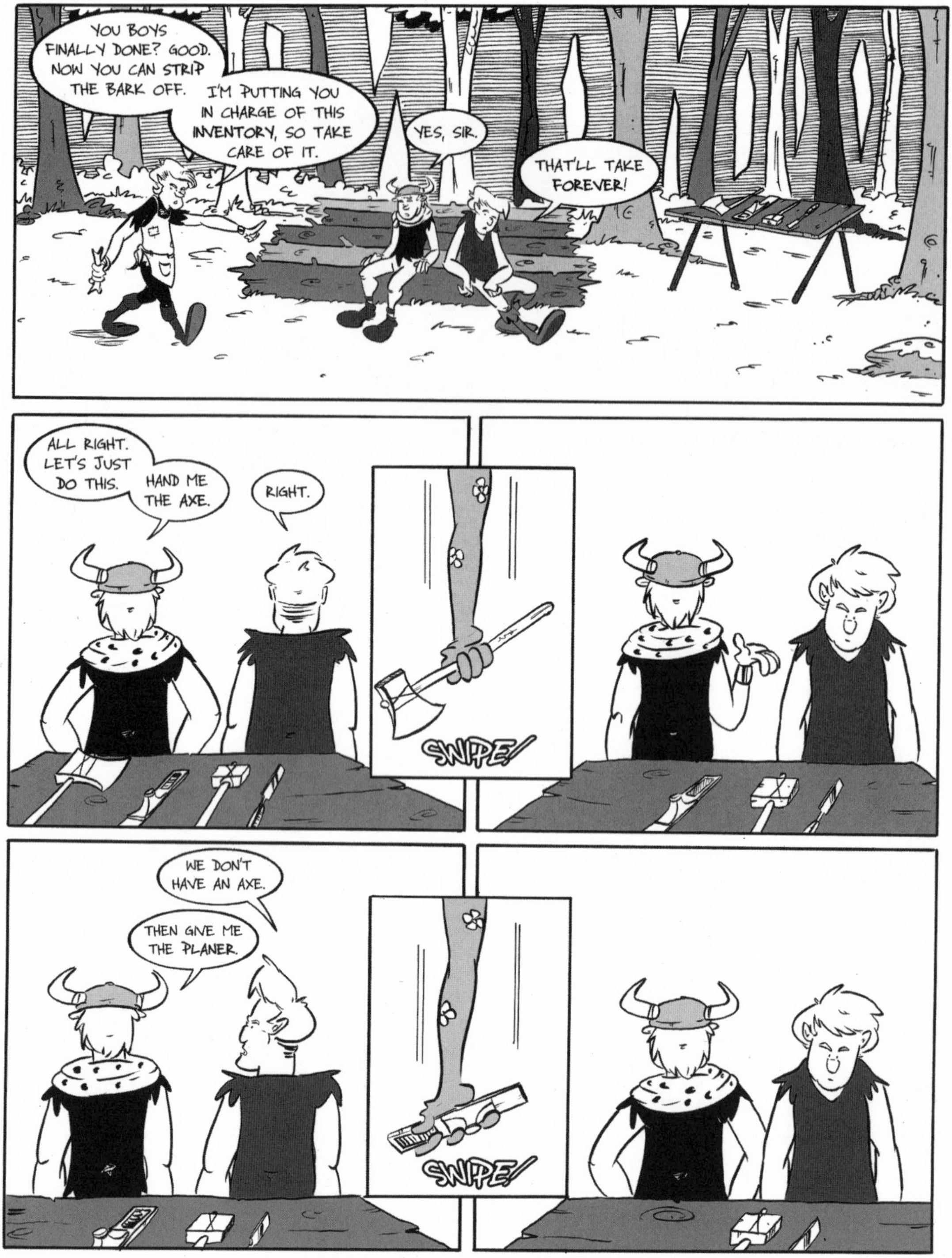
YOU BOYS FINALLY DONE? GOOD. NOW YOU CAN STRIP THE BARK OFF.
I'M PUTTING YOU IN CHARGE OF THIS INVENTORY, SO TAKE CARE OF IT.
YES, SIR.
THAT'LL TAKE FOREVER!
ALL RIGHT. LET'S JUST DO THIS.
HAND ME THE AXE.
RIGHT.
SWIPE!
WE DON'T HAVE AN AXE.
THEN GIVE ME THE PLANER.
SWIPE!

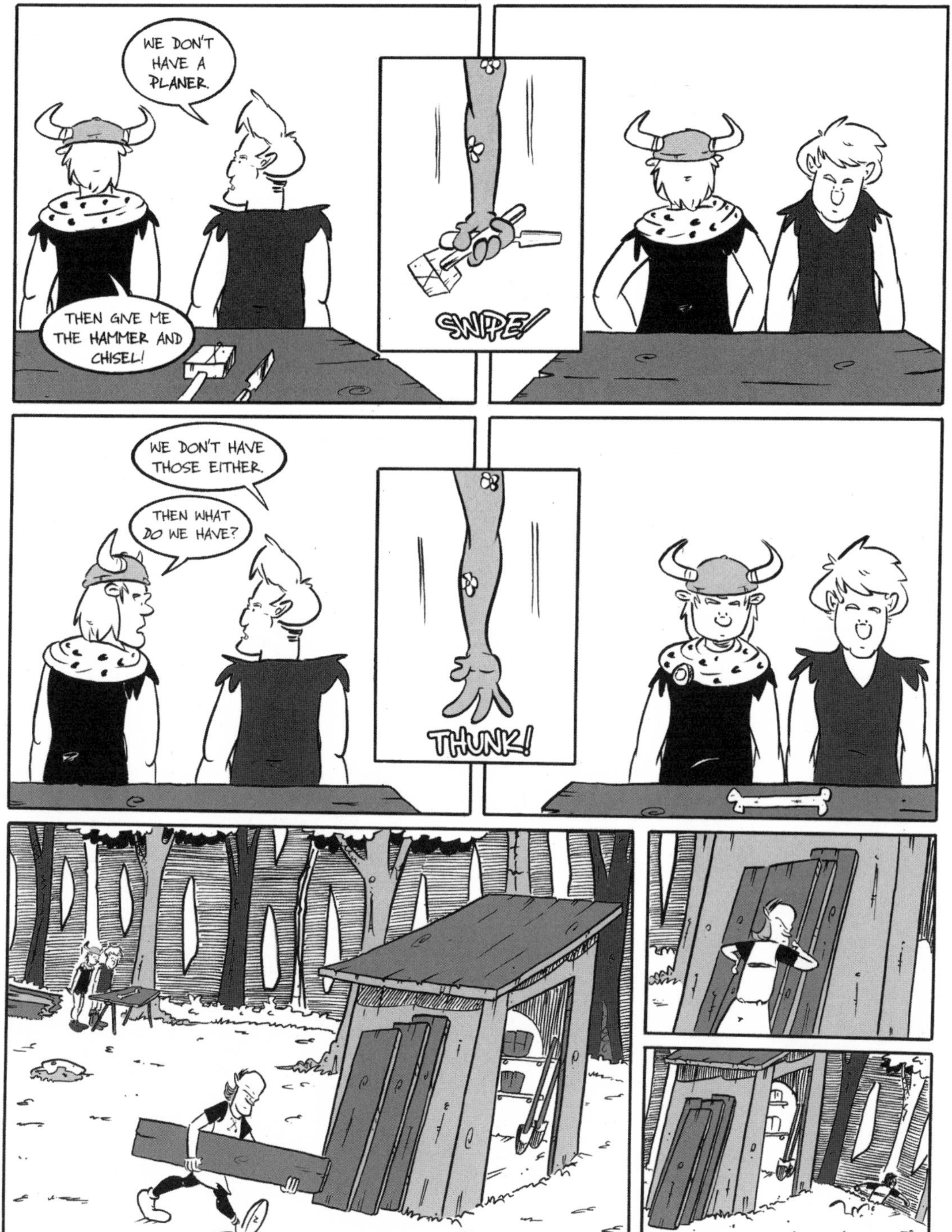

WE DON'T HAVE A PLANER.
THEN GIVE ME THE HAMMER AND CHISEL!
SWIPE!
WE DON'T HAVE THOSE EITHER.
THEN WHAT DO WE HAVE?
THUNK!

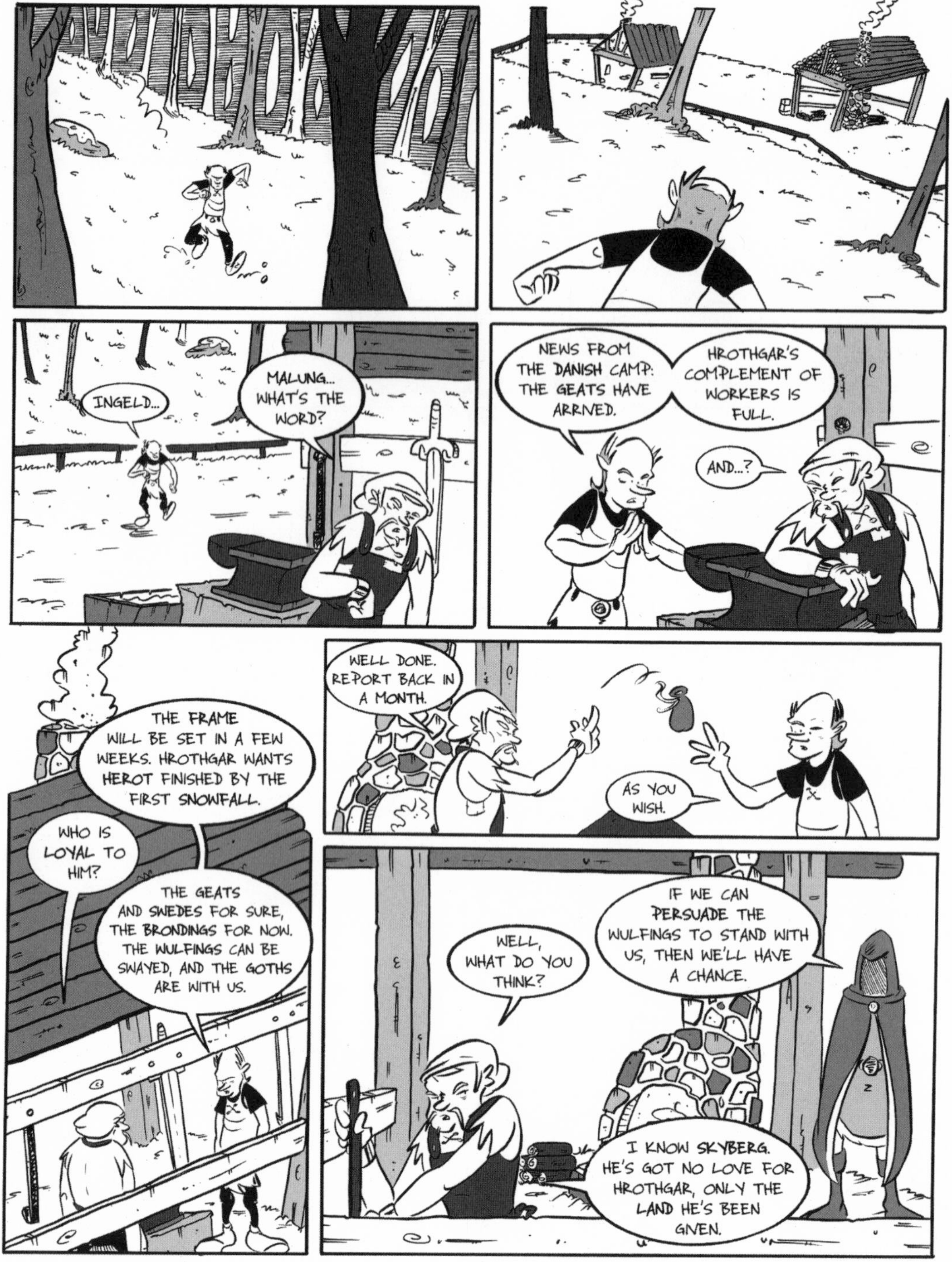
INGELD...
MALUNG... WHAT'S THE WORD?
NEWS FROM THE DANISH CAMP: THE GEATS HAVE ARRIVED.
HROTHGAR'S COMPLEMENT OF WORKERS IS FULL.
AND...?
THE FRAME WILL BE SET IN A FEW WEEKS. HROTHGAR WANTS HEROT FINISHED BY THE FIRST SNOWFALL.
WHO IS LOYAL TO HIM?
THE GEATS AND SWEDES FOR SURE, THE BRONDINGS FOR NOW. THE WULFINGS CAN BE SWAYED, AND THE GOTHS ARE WITH US.
WELL DONE. REPORT BACK IN A MONTH.
AS YOU WISH.
WELL, WHAT DO YOU THINK?
IF WE CAN PERSUADE THE WULFINGS TO STAND WITH US, THEN WE'LL HAVE A CHANCE.
I KNOW SKYBERG. HE'S GOT NO LOVE FOR HROTHGAR, ONLY THE LAND HE'S BEEN GIVEN.

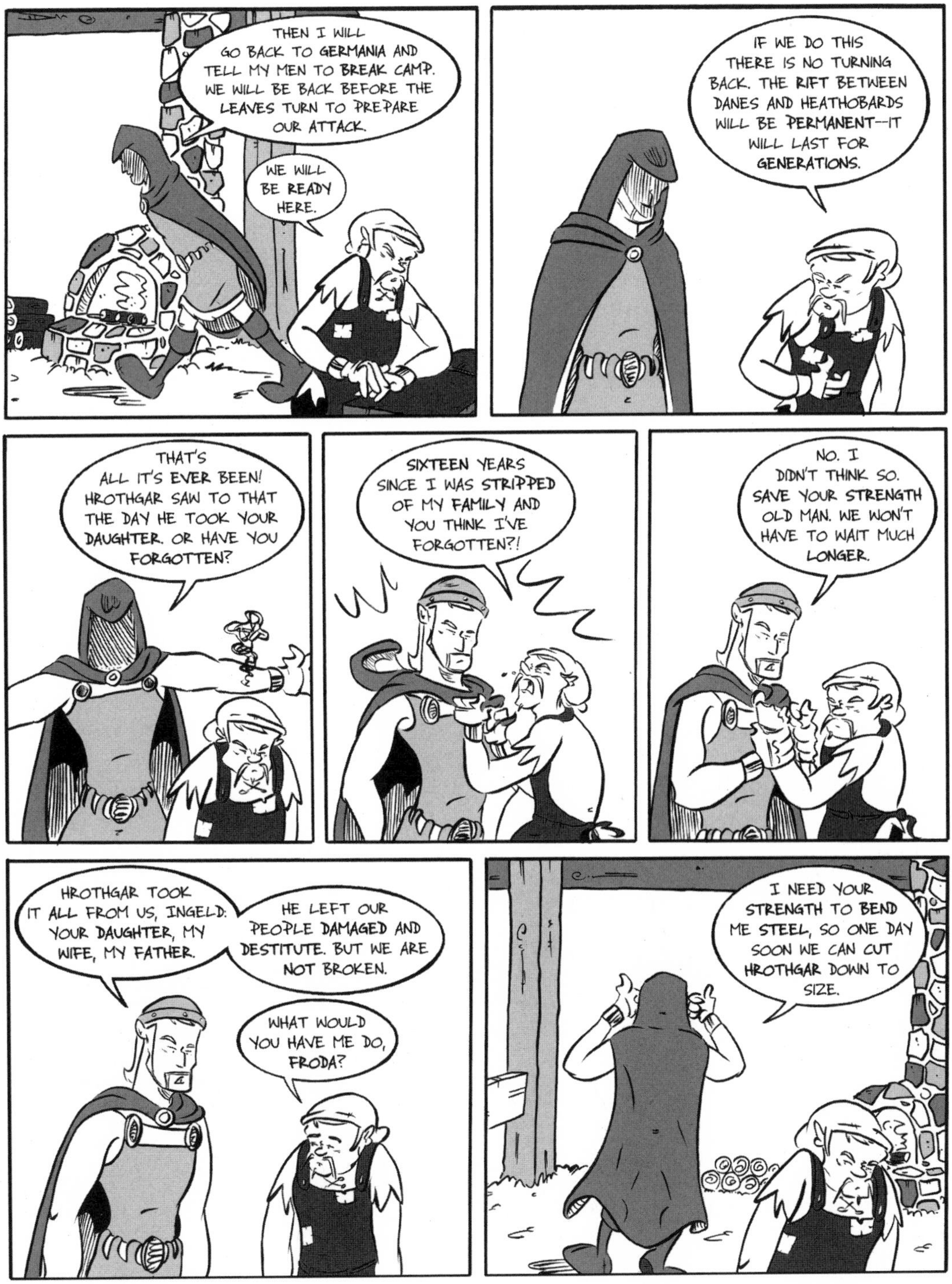
THEN I WILL GO BACK TO GERMANIA AND TELL MY MEN TO BREAK CAMP. WE WILL BE BACK BEFORE THE LEAVES TURN TO PREPARE OUR ATTACK.
WE WILL BE READY HERE.
IF WE DO THIS THERE IS NO TURNING BACK. THE RIFT BETWEEN DANES AND HEATHOBARDS WILL BE PERMANENT--IT WILL LAST FOR GENERATIONS.
THAT'S ALL IT'S EVER BEEN! HROTHGAR SAW TO THAT THE DAY HE TOOK YOUR DAUGHTER. OR HAVE YOU FORGOTTEN?
SIXTEEN YEARS SINCE I WAS STRIPPED OF MY FAMILY AND YOU THINK I'VE FORGOTTEN?!
NO. I DIDN'T THINK SO. SAVE YOUR STRENGTH OLD MAN. WE WON'T HAVE TO WAIT MUCH LONGER.
HROTHGAR TOOK IT ALL FROM US, INGELD. YOUR DAUGHTER, MY WIFE, MY FATHER.
HE LEFT OUR PEOPLE DAMAGED AND DESTITUTE. BUT WE ARE NOT BROKEN.
WHAT WOULD YOU HAVE ME DO, FRODA?
I NEED YOUR STRENGTH TO BEND ME STEEL, SO ONE DAY SOON WE CAN CUT HROTHGAR DOWN TO SIZE.

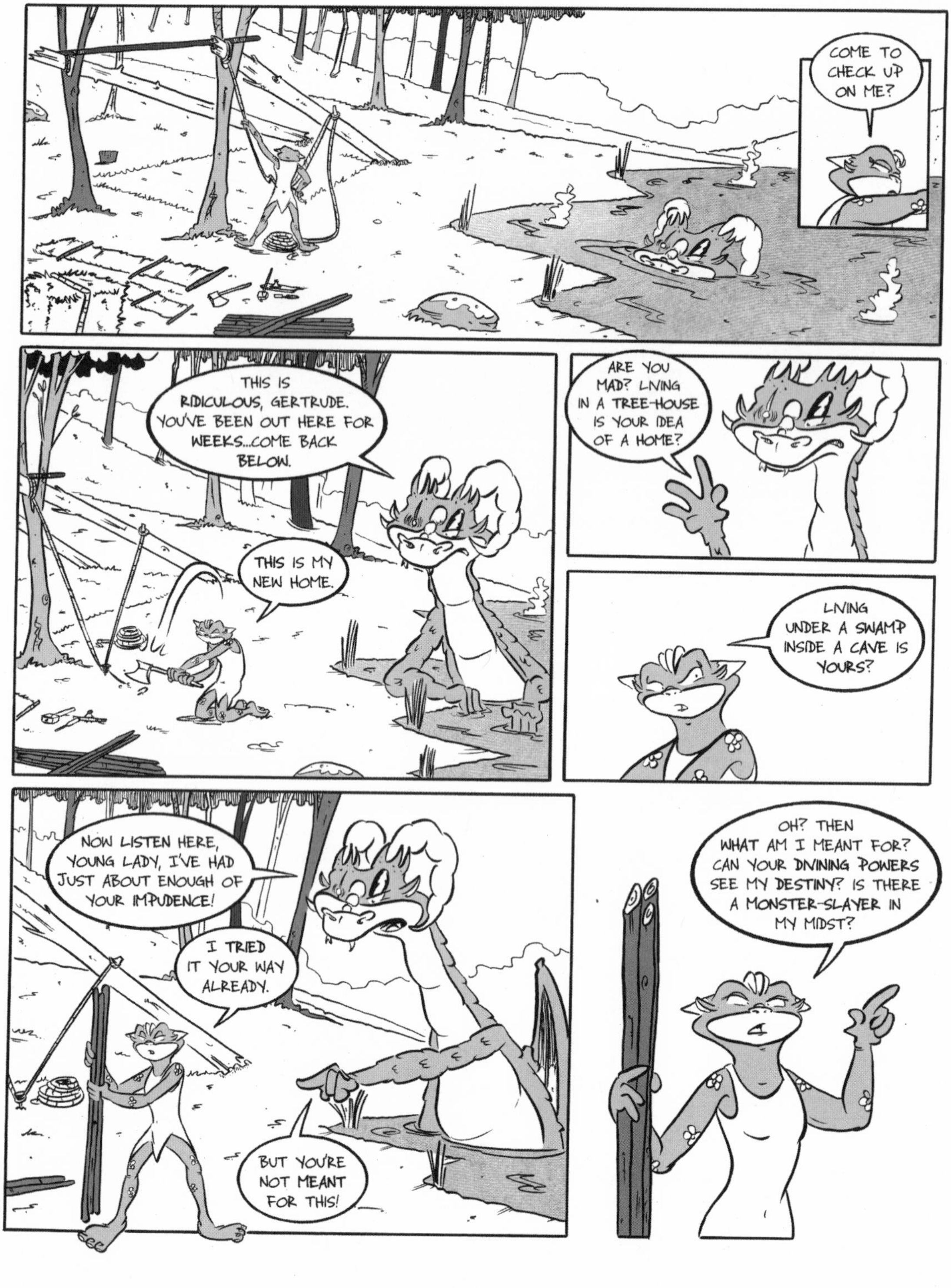
COME TO CHECK UP ON ME?
THIS IS RIDICULOUS, GERTRUDE. YOU'VE BEEN OUT HERE FOR WEEKS...COME BACK BELOW.
THIS IS MY NEW HOME.
ARE YOU MAD? LIVING IN A TREE-HOUSE IS YOUR IDEA OF A HOME?
LIVING UNDER A SWAMP INSIDE A CAVE IS YOURS?
NOW LISTEN HERE, YOUNG LADY, I'VE HAD JUST ABOUT ENOUGH OF YOUR IMPUDENCE!
I TRIED IT YOUR WAY ALREADY.
BUT YOU'RE NOT MEANT FOR THIS!
OH? THEN WHAT AM I MEANT FOR? CAN YOUR DIVINING POWERS SEE MY DESTINY? IS THERE A MONSTER-SLAYER IN MY MIDST?

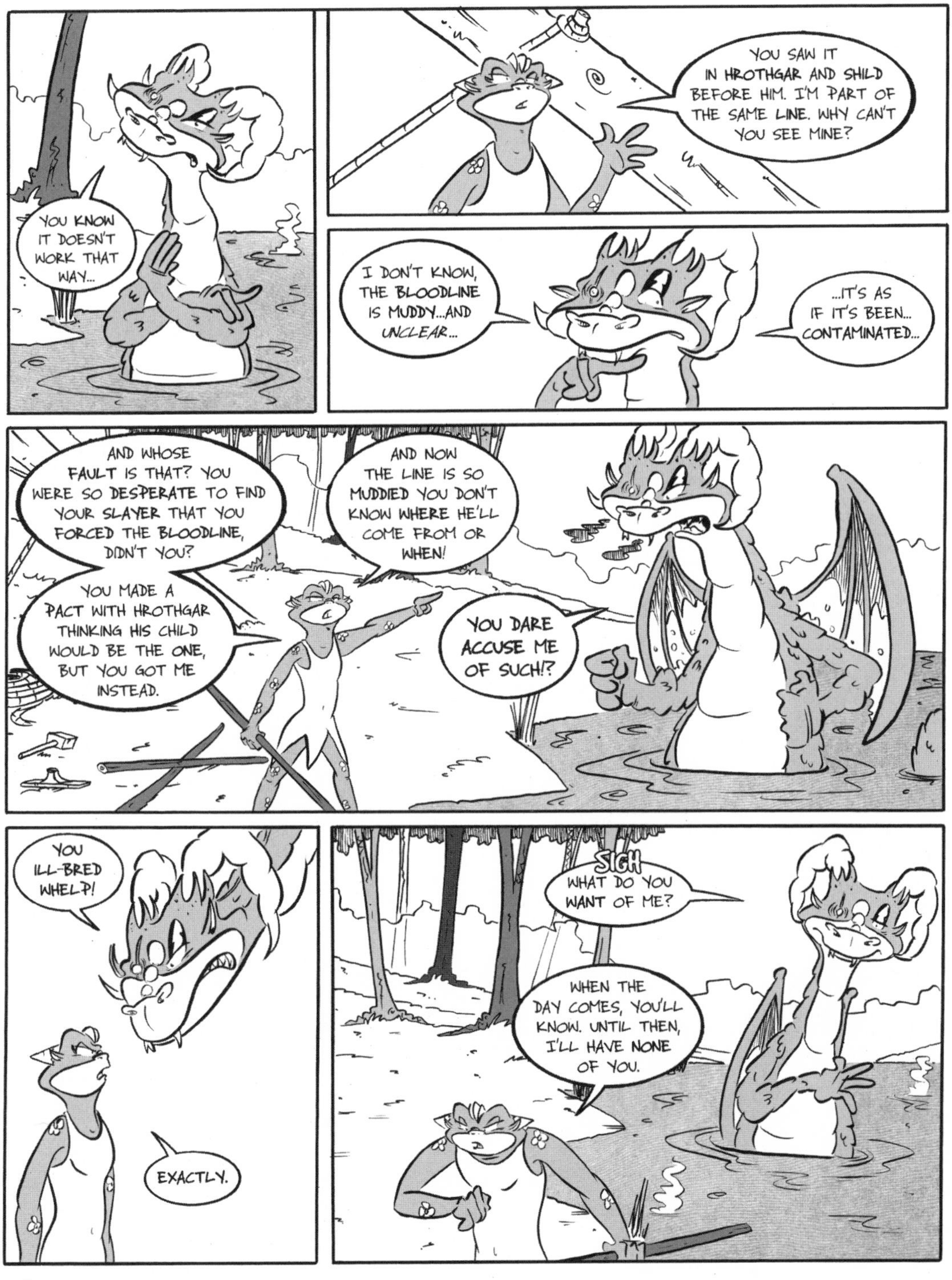
YOU KNOW IT DOESN'T WORK THAT WAY...
YOU SAW IT IN HROTHGAR AND SHILD BEFORE HIM. I'M PART OF THE SAME LINE. WHY CAN'T YOU SEE MINE?
I DON'T KNOW, THE BLOODLINE IS MUDDY...AND UNCLEAR...
...IT'S AS IF IT'S BEEN... CONTAMINATED...
AND WHOSE FAULT IS THAT? YOU WERE SO DESPERATE TO FIND YOUR SLAYER THAT YOU FORCED THE BLOODLINE, DIDN'T YOU?
YOU MADE A PACT WITH HROTHGAR THINKING HIS CHILD WOULD BE THE ONE, BUT YOU GOT ME INSTEAD.
AND NOW THE LINE IS SO MUDDIED YOU DON'T KNOW WHERE HE'LL COME FROM OR WHEN!
YOU DARE ACCUSE ME OF SUCH!?
YOU ILL-BRED WHELP!
EXACTLY.
SIGH
WHAT DO YOU WANT OF ME?
WHEN THE DAY COMES, YOU'LL KNOW. UNTIL THEN, I'LL HAVE NONE OF YOU.

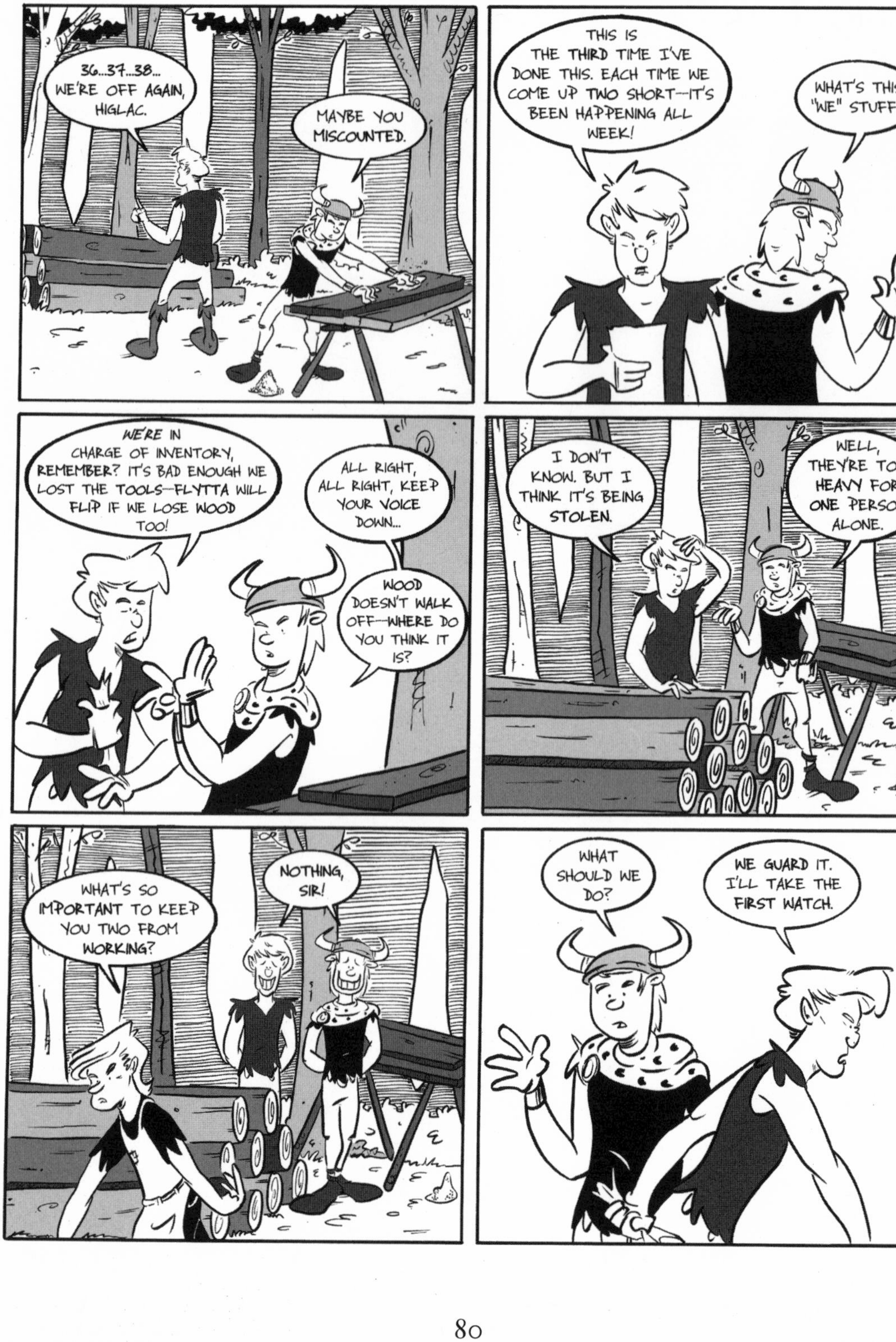
36...37...38... WE'RE OFF AGAIN, HIGLAC.
MAYBE YOU MISCOUNTED.
THIS IS THE THIRD TIME I'VE DONE THIS. EACH TIME WE COME UP TWO SHORT---IT'S BEEN HAPPENING ALL WEEK!
WHAT'S THIS "WE" STUFF?
WE'RE IN CHARGE OF INVENTORY, REMEMBER? IT'S BAD ENOUGH WE LOST THE TOOLS---FLYTTA WILL FLIP IF WE LOSE WOOD TOO!
ALL RIGHT, ALL RIGHT, KEEP YOUR VOICE DOWN...
WOOD DOESN'T WALK OFF---WHERE DO YOU THINK IT IS?
I DON'T KNOW. BUT I THINK IT'S BEING STOLEN.
WELL, THEY'RE TOO HEAVY FOR ONE PERSON ALONE.
WHAT'S SO IMPORTANT TO KEEP YOU TWO FROM WORKING?
NOTHING, SIR!
WHAT SHOULD WE DO?
WE GUARD IT. I'LL TAKE THE FIRST WATCH.

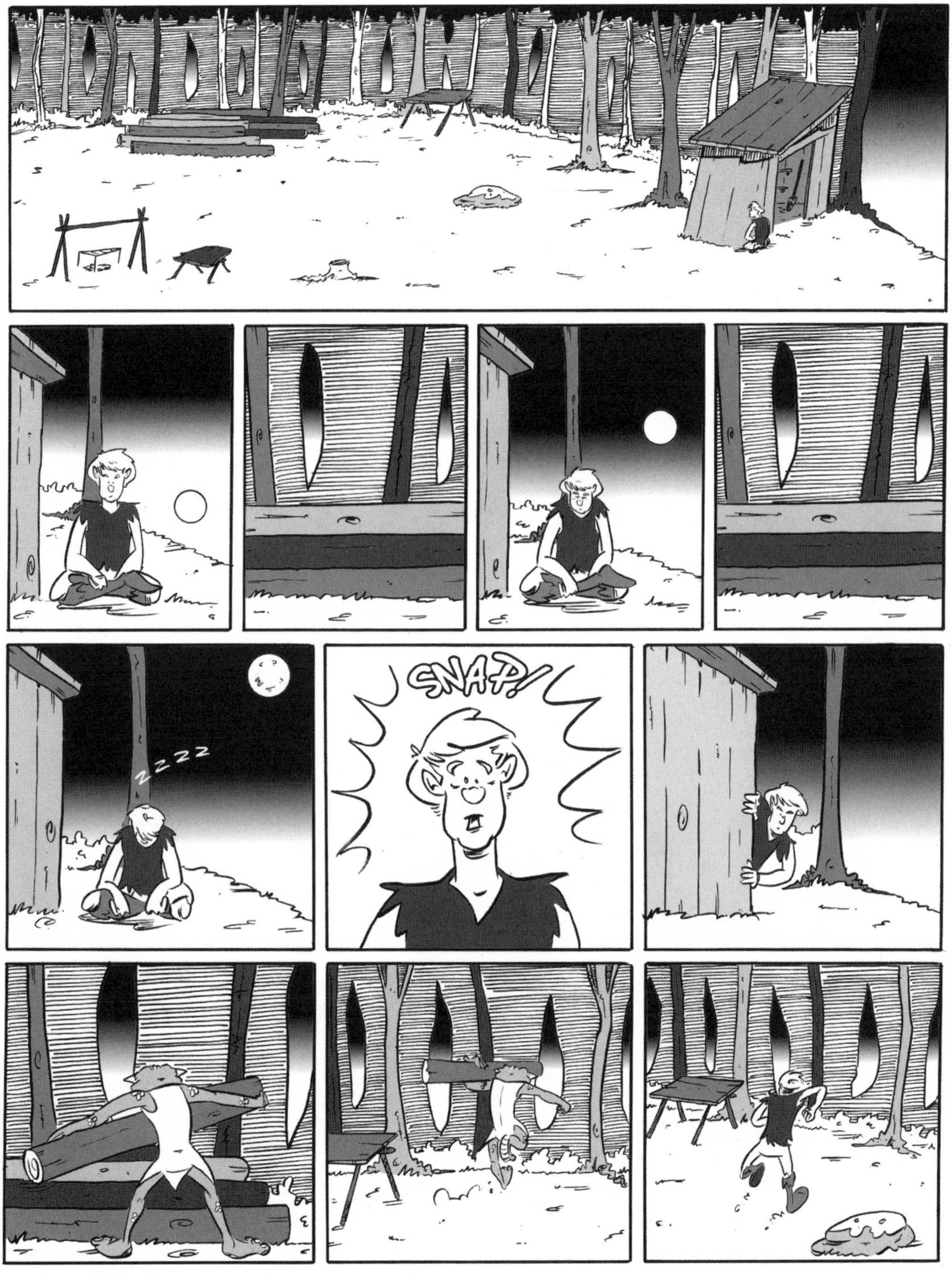
ZZZZ
SNAP!

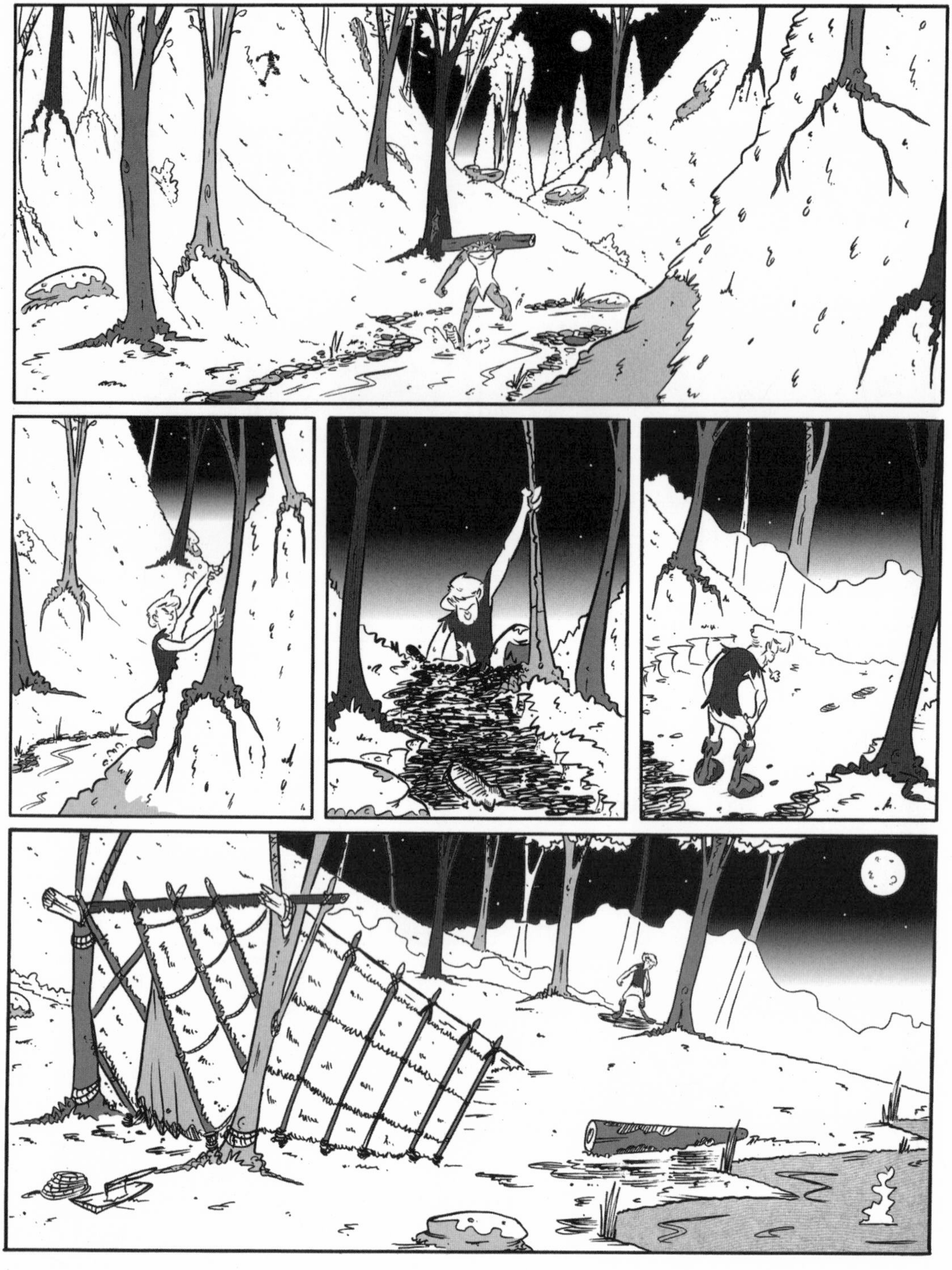

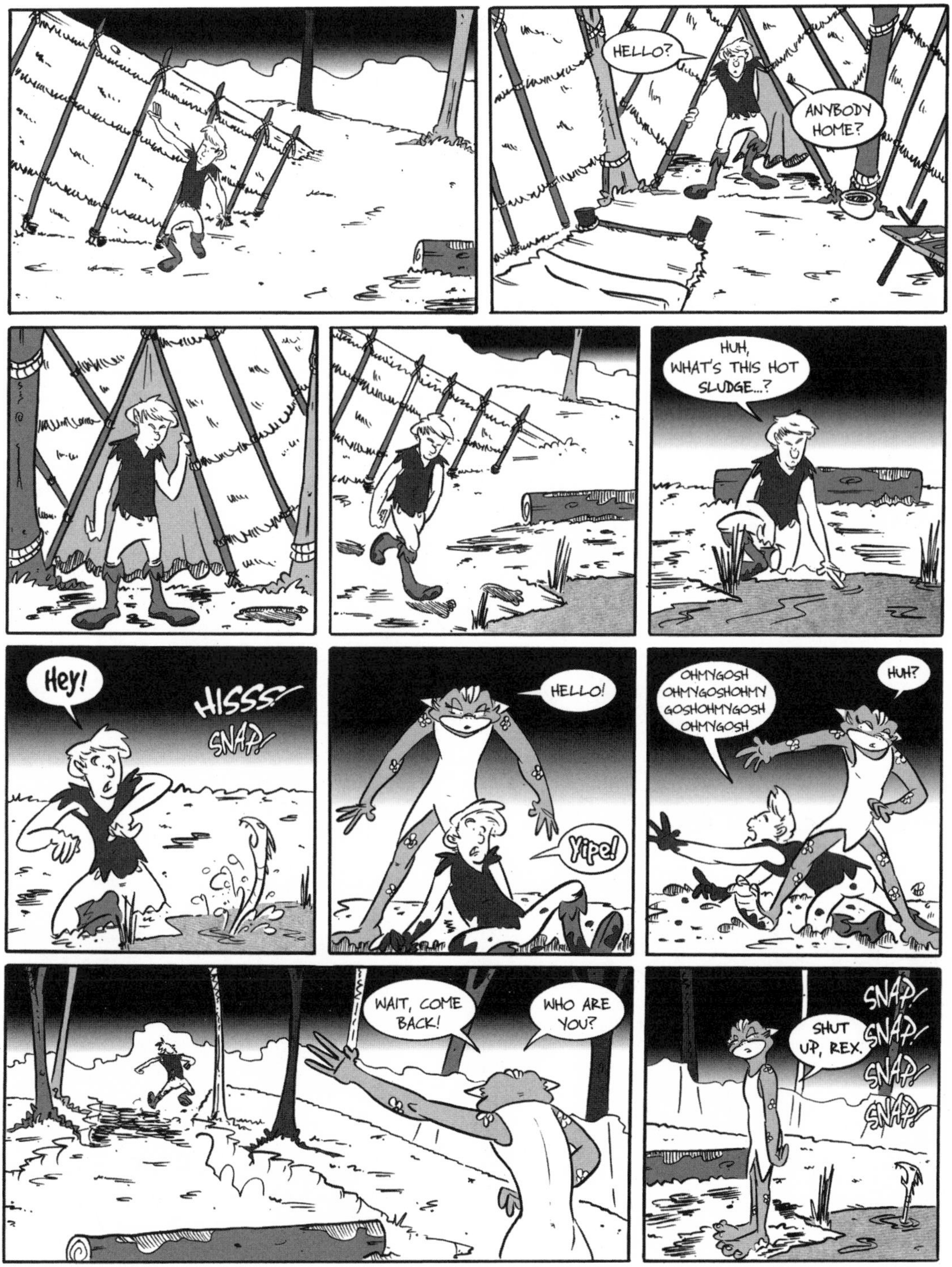
HELLO?
ANYBODY HOME?
HUH, WHAT'S THIS HOT SLUDGE...?
Hey!
HISSS!
SNAP!
HELLO!
Yipe!
OHMYGOSH OHMYGOSHOHMY GOSHOHMYGOSH OHMYGOSH
HUH?
WAIT, COME BACK!
WHO ARE YOU?
SHUT UP, REX.
SNAP! SNAP! SNAP! SNAP!

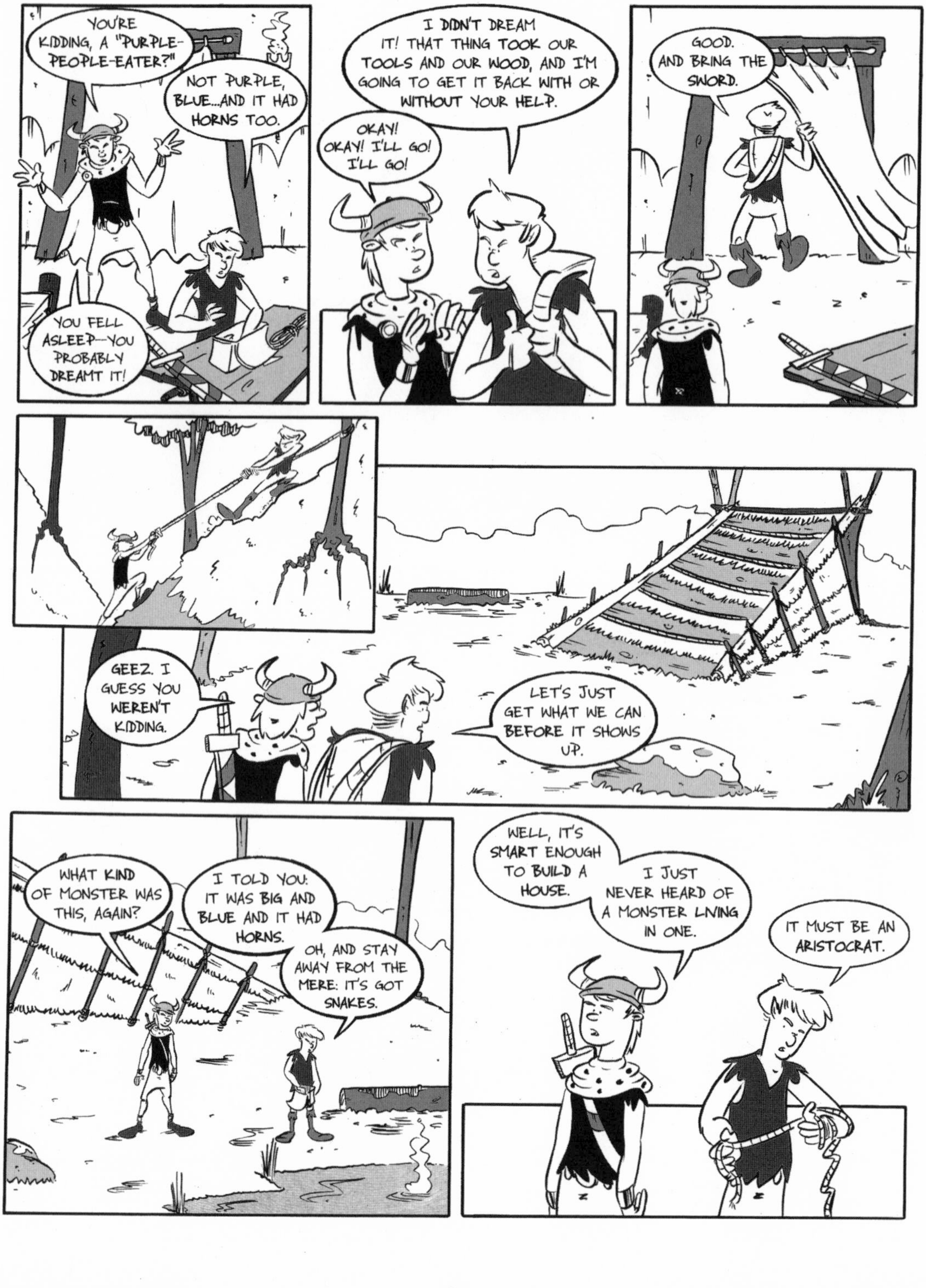
YOU'RE KIDDING, A "PURPLE-PEOPLE-EATER?"
NOT PURPLE, BLUE...AND IT HAD HORNS TOO.
YOU FELL ASLEEP--YOU PROBABLY DREAMT IT!
I DIDN'T DREAM IT! THAT THING TOOK OUR TOOLS AND OUR WOOD, AND I'M GOING TO GET IT BACK WITH OR WITHOUT YOUR HELP.
OKAY! OKAY! I'LL GO! I'LL GO!
GOOD. AND BRING THE SWORD.
GEEZ. I GUESS YOU WEREN'T KIDDING.
LET'S JUST GET WHAT WE CAN BEFORE IT SHOWS UP.
WHAT KIND OF MONSTER WAS THIS, AGAIN?
I TOLD YOU: IT WAS BIG AND BLUE AND IT HAD HORNS.
OH, AND STAY AWAY FROM THE MERE: IT'S GOT SNAKES.
WELL, IT'S SMART ENOUGH TO BUILD A HOUSE.
I JUST NEVER HEARD OF A MONSTER LIVING IN ONE.
IT MUST BE AN ARISTOCRAT.

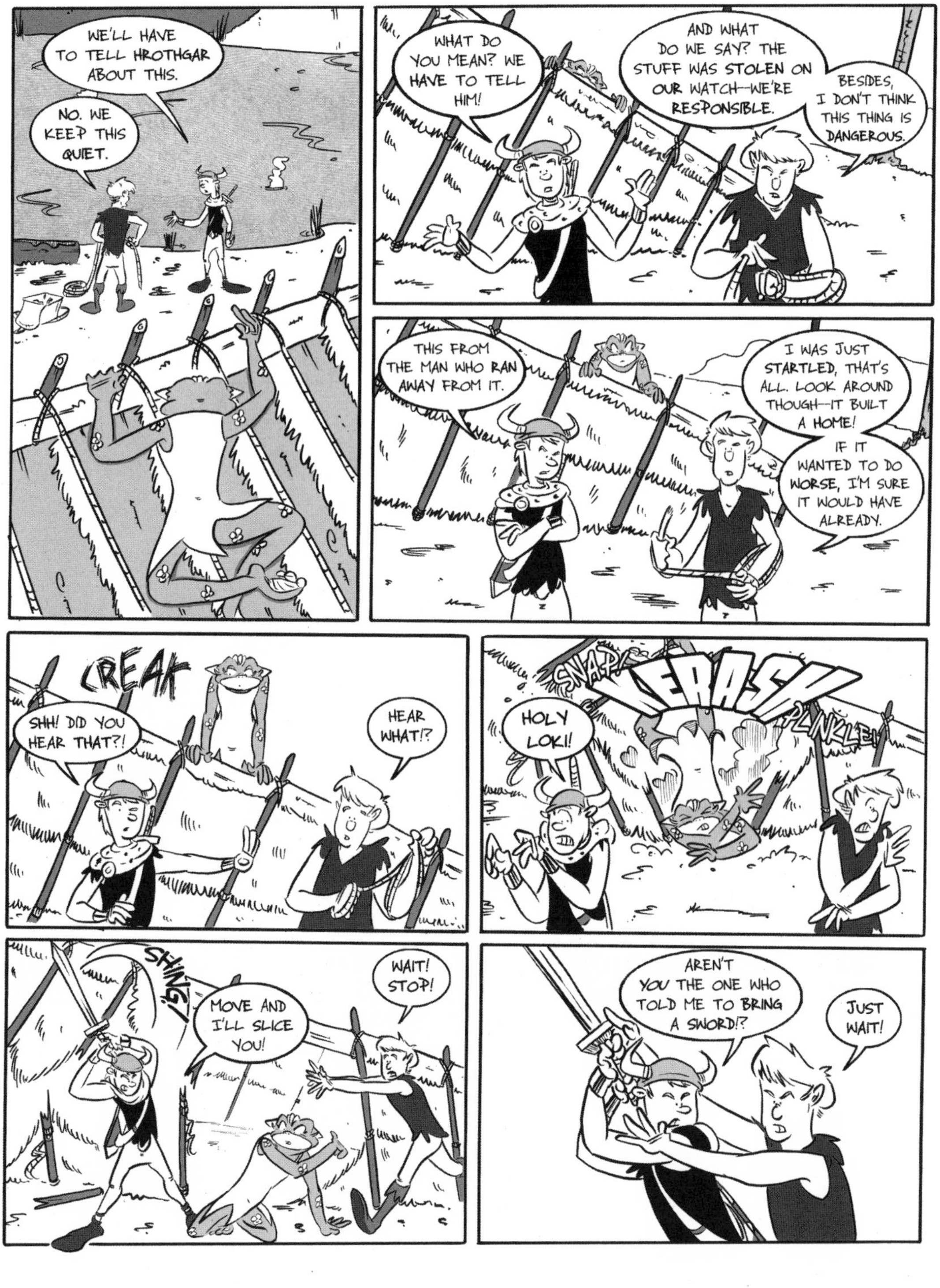
WE'LL HAVE TO TELL HROTHGAR ABOUT THIS.
NO. WE KEEP THIS QUIET.
WHAT DO YOU MEAN? WE HAVE TO TELL HIM!
AND WHAT DO WE SAY? THE STUFF WAS STOLEN ON OUR WATCH--WE'RE RESPONSIBLE.
BESIDES, I DON'T THINK THIS THING IS DANGEROUS.
THIS FROM THE MAN WHO RAN AWAY FROM IT.
I WAS JUST STARTLED, THAT'S ALL. LOOK AROUND THOUGH--IT BUILT A HOME!
IF IT WANTED TO DO WORSE, I'M SURE IT WOULD HAVE ALREADY.
CREAK
SHH! DID YOU HEAR THAT?!
HEAR WHAT!?
SNAP!
CRASH
PLINKLE!
HOLY LOKI!
SHING!
MOVE AND I'LL SLICE YOU!
WAIT! STOP!
AREN'T YOU THE ONE WHO TOLD ME TO BRING A SWORD!?
JUST WAIT!

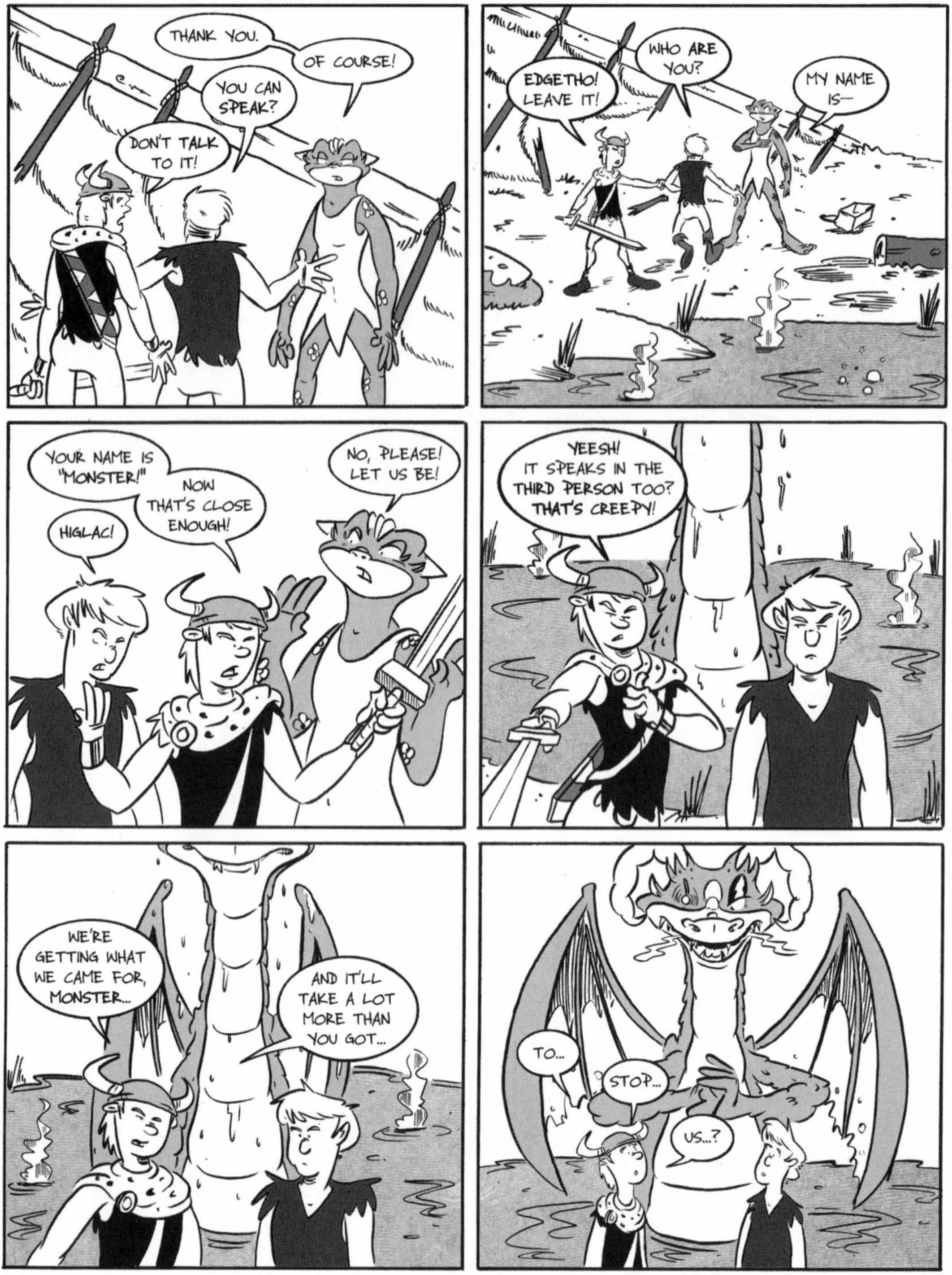
THANK YOU.
OF COURSE!
YOU CAN SPEAK?
DON'T TALK TO IT!
EDGETHO! LEAVE IT!
WHO ARE YOU?
MY NAME IS—
YOUR NAME IS "MONSTER!"
NOW THAT'S CLOSE ENOUGH!
HIGLAC!
NO, PLEASE! LET US BE!
YEESH! IT SPEAKS IN THE THIRD PERSON TOO? THAT'S CREEPY!
WE'RE GETTING WHAT WE CAME FOR, MONSTER...
AND IT'LL TAKE A LOT MORE THAN YOU GOT...
TO...
STOP...
US...?

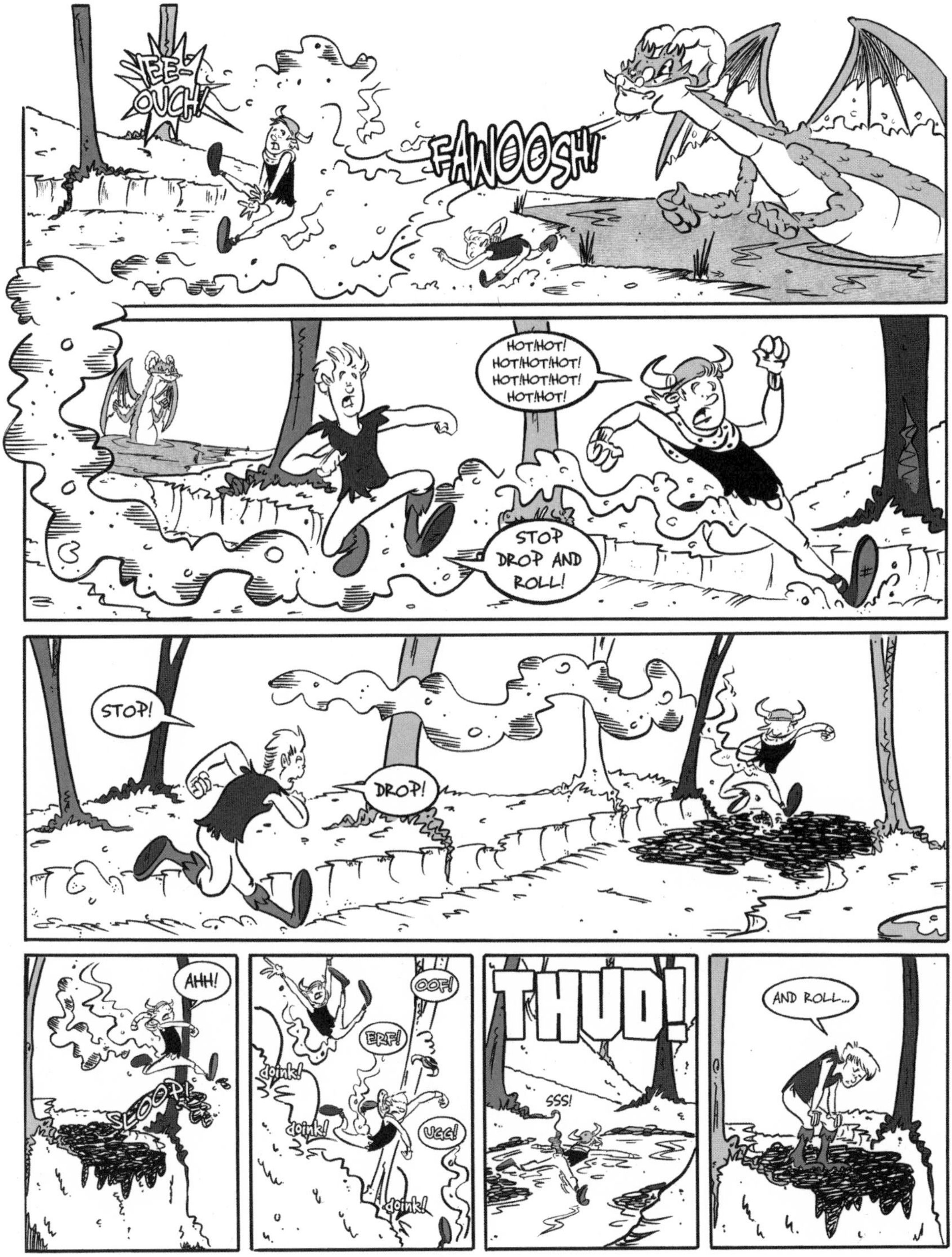
EE-OUCH!
FAWOOSH!
HOT!HOT! HOT!HOT!HOT! HOT!HOT!HOT! HOT!HOT!
STOP DROP AND ROLL!
STOP!
DROP!
AHH!
SLOOP!
OOF!
ERF!
doink!
doink!
UGG!
doink!
THUD!
SSS!
AND ROLL...

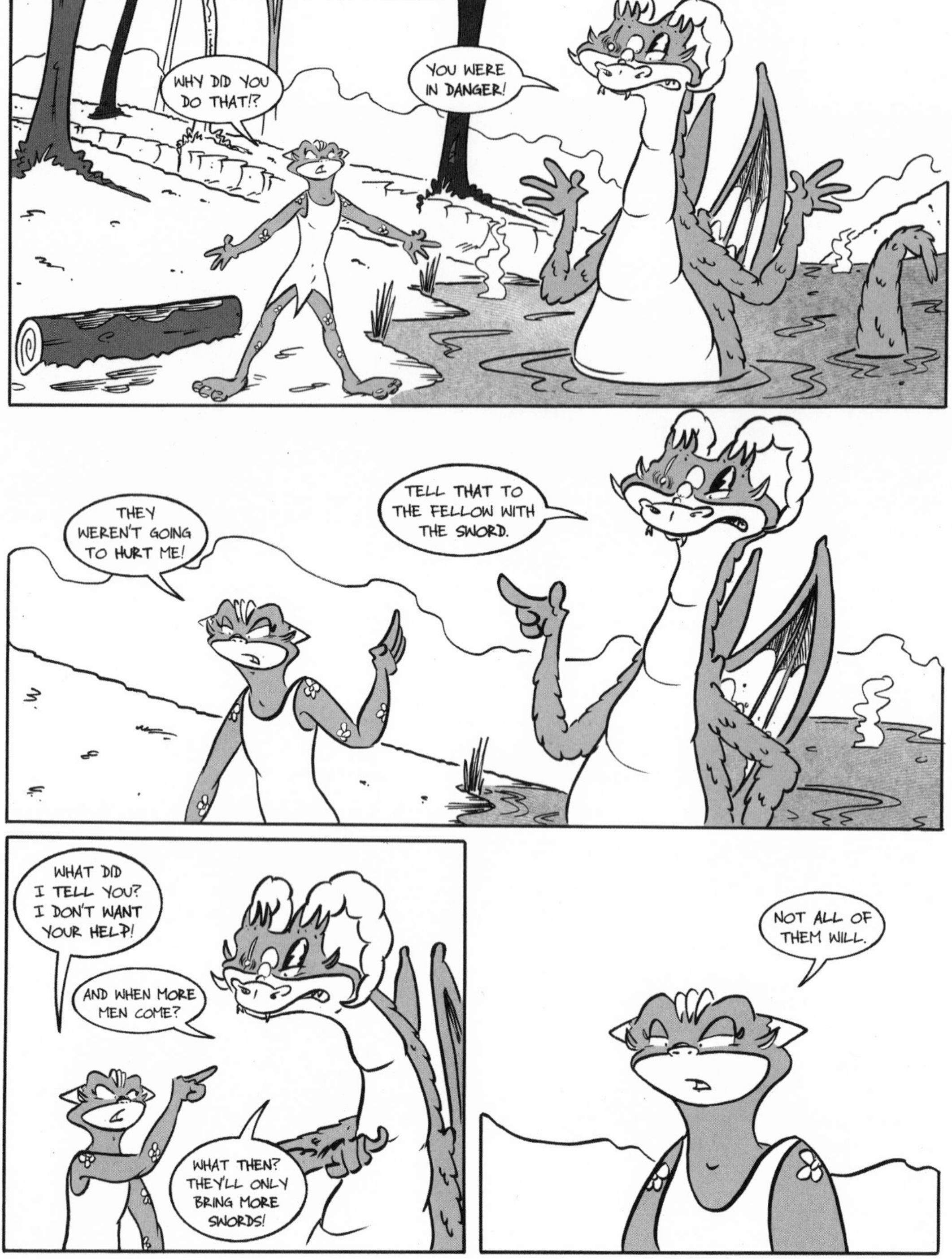
WHY DID YOU DO THAT!?
YOU WERE IN DANGER!
THEY WEREN'T GOING TO HURT ME!
TELL THAT TO THE FELLOW WITH THE SWORD.
WHAT DID I TELL YOU? I DON'T WANT YOUR HELP!
AND WHEN MORE MEN COME?
WHAT THEN? THEY'LL ONLY BRING MORE SWORDS!
NOT ALL OF THEM WILL.

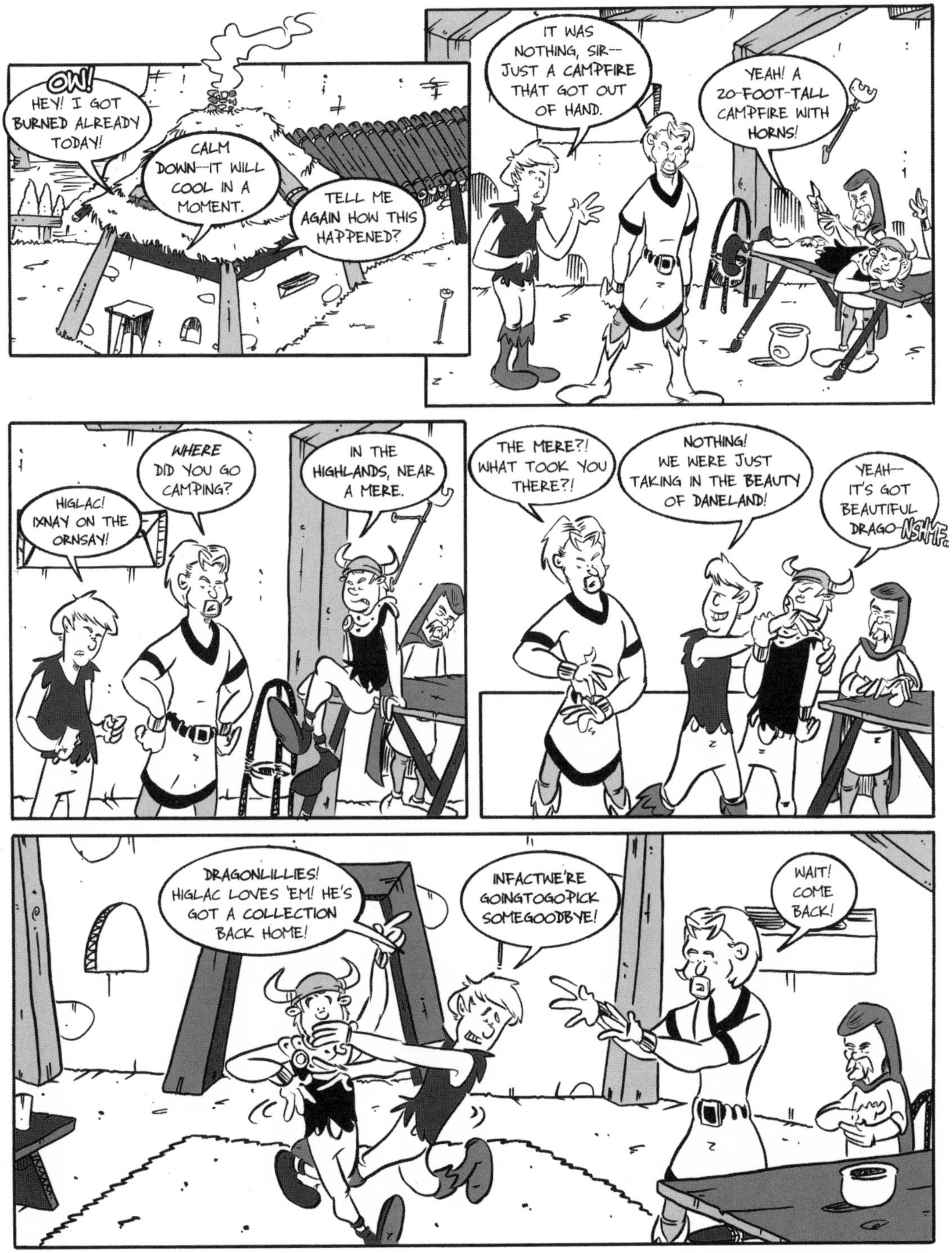
OW!
HEY! I GOT BURNED ALREADY TODAY!
CALM DOWN--IT WILL COOL IN A MOMENT.
TELL ME AGAIN HOW THIS HAPPENED?
IT WAS NOTHING, SIR--JUST A CAMPFIRE THAT GOT OUT OF HAND.
YEAH! A 20-FOOT-TALL CAMPFIRE WITH HORNS!
WHERE DID YOU GO CAMPING?
HIGLAC! IXNAY ON THE ORNSAY!
IN THE HIGHLANDS, NEAR A MERE.
THE MERE?! WHAT TOOK YOU THERE?!
NOTHING! WE WERE JUST TAKING IN THE BEAUTY OF DANELAND!
YEAH-- IT'S GOT BEAUTIFUL DRAGO-NSHMF..
DRAGONLILLIES! HIGLAC LOVES 'EM! HE'S GOT A COLLECTION BACK HOME!
INFACTWE'RE GOINGTOGOPICK SOMEGOODBYE!
WAIT! COME BACK!

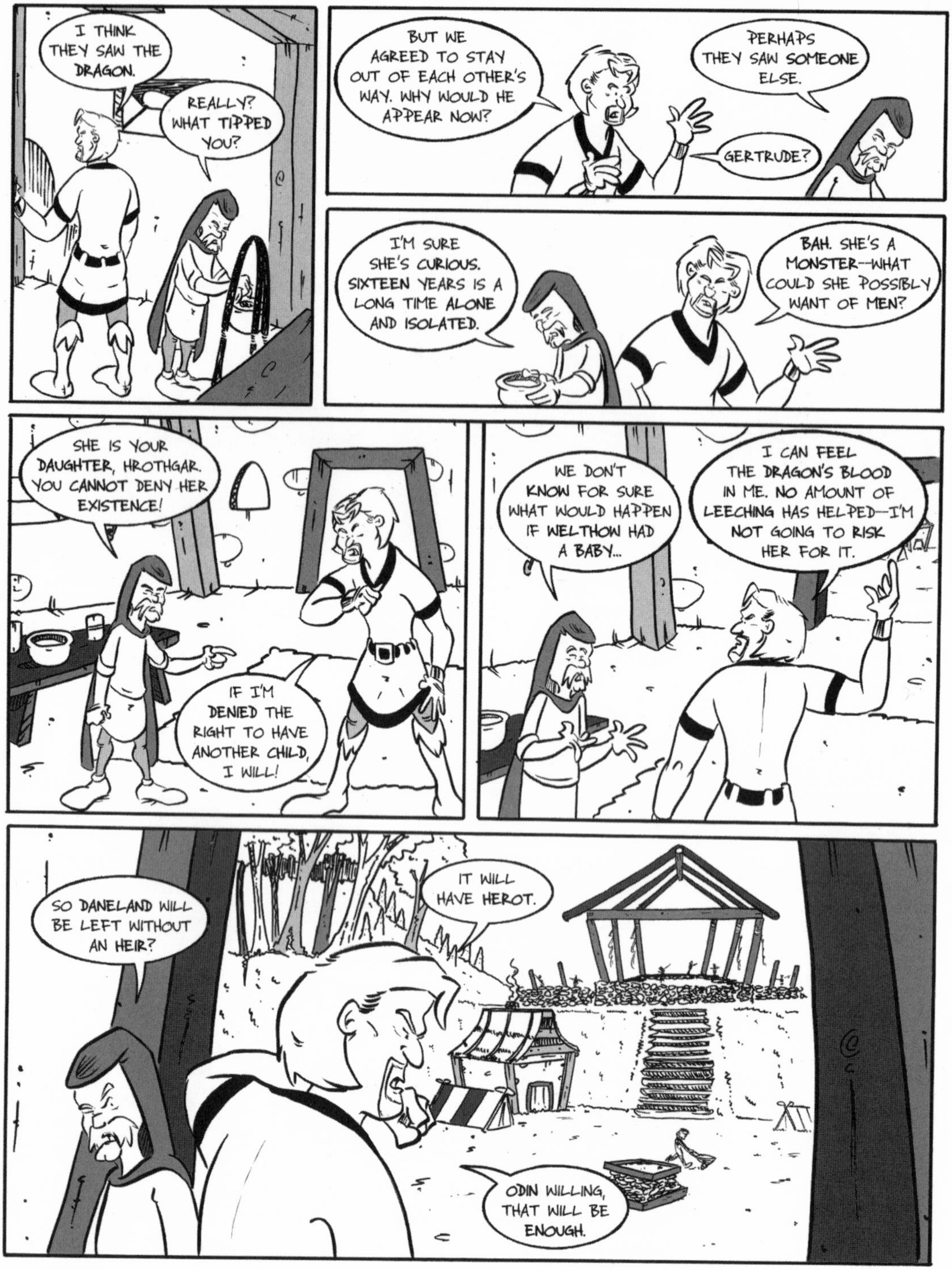
I THINK THEY SAW THE DRAGON.
REALLY? WHAT TIPPED YOU?
BUT WE AGREED TO STAY OUT OF EACH OTHER'S WAY. WHY WOULD HE APPEAR NOW?
PERHAPS THEY SAW SOMEONE ELSE.
GERTRUDE?
I'M SURE SHE'S CURIOUS. SIXTEEN YEARS IS A LONG TIME ALONE AND ISOLATED.
BAH. SHE'S A MONSTER--WHAT COULD SHE POSSIBLY WANT OF MEN?
SHE IS YOUR DAUGHTER, HROTHGAR. YOU CANNOT DENY HER EXISTENCE!
IF I'M DENIED THE RIGHT TO HAVE ANOTHER CHILD, I WILL!
WE DON'T KNOW FOR SURE WHAT WOULD HAPPEN IF WELTHOW HAD A BABY...
I CAN FEEL THE DRAGON'S BLOOD IN ME. NO AMOUNT OF LEECHING HAS HELPED--I'M NOT GOING TO RISK HER FOR IT.
SO DANELAND WILL BE LEFT WITHOUT AN HEIR?
IT WILL HAVE HEROT.
ODIN WILLING, THAT WILL BE ENOUGH.

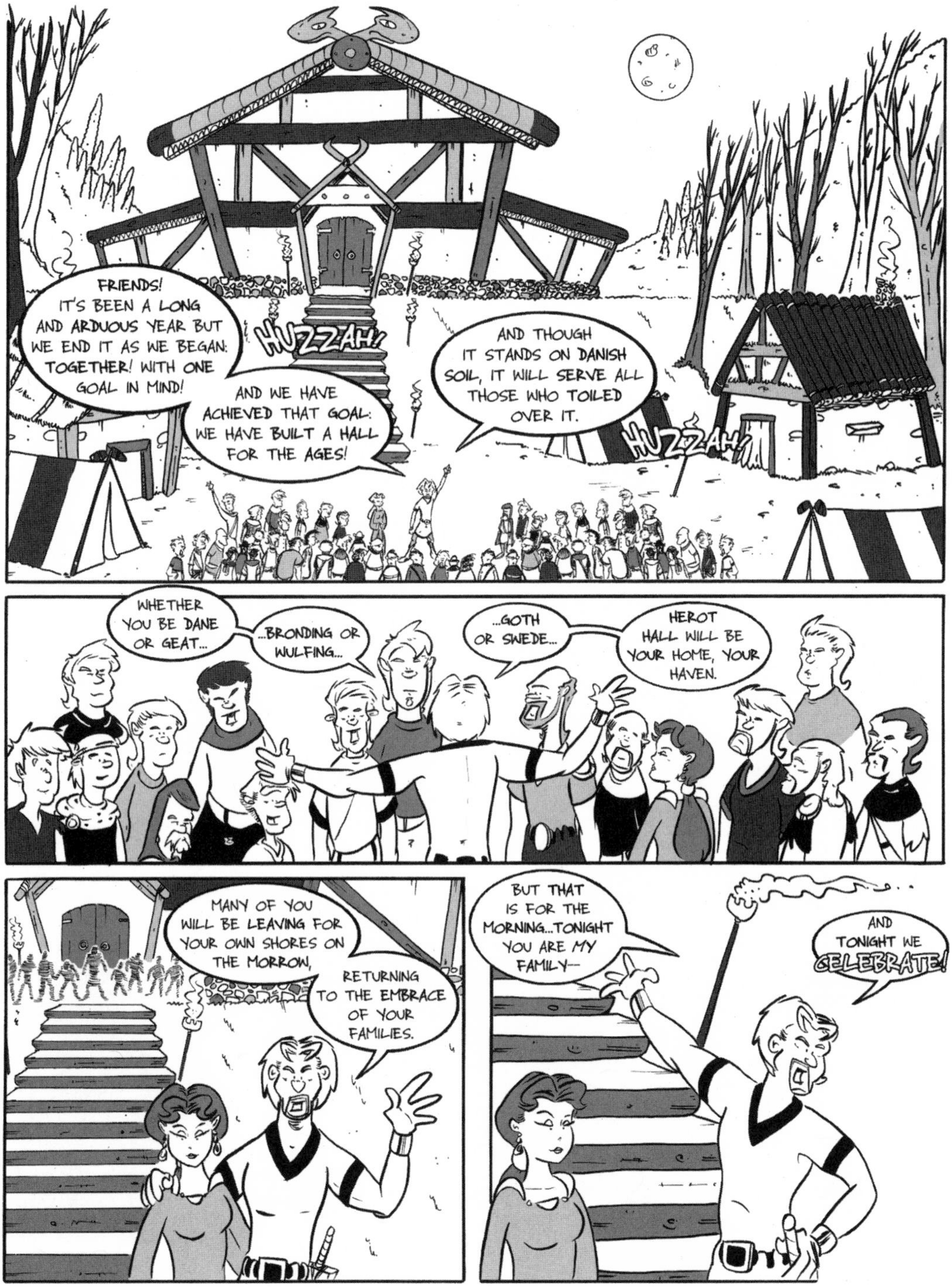

FRIENDS! IT'S BEEN A LONG AND ARDUOUS YEAR BUT WE END IT AS WE BEGAN: TOGETHER! WITH ONE GOAL IN MIND!
AND WE HAVE ACHIEVED THAT GOAL: WE HAVE BUILT A HALL FOR THE AGES!
HUZZAH!
AND THOUGH IT STANDS ON DANISH SOIL, IT WILL SERVE ALL THOSE WHO TOILED OVER IT.
HUZZAH!
WHETHER YOU BE DANE OR GEAT...
...BRONDING OR WULFING...
...GOTH OR SWEDE...
HEROT HALL WILL BE YOUR HOME, YOUR HAVEN.
MANY OF YOU WILL BE LEAVING FOR YOUR OWN SHORES ON THE MORROW,
RETURNING TO THE EMBRACE OF YOUR FAMILIES.
BUT THAT IS FOR THE MORNING...TONIGHT YOU ARE MY FAMILY--
AND TONIGHT WE CELEBRATE!

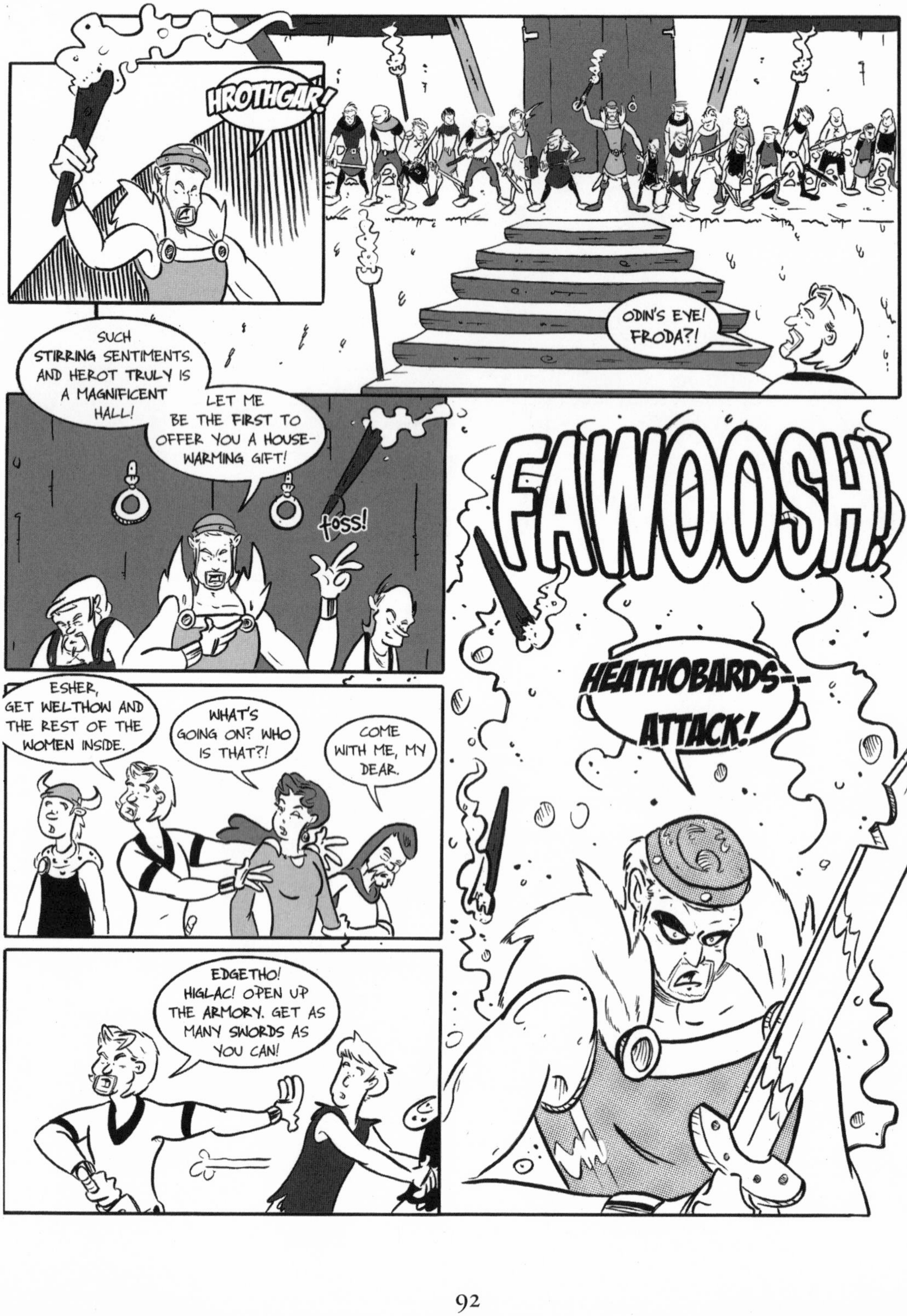
HROTHGAR!
ODIN'S EYE! FRODA?!
SUCH STIRRING SENTIMENTS. AND HEROT TRULY IS A MAGNIFICENT HALL!
LET ME BE THE FIRST TO OFFER YOU A HOUSE-WARMING GIFT!
toss!
FAWOOSH!
HEATHOBARDS-- ATTACK!
ESHER, GET WELTHOW AND THE REST OF THE WOMEN INSIDE.
WHAT'S GOING ON? WHO IS THAT?!
COME WITH ME, MY DEAR.
EDGETHO! HIGLAC! OPEN UP THE ARMORY. GET AS MANY SWORDS AS YOU CAN!

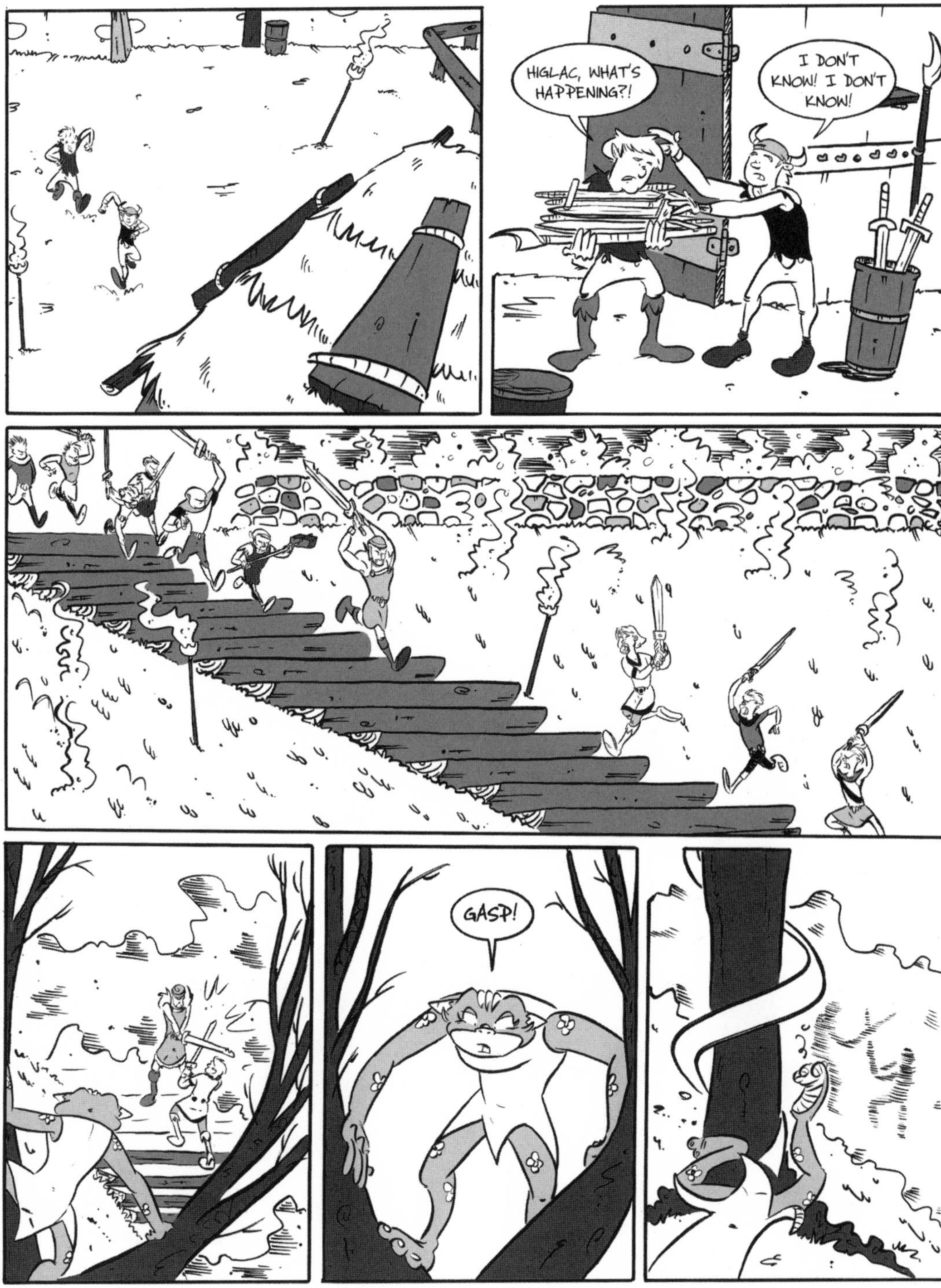
HIGLAC, WHAT'S HAPPENING?!
I DON'T KNOW! I DON'T KNOW!
GASP!

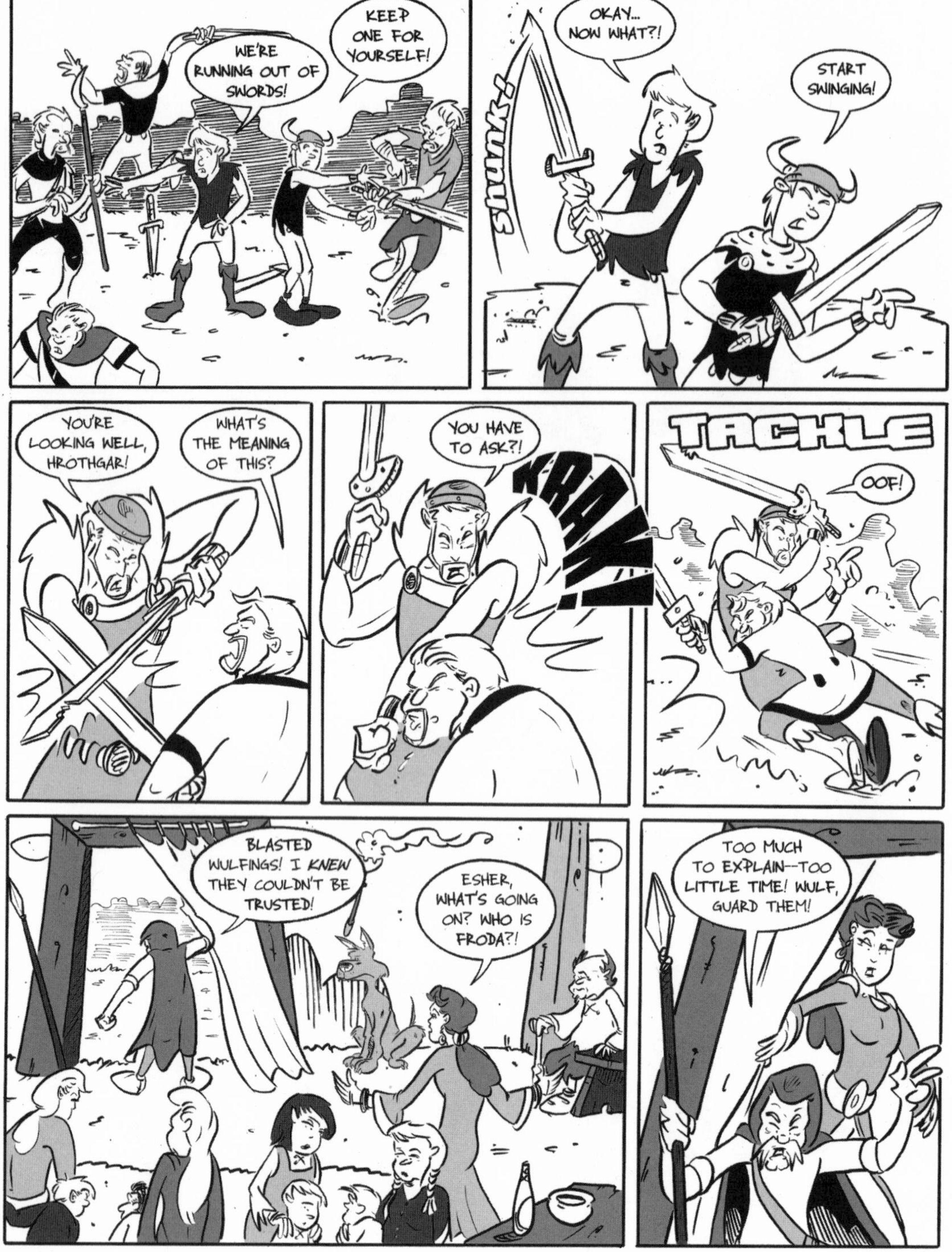
WE'RE RUNNING OUT OF SWORDS!
KEEP ONE FOR YOURSELF!
SHUNK!
OKAY... NOW WHAT?!
START SWINGING!
YOU'RE LOOKING WELL, HROTHGAR!
WHAT'S THE MEANING OF THIS?
YOU HAVE TO ASK?!
KRAW!!
TACKLE
OOF!
BLASTED WULFINGS! I *KNEW* THEY COULDN'T BE TRUSTED!
ESHER, WHAT'S GOING ON? WHO IS FRODA?!
TOO MUCH TO EXPLAIN--TOO LITTLE TIME! WULF, GUARD THEM!

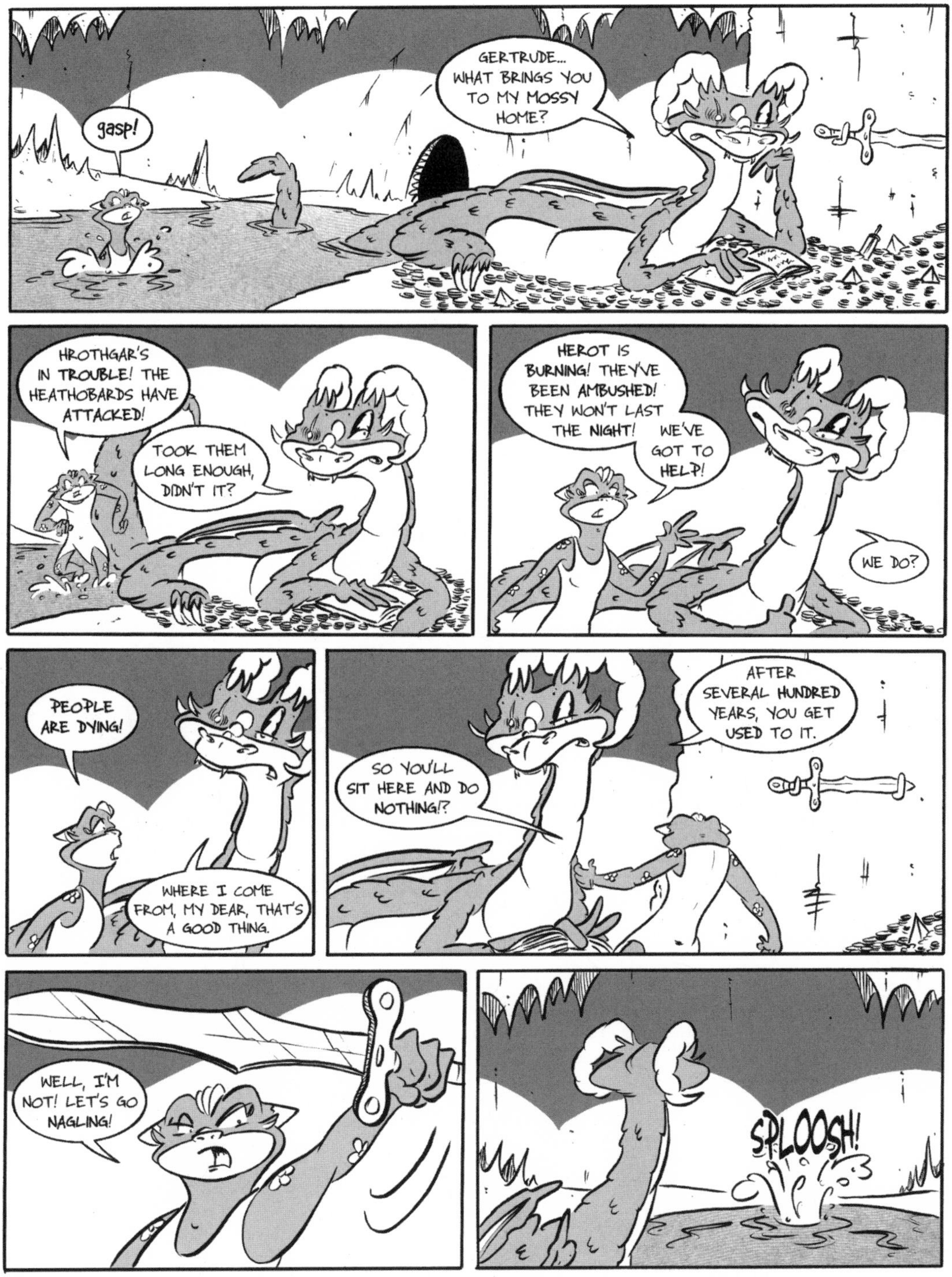
gasp!
GERTRUDE... WHAT BRINGS YOU TO MY MOSSY HOME?
HROTHGAR'S IN TROUBLE! THE HEATHOBARDS HAVE ATTACKED!
TOOK THEM LONG ENOUGH, DIDN'T IT?
HEROT IS BURNING! THEY'VE BEEN AMBUSHED! THEY WON'T LAST THE NIGHT!
WE'VE GOT TO HELP!
WE DO?
PEOPLE ARE DYING!
WHERE I COME FROM, MY DEAR, THAT'S A GOOD THING.
SO YOU'LL SIT HERE AND DO NOTHING!?
AFTER SEVERAL HUNDRED YEARS, YOU GET USED TO IT.
WELL, I'M NOT! LET'S GO NAGLING!
SPLOOSH!

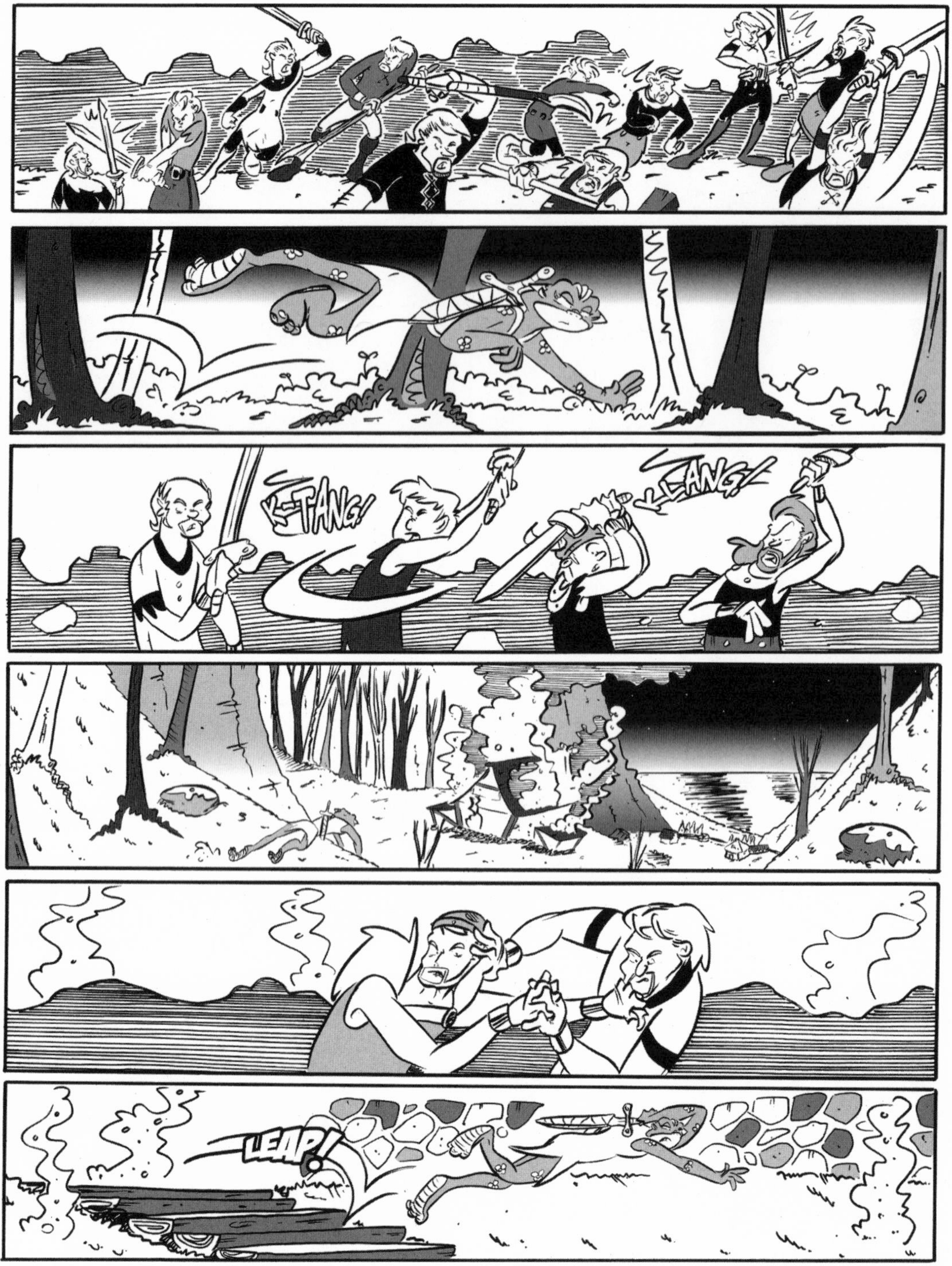
K-TANG!
K-LANG!
LEAP!

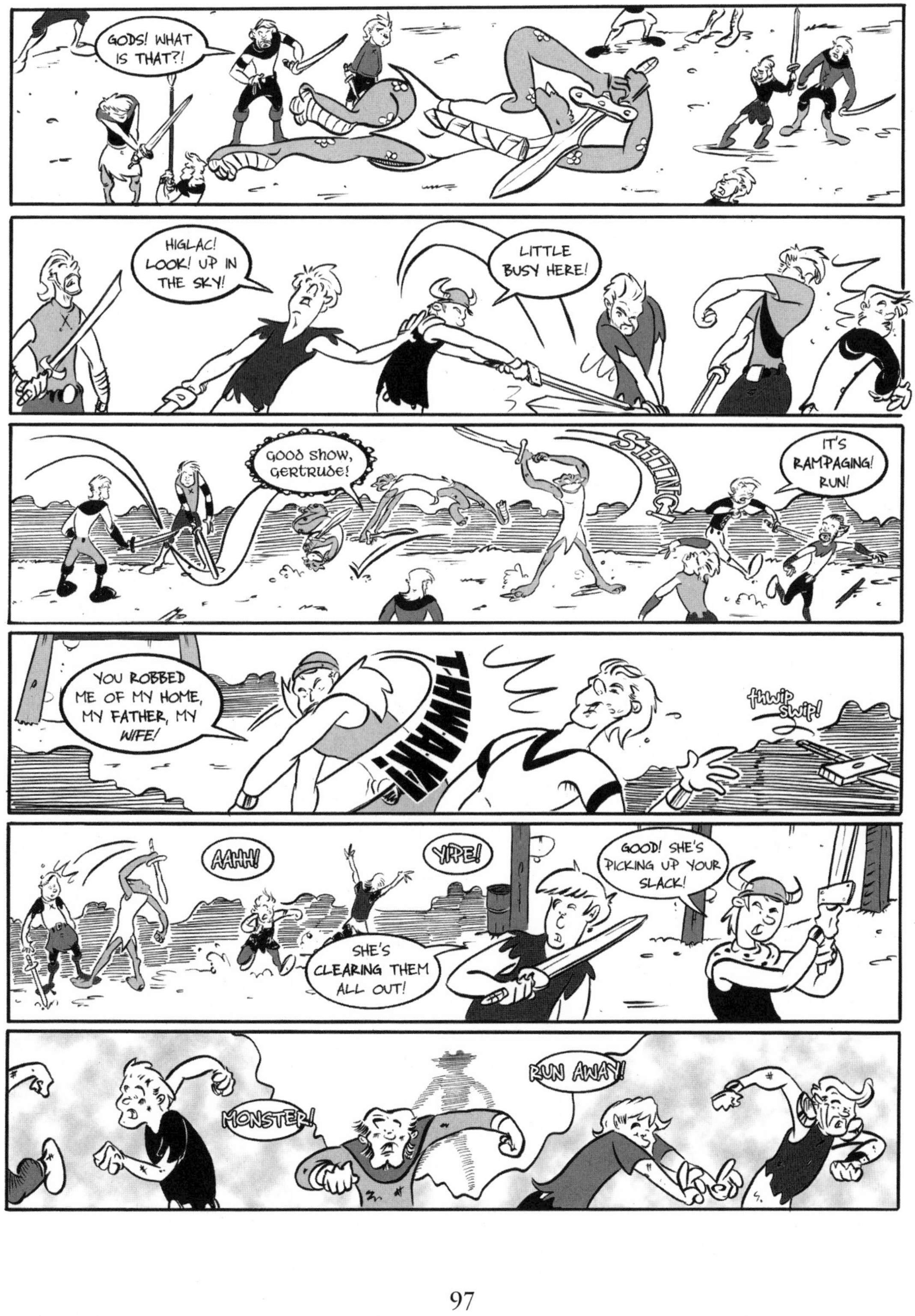
GODS! WHAT IS THAT?!
HIGLAC! LOOK! UP IN THE SKY!
LITTLE BUSY HERE!
GOOD SHOW, GERTRUDE!
SHING
IT'S RAMPAGING! RUN!
YOU ROBBED ME OF MY HOME, MY FATHER, MY WIFE!
THWAK!
thwip swip!
AAHH!
YIPE!
GOOD! SHE'S PICKING UP YOUR SLACK!
SHE'S CLEARING THEM ALL OUT!
MONSTER!
RUN AWAY!

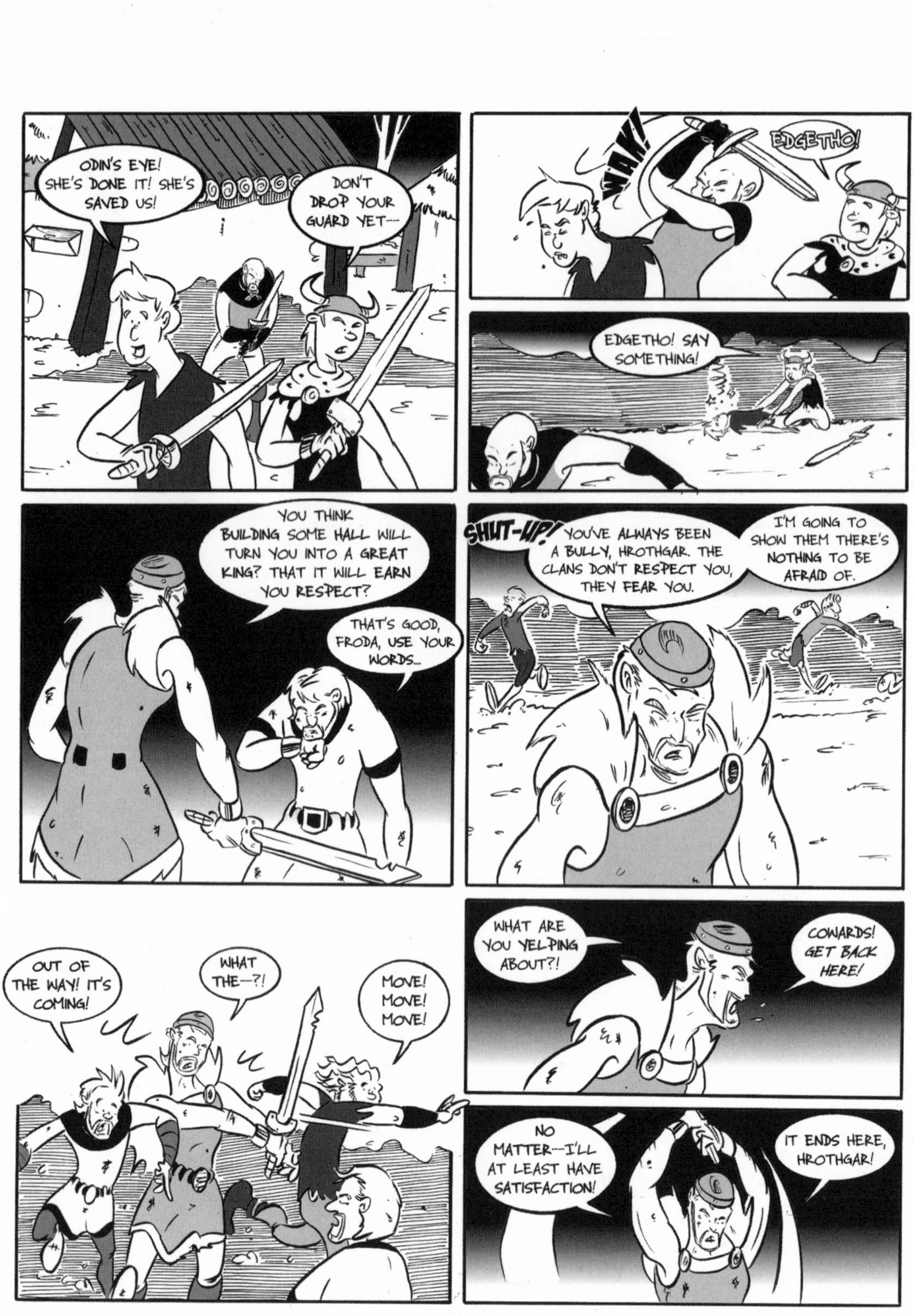
ODIN'S EYE! SHE'S DONE IT! SHE'S SAVED US!
DON'T DROP YOUR GUARD YET--
WAK!
EDGETHO!
EDGETHO! SAY SOMETHING!
YOU THINK BUILDING SOME HALL WILL TURN YOU INTO A GREAT KING? THAT IT WILL EARN YOU RESPECT?
THAT'S GOOD, FRODA, USE YOUR WORDS...
SHUT-UP!
YOU'VE ALWAYS BEEN A BULLY, HROTHGAR. THE CLANS DON'T RESPECT YOU, THEY FEAR YOU.
I'M GOING TO SHOW THEM THERE'S NOTHING TO BE AFRAID OF.
OUT OF THE WAY! IT'S COMING!
WHAT THE--?!
MOVE! MOVE! MOVE!
WHAT ARE YOU YELPING ABOUT?!
COWARDS! GET BACK HERE!
NO MATTER--I'LL AT LEAST HAVE SATISFACTION!
IT ENDS HERE, HROTHGAR!

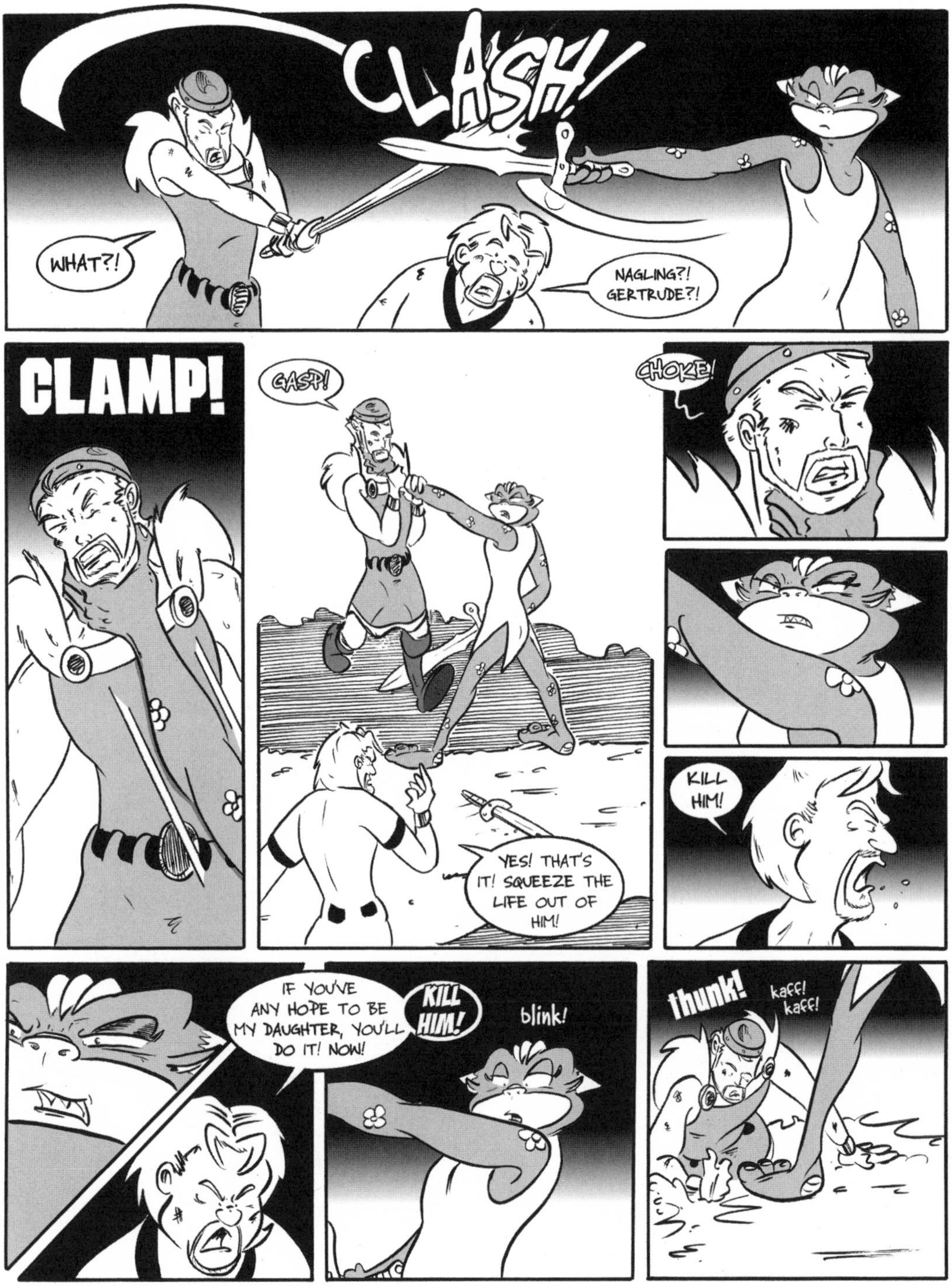
CLASH!
WHAT?!
NAGLING?!
GERTRUDE?!
CLAMP!
GASP!
CHOKE!
KILL HIM!
YES! THAT'S IT! SQUEEZE THE LIFE OUT OF HIM!
IF YOU'VE ANY HOPE TO BE MY DAUGHTER, YOU'LL DO IT! NOW!
KILL HIM!
blink!
thunk!
kaff! kaff!

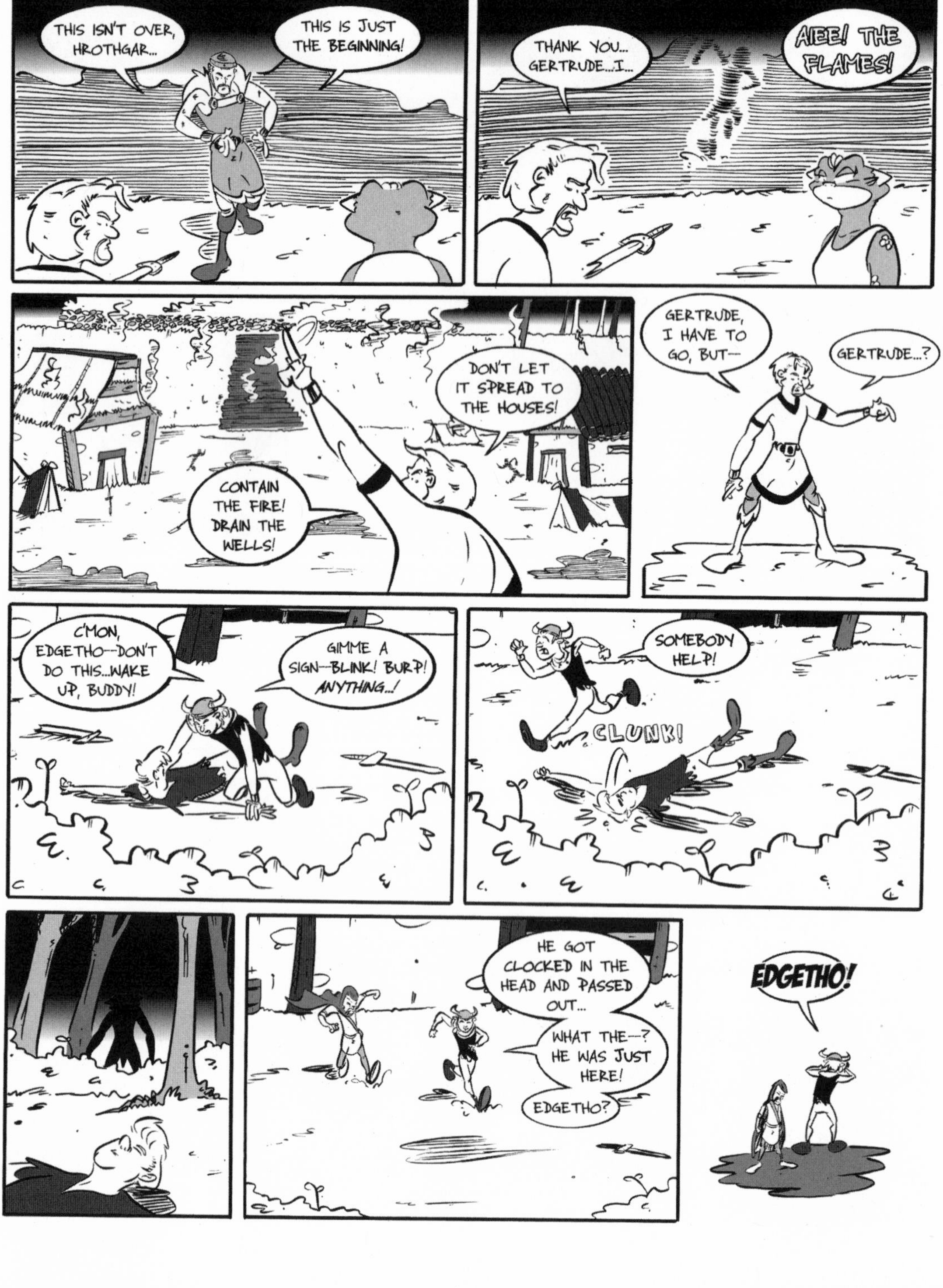
THIS ISN'T OVER, HROTHGAR...
THIS IS JUST THE BEGINNING!
THANK YOU... GERTRUDE...I...
AIEE! THE FLAMES!
DON'T LET IT SPREAD TO THE HOUSES!
CONTAIN THE FIRE! DRAIN THE WELLS!
GERTRUDE, I HAVE TO GO, BUT—
GERTRUDE...?
C'MON, EDGETHO—DON'T DO THIS...WAKE UP, BUDDY!
GIMME A SIGN—BLINK! BURP! ANYTHING...!
SOMEBODY HELP!
CLUNK!
HE GOT CLOCKED IN THE HEAD AND PASSED OUT...
WHAT THE—? HE WAS JUST HERE!
EDGETHO?
EDGETHO!

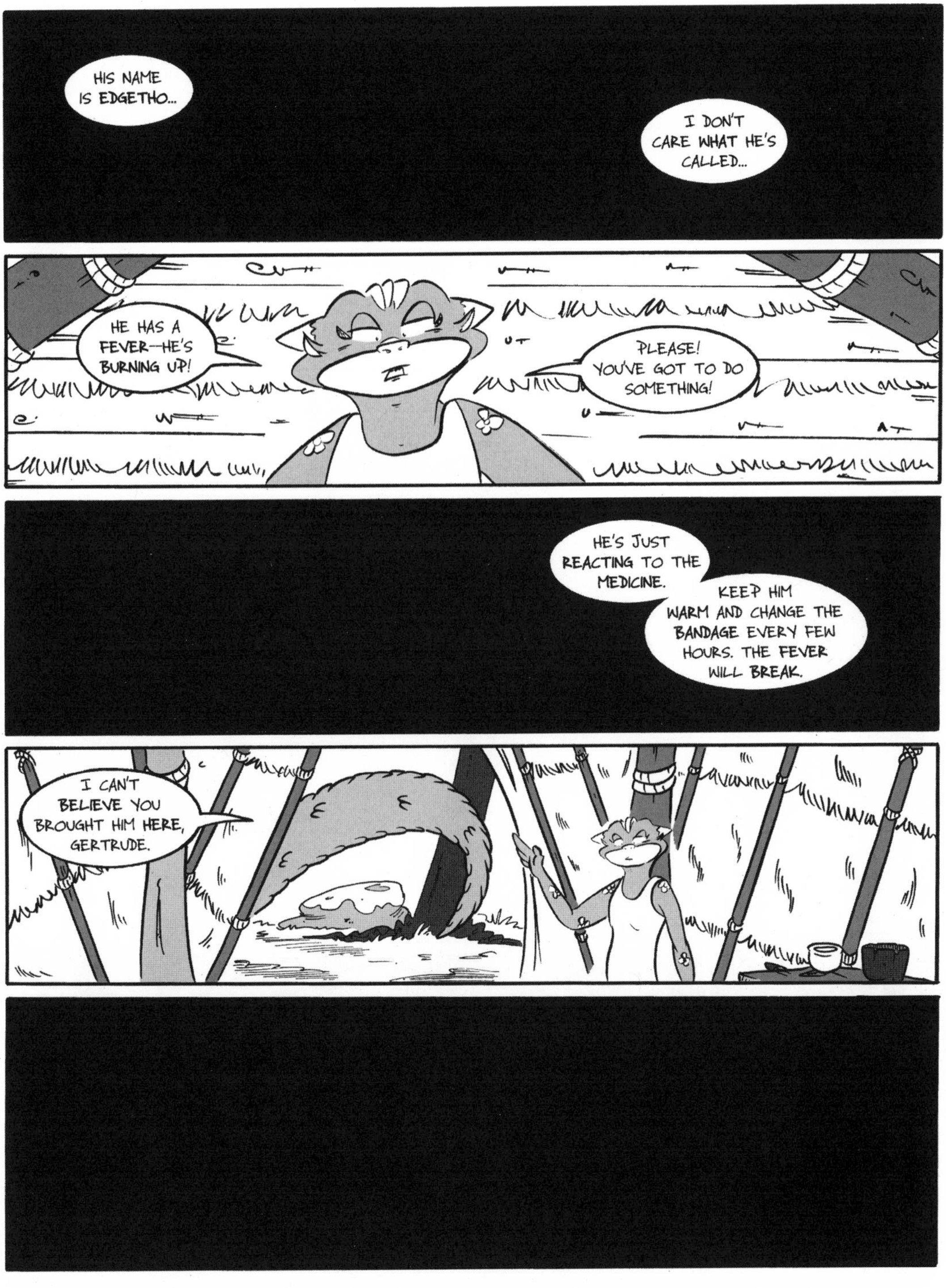
HIS NAME IS EDGETHO...
I DON'T CARE WHAT HE'S CALLED...
HE HAS A FEVER—HE'S BURNING UP!
PLEASE! YOU'VE GOT TO DO SOMETHING!
HE'S JUST REACTING TO THE MEDICINE.
KEEP HIM WARM AND CHANGE THE BANDAGE EVERY FEW HOURS. THE FEVER WILL BREAK.
I CAN'T BELIEVE YOU BROUGHT HIM HERE, GERTRUDE.

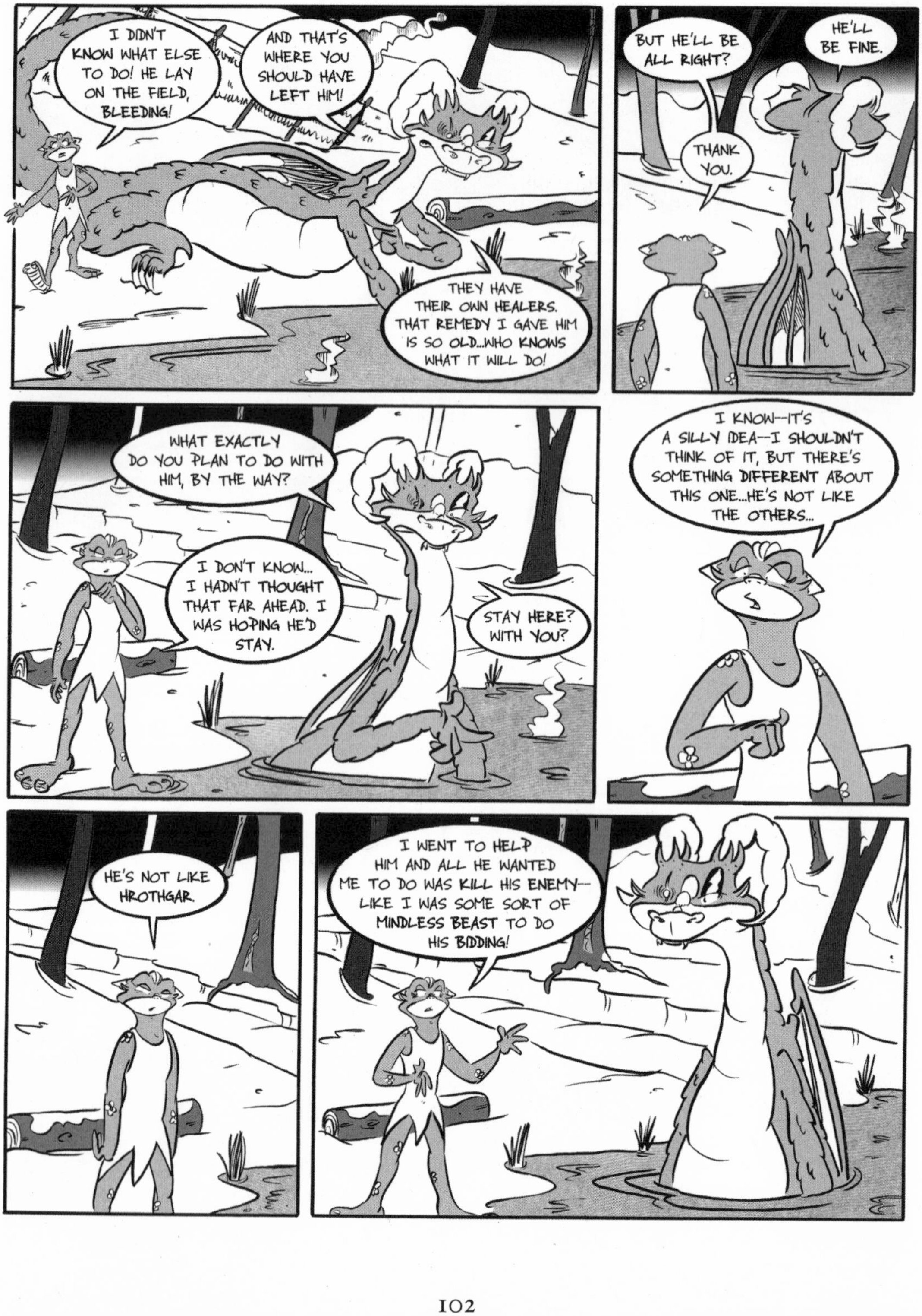

I DIDN'T KNOW WHAT ELSE TO DO! HE LAY ON THE FIELD, BLEEDING!
AND THAT'S WHERE YOU SHOULD HAVE LEFT HIM!
THEY HAVE THEIR OWN HEALERS. THAT REMEDY I GAVE HIM IS SO OLD...WHO KNOWS WHAT IT WILL DO!
BUT HE'LL BE ALL RIGHT?
HE'LL BE FINE.
THANK YOU.
WHAT EXACTLY DO YOU PLAN TO DO WITH HIM, BY THE WAY?
I DON'T KNOW... I HADN'T THOUGHT THAT FAR AHEAD. I WAS HOPING HE'D STAY.
STAY HERE? WITH YOU?
I KNOW--IT'S A SILLY IDEA--I SHOULDN'T THINK OF IT, BUT THERE'S SOMETHING DIFFERENT ABOUT THIS ONE...HE'S NOT LIKE THE OTHERS...
HE'S NOT LIKE HROTHGAR.
I WENT TO HELP HIM AND ALL HE WANTED ME TO DO WAS KILL HIS ENEMY--LIKE I WAS SOME SORT OF MINDLESS BEAST TO DO HIS BIDDING!

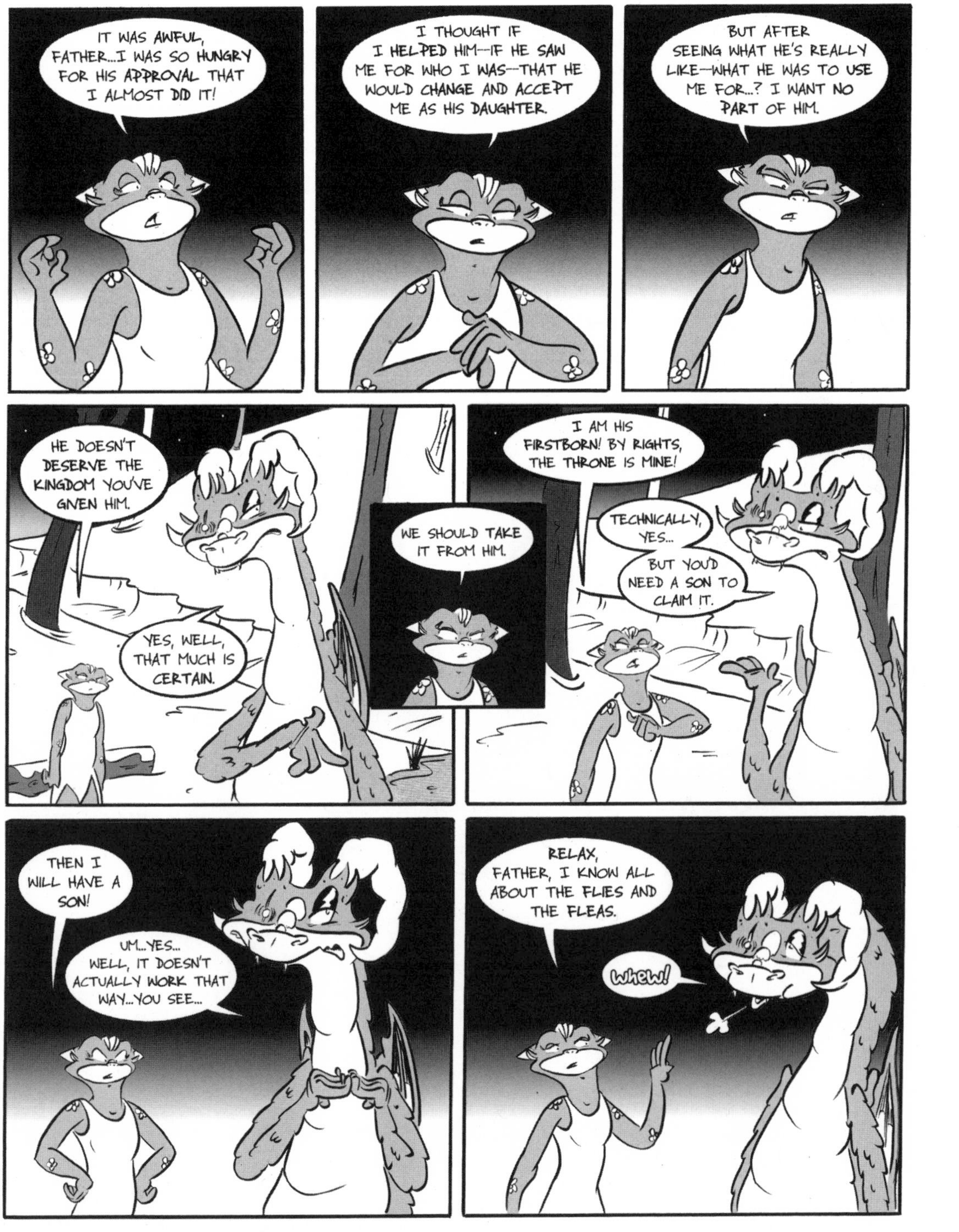
IT WAS AWFUL, FATHER...I WAS SO HUNGRY FOR HIS APPROVAL THAT I ALMOST DID IT!
I THOUGHT IF I HELPED HIM--IF HE SAW ME FOR WHO I WAS--THAT HE WOULD CHANGE AND ACCEPT ME AS HIS DAUGHTER.
BUT AFTER SEEING WHAT HE'S REALLY LIKE--WHAT HE WAS TO USE ME FOR...? I WANT NO PART OF HIM.
HE DOESN'T DESERVE THE KINGDOM YOU'VE GIVEN HIM.
YES, WELL, THAT MUCH IS CERTAIN.
WE SHOULD TAKE IT FROM HIM.
I AM HIS FIRSTBORN! BY RIGHTS, THE THRONE IS MINE!
TECHNICALLY, YES...
BUT YOU'D NEED A SON TO CLAIM IT.
THEN I WILL HAVE A SON!
UM...YES... WELL, IT DOESN'T ACTUALLY WORK THAT WAY...YOU SEE...
RELAX, FATHER, I KNOW ALL ABOUT THE FLIES AND THE FLEAS.
Whew!

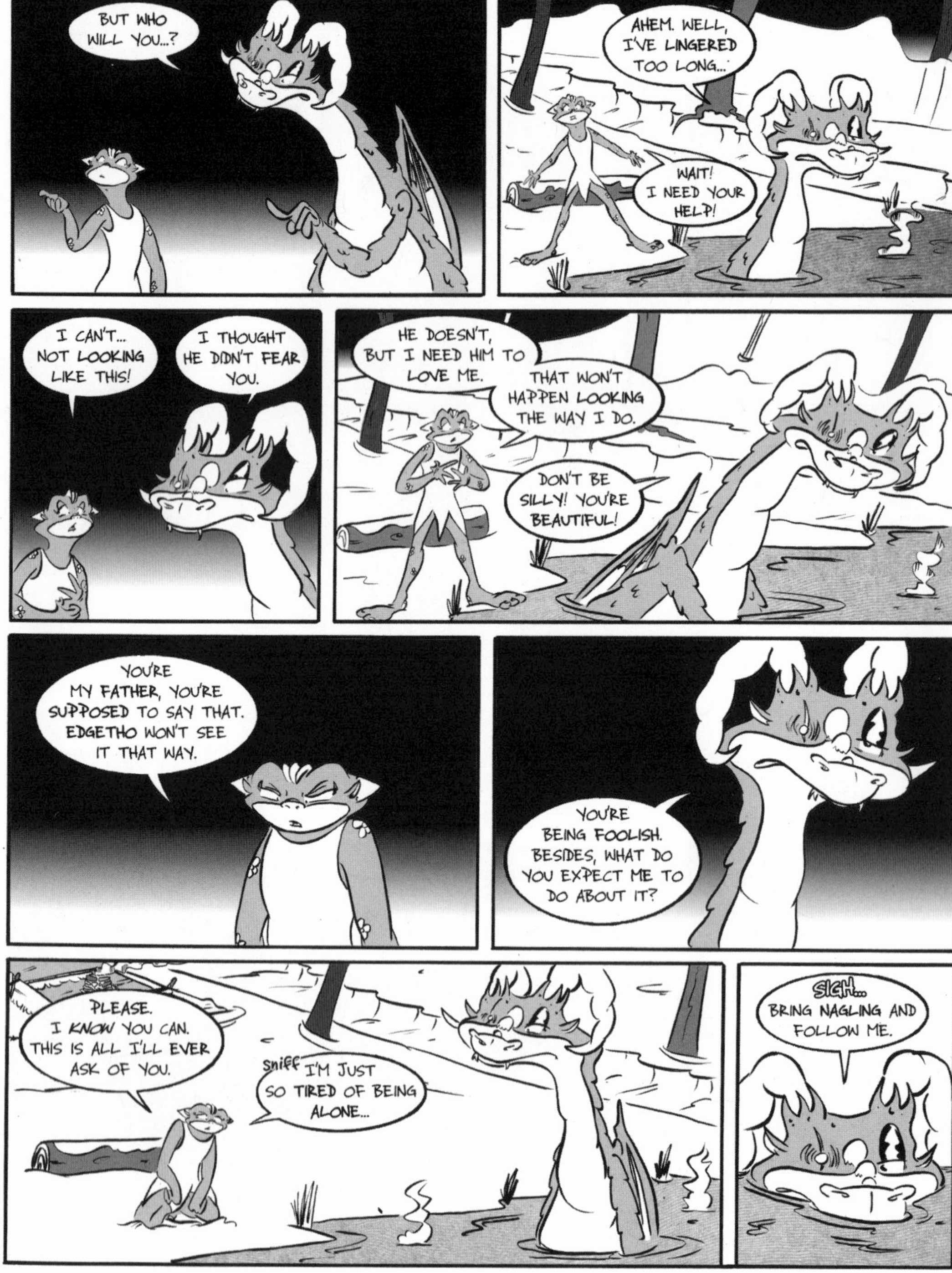

BUT WHO WILL YOU...?
AHEM. WELL, I'VE LINGERED TOO LONG...
WAIT! I NEED YOUR HELP!
I CAN'T... NOT LOOKING LIKE THIS!
I THOUGHT HE DIDN'T FEAR YOU.
HE DOESN'T, BUT I NEED HIM TO LOVE ME.
THAT WON'T HAPPEN LOOKING THE WAY I DO.
DON'T BE SILLY! YOU'RE BEAUTIFUL!
YOU'RE MY FATHER, YOU'RE SUPPOSED TO SAY THAT. EDGETHO WON'T SEE IT THAT WAY.
YOU'RE BEING FOOLISH. BESIDES, WHAT DO YOU EXPECT ME TO DO ABOUT IT?
PLEASE. I KNOW YOU CAN. THIS IS ALL I'LL EVER ASK OF YOU.
SNIFF I'M JUST SO TIRED OF BEING ALONE...
SIGH... BRING NAGLING AND FOLLOW ME.

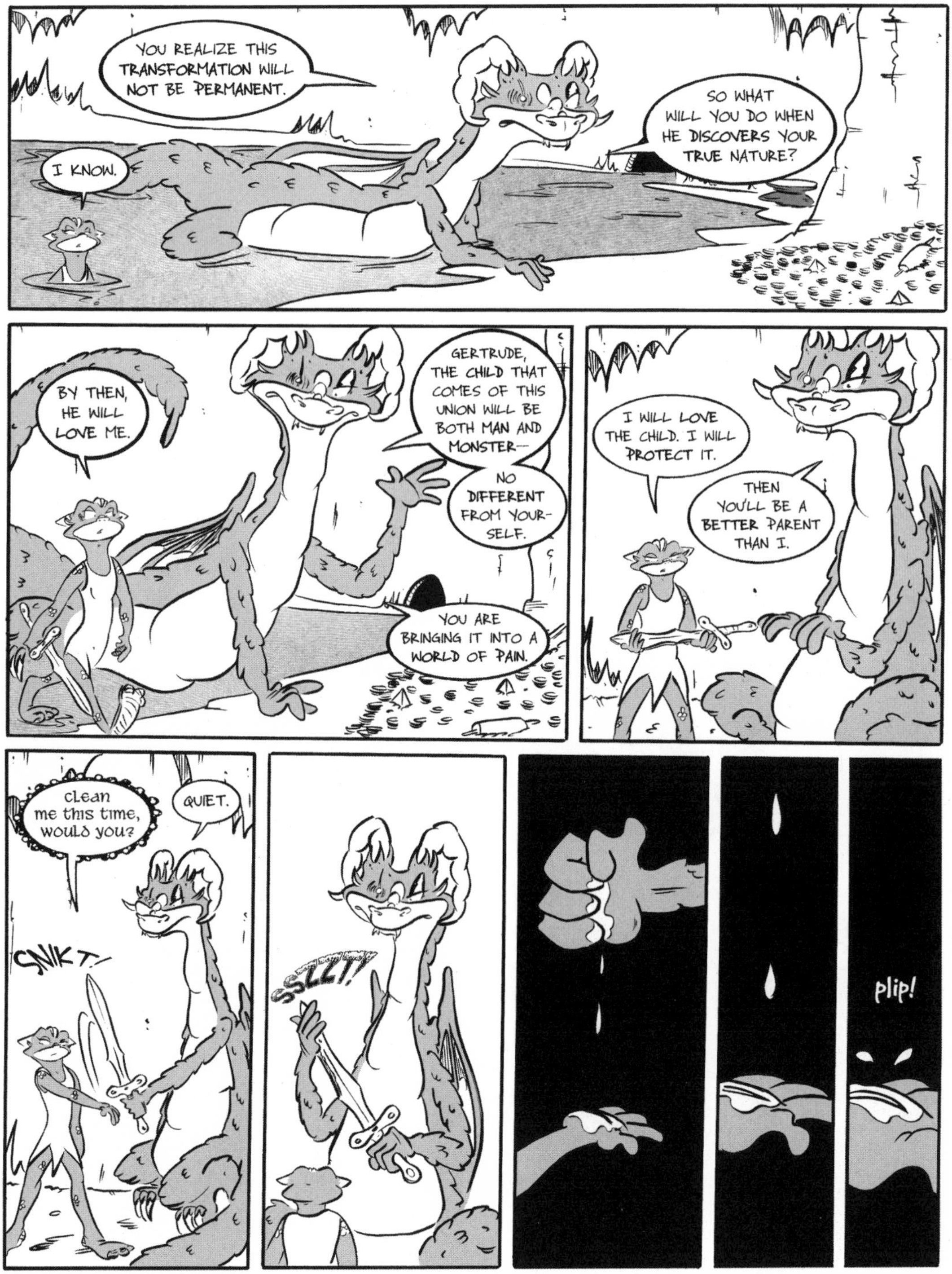
YOU REALIZE THIS TRANSFORMATION WILL NOT BE PERMANENT.
I KNOW.
SO WHAT WILL YOU DO WHEN HE DISCOVERS YOUR TRUE NATURE?
BY THEN, HE WILL LOVE ME.
GERTRUDE, THE CHILD THAT COMES OF THIS UNION WILL BE BOTH MAN AND MONSTER--
NO DIFFERENT FROM YOURSELF.
YOU ARE BRINGING IT INTO A WORLD OF PAIN.
I WILL LOVE THE CHILD. I WILL PROTECT IT.
THEN YOU'LL BE A BETTER PARENT THAN I.
clean me this time, would you?
QUIET.
SNIKT!
SSLLT!
plip!

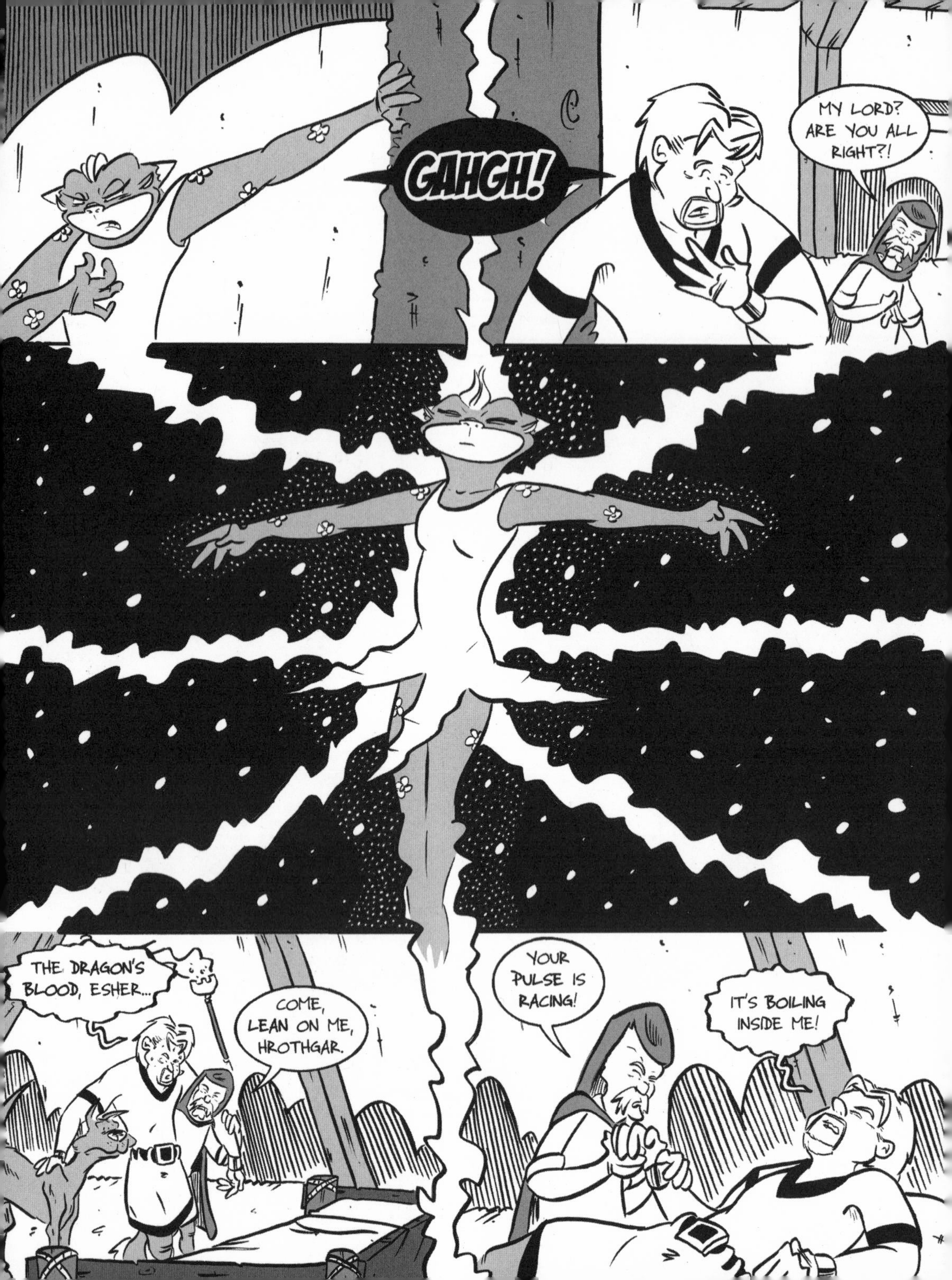
GAHGH!
MY LORD? ARE YOU ALL RIGHT?!
THE DRAGON'S BLOOD, ESHER...
COME, LEAN ON ME, HROTHGAR.
YOUR PULSE IS RACING!
IT'S BOILING INSIDE ME!

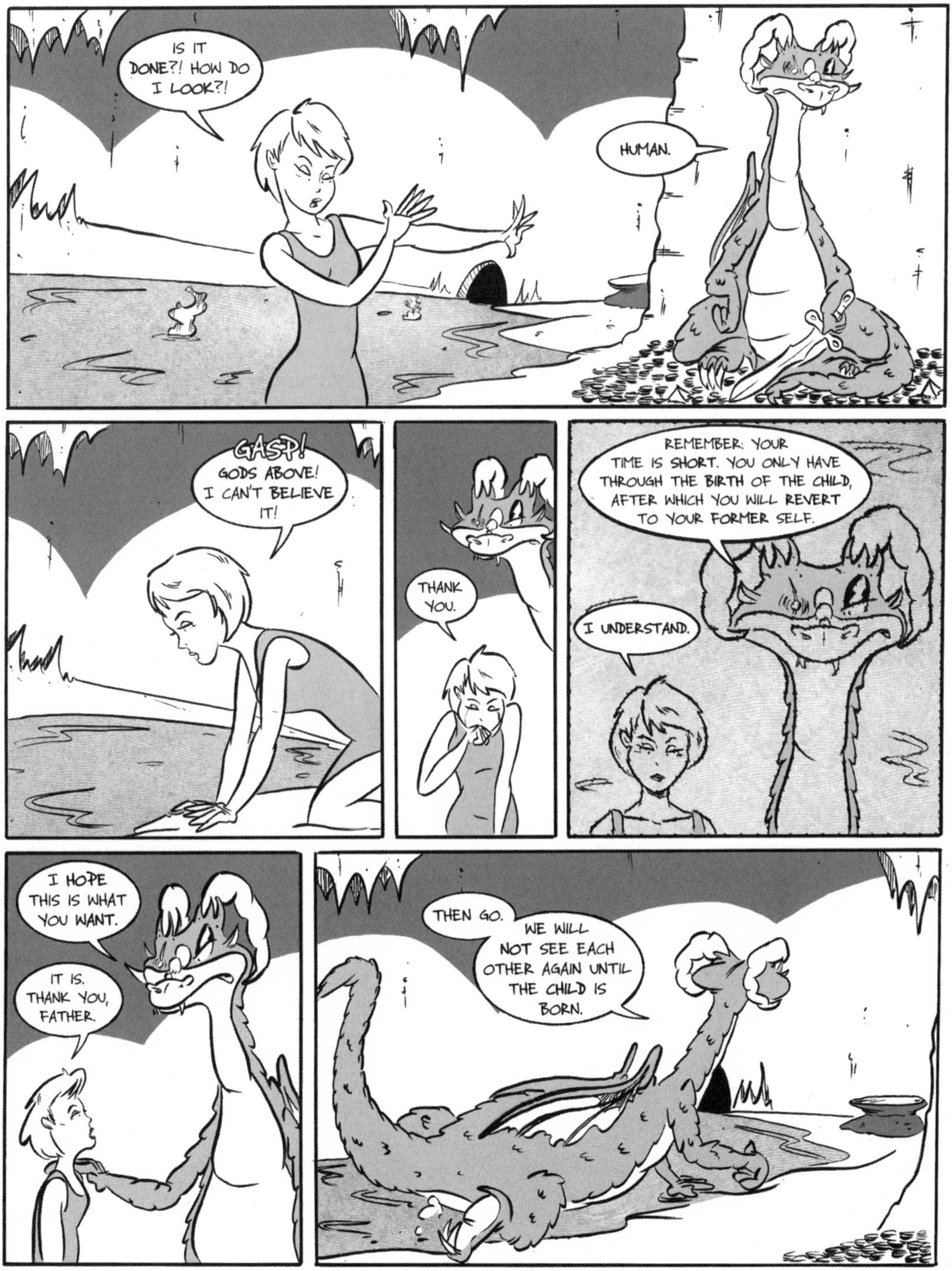
IS IT DONE?! HOW DO I LOOK?!
HUMAN.
GASP! GODS ABOVE! I CAN'T BELIEVE IT!
THANK YOU.
REMEMBER: YOUR TIME IS SHORT. YOU ONLY HAVE THROUGH THE BIRTH OF THE CHILD, AFTER WHICH YOU WILL REVERT TO YOUR FORMER SELF.
I UNDERSTAND.
I HOPE THIS IS WHAT YOU WANT.
IT IS. THANK YOU, FATHER.
THEN GO.
WE WILL NOT SEE EACH OTHER AGAIN UNTIL THE CHILD IS BORN.

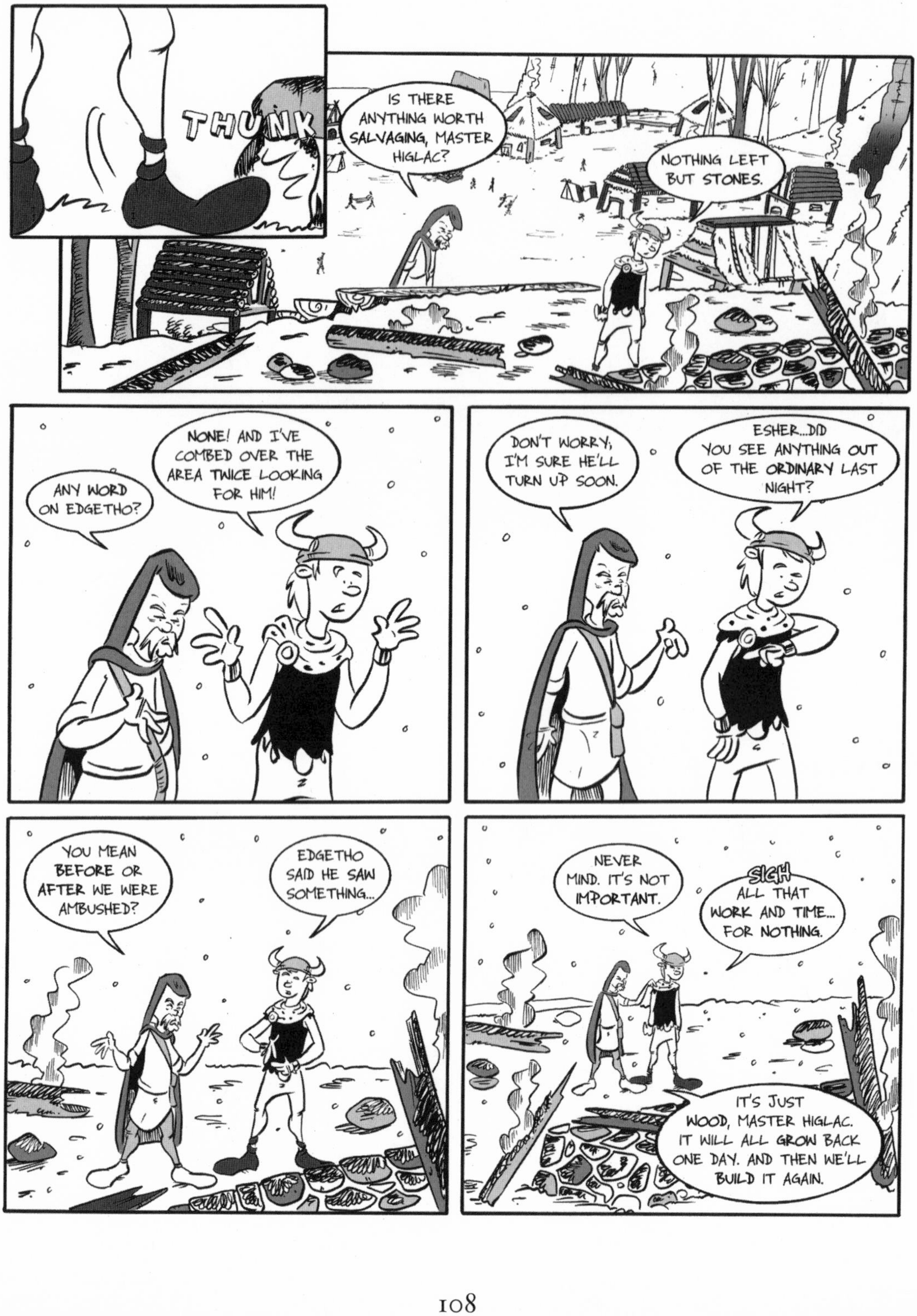
THUNK
IS THERE ANYTHING WORTH SALVAGING, MASTER HIGLAC?
NOTHING LEFT BUT STONES.
ANY WORD ON EDGETHO?
NONE! AND I'VE COMBED OVER THE AREA TWICE LOOKING FOR HIM!
DON'T WORRY; I'M SURE HE'LL TURN UP SOON.
ESHER...DID YOU SEE ANYTHING OUT OF THE ORDINARY LAST NIGHT?
YOU MEAN BEFORE OR AFTER WE WERE AMBUSHED?
EDGETHO SAID HE SAW SOMETHING...
NEVER MIND. IT'S NOT IMPORTANT.
SIGH
ALL THAT WORK AND TIME... FOR NOTHING.
IT'S JUST WOOD, MASTER HIGLAC. IT WILL ALL GROW BACK ONE DAY. AND THEN WE'LL BUILD IT AGAIN.

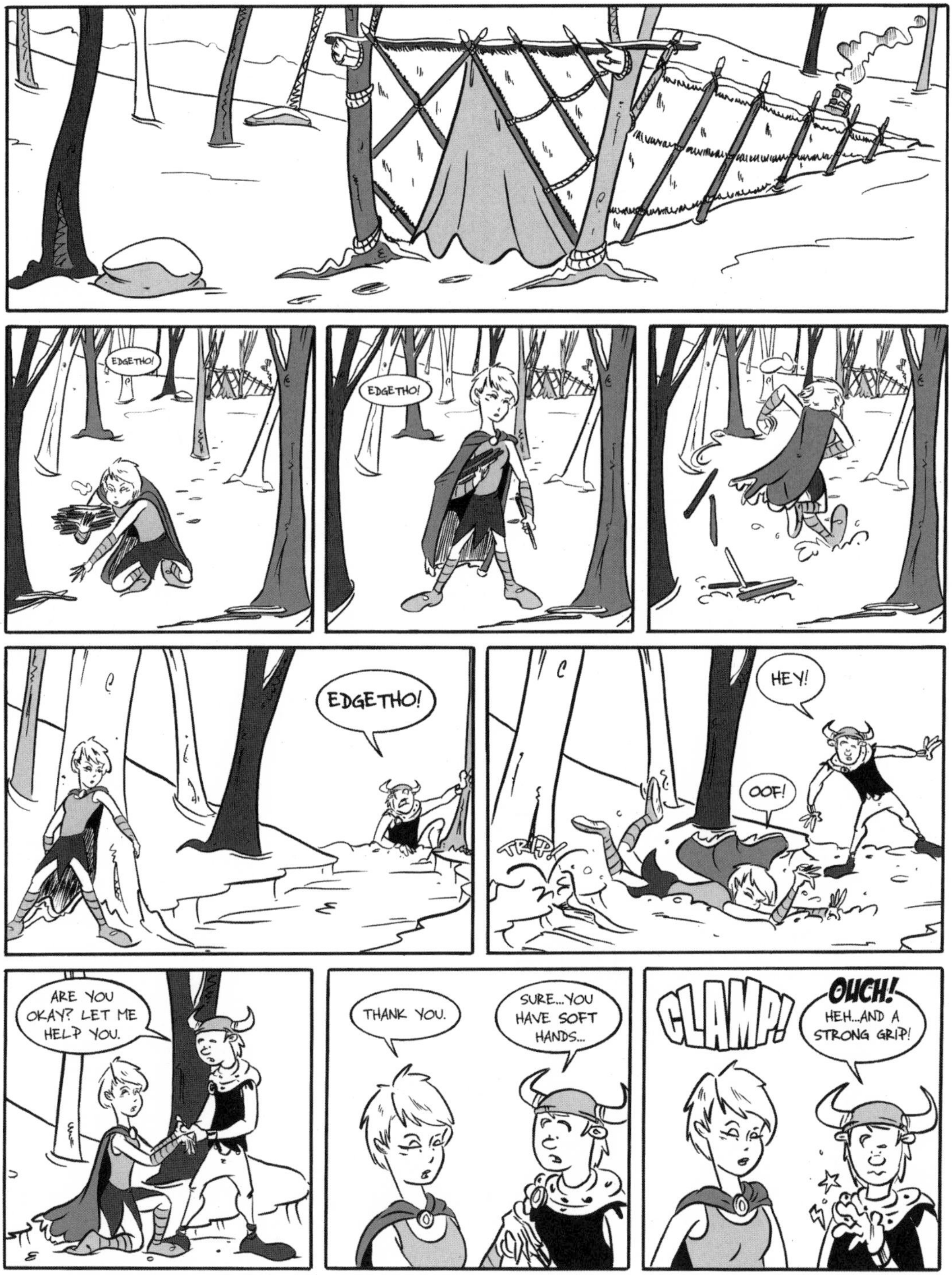
EDGETHO!
EDGETHO!
EDGETHO!
HEY!
OOF!
ARE YOU OKAY? LET ME HELP YOU.
THANK YOU.
SURE...YOU HAVE SOFT HANDS...
CLAMP!
OUCH! HEH...AND A STRONG GRIP!

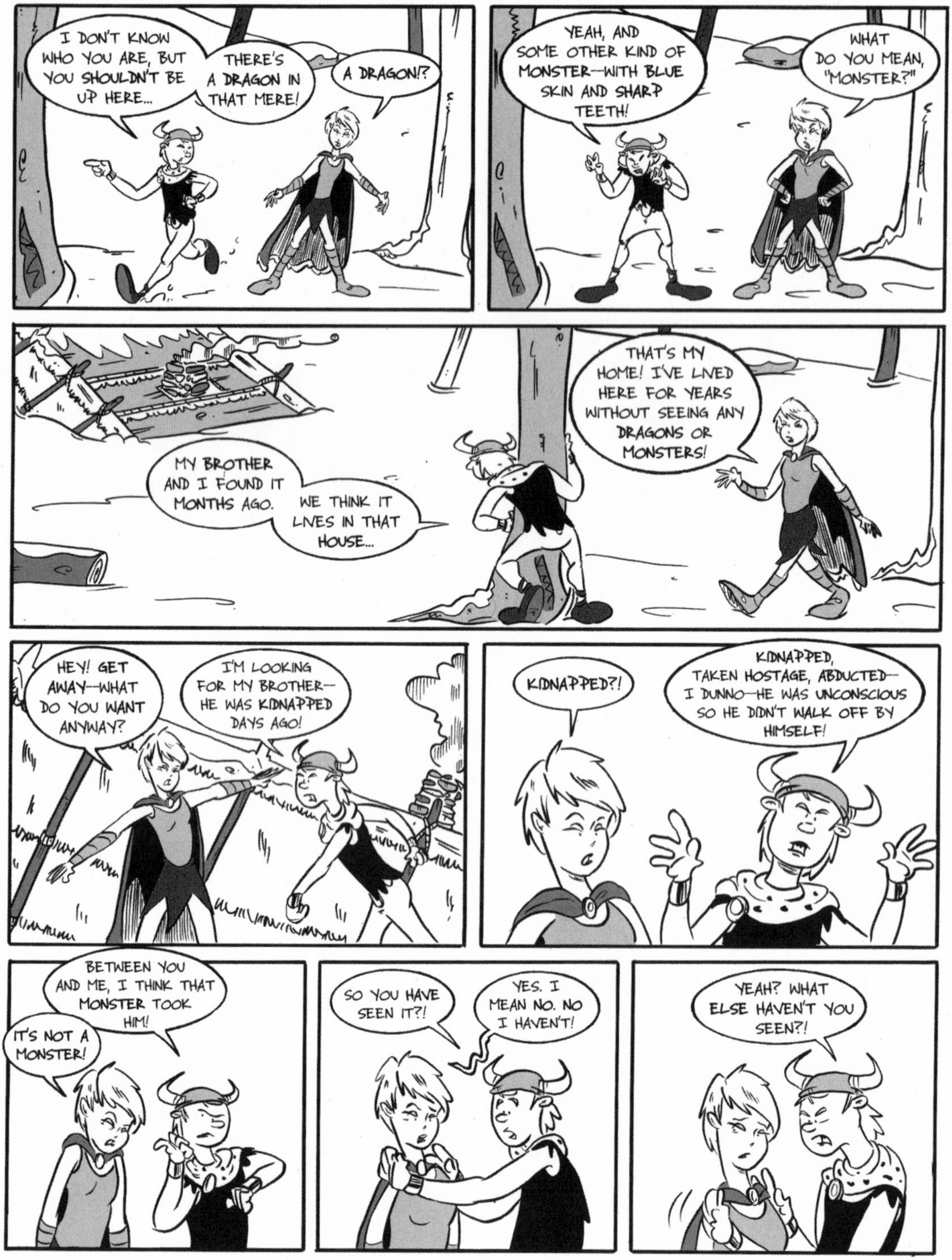
I DON'T KNOW WHO YOU ARE, BUT YOU SHOULDN'T BE UP HERE...
THERE'S A DRAGON IN THAT MERE!
A DRAGON!?
YEAH, AND SOME OTHER KIND OF MONSTER--WITH BLUE SKIN AND SHARP TEETH!
WHAT DO YOU MEAN, "MONSTER?"
MY BROTHER AND I FOUND IT MONTHS AGO.
WE THINK IT LIVES IN THAT HOUSE...
THAT'S MY HOME! I'VE LIVED HERE FOR YEARS WITHOUT SEEING ANY DRAGONS OR MONSTERS!
HEY! GET AWAY--WHAT DO YOU WANT ANYWAY?
I'M LOOKING FOR MY BROTHER-- HE WAS KIDNAPPED DAYS AGO!
KIDNAPPED?!
KIDNAPPED, TAKEN HOSTAGE, ABDUCTED-- I DUNNO--HE WAS UNCONSCIOUS SO HE DIDN'T WALK OFF BY HIMSELF!
BETWEEN YOU AND ME, I THINK THAT MONSTER TOOK HIM!
IT'S NOT A MONSTER!
SO YOU HAVE SEEN IT?!
YES. I MEAN NO. NO I HAVEN'T!
YEAH? WHAT ELSE HAVEN'T YOU SEEN?!

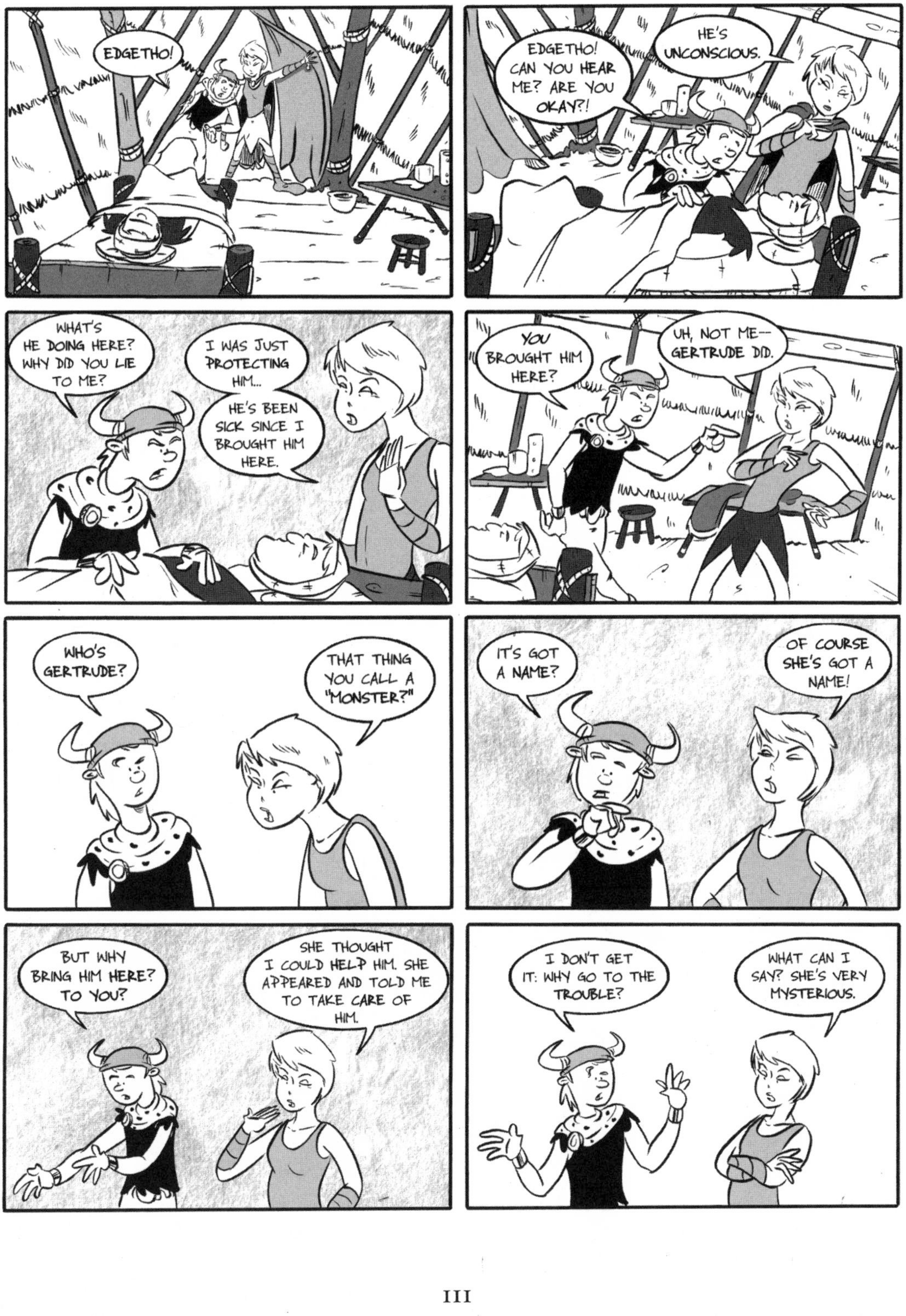
EDGETHO!
EDGETHO! CAN YOU HEAR ME? ARE YOU OKAY?!
HE'S UNCONSCIOUS.
WHAT'S HE DOING HERE? WHY DID YOU LIE TO ME?
I WAS JUST PROTECTING HIM...
HE'S BEEN SICK SINCE I BROUGHT HIM HERE.
YOU BROUGHT HIM HERE?
UH, NOT ME--GERTRUDE DID.
WHO'S GERTRUDE?
THAT THING YOU CALL A "MONSTER?"
IT'S GOT A NAME?
OF COURSE SHE'S GOT A NAME!
BUT WHY BRING HIM HERE? TO YOU?
SHE THOUGHT I COULD HELP HIM. SHE APPEARED AND TOLD ME TO TAKE CARE OF HIM.
I DON'T GET IT: WHY GO TO THE TROUBLE?
WHAT CAN I SAY? SHE'S VERY MYSTERIOUS.

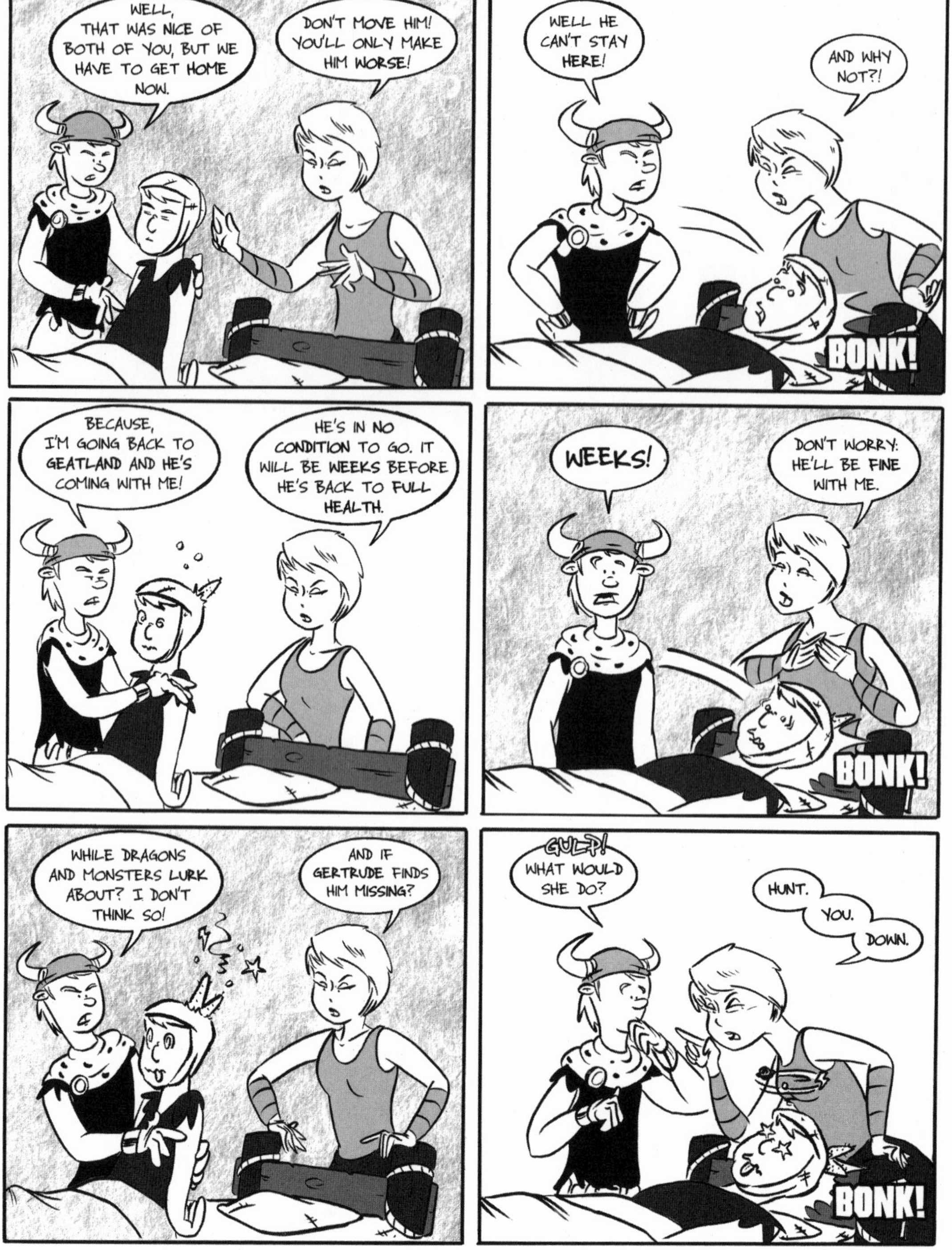

WELL, THAT WAS NICE OF BOTH OF YOU, BUT WE HAVE TO GET HOME NOW.
DON'T MOVE HIM! YOU'LL ONLY MAKE HIM WORSE!
WELL HE CAN'T STAY HERE!
AND WHY NOT?!
BONK!
BECAUSE, I'M GOING BACK TO GEATLAND AND HE'S COMING WITH ME!
HE'S IN NO CONDITION TO GO. IT WILL BE WEEKS BEFORE HE'S BACK TO FULL HEALTH.
WEEKS!
DON'T WORRY: HE'LL BE FINE WITH ME.
BONK!
WHILE DRAGONS AND MONSTERS LURK ABOUT? I DON'T THINK SO!
AND IF GERTRUDE FINDS HIM MISSING?
GULP!
WHAT WOULD SHE DO?
HUNT.
YOU.
DOWN.
BONK!

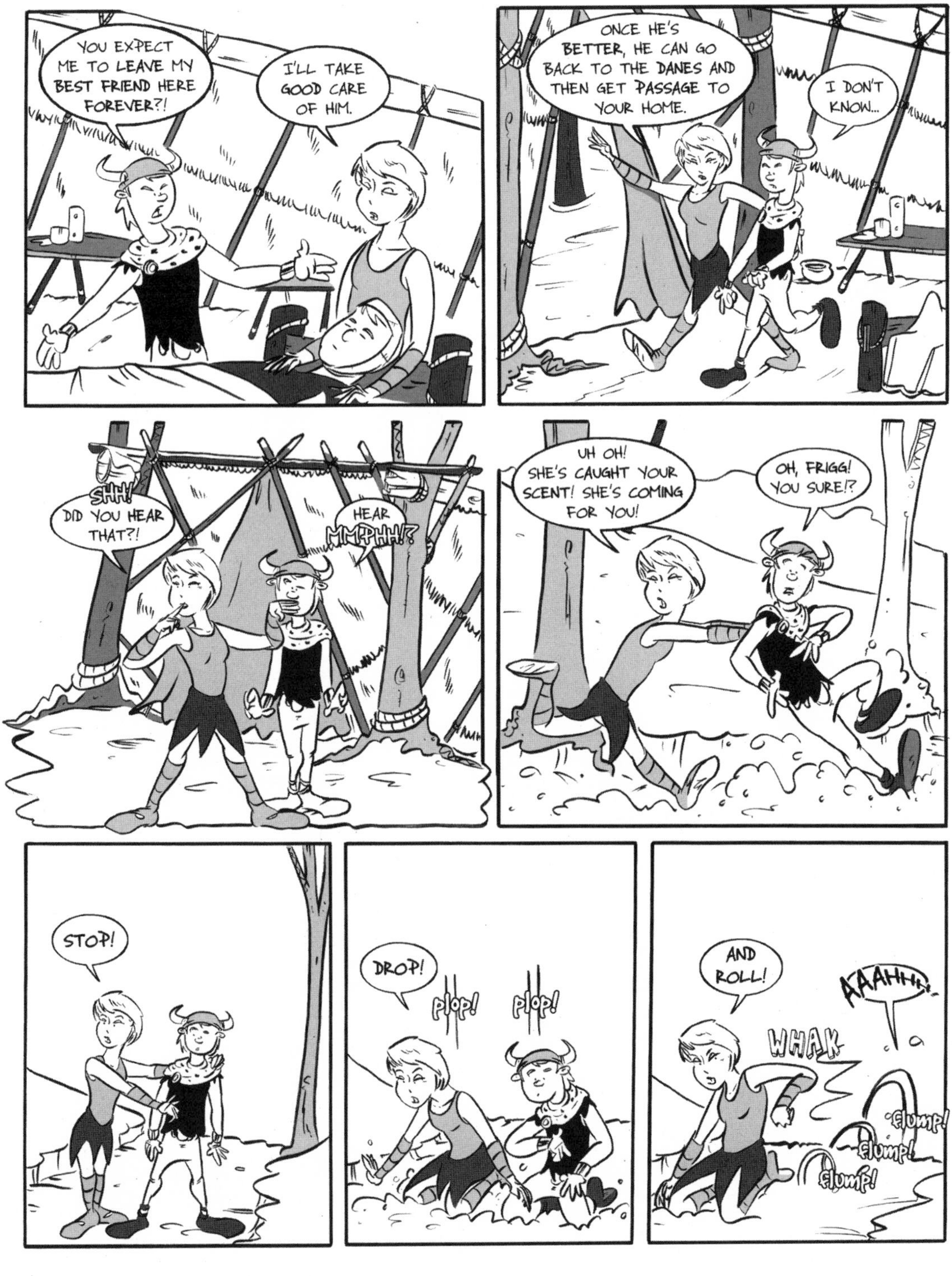
YOU EXPECT ME TO LEAVE MY BEST FRIEND HERE FOREVER?!
I'LL TAKE GOOD CARE OF HIM.
ONCE HE'S BETTER, HE CAN GO BACK TO THE DANES AND THEN GET PASSAGE TO YOUR HOME.
I DON'T KNOW...
SHH!
DID YOU HEAR THAT?!
HEAR MMPHH!?
UH OH! SHE'S CAUGHT YOUR SCENT! SHE'S COMING FOR YOU!
OH, FRIGG! YOU SURE!?
STOP!
DROP!
PLOP!
PLOP!
AND ROLL!
AAAHHH
WHAK
FLUMP!
FLUMP!
FLUMP!

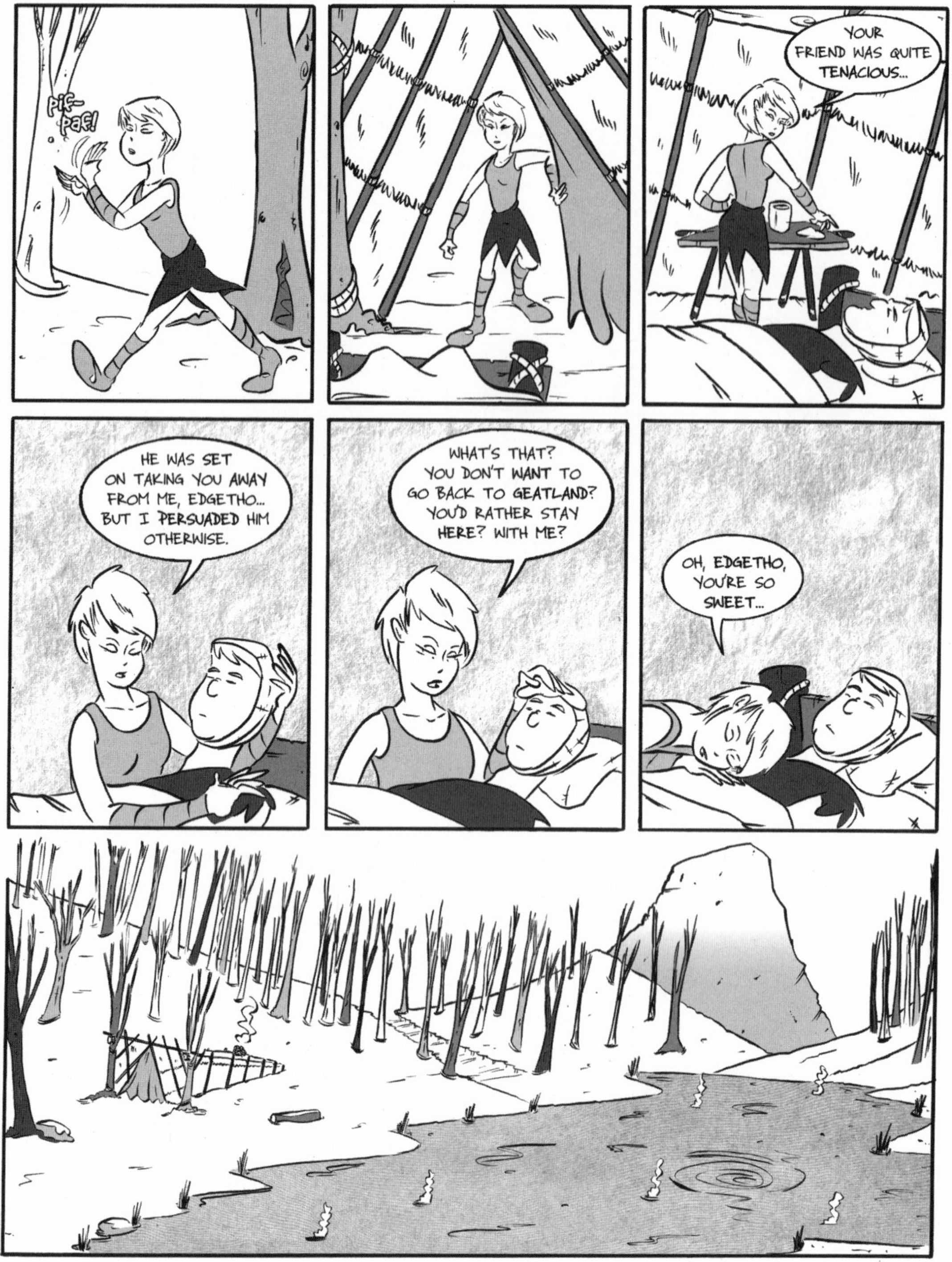
PIF-PAF!
YOUR FRIEND WAS QUITE TENACIOUS...
HE WAS SET ON TAKING YOU AWAY FROM ME, EDGETHO... BUT I PERSUADED HIM OTHERWISE.
WHAT'S THAT? YOU DON'T WANT TO GO BACK TO GEATLAND? YOU'D RATHER STAY HERE? WITH ME?
OH, EDGETHO, YOU'RE SO SWEET...

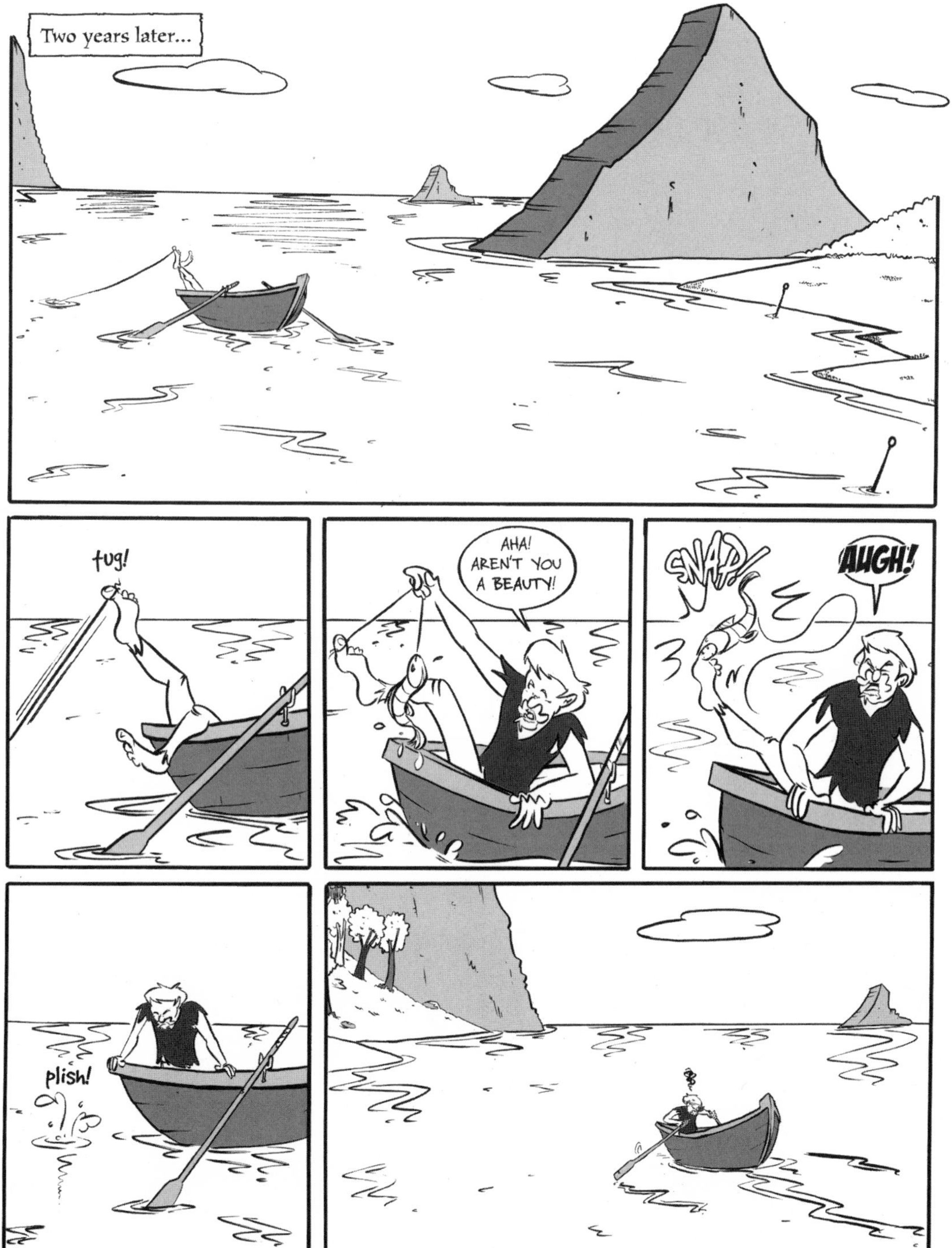
Two years later...
tug!
AHA! AREN'T YOU A BEAUTY!
SNAP!
AUGH!
plish!

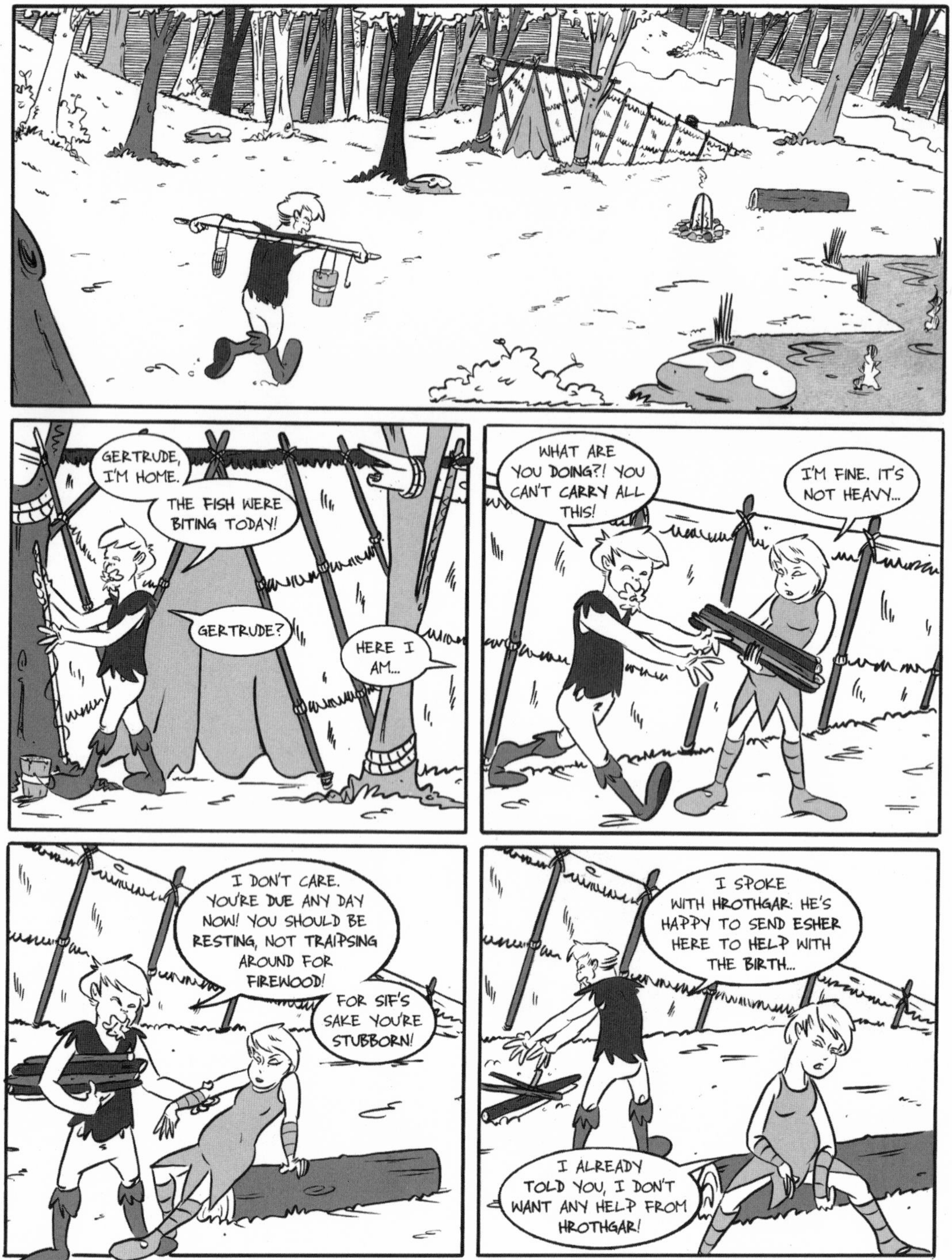
GERTRUDE, I'M HOME.
THE FISH WERE BITING TODAY!
GERTRUDE?
HERE I AM...
WHAT ARE YOU DOING?! YOU CAN'T CARRY ALL THIS!
I'M FINE. IT'S NOT HEAVY...
I DON'T CARE. YOU'RE DUE ANY DAY NOW! YOU SHOULD BE RESTING, NOT TRAIPSING AROUND FOR FIREWOOD!
FOR SIF'S SAKE YOU'RE STUBBORN!
I SPOKE WITH HROTHGAR: HE'S HAPPY TO SEND ESHER HERE TO HELP WITH THE BIRTH...
I ALREADY TOLD YOU, I DON'T WANT ANY HELP FROM HROTHGAR!

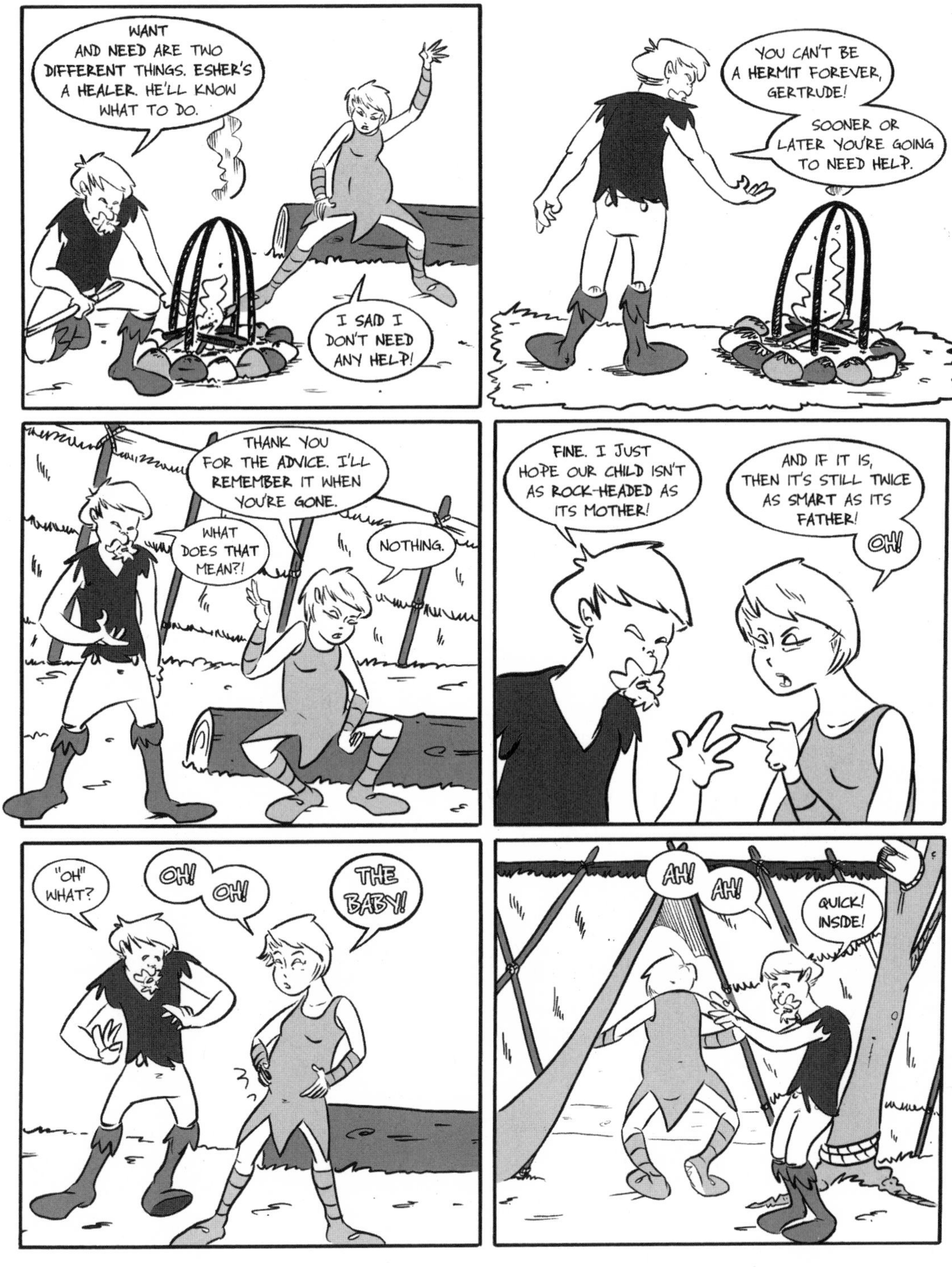
WANT AND NEED ARE TWO DIFFERENT THINGS. ESHER'S A HEALER. HE'LL KNOW WHAT TO DO.
I SAID I DON'T NEED ANY HELP!
YOU CAN'T BE A HERMIT FOREVER, GERTRUDE!
SOONER OR LATER YOU'RE GOING TO NEED HELP.
THANK YOU FOR THE ADVICE. I'LL REMEMBER IT WHEN YOU'RE GONE.
WHAT DOES THAT MEAN?!
NOTHING.
FINE. I JUST HOPE OUR CHILD ISN'T AS ROCK-HEADED AS ITS MOTHER!
AND IF IT IS, THEN IT'S STILL TWICE AS SMART AS ITS FATHER!
OH!
"OH" WHAT?
OH!
OH!
THE BABY!
AH!
AH!
QUICK! INSIDE!

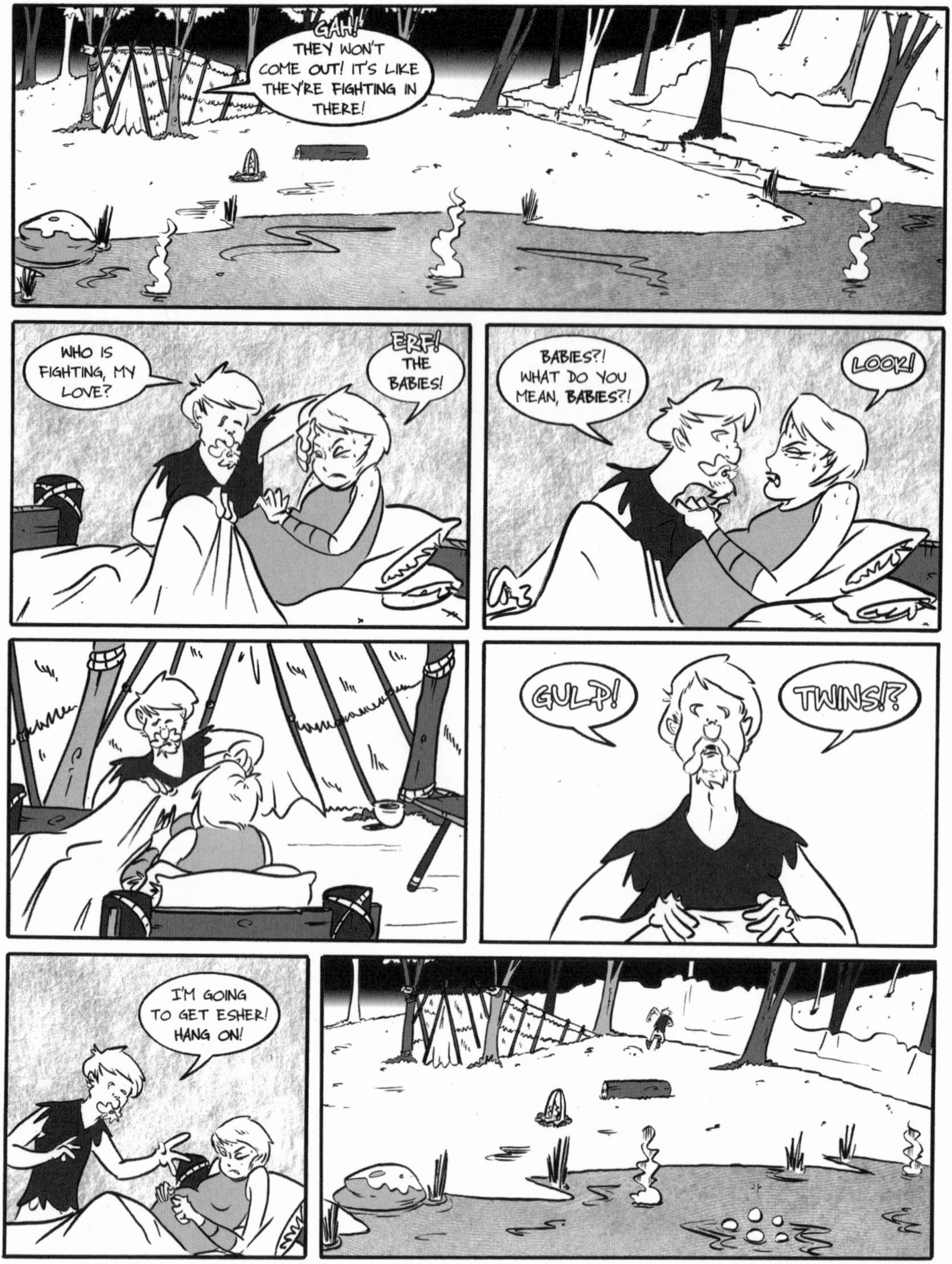
GAH!
THEY WON'T COME OUT! IT'S LIKE THEY'RE FIGHTING IN THERE!
WHO IS FIGHTING, MY LOVE?
ERF! THE BABIES!
BABIES?! WHAT DO YOU MEAN, BABIES?!
LOOK!
GULP!
TWINS!?
I'M GOING TO GET ESHER! HANG ON!

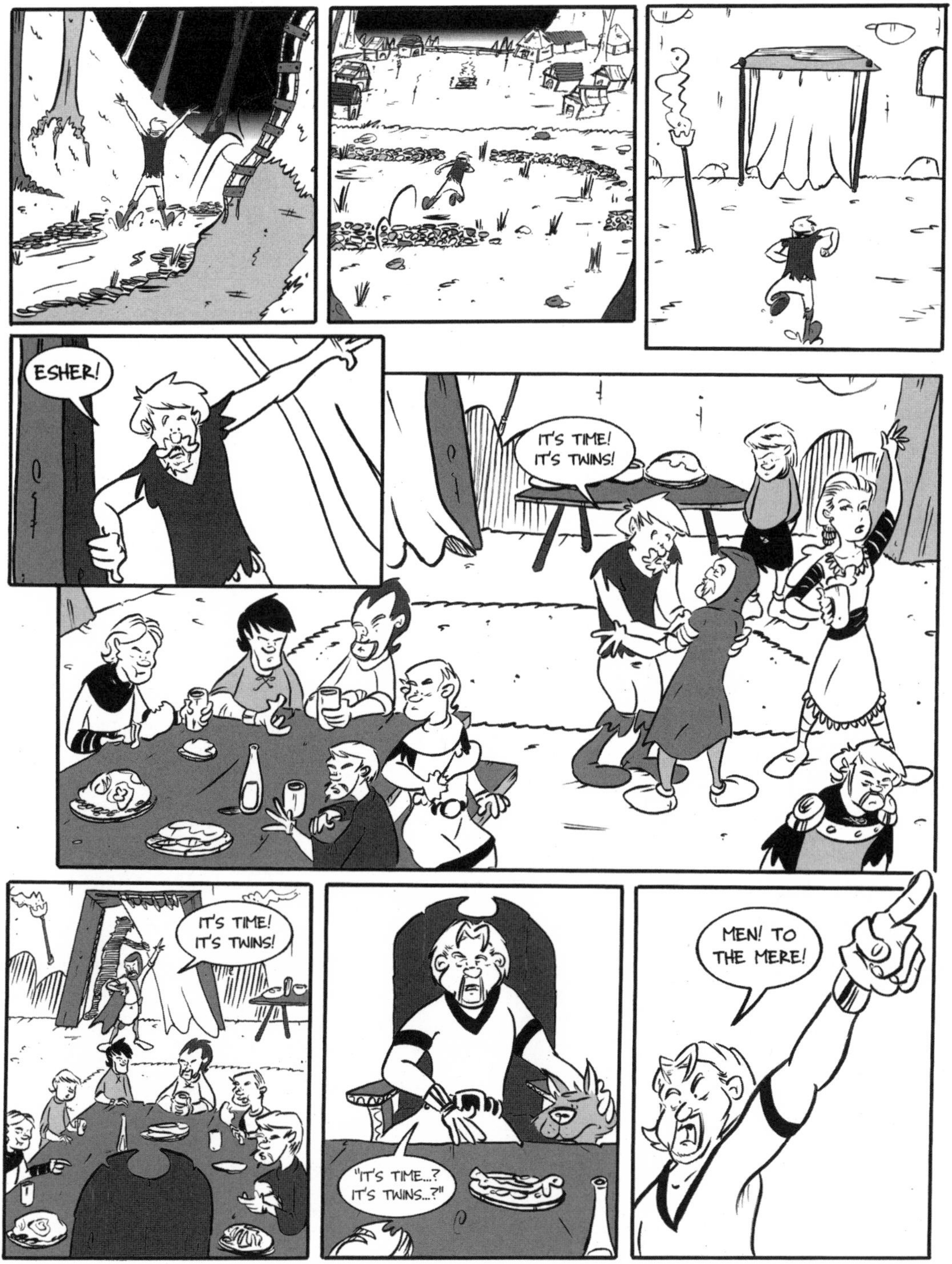
ESHER!
IT'S TIME! IT'S TWINS!
IT'S TIME! IT'S TWINS!
"IT'S TIME...? IT'S TWINS...?"
MEN! TO THE MERE!

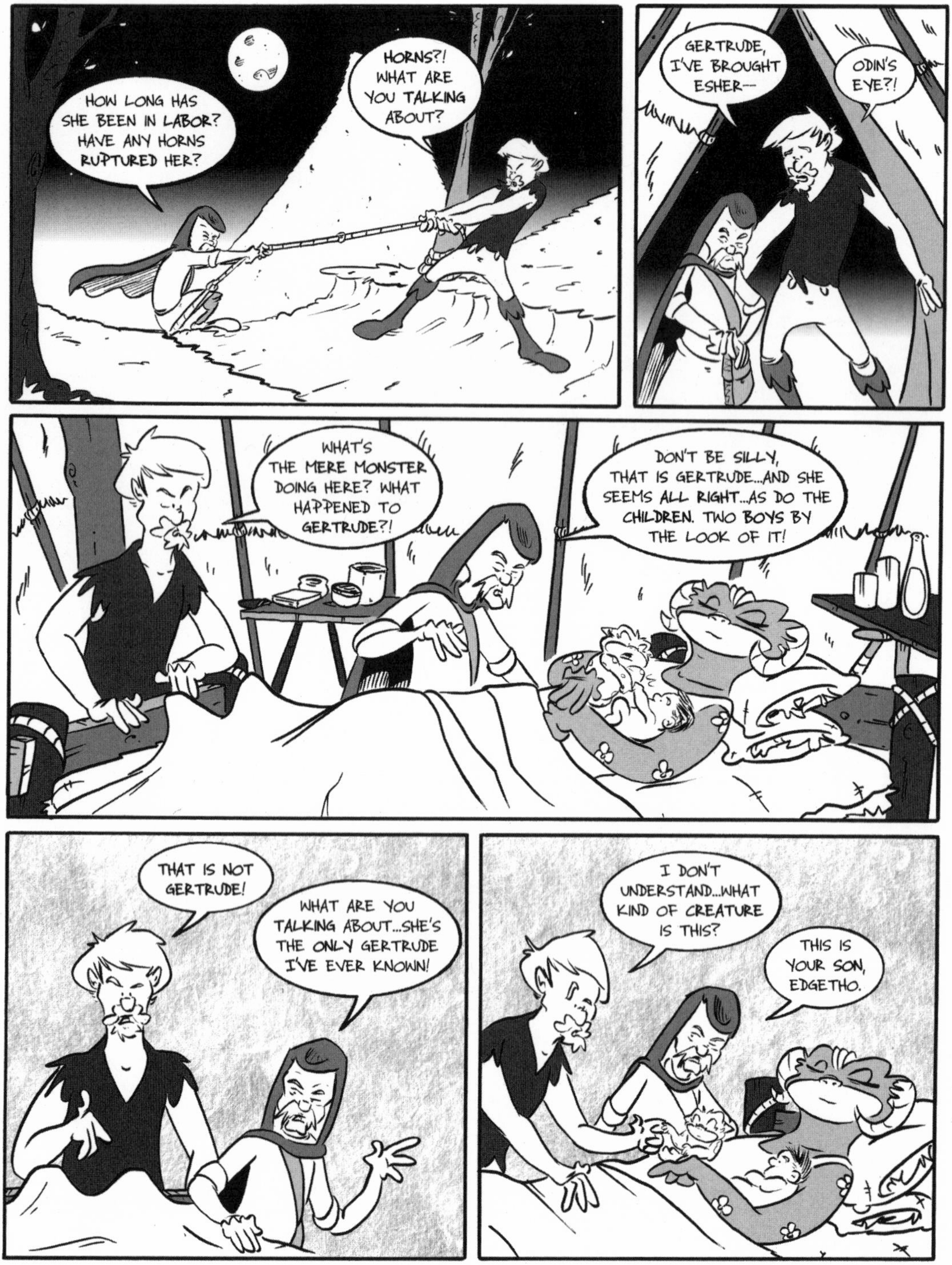
HOW LONG HAS SHE BEEN IN LABOR? HAVE ANY HORNS RUPTURED HER?
HORNS?! WHAT ARE YOU TALKING ABOUT?
GERTRUDE, I'VE BROUGHT ESHER--
ODIN'S EYE?!
WHAT'S THE MERE MONSTER DOING HERE? WHAT HAPPENED TO GERTRUDE?!
DON'T BE SILLY, THAT IS GERTRUDE...AND SHE SEEMS ALL RIGHT...AS DO THE CHILDREN. TWO BOYS BY THE LOOK OF IT!
THAT IS NOT GERTRUDE!
WHAT ARE YOU TALKING ABOUT...SHE'S THE ONLY GERTRUDE I'VE EVER KNOWN!
I DON'T UNDERSTAND...WHAT KIND OF CREATURE IS THIS?
THIS IS YOUR SON, EDGETHO.

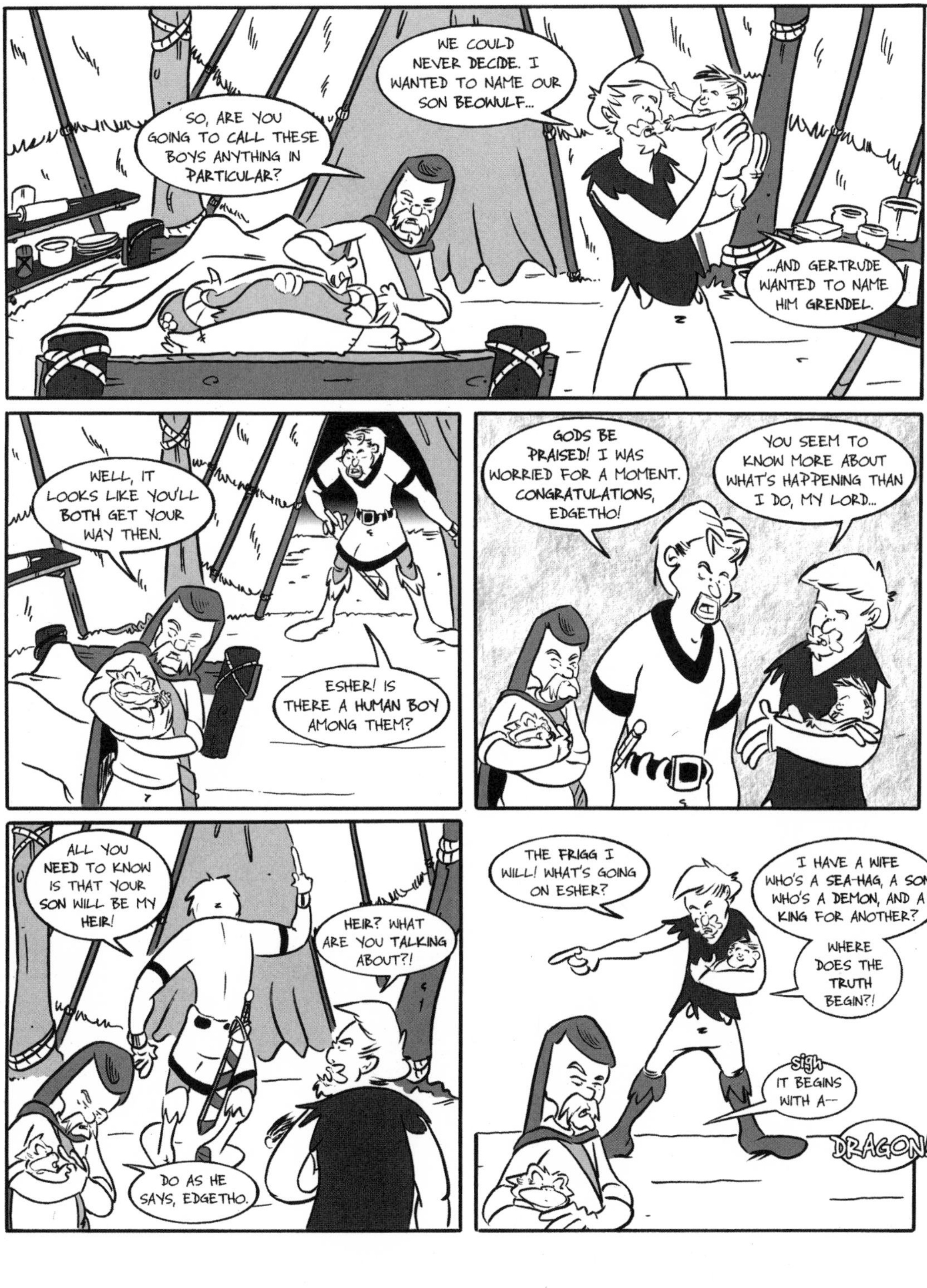
SO, ARE YOU GOING TO CALL THESE BOYS ANYTHING IN PARTICULAR?
WE COULD NEVER DECIDE. I WANTED TO NAME OUR SON BEOWULF...
...AND GERTRUDE WANTED TO NAME HIM GRENDEL.
WELL, IT LOOKS LIKE YOU'LL BOTH GET YOUR WAY THEN.
ESHER! IS THERE A HUMAN BOY AMONG THEM?
GODS BE PRAISED! I WAS WORRIED FOR A MOMENT. CONGRATULATIONS, EDGETHO!
YOU SEEM TO KNOW MORE ABOUT WHAT'S HAPPENING THAN I DO, MY LORD...
ALL YOU NEED TO KNOW IS THAT YOUR SON WILL BE MY HEIR!
HEIR? WHAT ARE YOU TALKING ABOUT?!
DO AS HE SAYS, EDGETHO.
THE FRIGG I WILL! WHAT'S GOING ON ESHER?
I HAVE A WIFE WHO'S A SEA-HAG, A SON WHO'S A DEMON, AND A KING FOR ANOTHER?
WHERE DOES THE TRUTH BEGIN?!
sigh
IT BEGINS WITH A--
DRAGON!

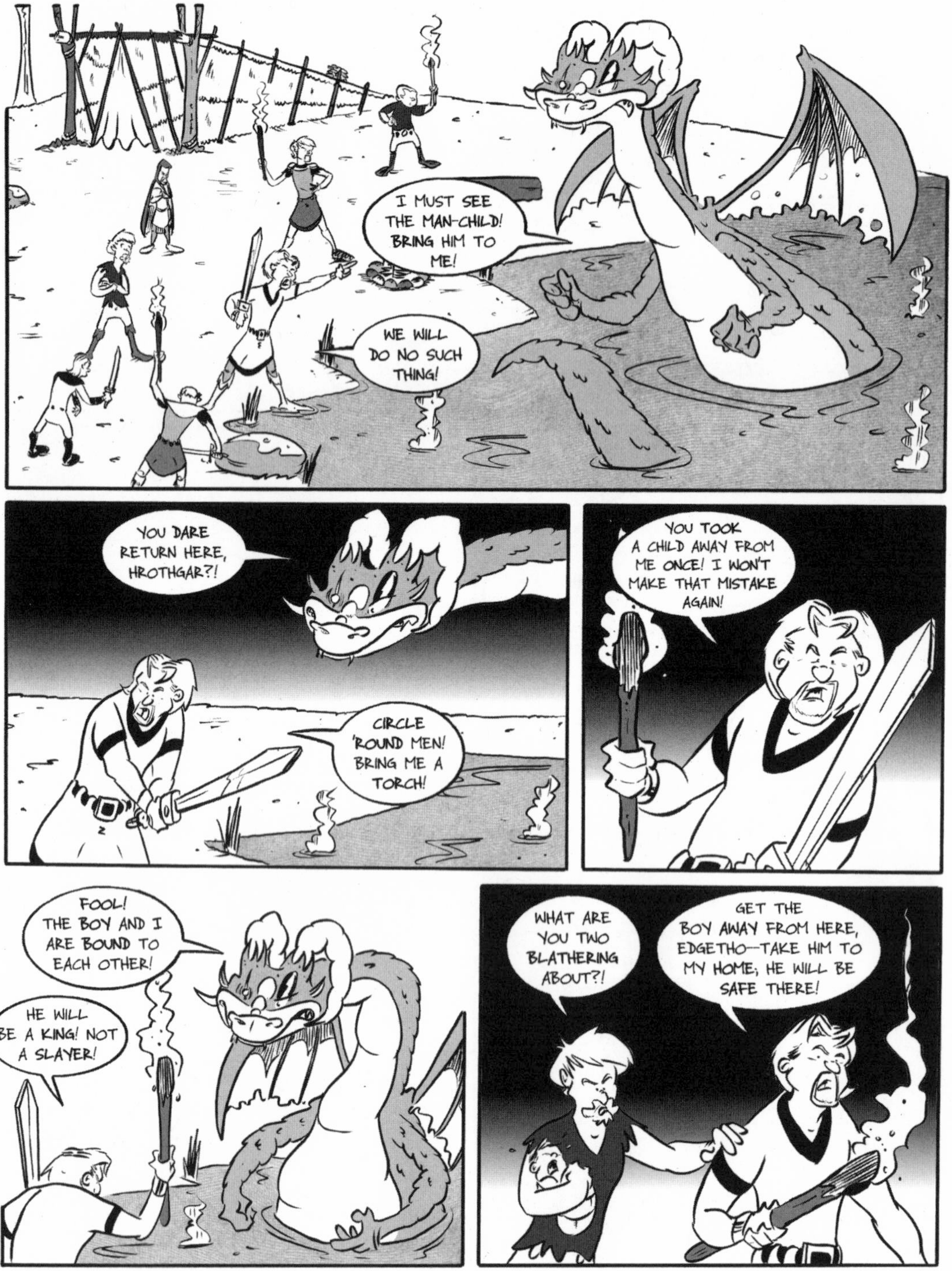
I MUST SEE THE MAN-CHILD! BRING HIM TO ME!
WE WILL DO NO SUCH THING!
YOU DARE RETURN HERE, HROTHGAR?!
CIRCLE 'ROUND MEN! BRING ME A TORCH!
YOU TOOK A CHILD AWAY FROM ME ONCE! I WON'T MAKE THAT MISTAKE AGAIN!
FOOL! THE BOY AND I ARE BOUND TO EACH OTHER!
HE WILL BE A KING! NOT A SLAYER!
WHAT ARE YOU TWO BLATHERING ABOUT?!
GET THE BOY AWAY FROM HERE, EDGETHO--TAKE HIM TO MY HOME; HE WILL BE SAFE THERE!

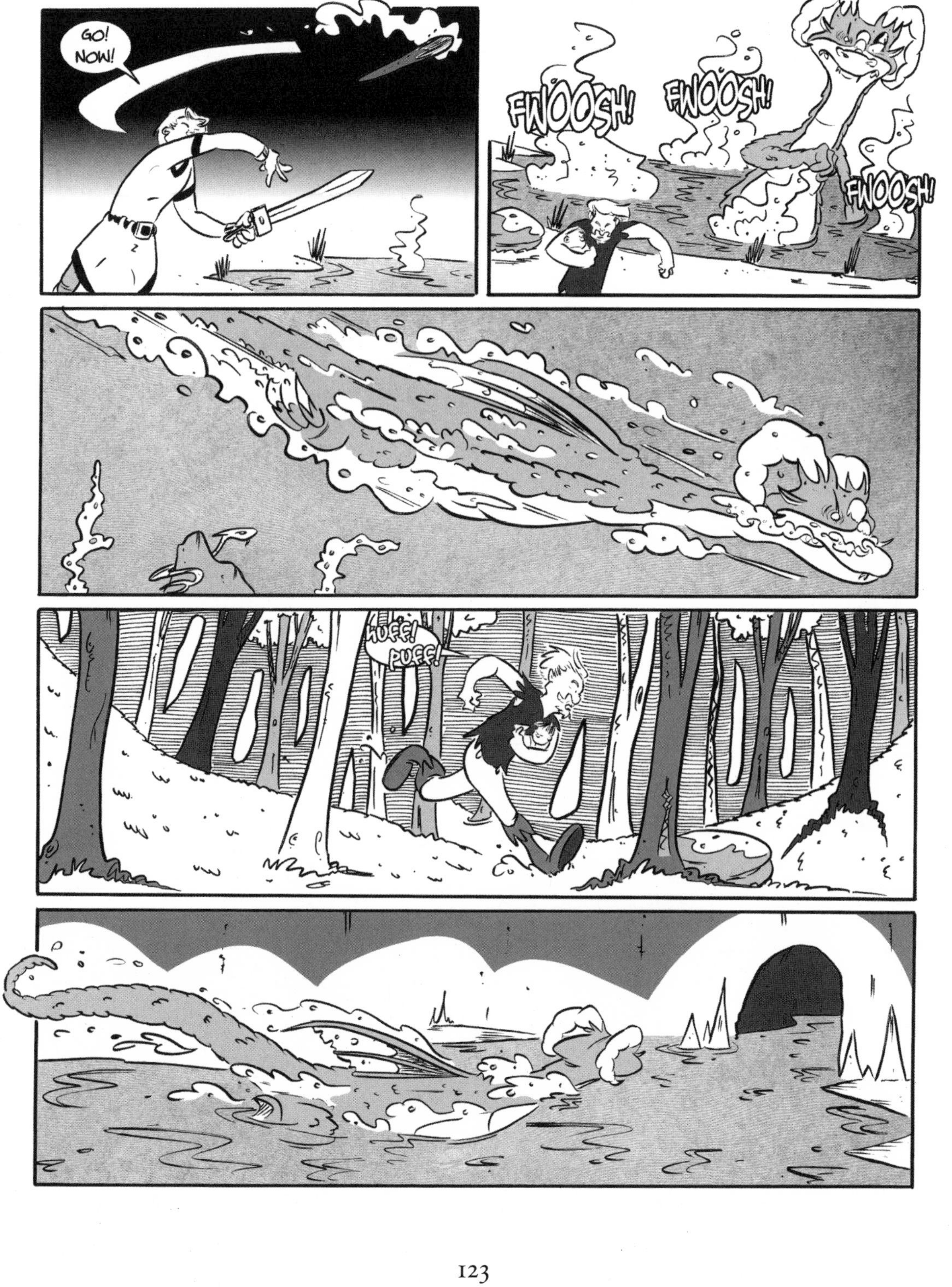
GO! NOW!
FWOOSH!
FWOOSH!
FWOOSH!
HUFF! PUFF!

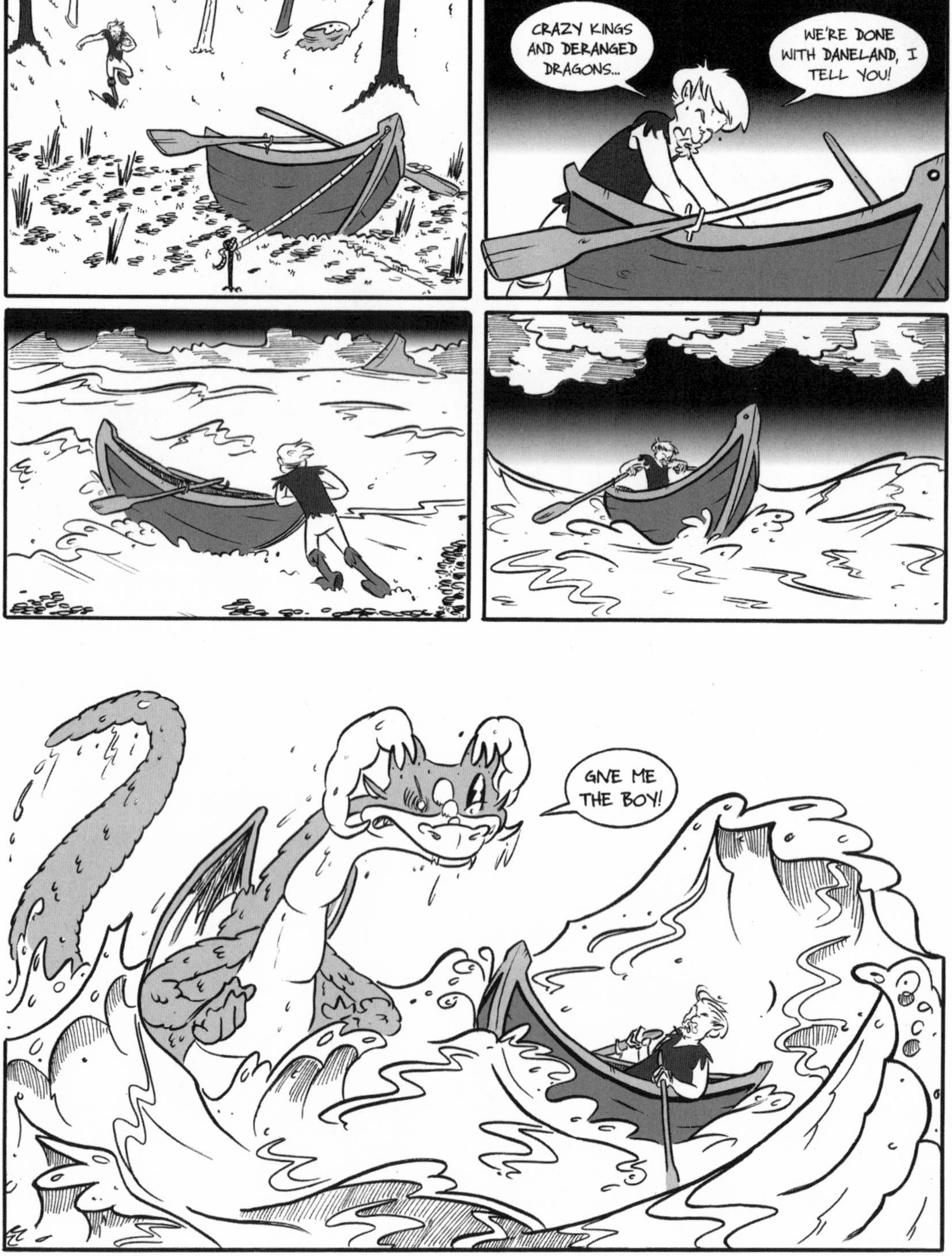
CRAZY KINGS AND DERANGED DRAGONS...
WE'RE DONE WITH DANELAND, I TELL YOU!
GIVE ME THE BOY!

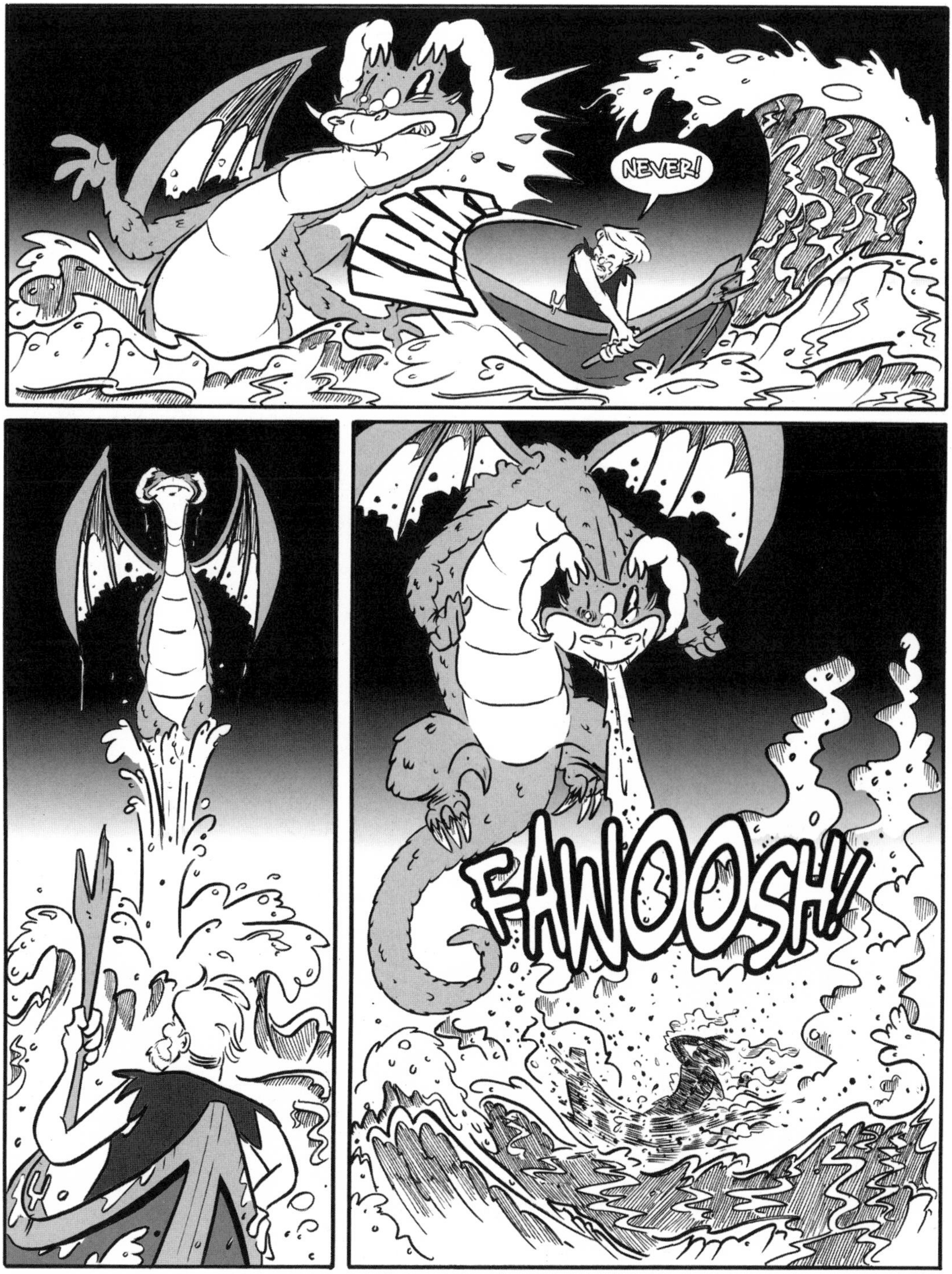
NEVER!
FAWOOSH!

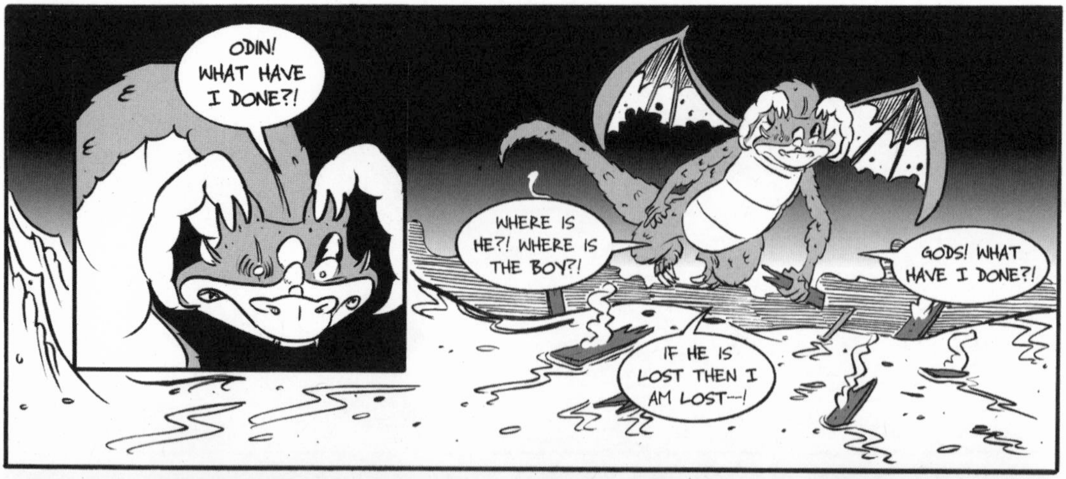
ODIN! WHAT HAVE I DONE?!
WHERE IS HE?! WHERE IS THE BOY?!
IF HE IS LOST THEN I AM LOST--!
GODS! WHAT HAVE I DONE?!

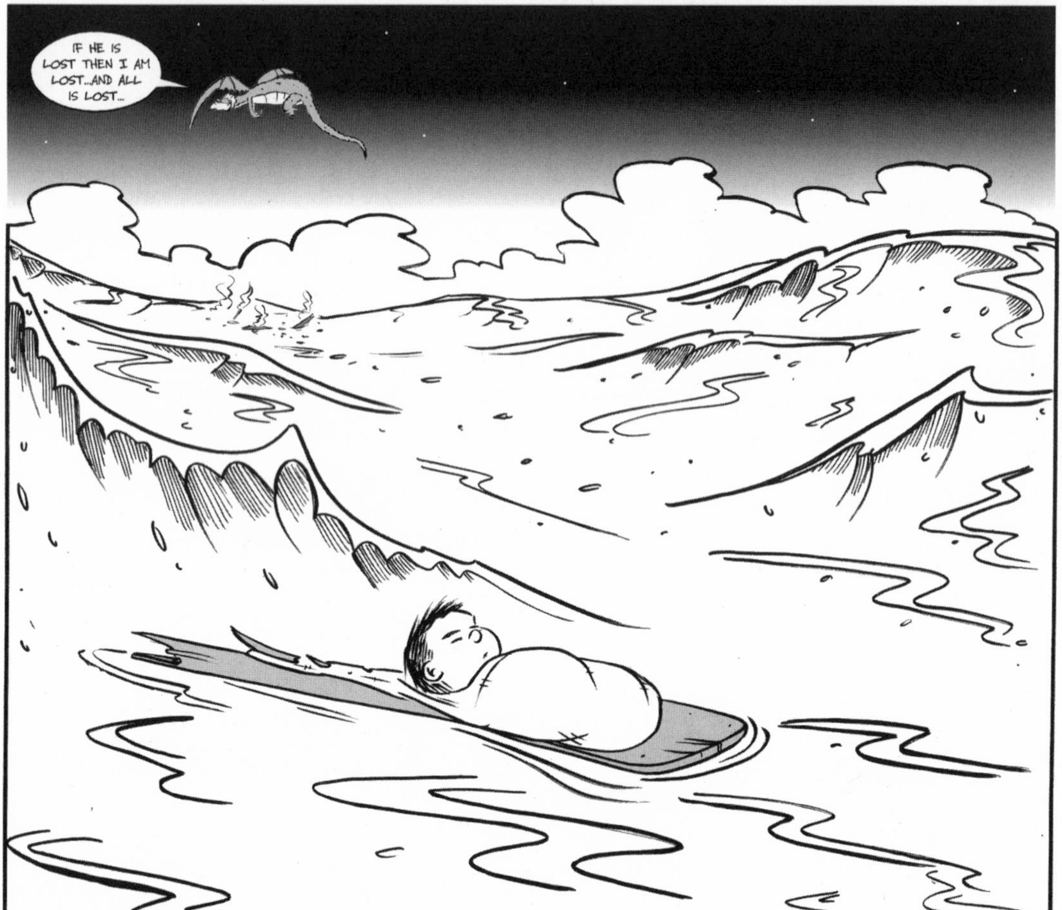
IF HE IS LOST THEN I AM LOST...AND ALL IS LOST...

Part Three

the future

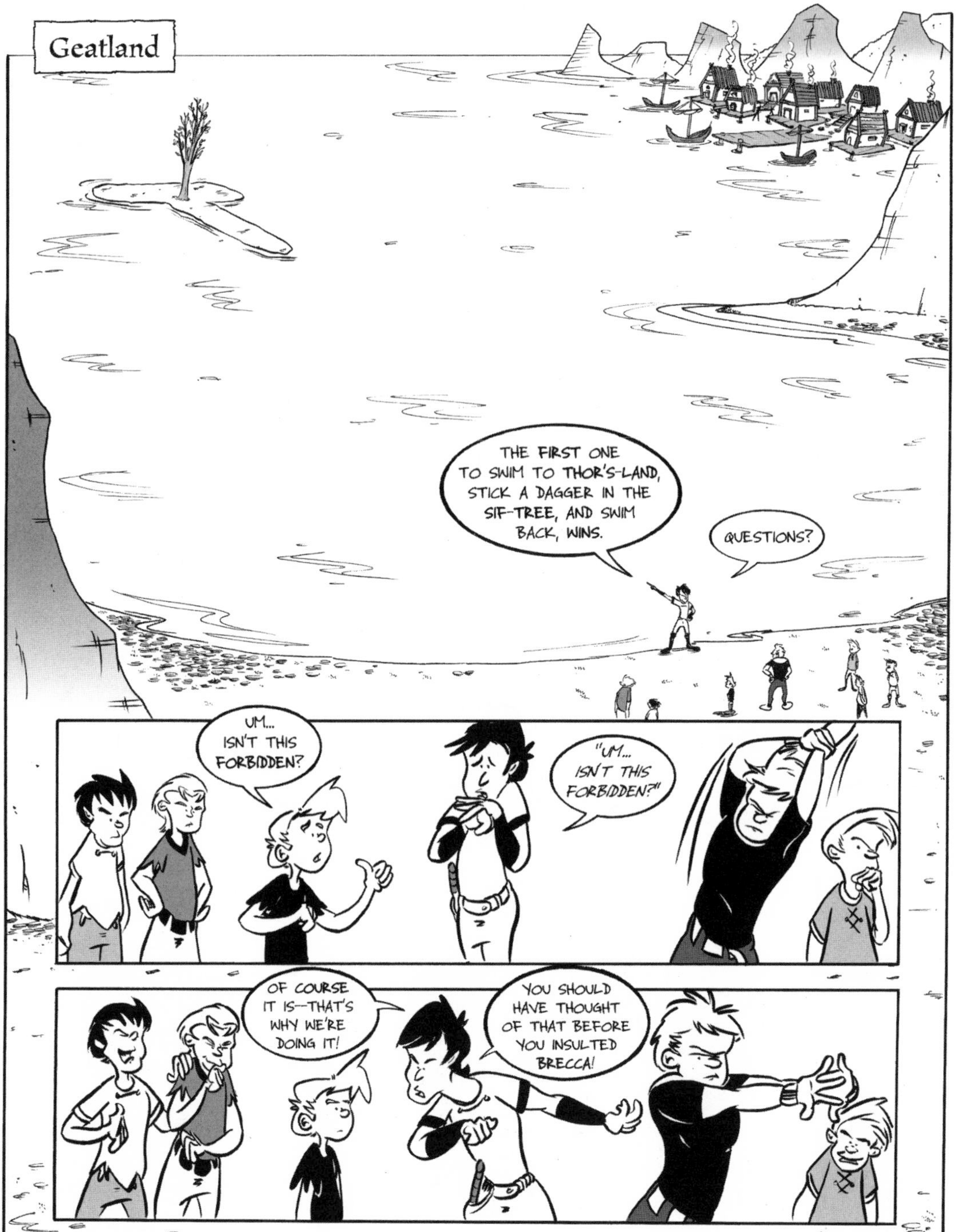
Geatland
THE FIRST ONE TO SWIM TO THOR'S-LAND, STICK A DAGGER IN THE SIF-TREE, AND SWIM BACK, WINS.
QUESTIONS?
UM... ISN'T THIS FORBIDDEN?
"UM... ISN'T THIS FORBIDDEN?"
OF COURSE IT IS--THAT'S WHY WE'RE DOING IT!
YOU SHOULD HAVE THOUGHT OF THAT BEFORE YOU INSULTED BRECCA!

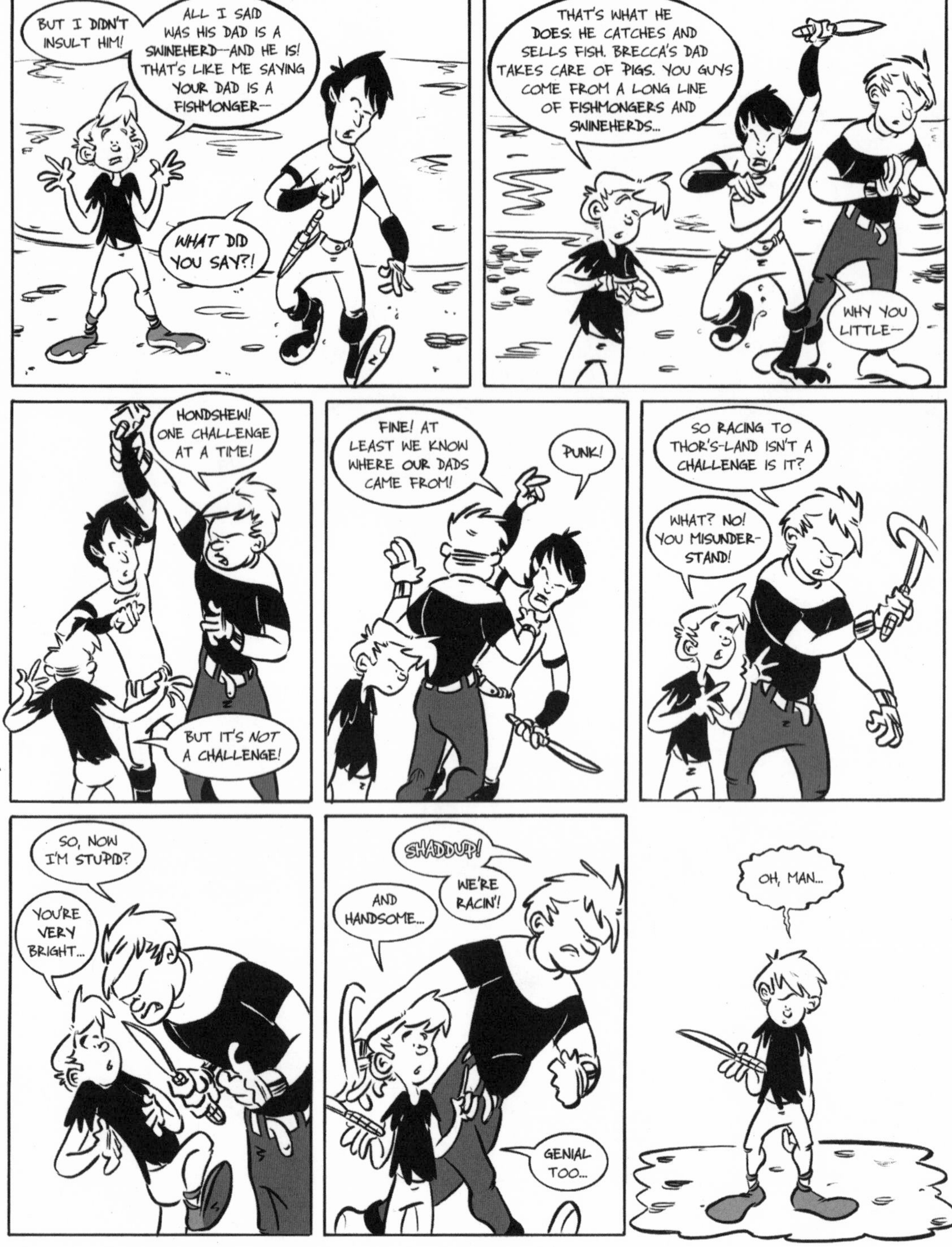
BUT I DIDN'T INSULT HIM!
ALL I SAID WAS HIS DAD IS A SWINEHERD--AND HE IS! THAT'S LIKE ME SAYING YOUR DAD IS A FISHMONGER--
WHAT DID YOU SAY?!
THAT'S WHAT HE DOES: HE CATCHES AND SELLS FISH. BRECCA'S DAD TAKES CARE OF PIGS. YOU GUYS COME FROM A LONG LINE OF FISHMONGERS AND SWINEHERDS...
WHY YOU LITTLE--
HONDSHEW! ONE CHALLENGE AT A TIME!
BUT IT'S NOT A CHALLENGE!
FINE! AT LEAST WE KNOW WHERE OUR DADS CAME FROM!
PUNK!
SO RACING TO THOR'S-LAND ISN'T A CHALLENGE IS IT?
WHAT? NO! YOU MISUNDER-STAND!
SO, NOW I'M STUPID?
YOU'RE VERY BRIGHT...
SHADDUP!
WE'RE RACIN'!
AND HANDSOME...
GENIAL TOO...
OH, MAN...

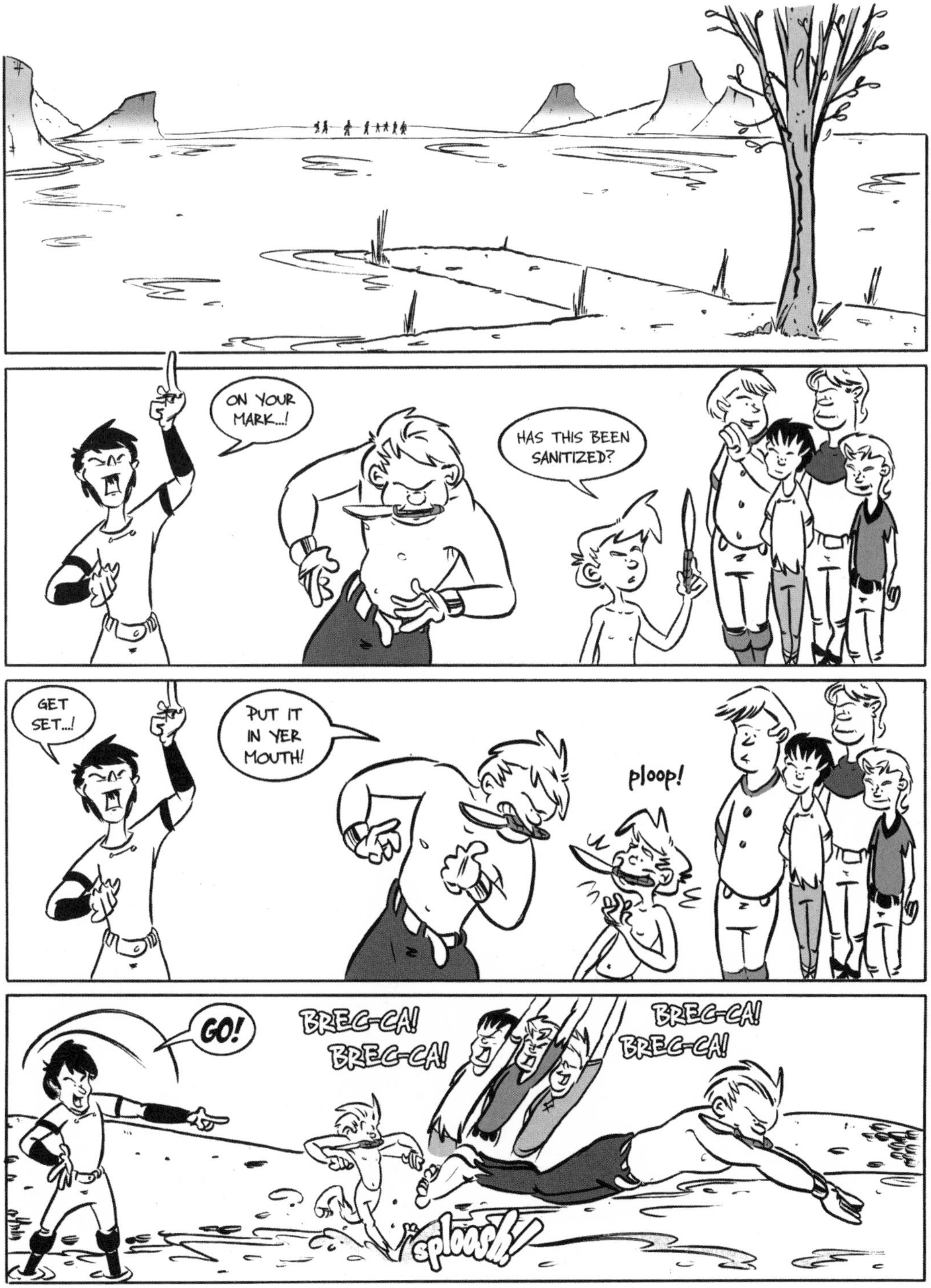

ON YOUR MARK...!
HAS THIS BEEN SANITIZED?
GET SET...!
PUT IT IN YER MOUTH!
ploop!
GO!
BREC-CA!
BREC-CA!
BREC-CA!
BREC-CA!
sploosh!

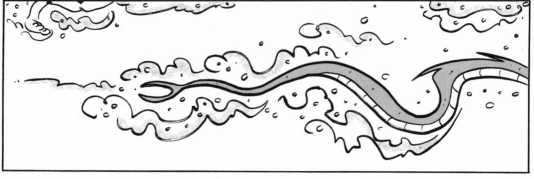

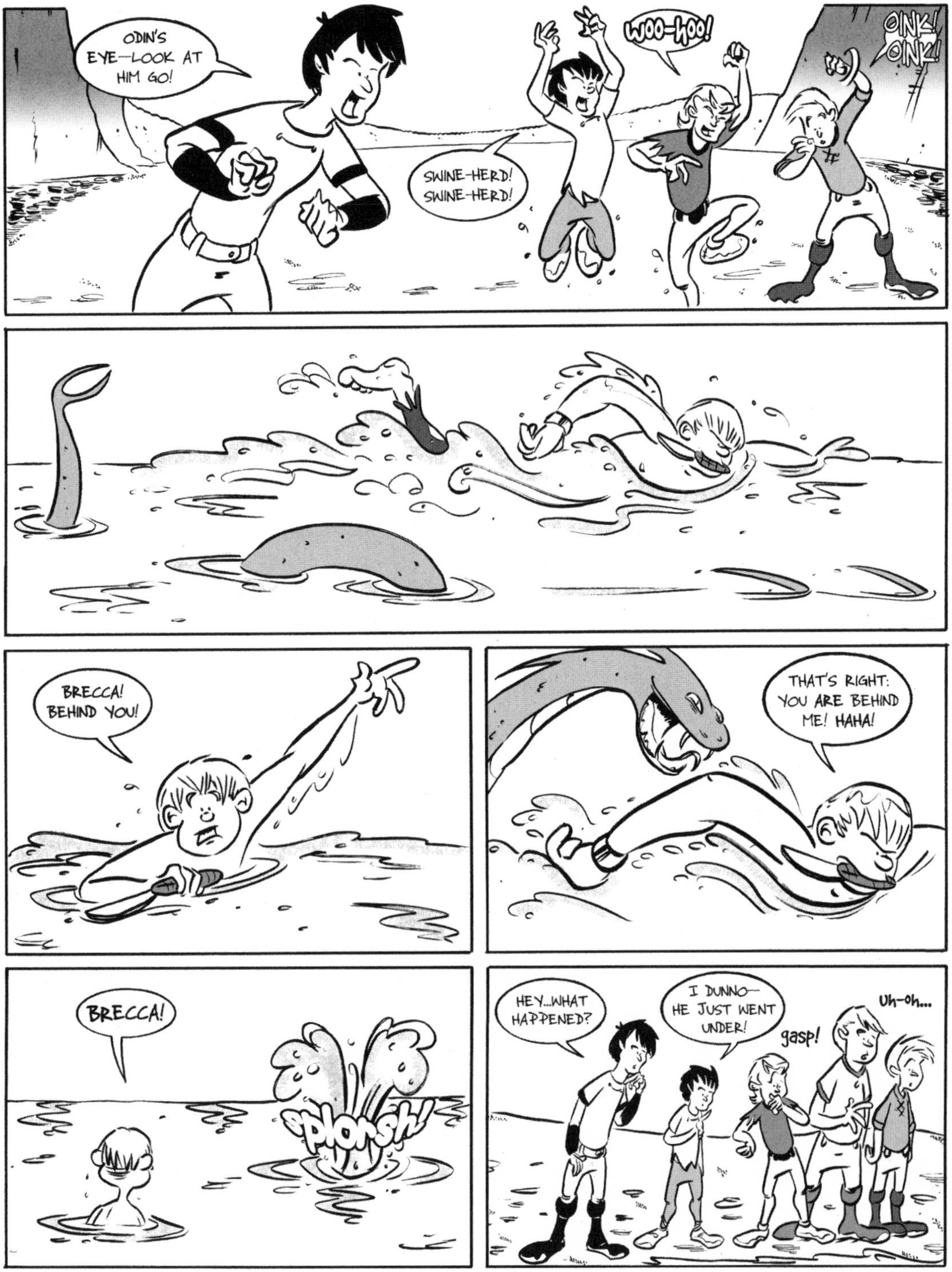
ODIN'S EYE--LOOK AT HIM GO!
SWINE-HERD! SWINE-HERD!
WOO-HOO!
OINK! OINK!
BRECCA! BEHIND YOU!
THAT'S RIGHT: YOU ARE BEHIND ME! HAHA!
BRECCA!
sploosh!
HEY...WHAT HAPPENED?
I DUNNO--HE JUST WENT UNDER!
gasp!
Uh-oh...

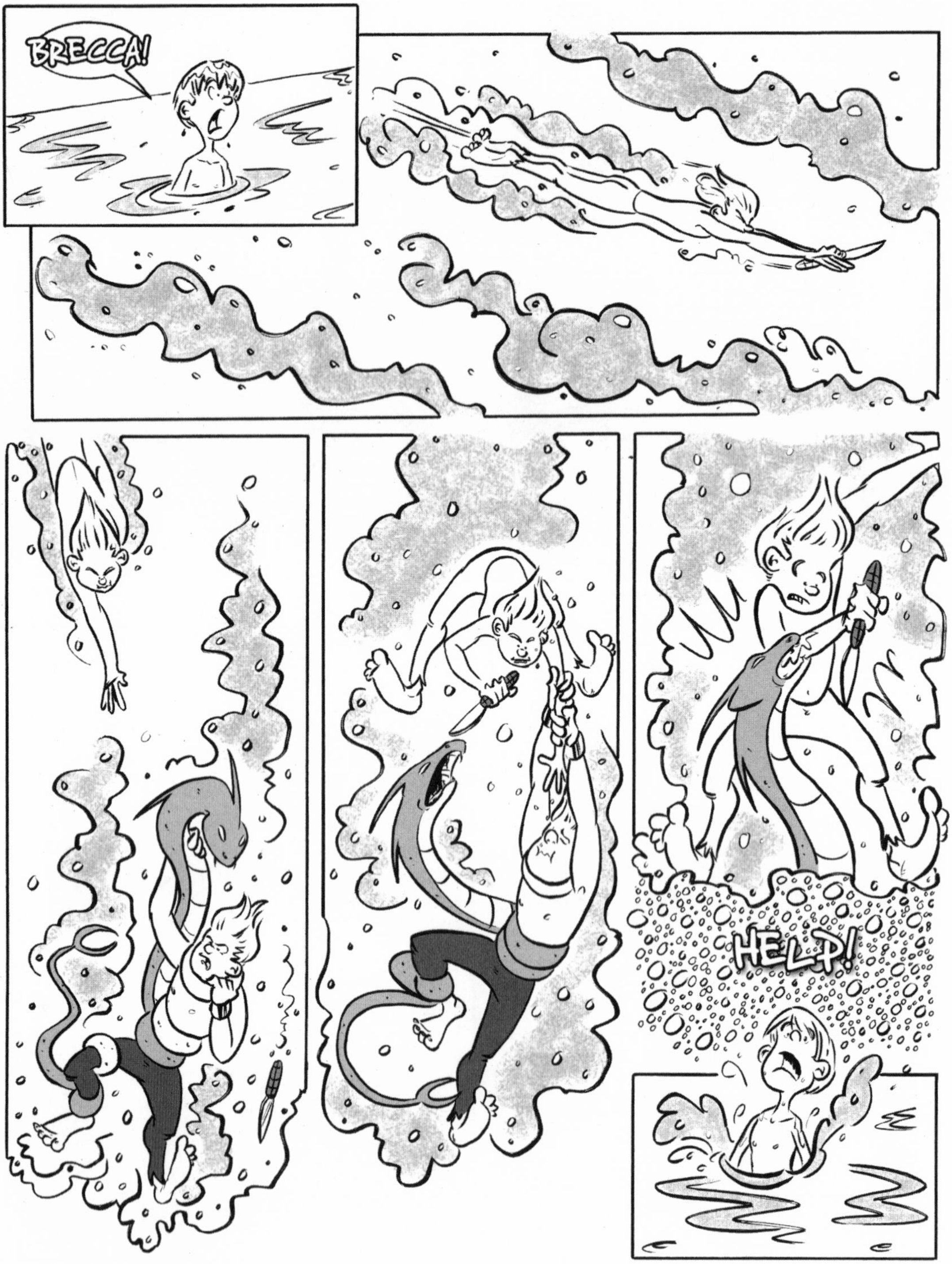
BRECCA!
HELP!

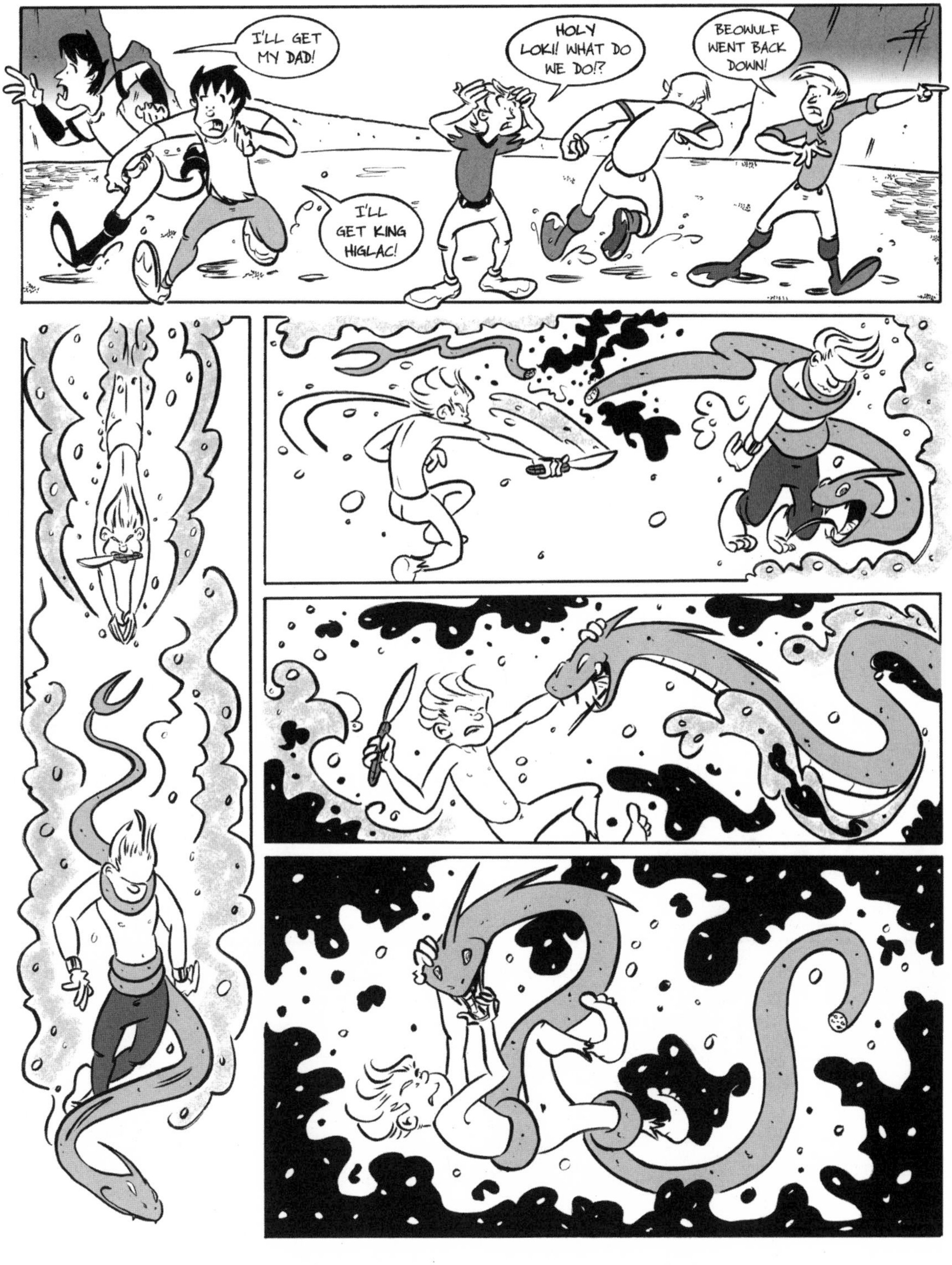
I'LL GET MY DAD!
I'LL GET KING HIGLAC!
HOLY LOKI! WHAT DO WE DO!?
BEOWULF WENT BACK DOWN!

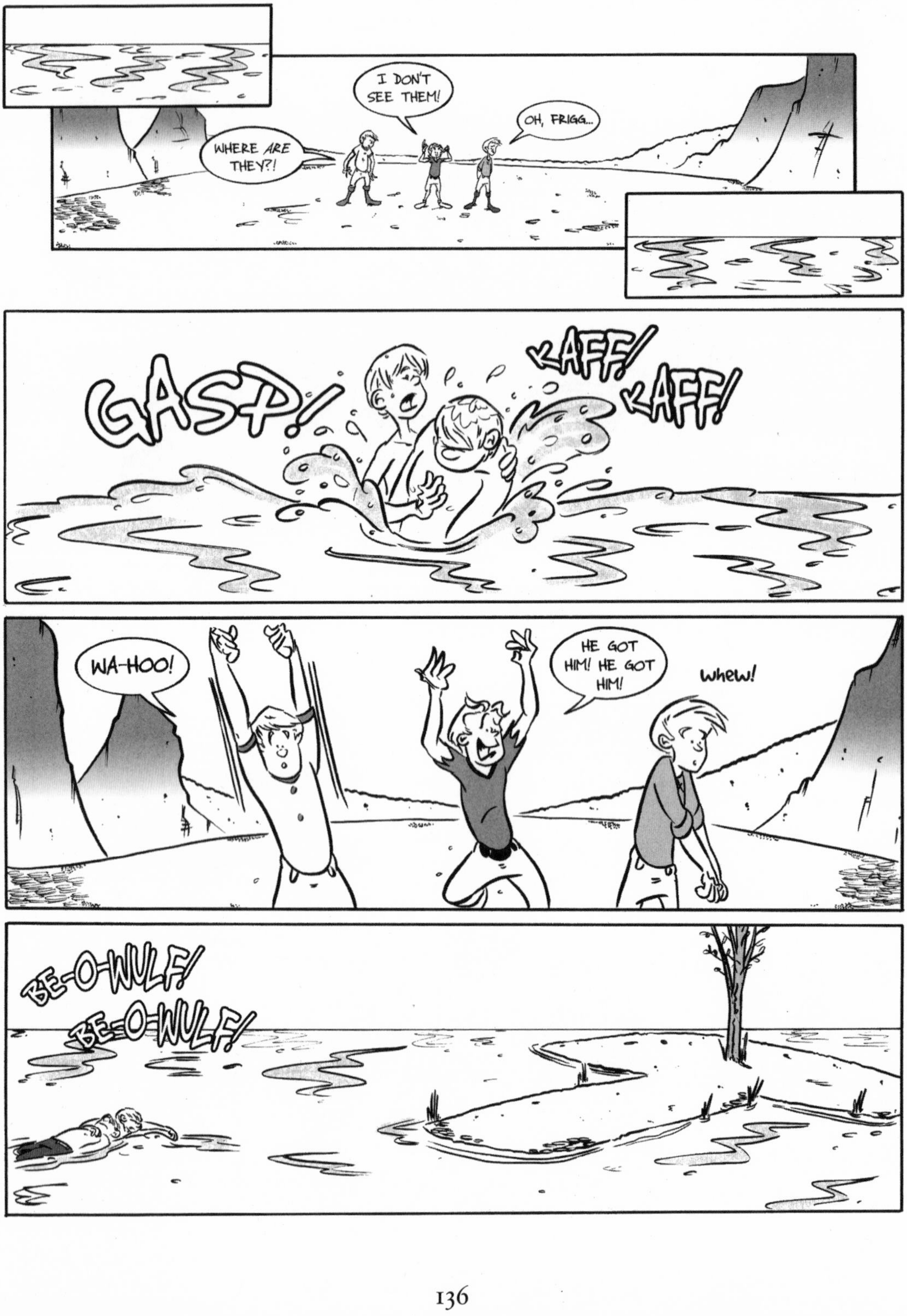
WHERE ARE THEY?!
I DON'T SEE THEM!
OH, FRIGG...
GASP!
KAFF! KAFF!
WA-HOO!
HE GOT HIM! HE GOT HIM!
whew!
BE-O-WULF! BE-O-WULF!

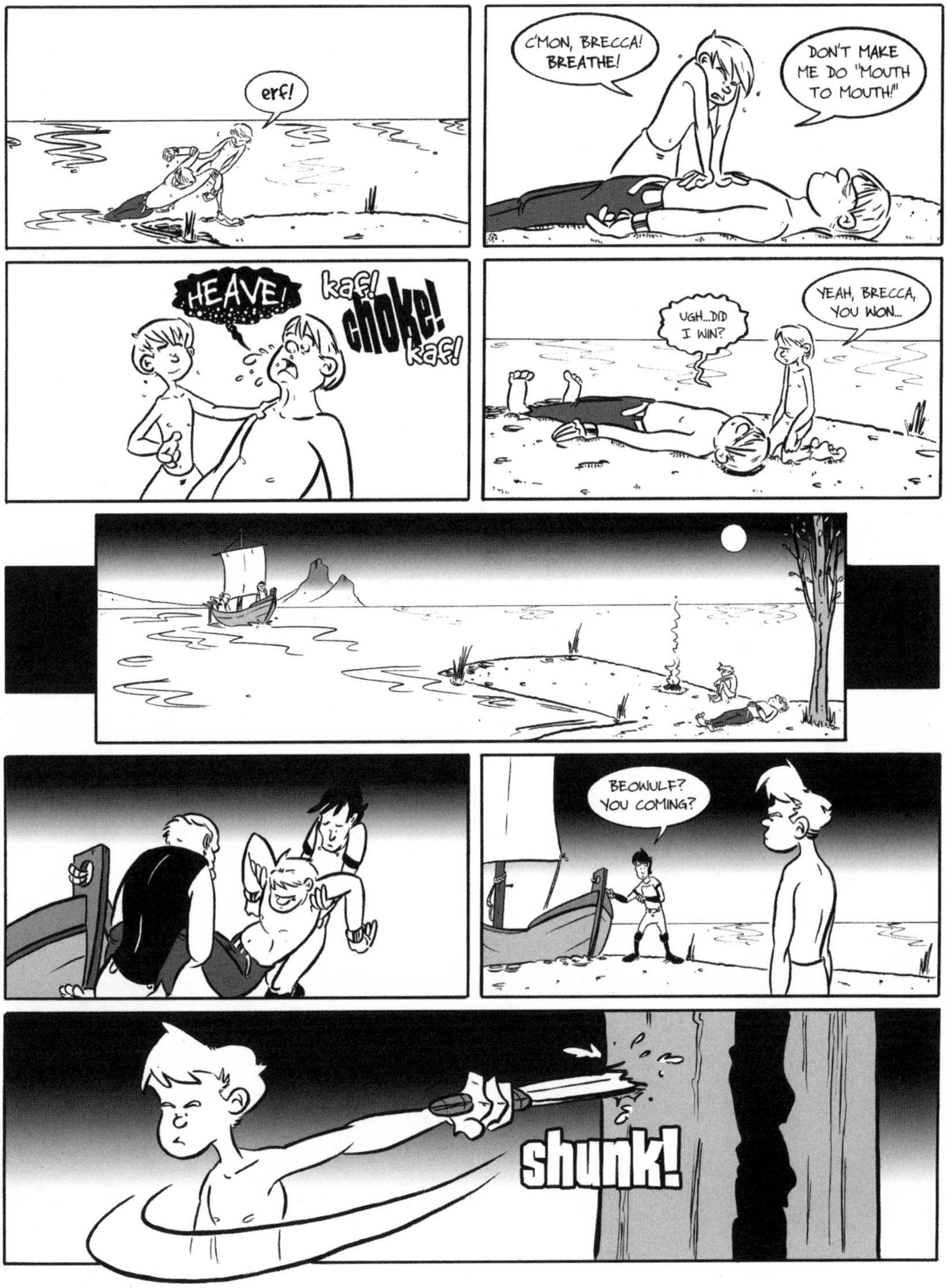
erf!
C'MON, BRECCA! BREATHE!
DON'T MAKE ME DO "MOUTH TO MOUTH!"
HEAVE!
kaf!
choke!
kaf!
UGH...DID I WIN?
YEAH, BRECCA, YOU WON...
BEOWULF? YOU COMING?
shunk!

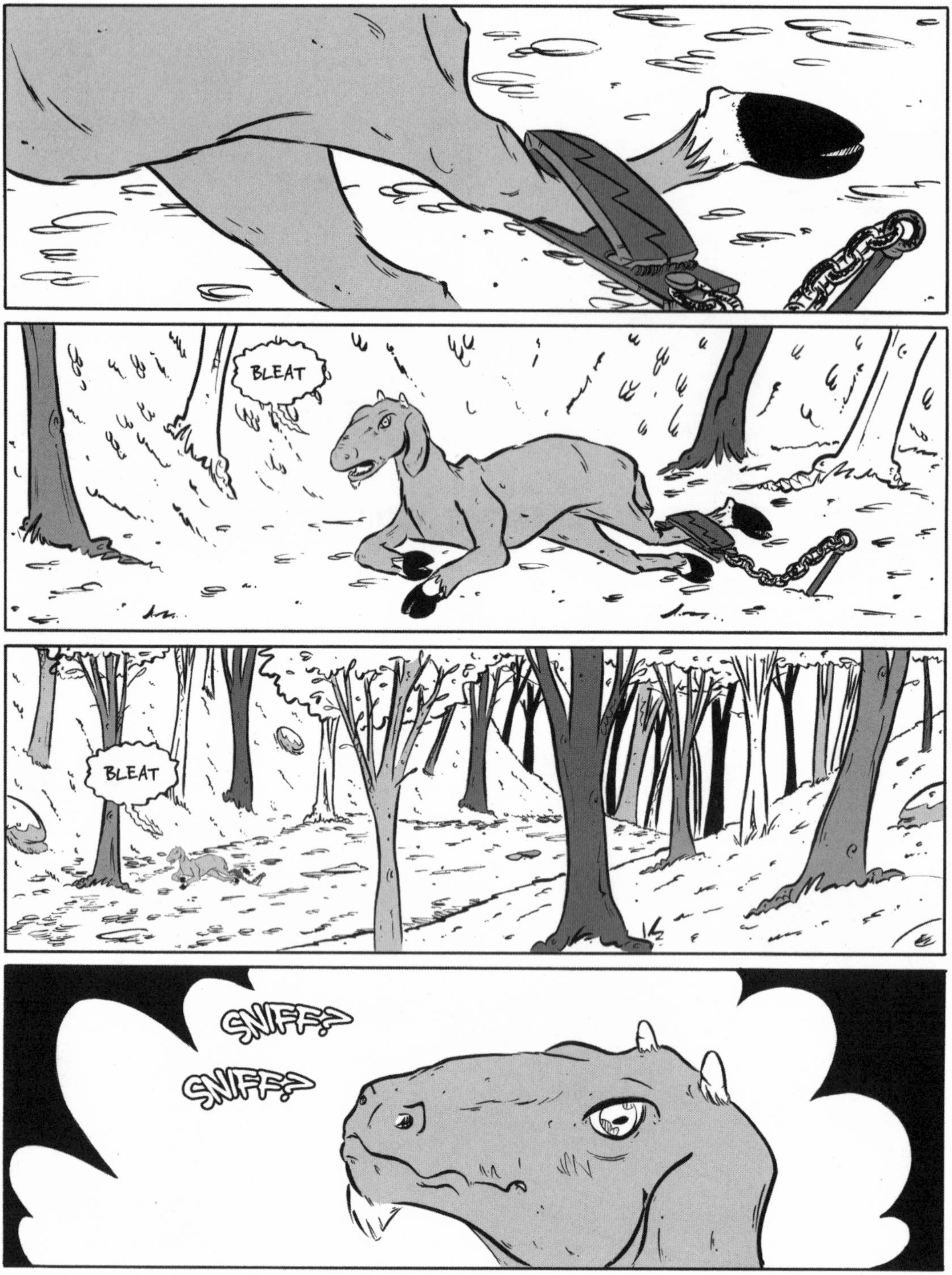
BLEAT
BLEAT
SNIFF?
SNIFF?

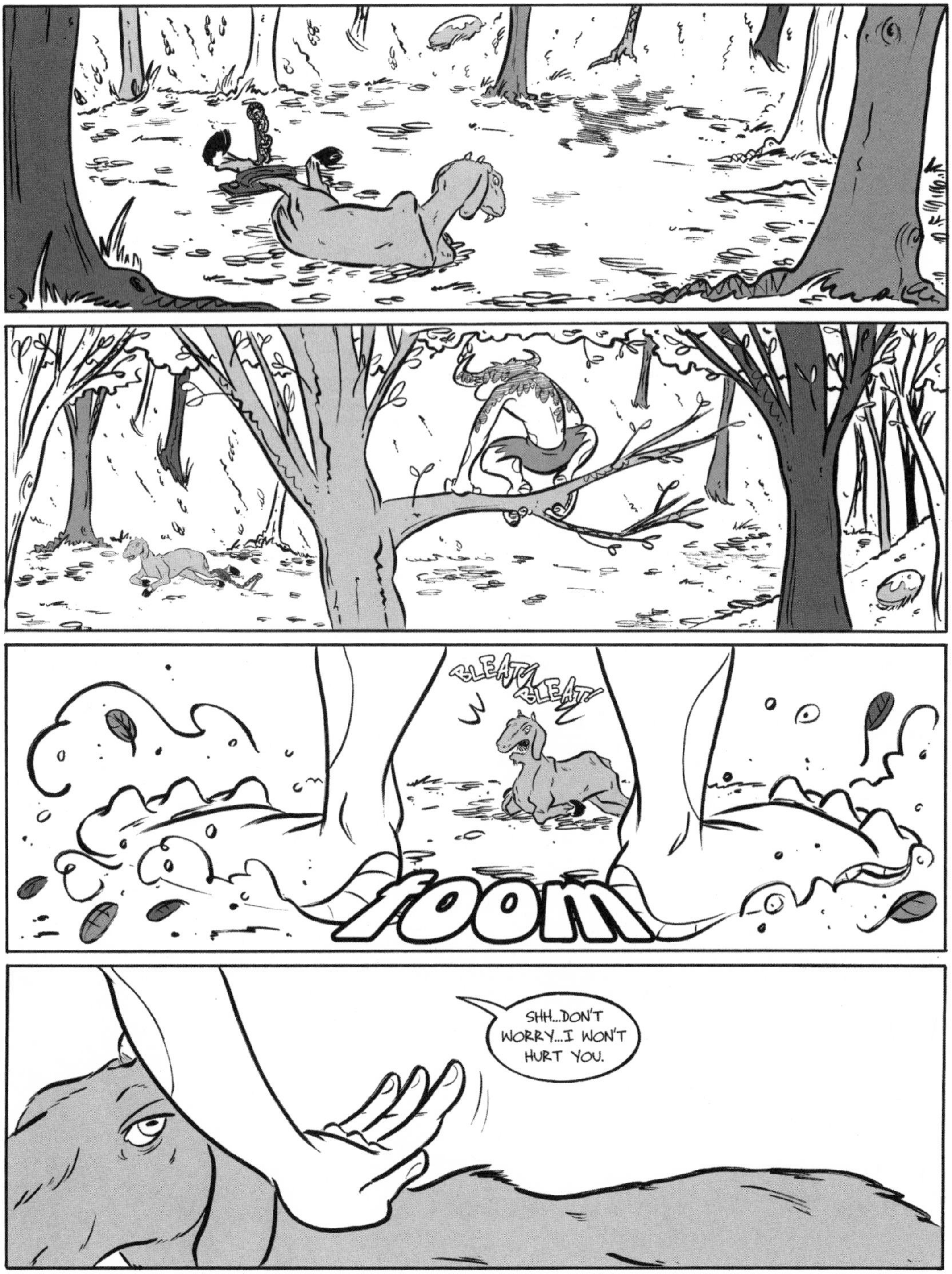
BLEAT! BLEAT!
TOOM
SHH...DON'T WORRY...I WON'T HURT YOU.

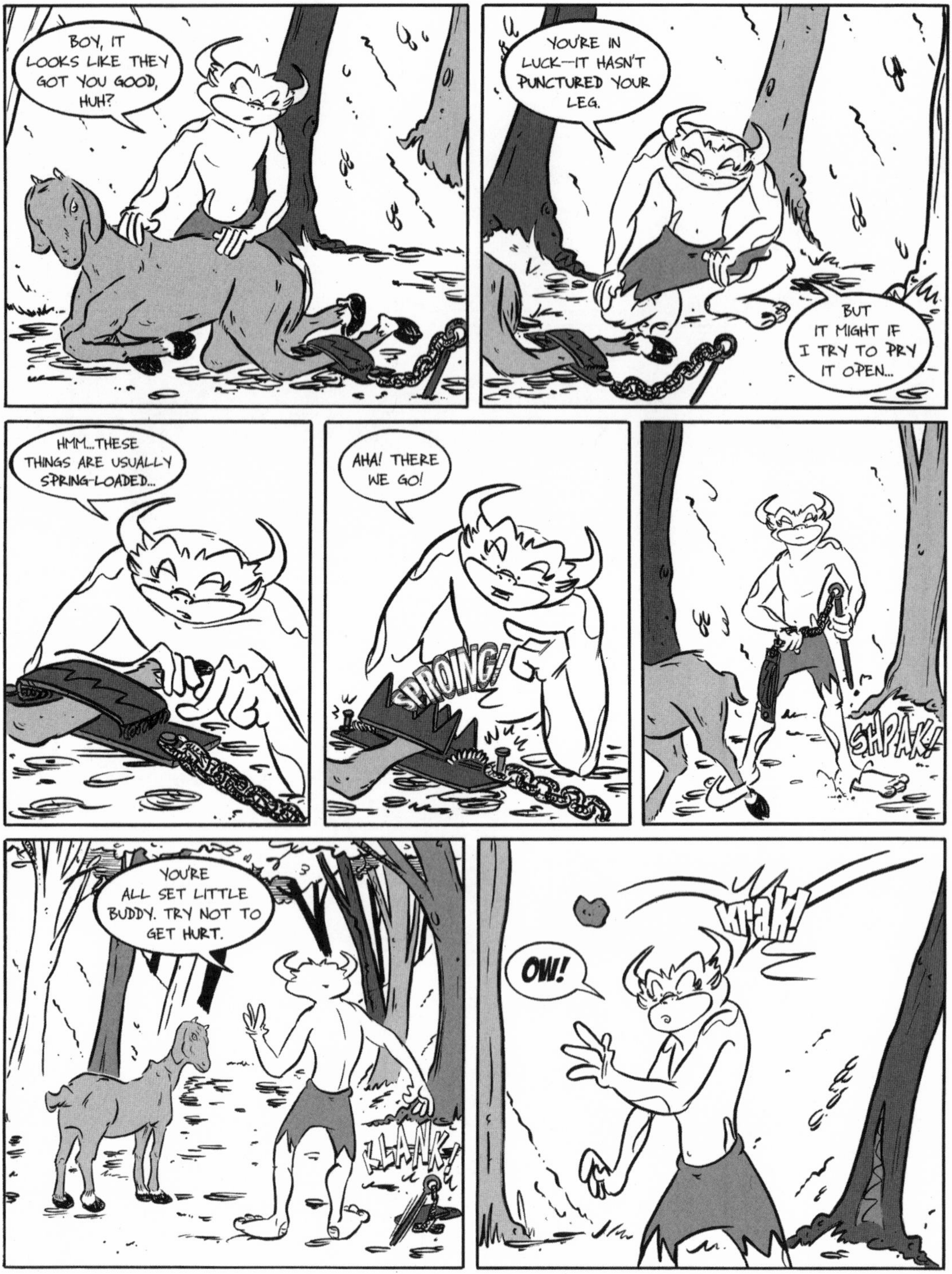
BOY, IT LOOKS LIKE THEY GOT YOU GOOD, HUH?
YOU'RE IN LUCK--IT HASN'T PUNCTURED YOUR LEG.
BUT IT MIGHT IF I TRY TO PRY IT OPEN...
HMM...THESE THINGS ARE USUALLY SPRING-LOADED...
AHA! THERE WE GO!
SPROING!
SHPAK!
YOU'RE ALL SET LITTLE BUDDY. TRY NOT TO GET HURT.
KLANK!
KRAK!
OW!

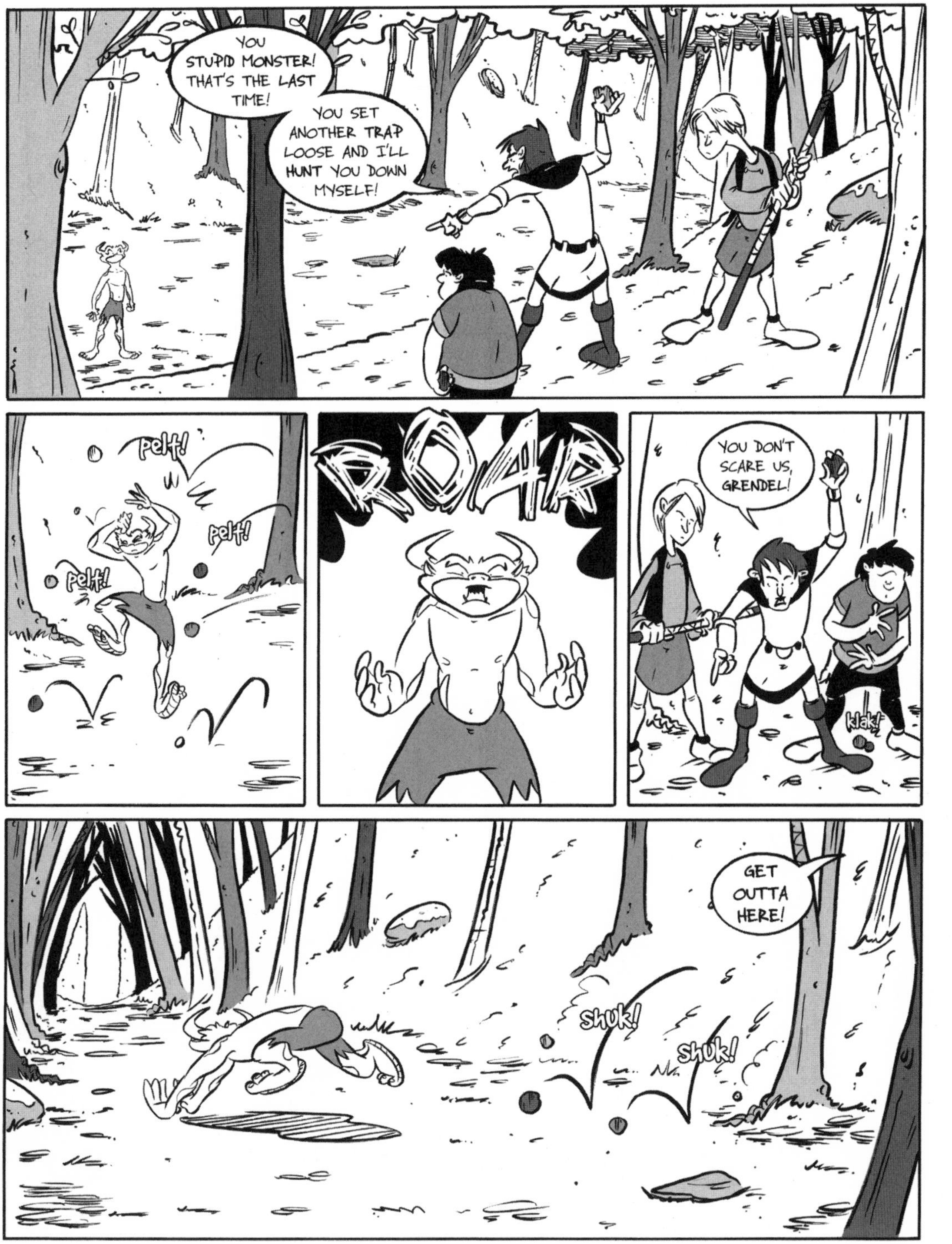
YOU STUPID MONSTER! THAT'S THE LAST TIME!
YOU SET ANOTHER TRAP LOOSE AND I'LL HUNT YOU DOWN MYSELF!
pelt!
pelt!
pelt!
ROAR
YOU DON'T SCARE US, GRENDEL!
klak!
GET OUTTA HERE!
SHUK!
SHUK!

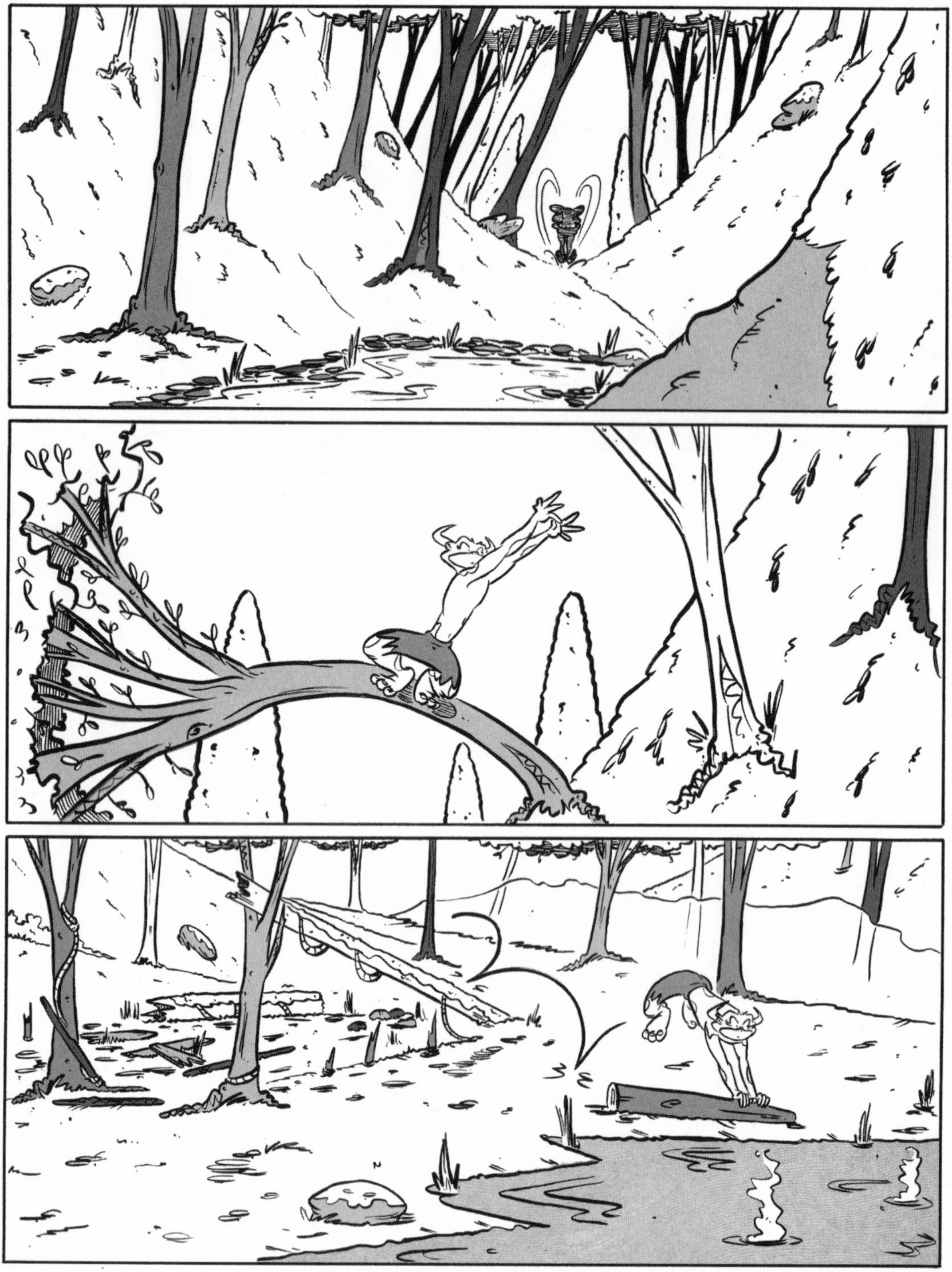

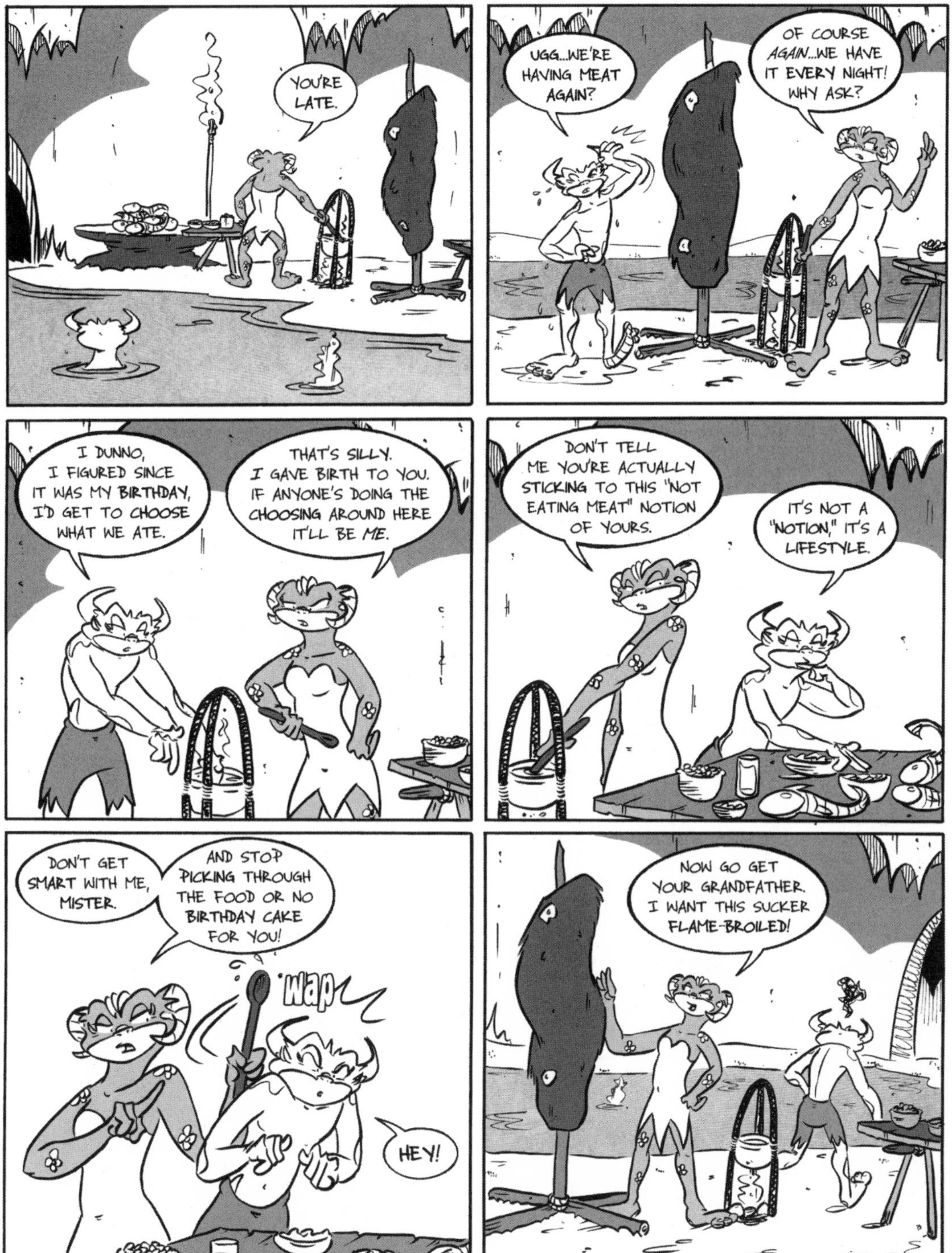
YOU'RE LATE.
UGG...WE'RE HAVING MEAT AGAIN?
OF COURSE AGAIN...WE HAVE IT EVERY NIGHT! WHY ASK?
I DUNNO, I FIGURED SINCE IT WAS MY BIRTHDAY, I'D GET TO CHOOSE WHAT WE ATE.
THAT'S SILLY. I GAVE BIRTH TO YOU. IF ANYONE'S DOING THE CHOOSING AROUND HERE IT'LL BE ME.
DON'T TELL ME YOU'RE ACTUALLY STICKING TO THIS "NOT EATING MEAT" NOTION OF YOURS.
IT'S NOT A "NOTION," IT'S A LIFESTYLE.
DON'T GET SMART WITH ME, MISTER.
AND STOP PICKING THROUGH THE FOOD OR NO BIRTHDAY CAKE FOR YOU!
WAP
HEY!
NOW GO GET YOUR GRANDFATHER. I WANT THIS SUCKER FLAME-BROILED!

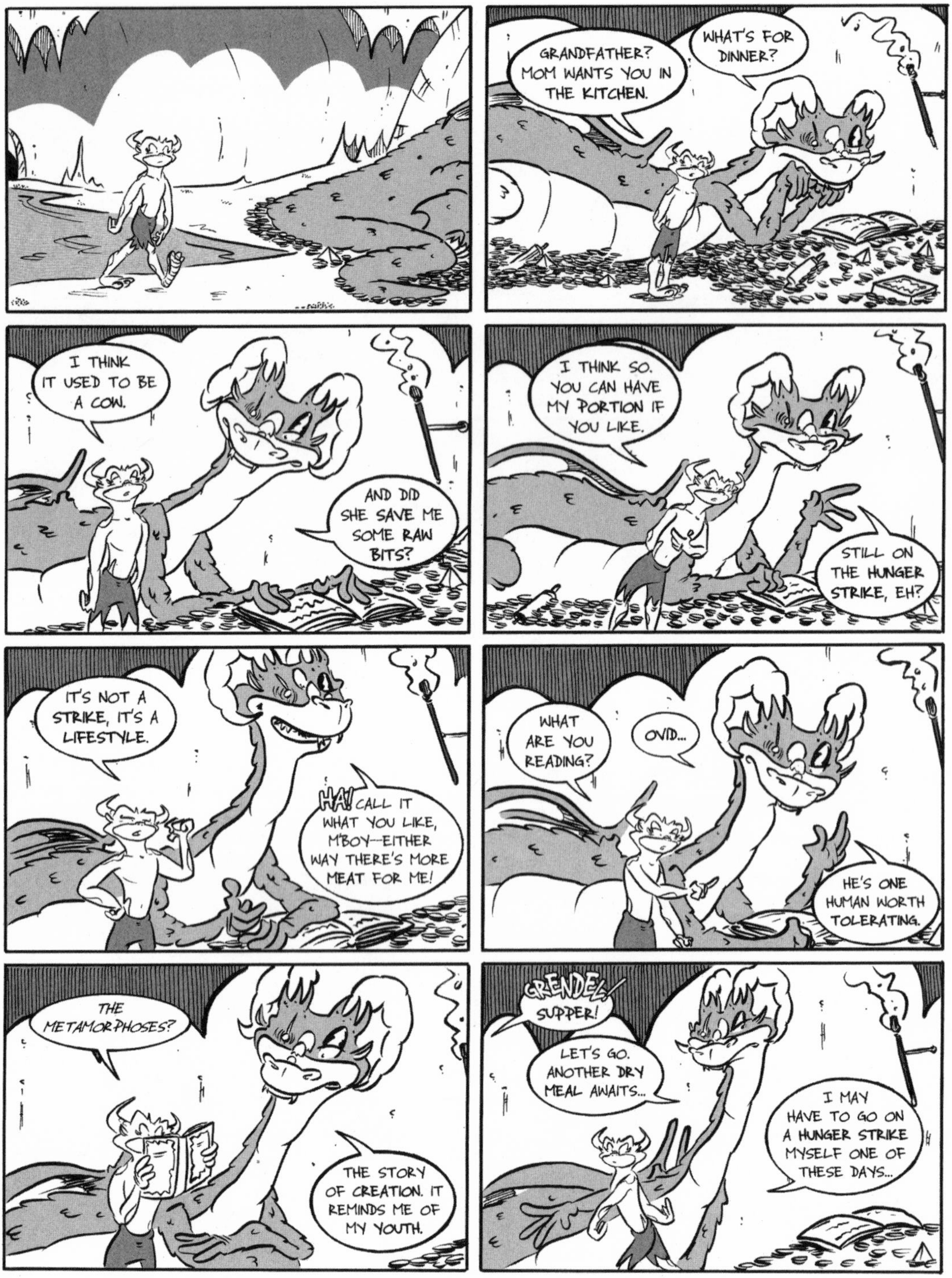
GRANDFATHER? MOM WANTS YOU IN THE KITCHEN.
WHAT'S FOR DINNER?
I THINK IT USED TO BE A COW.
AND DID SHE SAVE ME SOME RAW BITS?
I THINK SO. YOU CAN HAVE MY PORTION IF YOU LIKE.
STILL ON THE HUNGER STRIKE, EH?
IT'S NOT A STRIKE, IT'S A LIFESTYLE.
HA! CALL IT WHAT YOU LIKE, M'BOY--EITHER WAY THERE'S MORE MEAT FOR ME!
WHAT ARE YOU READING?
OVID...
HE'S ONE HUMAN WORTH TOLERATING.
THE METAMORPHOSES?
THE STORY OF CREATION. IT REMINDS ME OF MY YOUTH.
GRENDEL! SUPPER!
LET'S GO. ANOTHER DRY MEAL AWAITS...
I MAY HAVE TO GO ON A HUNGER STRIKE MYSELF ONE OF THESE DAYS...

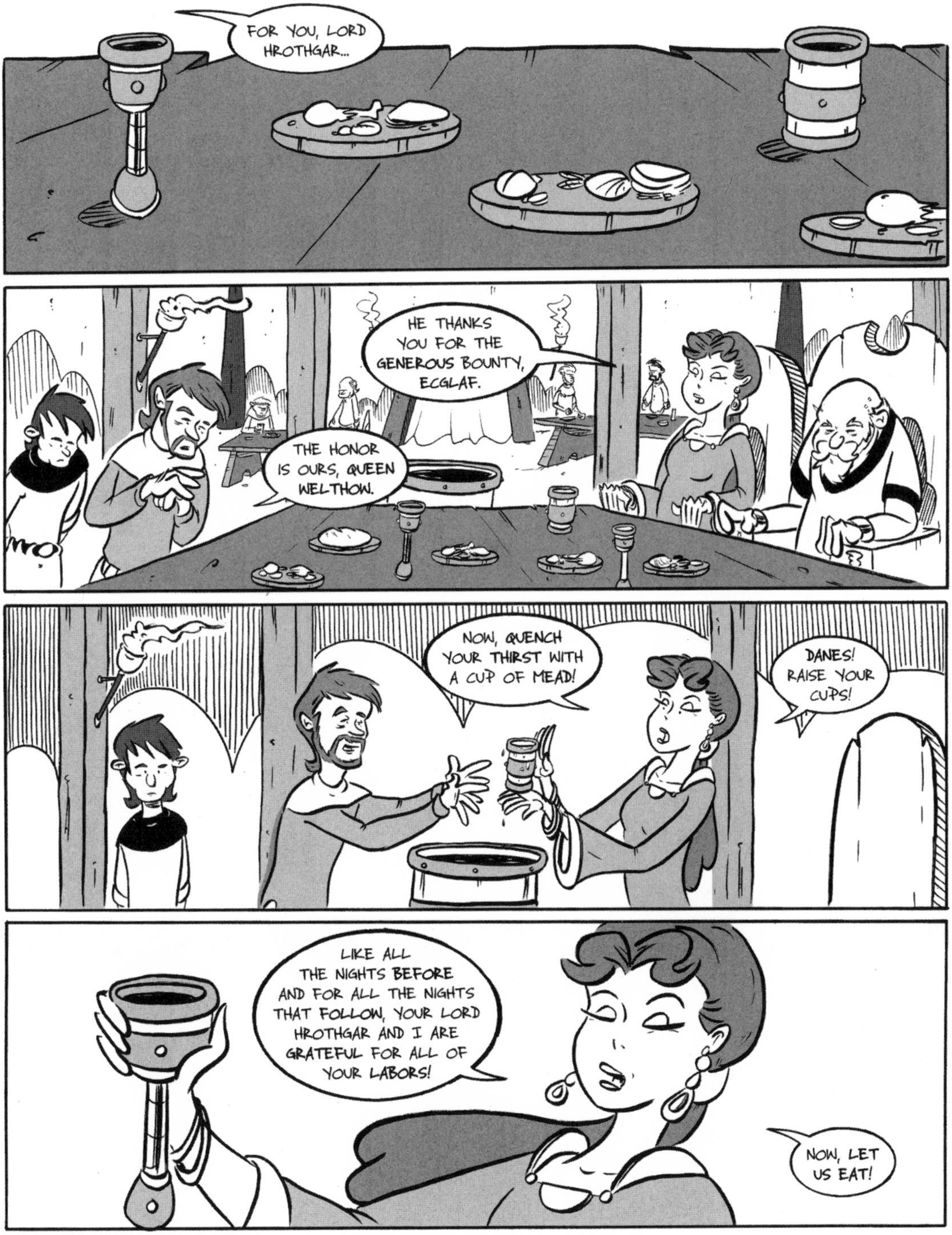
FOR YOU, LORD HROTHGAR...
HE THANKS YOU FOR THE GENEROUS BOUNTY, ECGLAF.
THE HONOR IS OURS, QUEEN WELTHOW.
NOW, QUENCH YOUR THIRST WITH A CUP OF MEAD!
DANES! RAISE YOUR CUPS!
LIKE ALL THE NIGHTS BEFORE AND FOR ALL THE NIGHTS THAT FOLLOW, YOUR LORD HROTHGAR AND I ARE GRATEFUL FOR ALL OF YOUR LABORS!
NOW, LET US EAT!

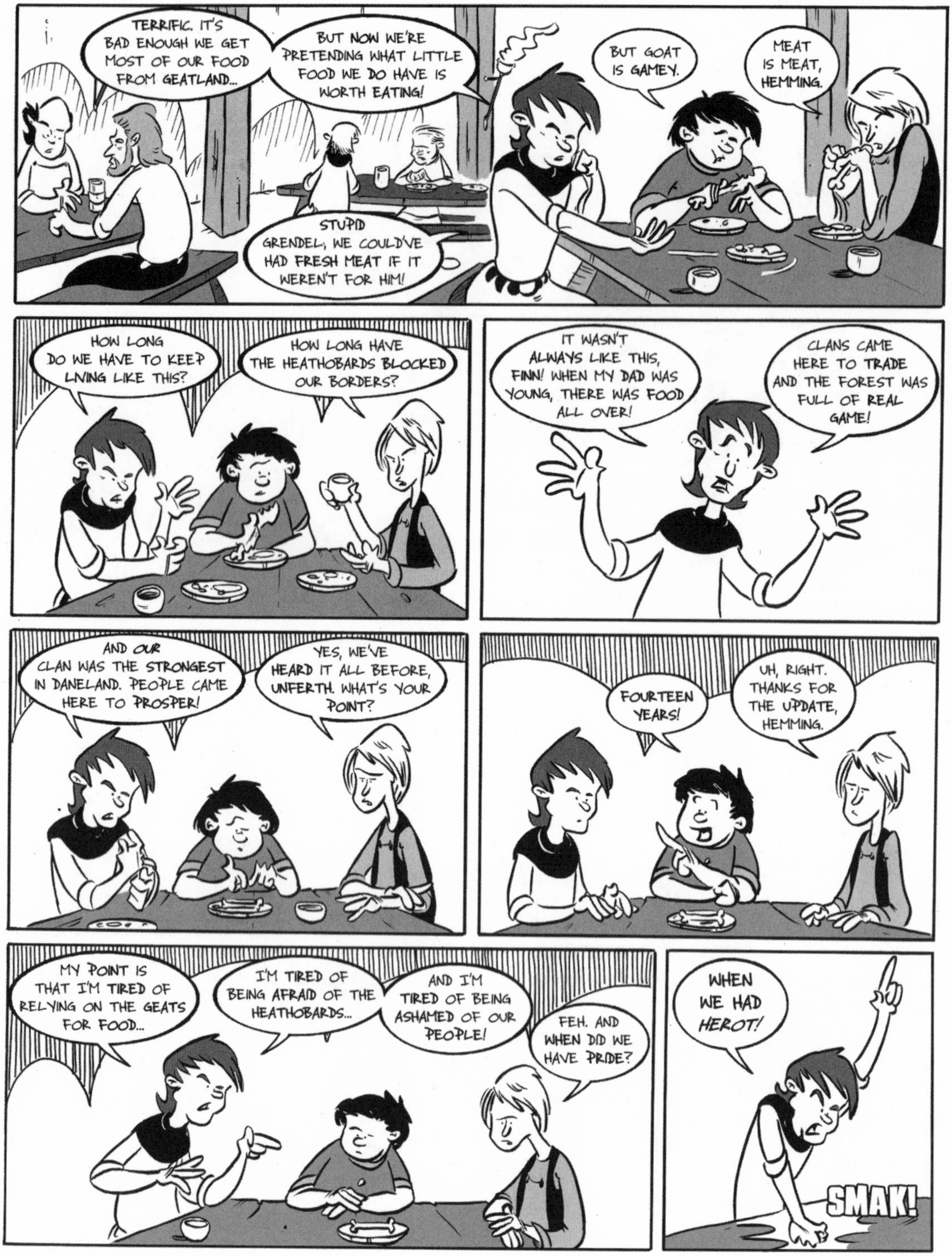
TERRIFIC. IT'S BAD ENOUGH WE GET MOST OF OUR FOOD FROM GEATLAND...
BUT NOW WE'RE PRETENDING WHAT LITTLE FOOD WE DO HAVE IS WORTH EATING!
STUPID GRENDEL, WE COULD'VE HAD FRESH MEAT IF IT WEREN'T FOR HIM!
BUT GOAT IS GAMEY.
MEAT IS MEAT, HEMMING.
HOW LONG DO WE HAVE TO KEEP LIVING LIKE THIS?
HOW LONG HAVE THE HEATHOBARDS BLOCKED OUR BORDERS?
IT WASN'T ALWAYS LIKE THIS, FINN! WHEN MY DAD WAS YOUNG, THERE WAS FOOD ALL OVER!
CLANS CAME HERE TO TRADE AND THE FOREST WAS FULL OF REAL GAME!
AND OUR CLAN WAS THE STRONGEST IN DANELAND. PEOPLE CAME HERE TO PROSPER!
YES, WE'VE HEARD IT ALL BEFORE, UNFERTH. WHAT'S YOUR POINT?
FOURTEEN YEARS!
UH, RIGHT. THANKS FOR THE UPDATE, HEMMING.
MY POINT IS THAT I'M TIRED OF RELYING ON THE GEATS FOR FOOD...
I'M TIRED OF BEING AFRAID OF THE HEATHOBARDS...
AND I'M TIRED OF BEING ASHAMED OF OUR PEOPLE!
FEH. AND WHEN DID WE HAVE PRIDE?
WHEN WE HAD HEROT!
SMAK!

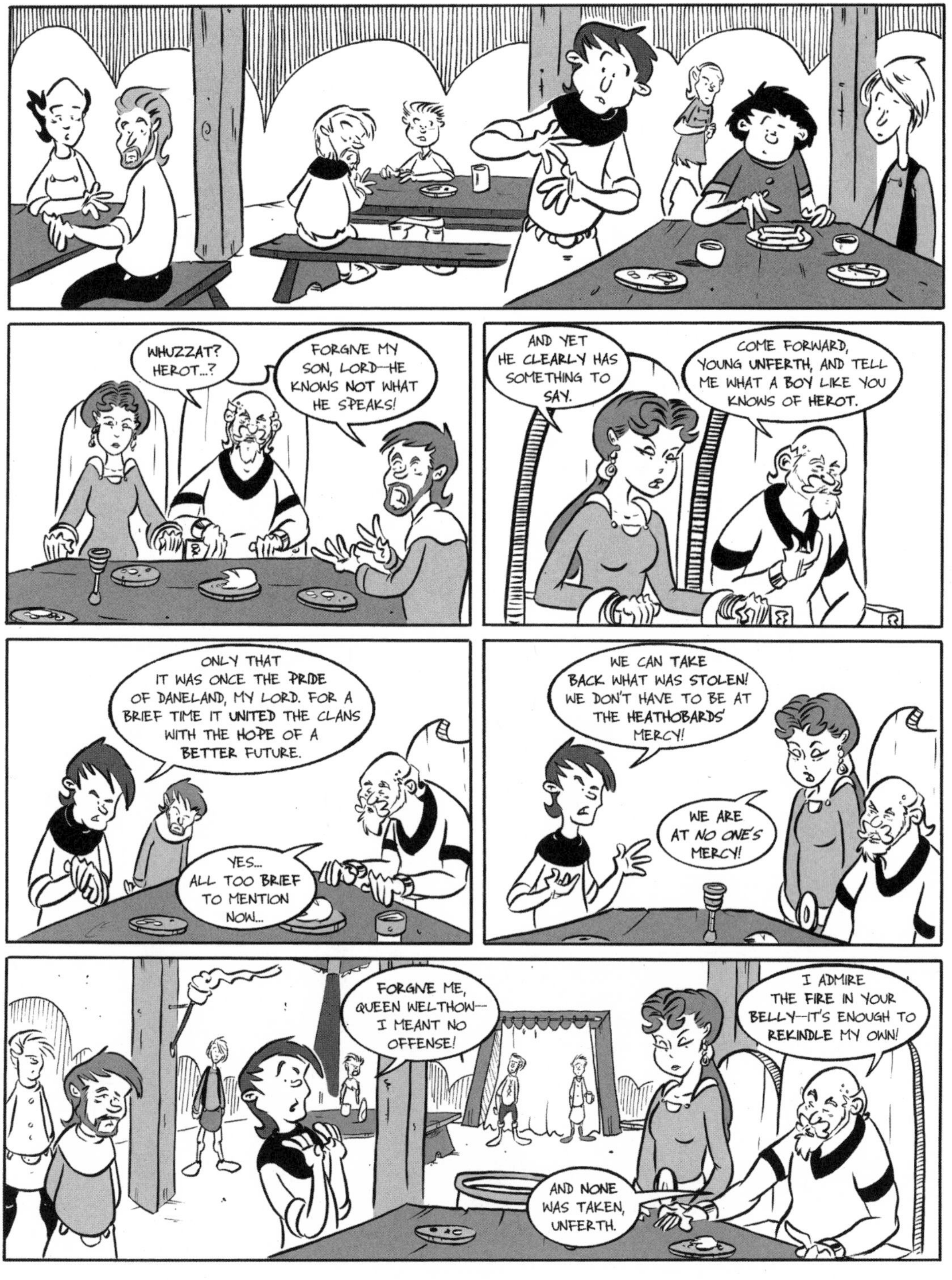
WHUZZAT? HEROT...?
FORGIVE MY SON, LORD--HE KNOWS NOT WHAT HE SPEAKS!
AND YET HE CLEARLY HAS SOMETHING TO SAY.
COME FORWARD, YOUNG UNFERTH, AND TELL ME WHAT A BOY LIKE YOU KNOWS OF HEROT.
ONLY THAT IT WAS ONCE THE PRIDE OF DANELAND, MY LORD. FOR A BRIEF TIME IT UNITED THE CLANS WITH THE HOPE OF A BETTER FUTURE.
YES... ALL TOO BRIEF TO MENTION NOW...
WE CAN TAKE BACK WHAT WAS STOLEN! WE DON'T HAVE TO BE AT THE HEATHOBARDS' MERCY!
WE ARE AT NO ONE'S MERCY!
FORGIVE ME, QUEEN WELTHOW-- I MEANT NO OFFENSE!
I ADMIRE THE FIRE IN YOUR BELLY--IT'S ENOUGH TO REKINDLE MY OWN!
AND NONE WAS TAKEN, UNFERTH.

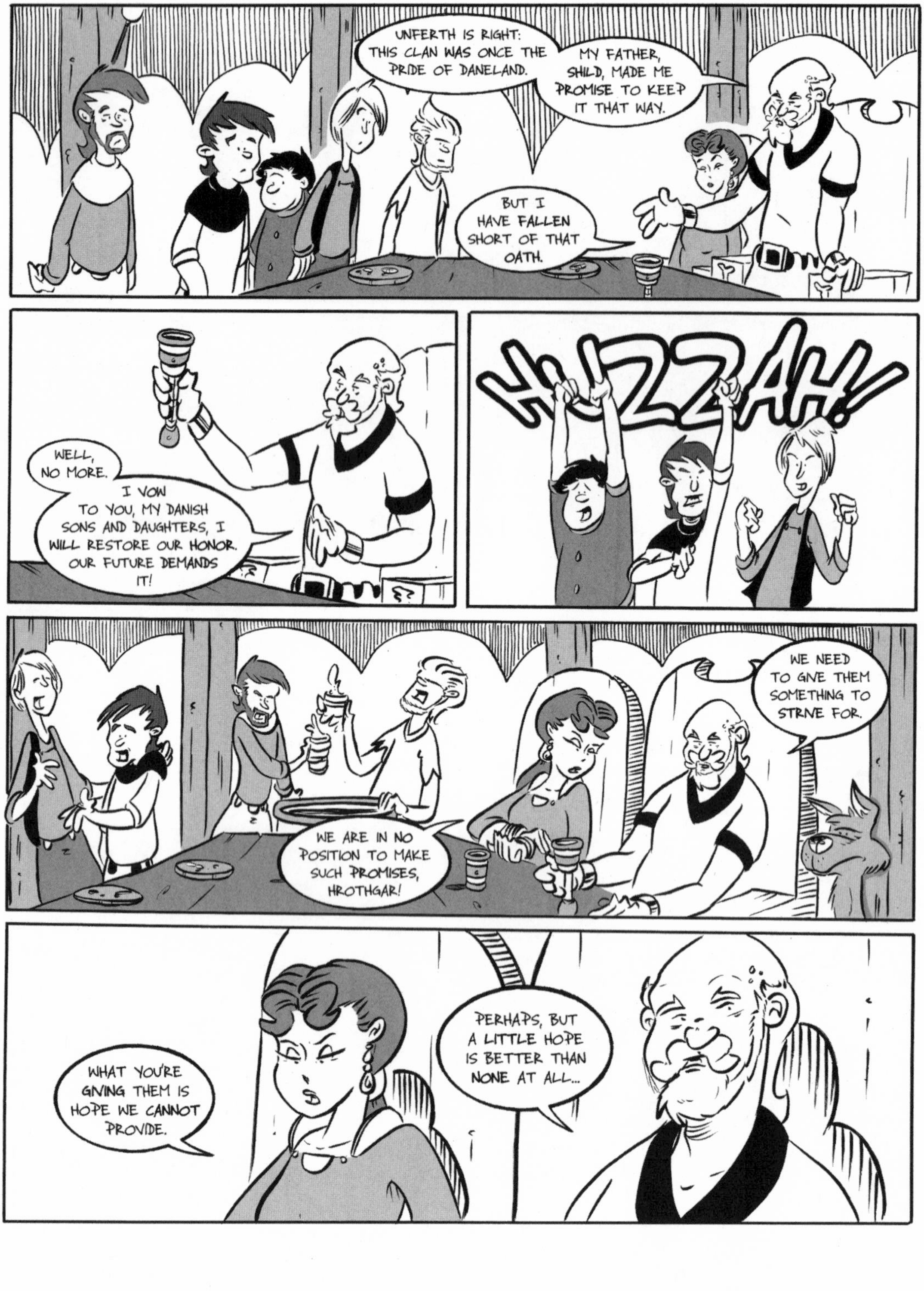
UNFERTH IS RIGHT: THIS CLAN WAS ONCE THE PRIDE OF DANELAND.
MY FATHER, SHILD, MADE ME PROMISE TO KEEP IT THAT WAY.
BUT I HAVE FALLEN SHORT OF THAT OATH.
WELL, NO MORE.
I VOW TO YOU, MY DANISH SONS AND DAUGHTERS, I WILL RESTORE OUR HONOR. OUR FUTURE DEMANDS IT!
HUZZAH!
WE ARE IN NO POSITION TO MAKE SUCH PROMISES, HROTHGAR!
WE NEED TO GIVE THEM SOMETHING TO STRIVE FOR.
WHAT YOU'RE GIVING THEM IS HOPE WE CANNOT PROVIDE.
PERHAPS, BUT A LITTLE HOPE IS BETTER THAN NONE AT ALL...

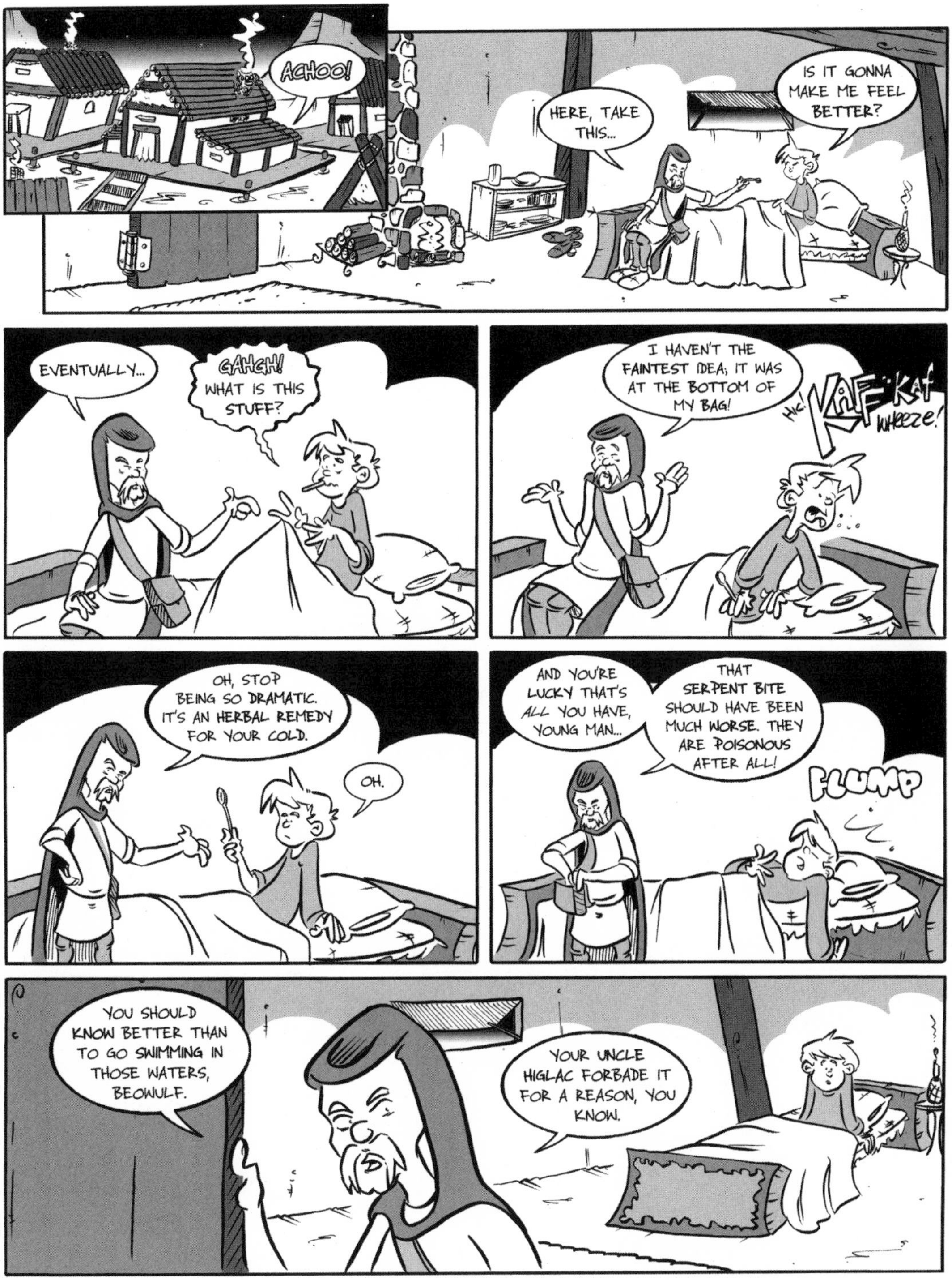
ACHOO!
HERE, TAKE THIS...
IS IT GONNA MAKE ME FEEL BETTER?
EVENTUALLY...
GAHGH! WHAT IS THIS STUFF?
I HAVEN'T THE FAINTEST IDEA; IT WAS AT THE BOTTOM OF MY BAG!
HIC! KAF KAF WHEEZE!
OH, STOP BEING SO DRAMATIC. IT'S AN HERBAL REMEDY FOR YOUR COLD.
OH.
AND YOU'RE LUCKY THAT'S ALL YOU HAVE, YOUNG MAN...
THAT SERPENT BITE SHOULD HAVE BEEN MUCH WORSE. THEY ARE POISONOUS AFTER ALL!
FLUMP
YOU SHOULD KNOW BETTER THAN TO GO SWIMMING IN THOSE WATERS, BEOWULF.
YOUR UNCLE HIGLAC FORBADE IT FOR A REASON, YOU KNOW.

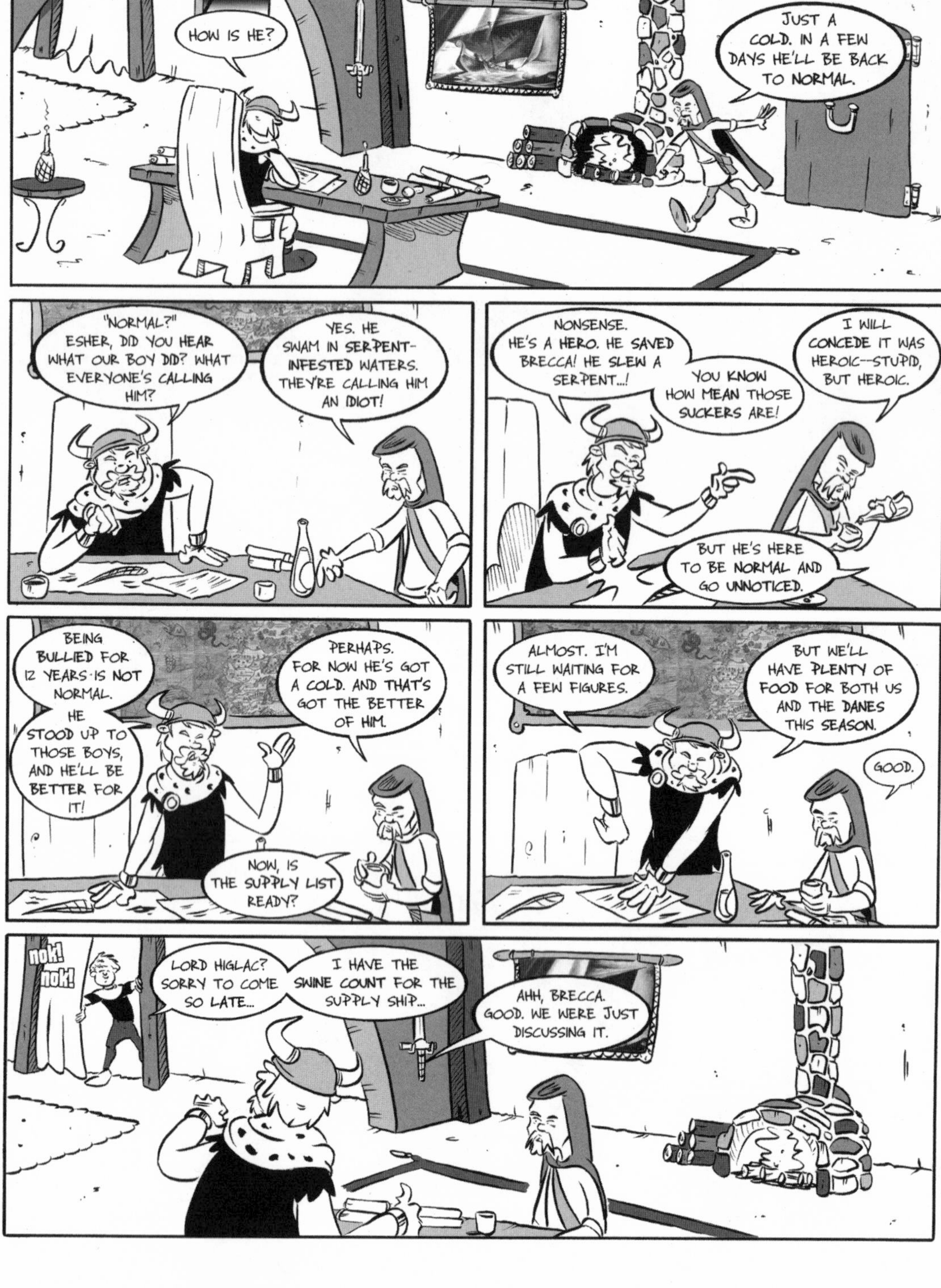
HOW IS HE?
JUST A COLD. IN A FEW DAYS HE'LL BE BACK TO NORMAL.
"NORMAL?" ESHER, DID YOU HEAR WHAT OUR BOY DID? WHAT EVERYONE'S CALLING HIM?
YES. HE SWAM IN SERPENT-INFESTED WATERS. THEY'RE CALLING HIM AN IDIOT!
NONSENSE. HE'S A HERO. HE SAVED BRECCA! HE SLEW A SERPENT...!
YOU KNOW HOW MEAN THOSE SUCKERS ARE!
I WILL CONCEDE IT WAS HEROIC--STUPID, BUT HEROIC.
BUT HE'S HERE TO BE NORMAL AND GO UNNOTICED.
BEING BULLIED FOR 12 YEARS IS NOT NORMAL.
HE STOOD UP TO THOSE BOYS, AND HE'LL BE BETTER FOR IT!
PERHAPS. FOR NOW HE'S GOT A COLD. AND THAT'S GOT THE BETTER OF HIM.
NOW, IS THE SUPPLY LIST READY?
ALMOST. I'M STILL WAITING FOR A FEW FIGURES.
BUT WE'LL HAVE PLENTY OF FOOD FOR BOTH US AND THE DANES THIS SEASON.
GOOD.
nok! nok!
LORD HIGLAC? SORRY TO COME SO LATE...
I HAVE THE SWINE COUNT FOR THE SUPPLY SHIP...
AHH, BRECCA. GOOD. WE WERE JUST DISCUSSING IT.

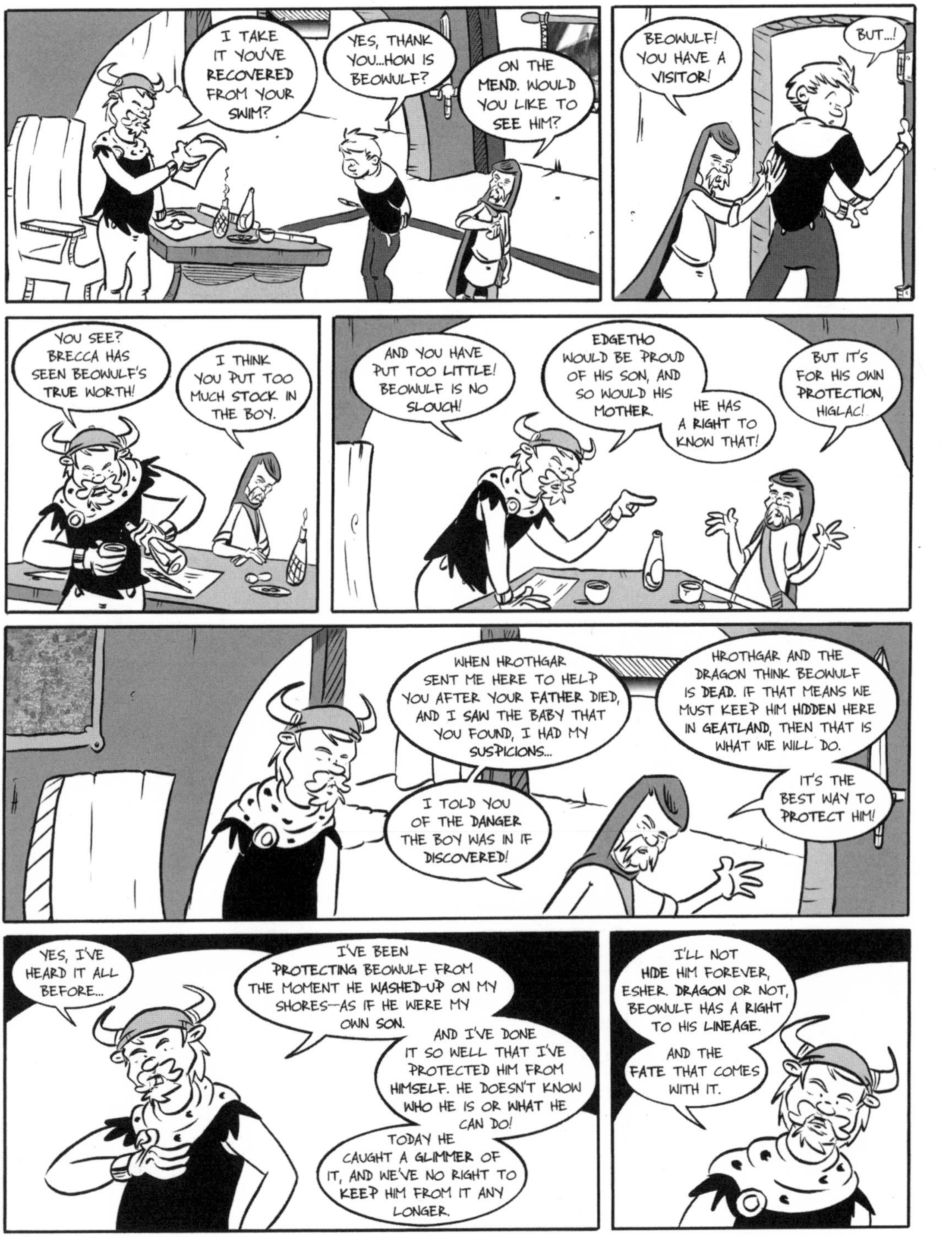
I TAKE IT YOU'VE RECOVERED FROM YOUR SWIM?
YES, THANK YOU...HOW IS BEOWULF?
ON THE MEND. WOULD YOU LIKE TO SEE HIM?
BEOWULF! YOU HAVE A VISITOR!
BUT...!
YOU SEE? BRECCA HAS SEEN BEOWULF'S TRUE WORTH!
I THINK YOU PUT TOO MUCH STOCK IN THE BOY.
AND YOU HAVE PUT TOO LITTLE! BEOWULF IS NO SLOUCH!
EDGETHO WOULD BE PROUD OF HIS SON, AND SO WOULD HIS MOTHER.
HE HAS A RIGHT TO KNOW THAT!
BUT IT'S FOR HIS OWN PROTECTION, HIGLAC!
WHEN HROTHGAR SENT ME HERE TO HELP YOU AFTER YOUR FATHER DIED, AND I SAW THE BABY THAT YOU FOUND, I HAD MY SUSPICIONS...
I TOLD YOU OF THE DANGER THE BOY WAS IN IF DISCOVERED!
HROTHGAR AND THE DRAGON THINK BEOWULF IS DEAD. IF THAT MEANS WE MUST KEEP HIM HIDDEN HERE IN GEATLAND, THEN THAT IS WHAT WE WILL DO.
IT'S THE BEST WAY TO PROTECT HIM!
YES, I'VE HEARD IT ALL BEFORE...
I'VE BEEN PROTECTING BEOWULF FROM THE MOMENT HE WASHED-UP ON MY SHORES—AS IF HE WERE MY OWN SON.
AND I'VE DONE IT SO WELL THAT I'VE PROTECTED HIM FROM HIMSELF. HE DOESN'T KNOW WHO HE IS OR WHAT HE CAN DO!
TODAY HE CAUGHT A GLIMMER OF IT, AND WE'VE NO RIGHT TO KEEP HIM FROM IT ANY LONGER.
I'LL NOT HIDE HIM FOREVER, ESHER. DRAGON OR NOT, BEOWULF HAS A RIGHT TO HIS LINEAGE.
AND THE FATE THAT COMES WITH IT.

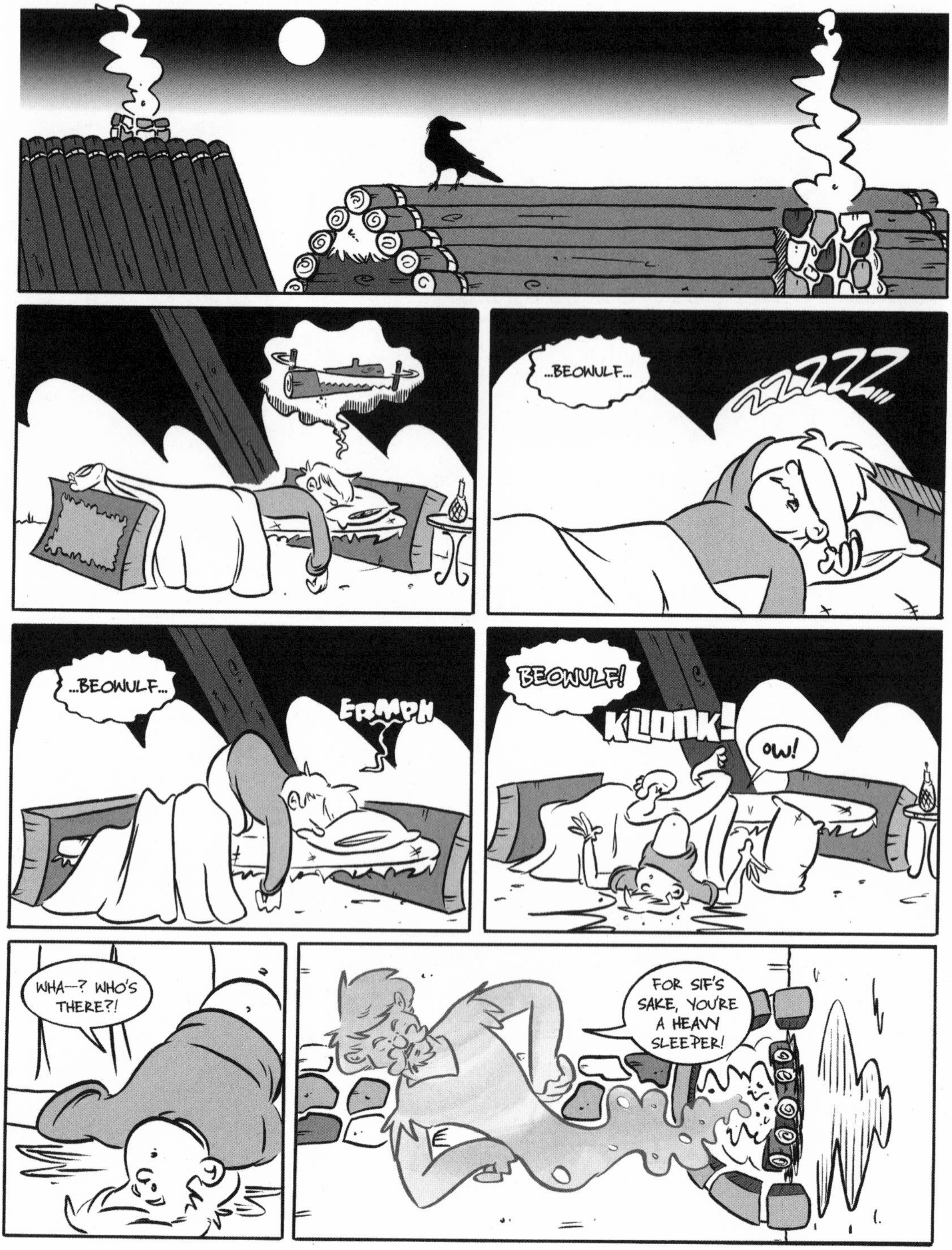
...BEOWULF...
ZZZZZZ
...BEOWULF...
ERMPH
BEOWULF!
KLONK!
OW!
WHA--? WHO'S THERE?!
FOR SIF'S SAKE, YOU'RE A HEAVY SLEEPER!

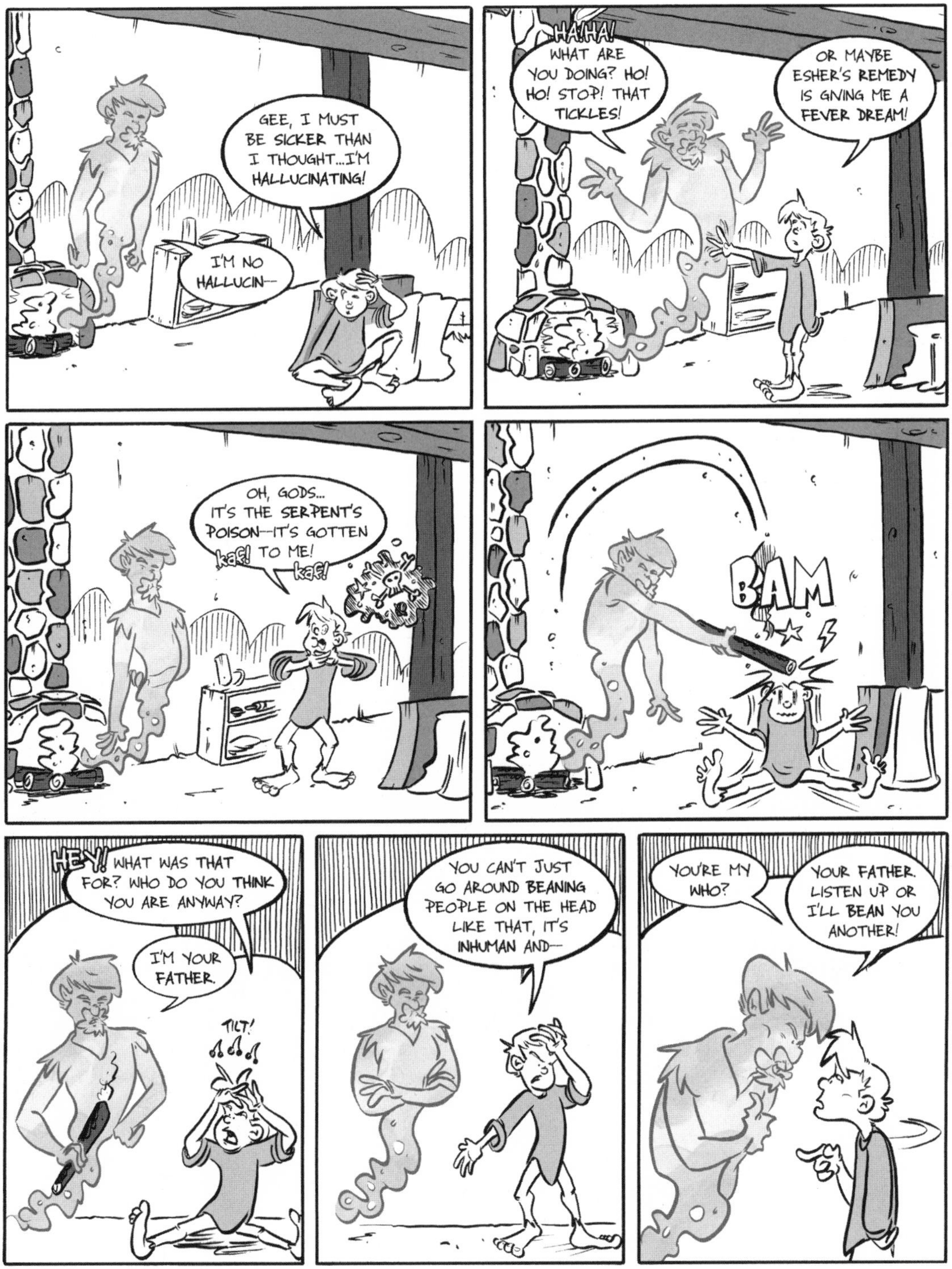
GEE, I MUST BE SICKER THAN I THOUGHT...I'M HALLUCINATING!
I'M NO HALLUCIN---
HA!HA!
WHAT ARE YOU DOING? HO! HO! STOP! THAT TICKLES!
OR MAYBE ESHER'S REMEDY IS GIVING ME A FEVER DREAM!
OH, GODS... IT'S THE SERPENT'S POISON---IT'S GOTTEN TO ME!
kaf!
kaf!
BAM
HEY!
WHAT WAS THAT FOR? WHO DO YOU THINK YOU ARE ANYWAY?
I'M YOUR FATHER.
TILT!
YOU CAN'T JUST GO AROUND BEANING PEOPLE ON THE HEAD LIKE THAT, IT'S INHUMAN AND---
YOU'RE MY WHO?
YOUR FATHER. LISTEN UP OR I'LL BEAN YOU ANOTHER!

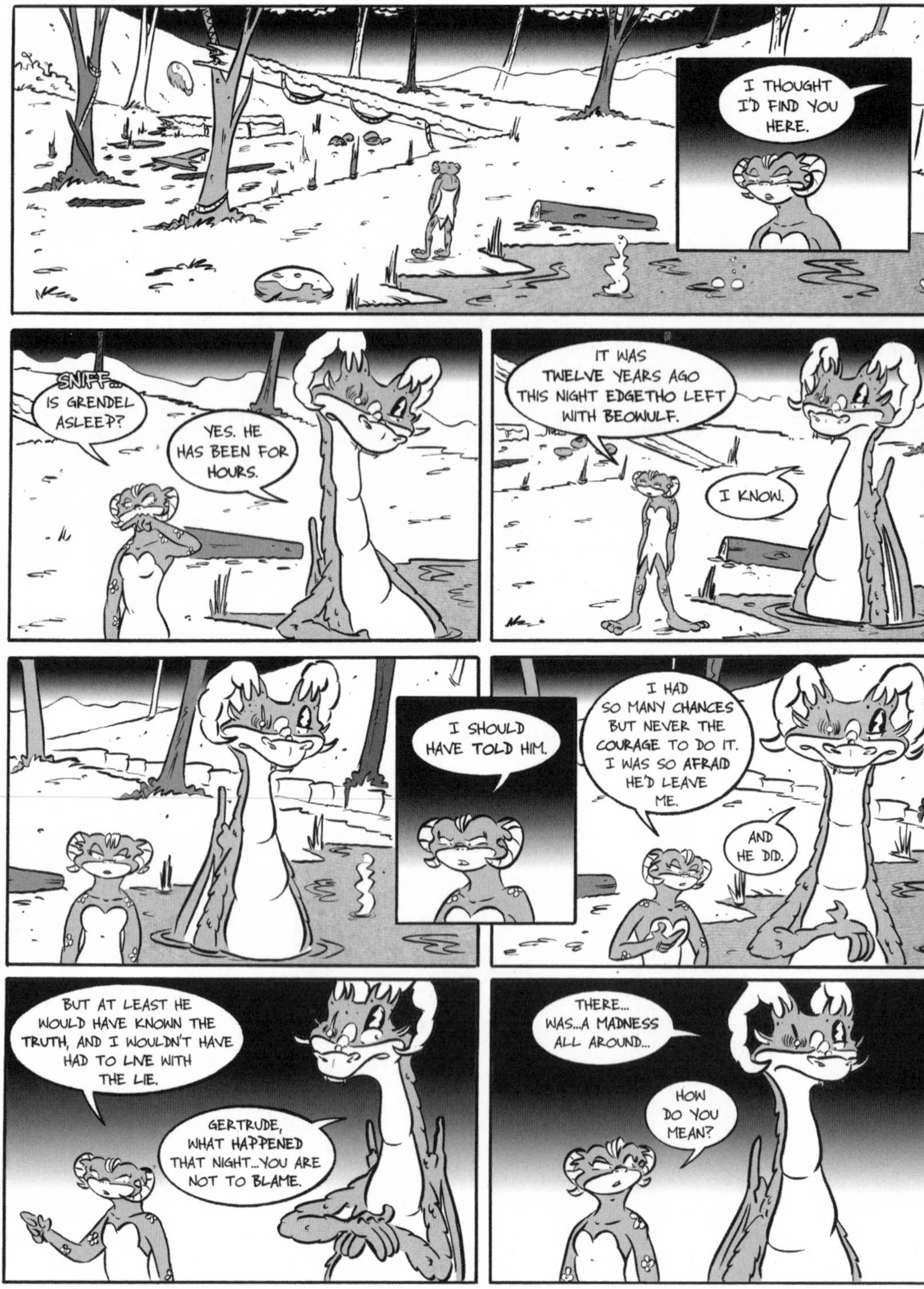
I THOUGHT I'D FIND YOU HERE.
SNIFF... IS GRENDEL ASLEEP?
YES. HE HAS BEEN FOR HOURS.
IT WAS TWELVE YEARS AGO THIS NIGHT EDGETHO LEFT WITH BEOWULF.
I KNOW.
I SHOULD HAVE TOLD HIM.
I HAD SO MANY CHANCES BUT NEVER THE COURAGE TO DO IT. I WAS SO AFRAID HE'D LEAVE ME.
AND HE DID.
BUT AT LEAST HE WOULD HAVE KNOWN THE TRUTH, AND I WOULDN'T HAVE HAD TO LIVE WITH THE LIE.
GERTRUDE, WHAT HAPPENED THAT NIGHT...YOU ARE NOT TO BLAME.
THERE... WAS...A MADNESS ALL AROUND...
HOW DO YOU MEAN?

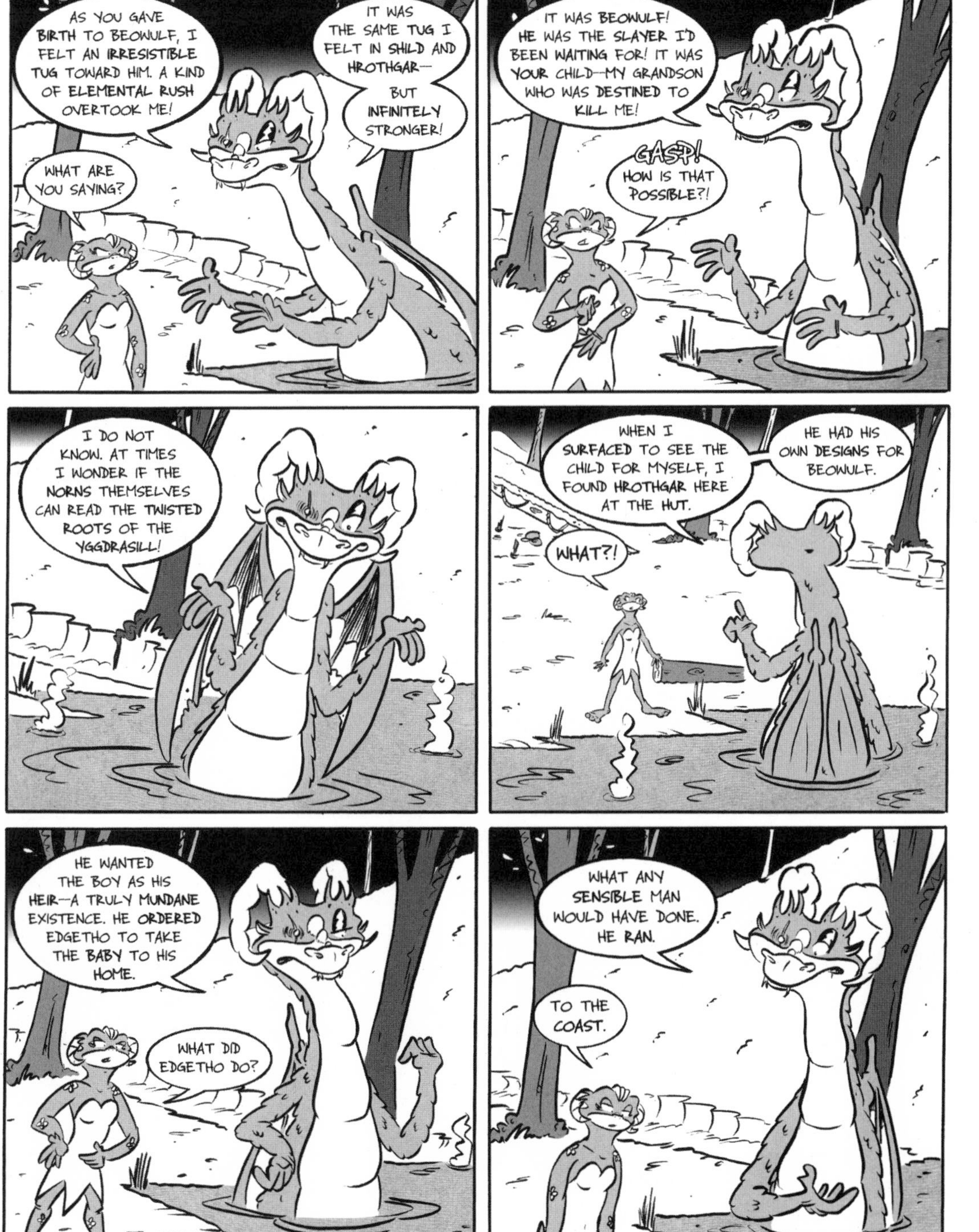
AS YOU GAVE BIRTH TO BEOWULF, I FELT AN IRRESISTIBLE TUG TOWARD HIM. A KIND OF ELEMENTAL RUSH OVERTOOK ME!
IT WAS THE SAME TUG I FELT IN SHILD AND HROTHGAR--
BUT INFINITELY STRONGER!
WHAT ARE YOU SAYING?
IT WAS BEOWULF! HE WAS THE SLAYER I'D BEEN WAITING FOR! IT WAS YOUR CHILD--MY GRANDSON WHO WAS DESTINED TO KILL ME!
GASP!
HOW IS THAT POSSIBLE?!
I DO NOT KNOW. AT TIMES I WONDER IF THE NORNS THEMSELVES CAN READ THE TWISTED ROOTS OF THE YGGDRASILL!
WHEN I SURFACED TO SEE THE CHILD FOR MYSELF, I FOUND HROTHGAR HERE AT THE HUT.
HE HAD HIS OWN DESIGNS FOR BEOWULF.
WHAT?!
HE WANTED THE BOY AS HIS HEIR--A TRULY MUNDANE EXISTENCE. HE ORDERED EDGETHO TO TAKE THE BABY TO HIS HOME.
WHAT DID EDGETHO DO?
WHAT ANY SENSIBLE MAN WOULD HAVE DONE. HE RAN.
TO THE COAST.

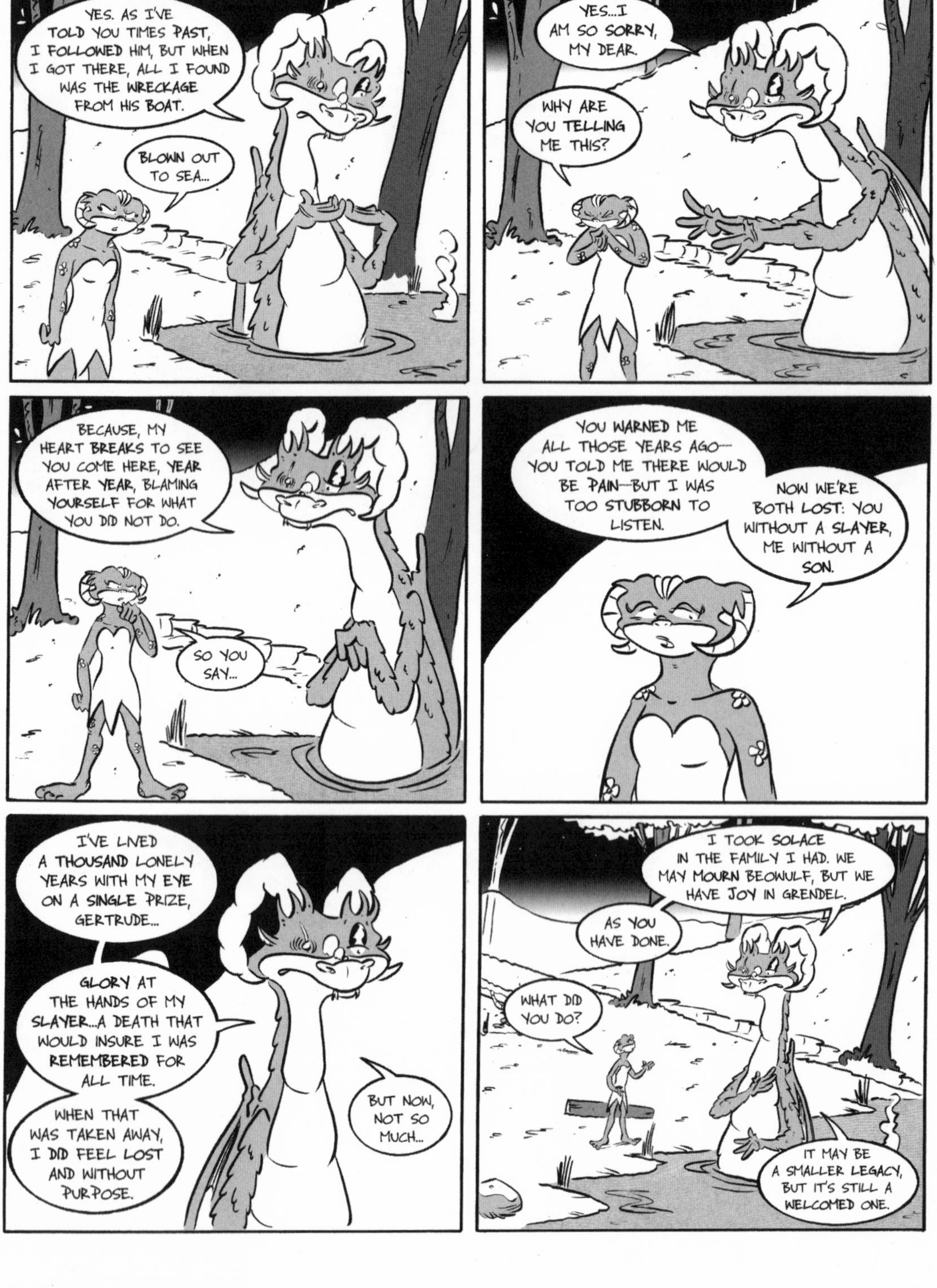
YES. AS I'VE TOLD YOU TIMES PAST, I FOLLOWED HIM, BUT WHEN I GOT THERE, ALL I FOUND WAS THE WRECKAGE FROM HIS BOAT.
BLOWN OUT TO SEA...
YES...I AM SO SORRY, MY DEAR.
WHY ARE YOU TELLING ME THIS?
BECAUSE, MY HEART BREAKS TO SEE YOU COME HERE, YEAR AFTER YEAR, BLAMING YOURSELF FOR WHAT YOU DID NOT DO.
SO YOU SAY...
YOU WARNED ME ALL THOSE YEARS AGO—YOU TOLD ME THERE WOULD BE PAIN—BUT I WAS TOO STUBBORN TO LISTEN.
NOW WE'RE BOTH LOST: YOU WITHOUT A SLAYER, ME WITHOUT A SON.
I'VE LIVED A THOUSAND LONELY YEARS WITH MY EYE ON A SINGLE PRIZE, GERTRUDE...
GLORY AT THE HANDS OF MY SLAYER...A DEATH THAT WOULD INSURE I WAS REMEMBERED FOR ALL TIME.
WHEN THAT WAS TAKEN AWAY, I DID FEEL LOST AND WITHOUT PURPOSE.
BUT NOW, NOT SO MUCH...
I TOOK SOLACE IN THE FAMILY I HAD. WE MAY MOURN BEOWULF, BUT WE HAVE JOY IN GRENDEL.
AS YOU HAVE DONE.
WHAT DID YOU DO?
IT MAY BE A SMALLER LEGACY, BUT IT'S STILL A WELCOMED ONE.

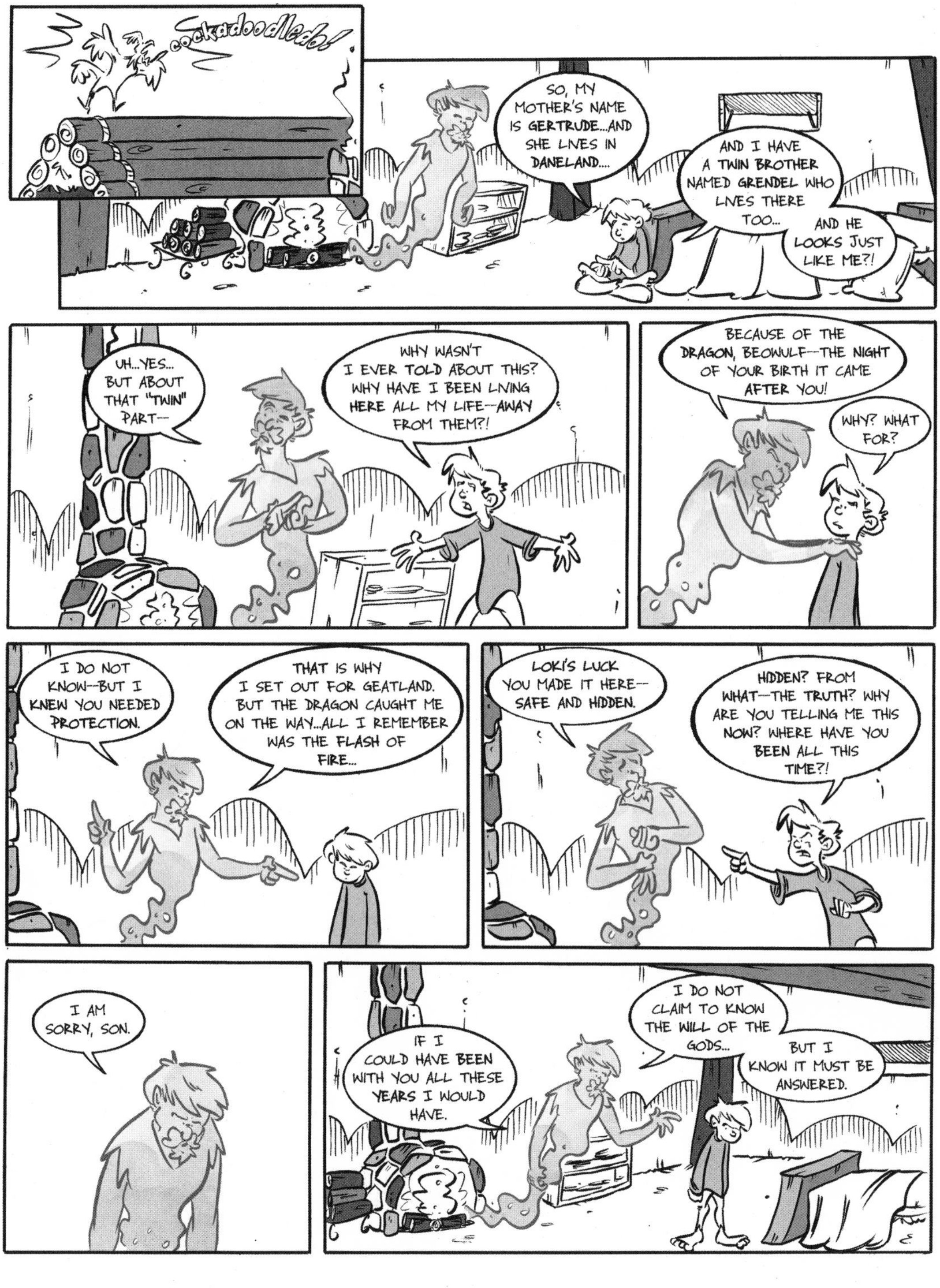
cockadoodledoo!
SO, MY MOTHER'S NAME IS GERTRUDE...AND SHE LIVES IN DANELAND....
AND I HAVE A TWIN BROTHER NAMED GRENDEL WHO LIVES THERE TOO...
AND HE LOOKS JUST LIKE ME?!
UH...YES... BUT ABOUT THAT "TWIN" PART--
WHY WASN'T I EVER TOLD ABOUT THIS? WHY HAVE I BEEN LIVING HERE ALL MY LIFE--AWAY FROM THEM?!
BECAUSE OF THE DRAGON, BEOWULF--THE NIGHT OF YOUR BIRTH IT CAME AFTER YOU!
WHY? WHAT FOR?
I DO NOT KNOW--BUT I KNEW YOU NEEDED PROTECTION.
THAT IS WHY I SET OUT FOR GEATLAND. BUT THE DRAGON CAUGHT ME ON THE WAY...ALL I REMEMBER WAS THE FLASH OF FIRE...
LOKI'S LUCK YOU MADE IT HERE--SAFE AND HIDDEN.
HIDDEN? FROM WHAT--THE TRUTH? WHY ARE YOU TELLING ME THIS NOW? WHERE HAVE YOU BEEN ALL THIS TIME?!
I AM SORRY, SON.
IF I COULD HAVE BEEN WITH YOU ALL THESE YEARS I WOULD HAVE.
I DO NOT CLAIM TO KNOW THE WILL OF THE GODS...
BUT I KNOW IT MUST BE ANSWERED.

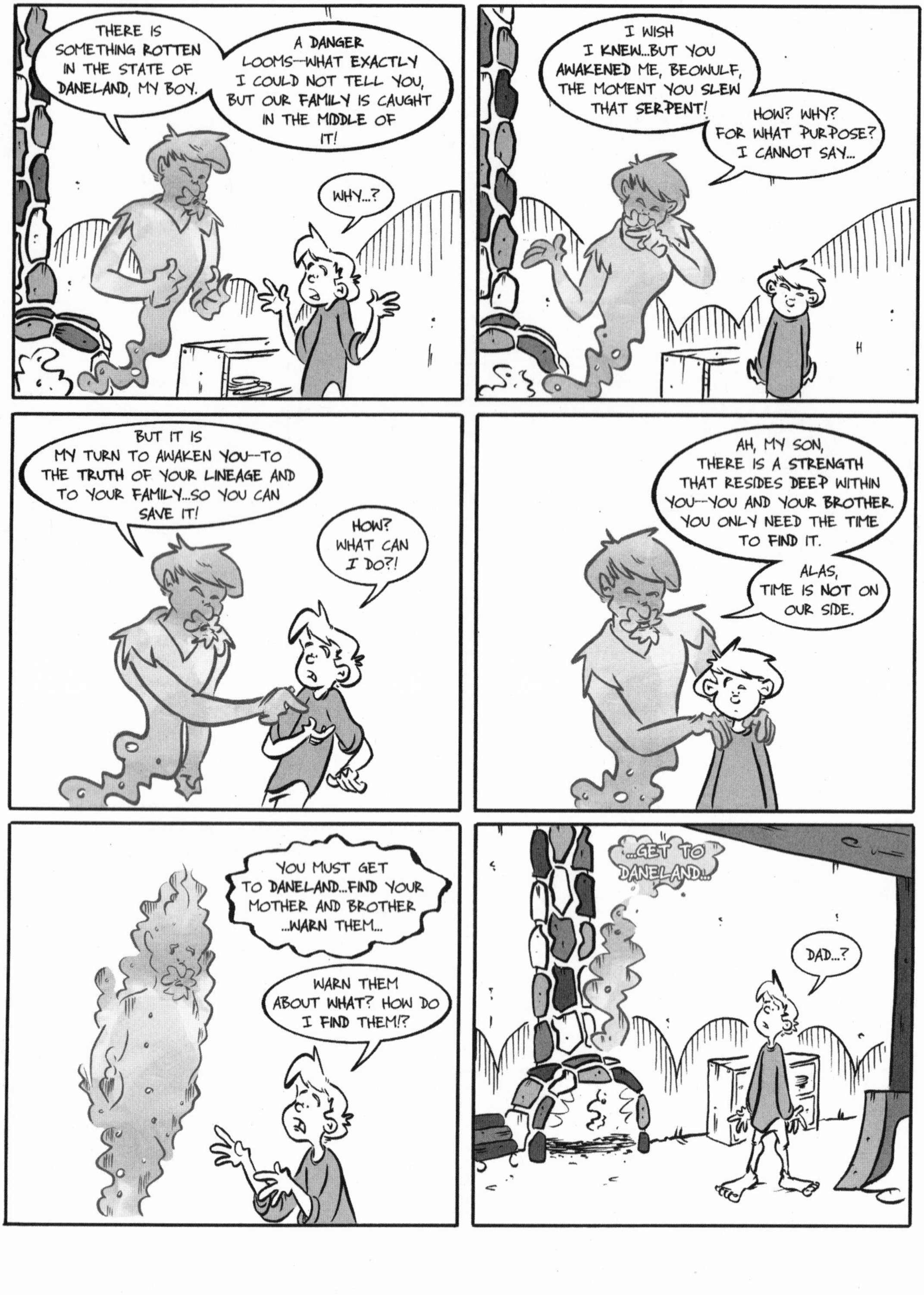
THERE IS SOMETHING ROTTEN IN THE STATE OF DANELAND, MY BOY.
A DANGER LOOMS--WHAT EXACTLY I COULD NOT TELL YOU, BUT OUR FAMILY IS CAUGHT IN THE MIDDLE OF IT!
WHY...?
I WISH I KNEW...BUT YOU AWAKENED ME, BEOWULF, THE MOMENT YOU SLEW THAT SERPENT!
HOW? WHY? FOR WHAT PURPOSE? I CANNOT SAY...
BUT IT IS MY TURN TO AWAKEN YOU--TO THE TRUTH OF YOUR LINEAGE AND TO YOUR FAMILY...SO YOU CAN SAVE IT!
HOW? WHAT CAN I DO?!
AH, MY SON, THERE IS A STRENGTH THAT RESIDES DEEP WITHIN YOU--YOU AND YOUR BROTHER. YOU ONLY NEED THE TIME TO FIND IT.
ALAS, TIME IS NOT ON OUR SIDE.
YOU MUST GET TO DANELAND...FIND YOUR MOTHER AND BROTHER ...WARN THEM...
WARN THEM ABOUT WHAT? HOW DO I FIND THEM!?
...GET TO DANELAND...
DAD...?

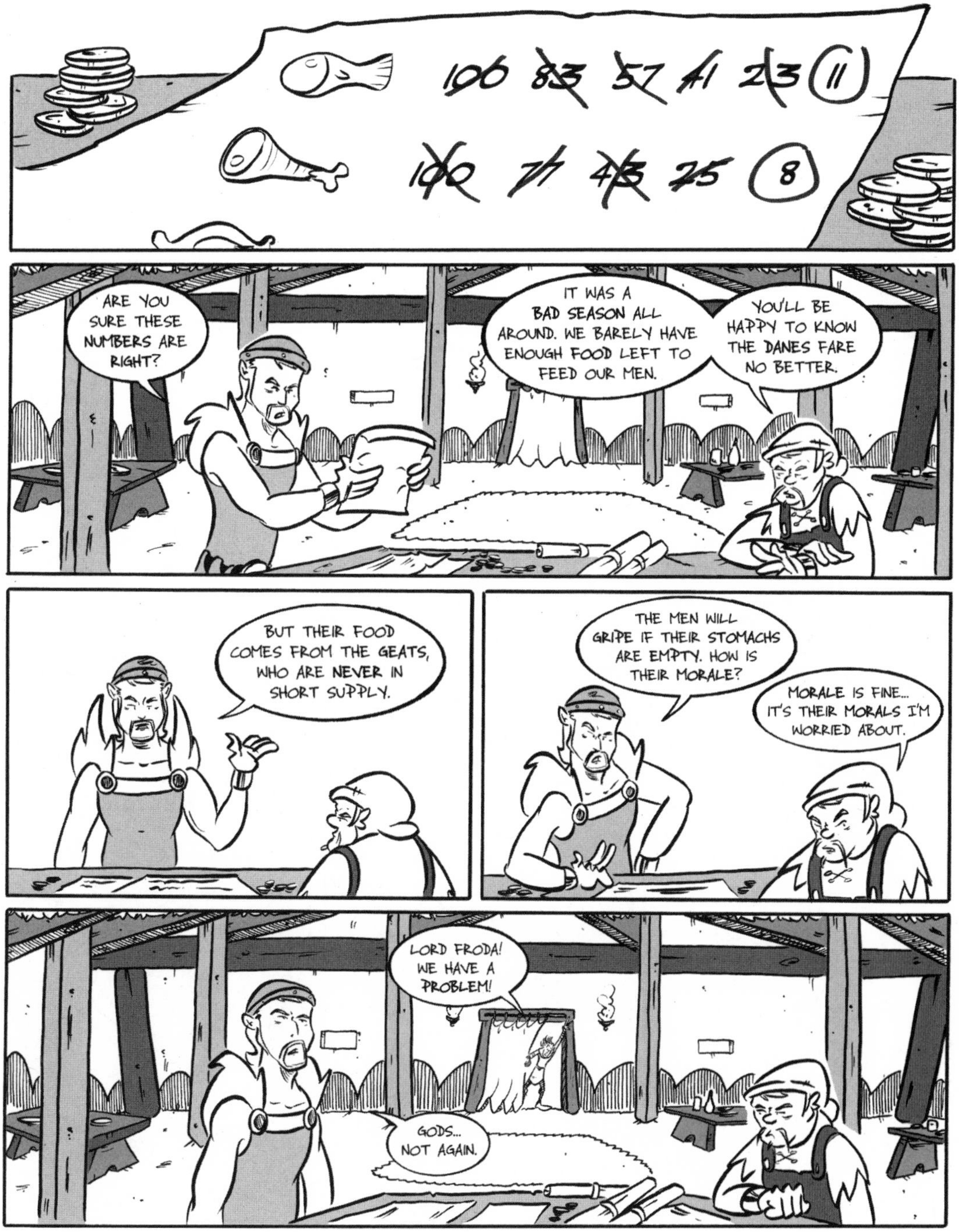
100 83 57 41 23 11
100 71 43 25 8
ARE YOU SURE THESE NUMBERS ARE RIGHT?
IT WAS A BAD SEASON ALL AROUND. WE BARELY HAVE ENOUGH FOOD LEFT TO FEED OUR MEN.
YOU'LL BE HAPPY TO KNOW THE DANES FARE NO BETTER.
BUT THEIR FOOD COMES FROM THE GEATS, WHO ARE NEVER IN SHORT SUPPLY.
THE MEN WILL GRIPE IF THEIR STOMACHS ARE EMPTY. HOW IS THEIR MORALE?
MORALE IS FINE... IT'S THEIR MORALS I'M WORRIED ABOUT.
LORD FRODA! WE HAVE A PROBLEM!
GODS... NOT AGAIN.

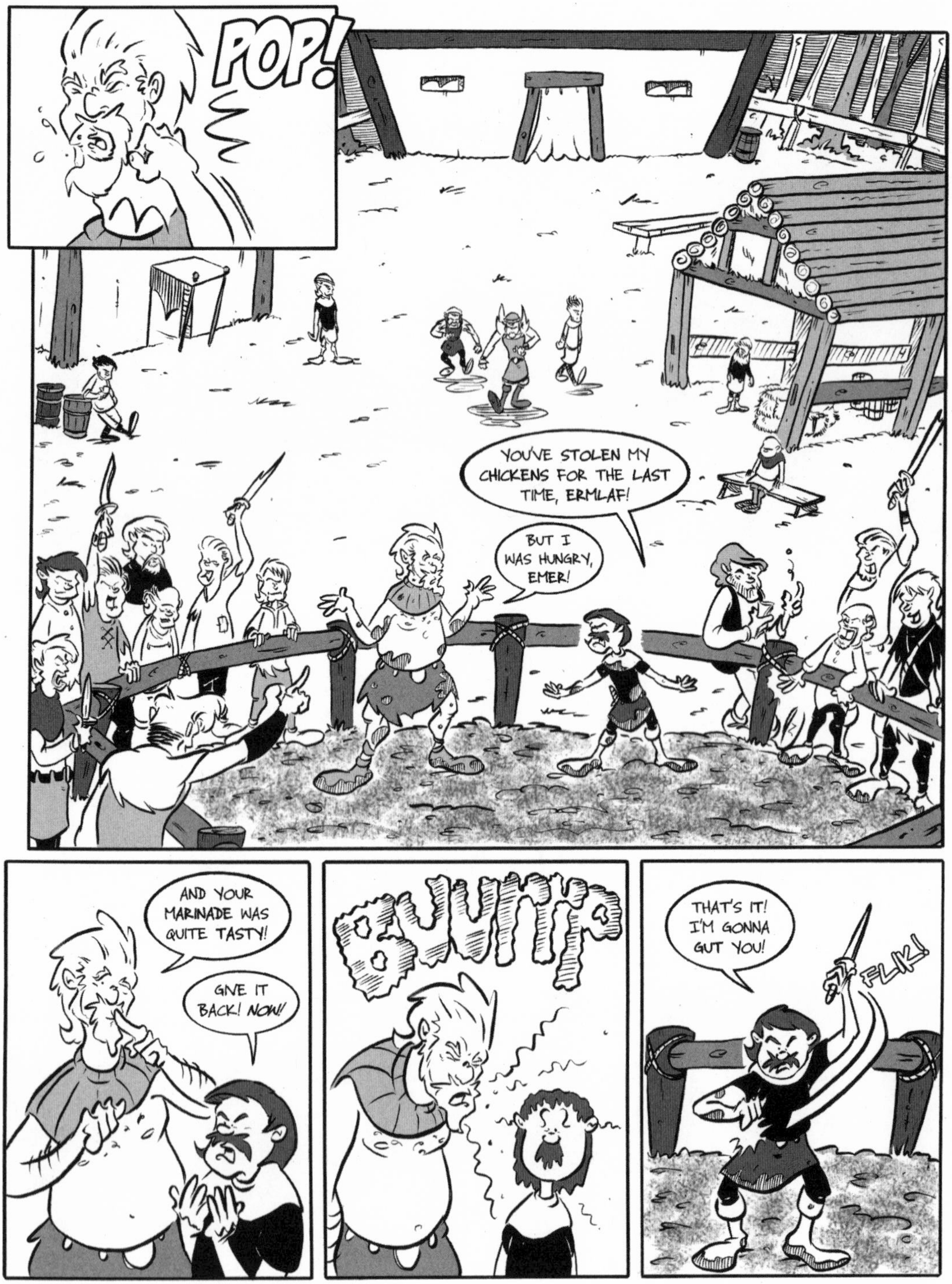
POP!
YOU'VE STOLEN MY CHICKENS FOR THE LAST TIME, ERMLAF!
BUT I WAS HUNGRY, EMER!
AND YOUR MARINADE WAS QUITE TASTY!
GIVE IT BACK! NOW!
BWUMP
THAT'S IT! I'M GONNA GUT YOU!
FLIK!

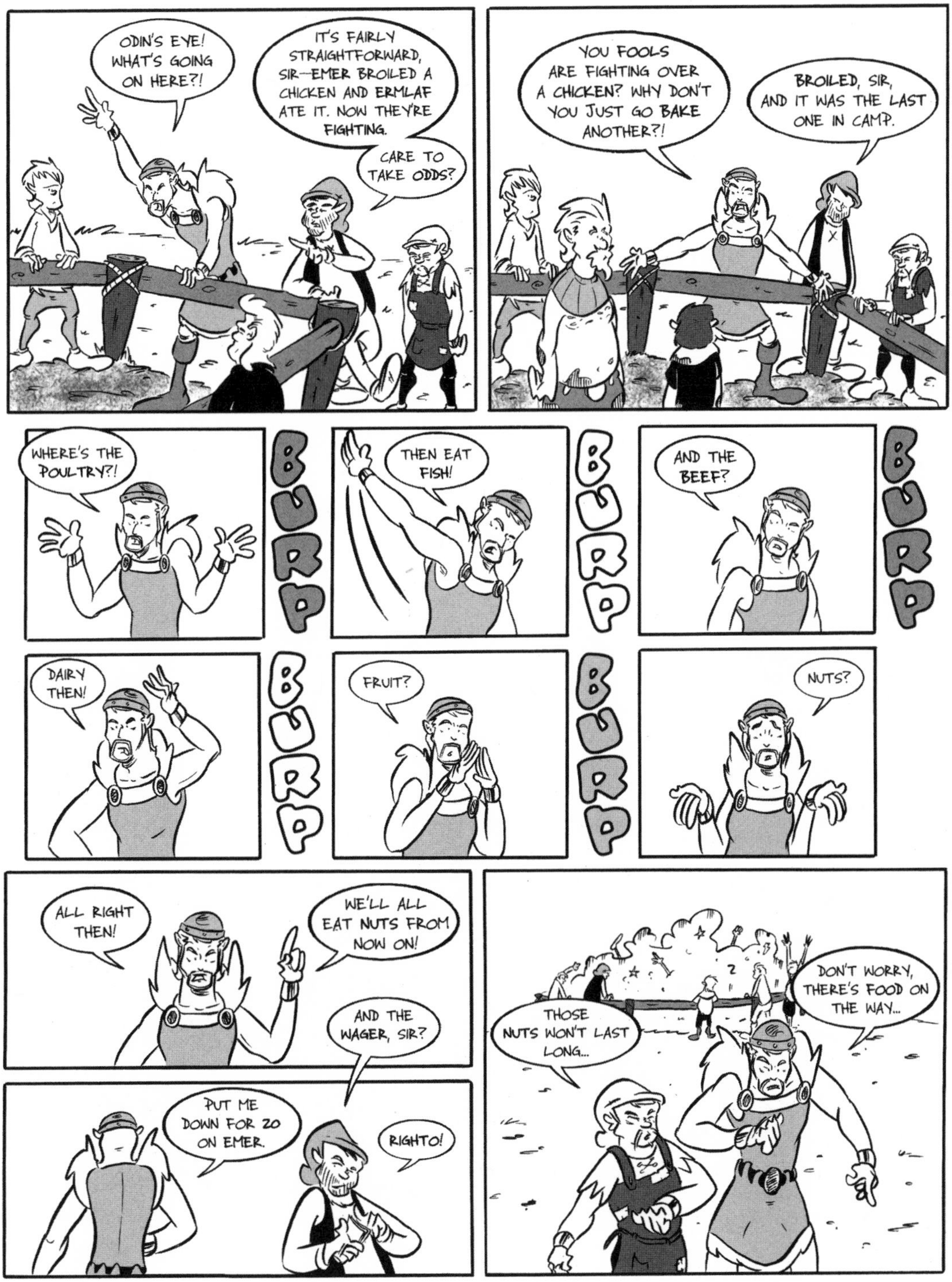
ODIN'S EYE! WHAT'S GOING ON HERE?!
IT'S FAIRLY STRAIGHTFORWARD, SIR—EMER BROILED A CHICKEN AND ERMLAF ATE IT. NOW THEY'RE FIGHTING.
CARE TO TAKE ODDS?
YOU FOOLS ARE FIGHTING OVER A CHICKEN? WHY DON'T YOU JUST GO BAKE ANOTHER?!
BROILED, SIR, AND IT WAS THE LAST ONE IN CAMP.
WHERE'S THE POULTRY?!
BURP
THEN EAT FISH!
BURP
AND THE BEEF?
BURP
DAIRY THEN!
BURP
FRUIT?
BURP
NUTS?
ALL RIGHT THEN!
WE'LL ALL EAT NUTS FROM NOW ON!
AND THE WAGER, SIR?
PUT ME DOWN FOR 20 ON EMER.
RIGHTO!
THOSE NUTS WON'T LAST LONG...
DON'T WORRY, THERE'S FOOD ON THE WAY...

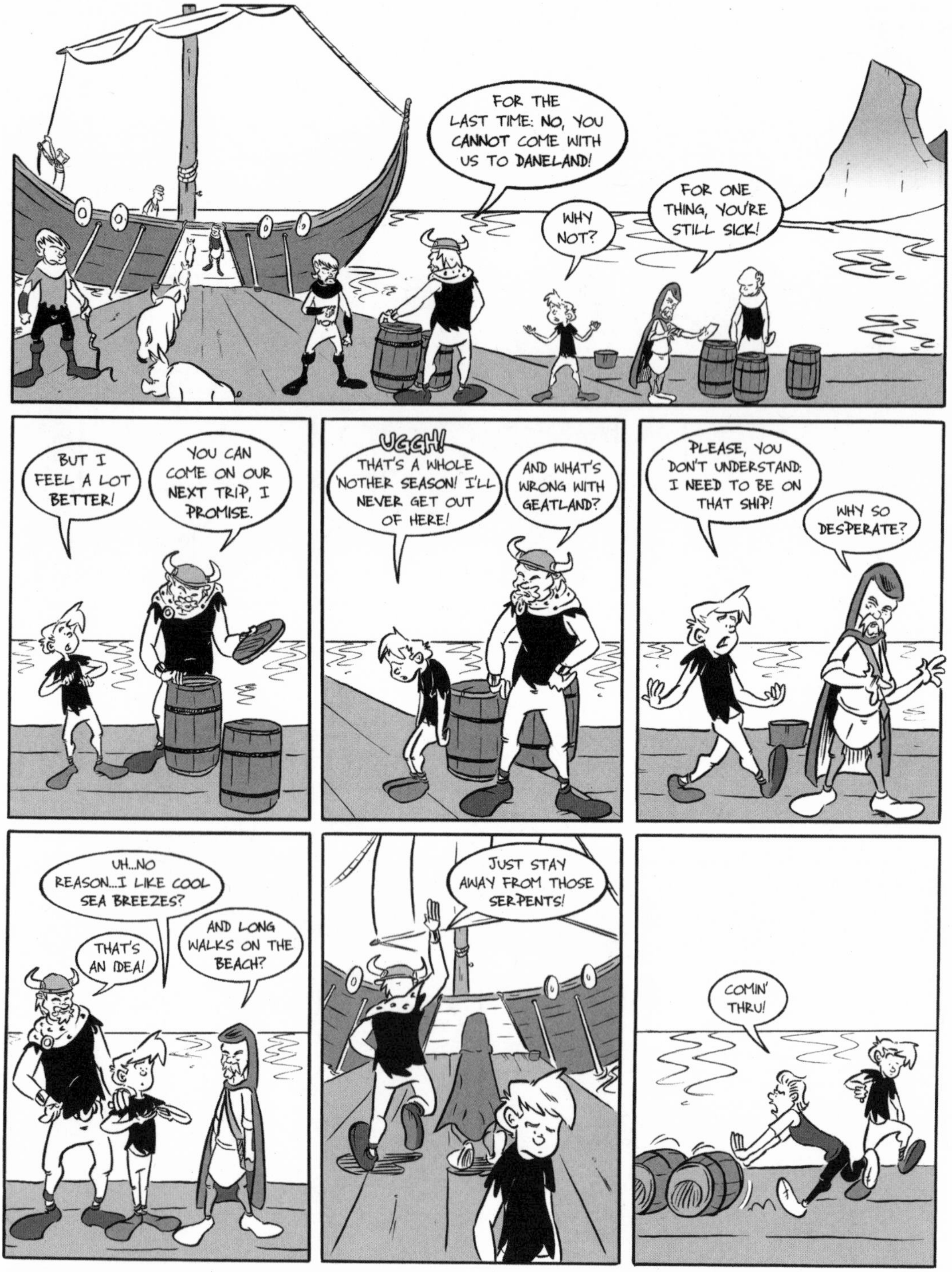
FOR THE LAST TIME: NO, YOU CANNOT COME WITH US TO DANELAND!
WHY NOT?
FOR ONE THING, YOU'RE STILL SICK!
BUT I FEEL A LOT BETTER!
YOU CAN COME ON OUR NEXT TRIP, I PROMISE.
UGGH!
THAT'S A WHOLE 'NOTHER SEASON! I'LL NEVER GET OUT OF HERE!
AND WHAT'S WRONG WITH GEATLAND?
PLEASE, YOU DON'T UNDERSTAND: I NEED TO BE ON THAT SHIP!
WHY SO DESPERATE?
UH...NO REASON...I LIKE COOL SEA BREEZES?
THAT'S AN IDEA!
AND LONG WALKS ON THE BEACH?
JUST STAY AWAY FROM THOSE SERPENTS!
COMIN' THRU!

SHUNK!

BLEAH.

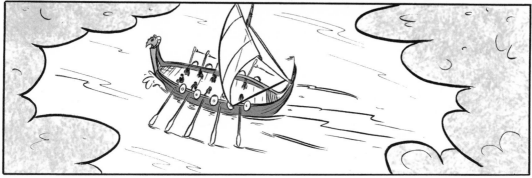

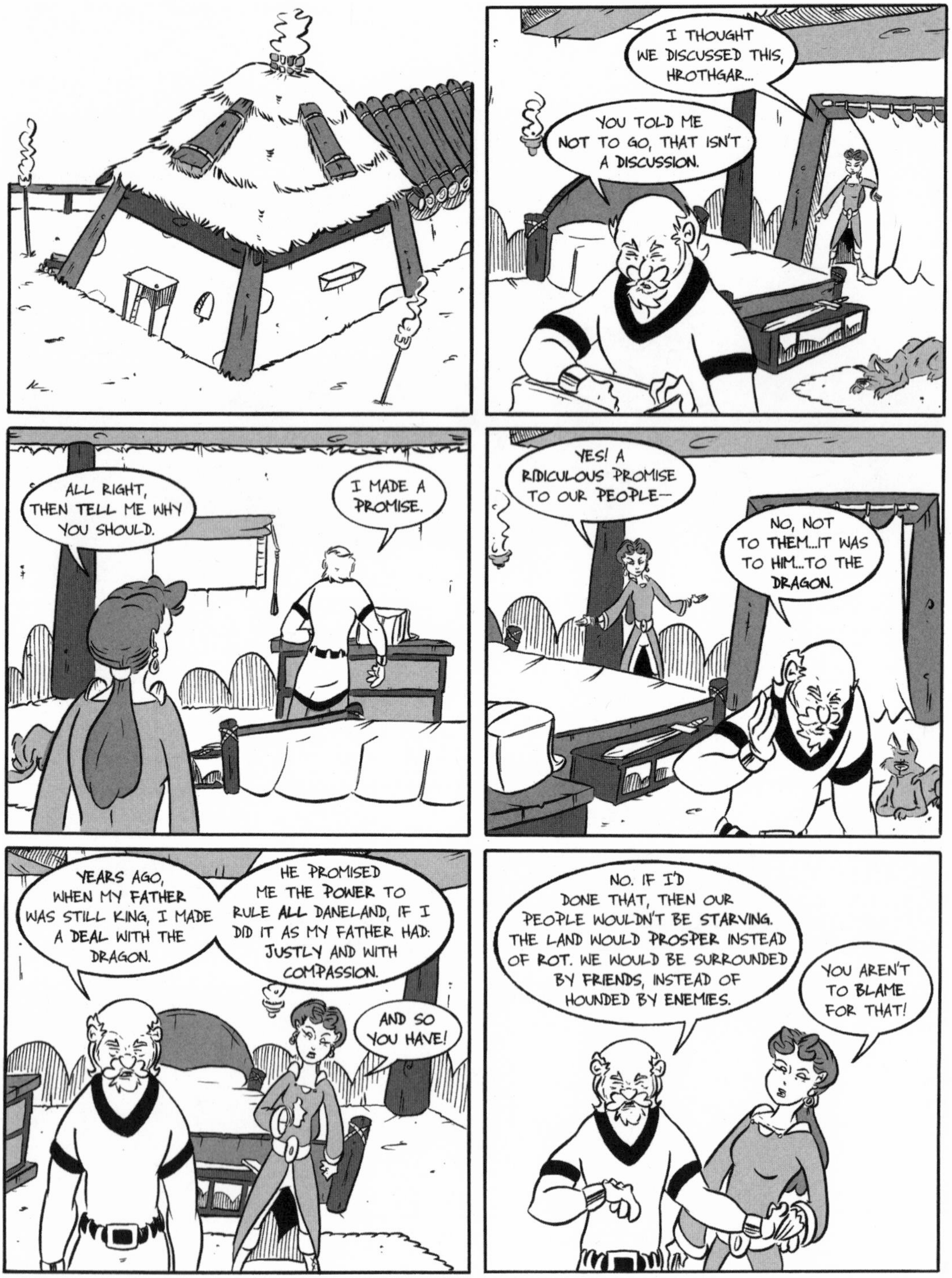
I THOUGHT WE DISCUSSED THIS, HROTHGAR...
YOU TOLD ME NOT TO GO, THAT ISN'T A DISCUSSION.
ALL RIGHT, THEN TELL ME WHY YOU SHOULD.
I MADE A PROMISE.
YES! A RIDICULOUS PROMISE TO OUR PEOPLE--
NO, NOT TO THEM...IT WAS TO HIM...TO THE DRAGON.
YEARS AGO, WHEN MY FATHER WAS STILL KING, I MADE A DEAL WITH THE DRAGON.
HE PROMISED ME THE POWER TO RULE ALL DANELAND, IF I DID IT AS MY FATHER HAD: JUSTLY AND WITH COMPASSION.
AND SO YOU HAVE!
NO. IF I'D DONE THAT, THEN OUR PEOPLE WOULDN'T BE STARVING. THE LAND WOULD PROSPER INSTEAD OF ROT. WE WOULD BE SURROUNDED BY FRIENDS, INSTEAD OF HOUNDED BY ENEMIES.
YOU AREN'T TO BLAME FOR THAT!

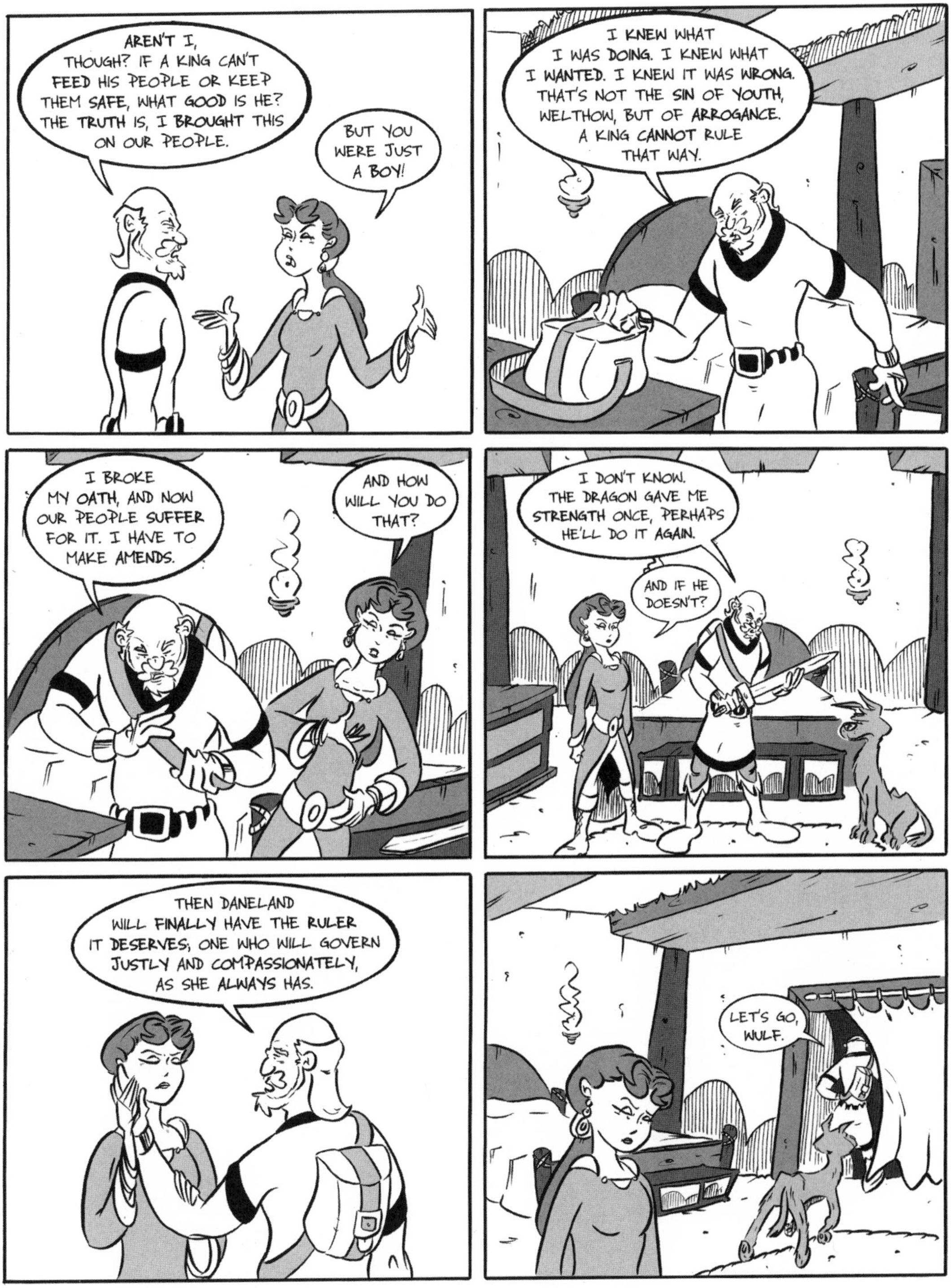
AREN'T I, THOUGH? IF A KING CAN'T FEED HIS PEOPLE OR KEEP THEM SAFE, WHAT GOOD IS HE? THE TRUTH IS, I BROUGHT THIS ON OUR PEOPLE.
BUT YOU WERE JUST A BOY!
I KNEW WHAT I WAS DOING. I KNEW WHAT I WANTED. I KNEW IT WAS WRONG. THAT'S NOT THE SIN OF YOUTH, WELTHOW, BUT OF ARROGANCE. A KING CANNOT RULE THAT WAY.
I BROKE MY OATH, AND NOW OUR PEOPLE SUFFER FOR IT. I HAVE TO MAKE AMENDS.
AND HOW WILL YOU DO THAT?
I DON'T KNOW. THE DRAGON GAVE ME STRENGTH ONCE, PERHAPS HE'LL DO IT AGAIN.
AND IF HE DOESN'T?
THEN DANELAND WILL FINALLY HAVE THE RULER IT DESERVES; ONE WHO WILL GOVERN JUSTLY AND COMPASSIONATELY, AS SHE ALWAYS HAS.
LET'S GO, WULF.

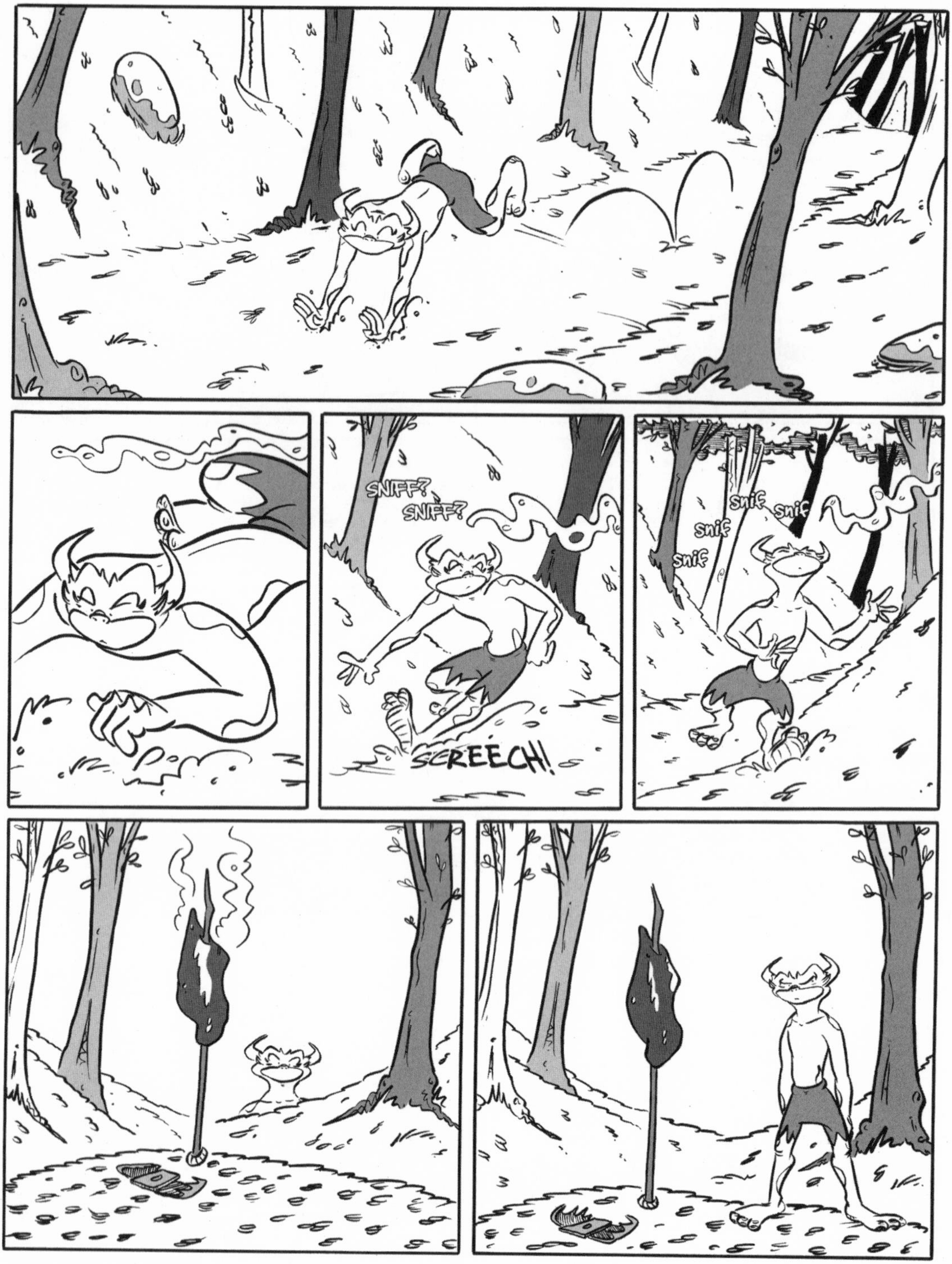
SNIFF?
SNIFF?
SCREECH!
snif
snif
snif
snif

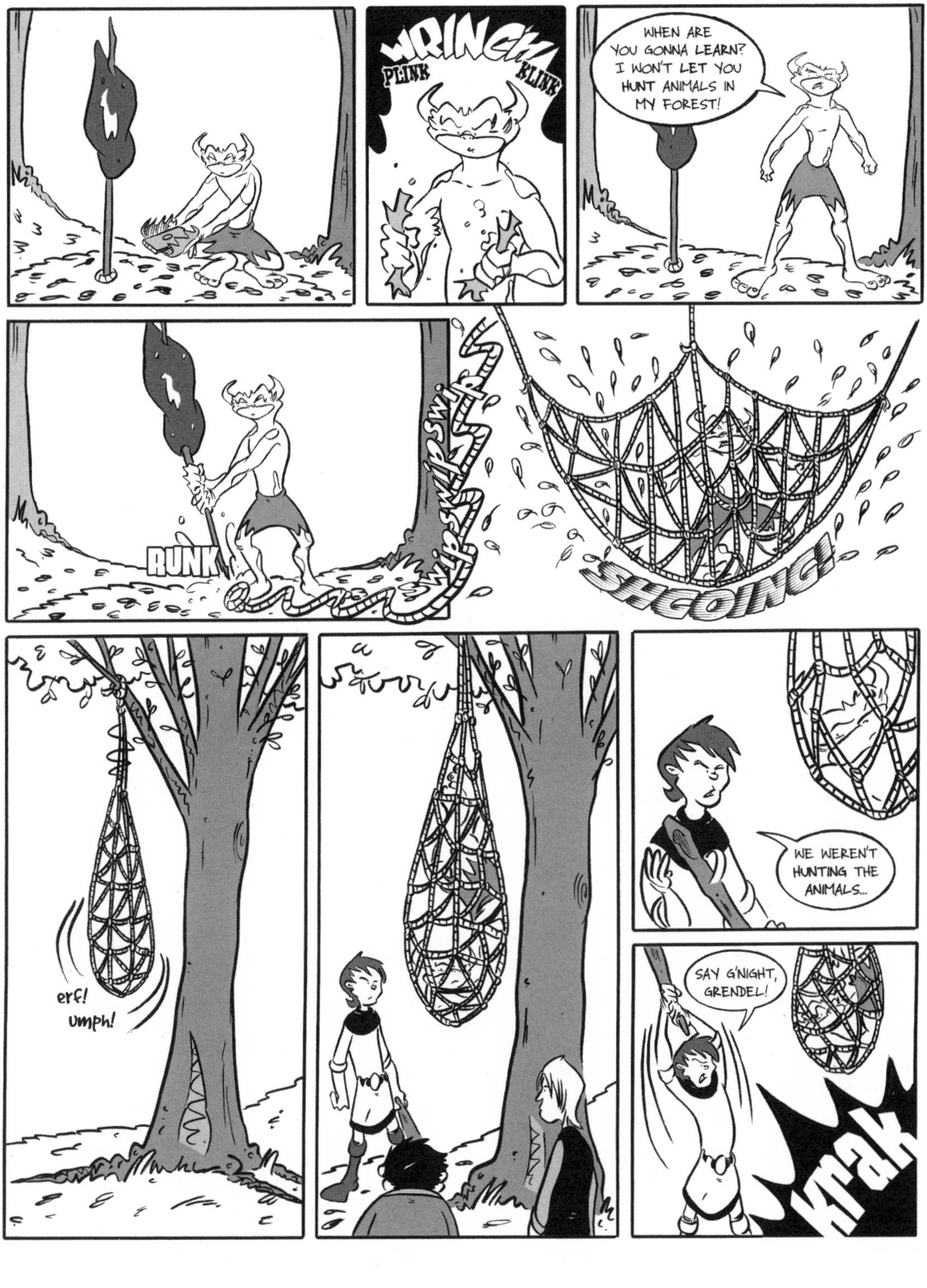
WRINCH
PLINK
KLINK
WHEN ARE YOU GONNA LEARN? I WON'T LET YOU HUNT ANIMALS IN MY FOREST!
RUNK
SHGOING!
erf!
umph!
WE WEREN'T HUNTING THE ANIMALS...
SAY G'NIGHT, GRENDEL!
krak

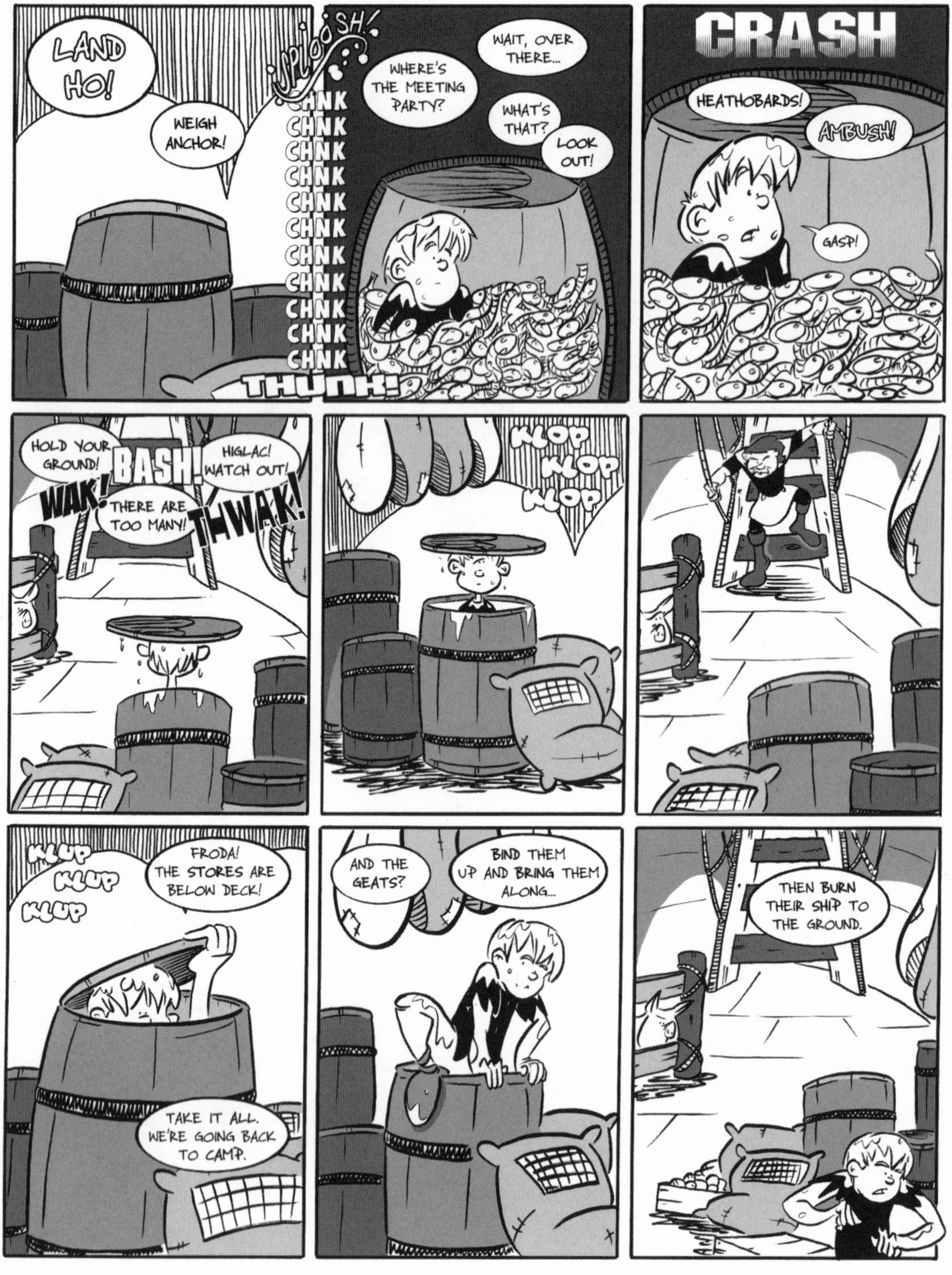
LAND HO!
WEIGH ANCHOR!
SPLOOSH!
CHNK CHNK CHNK CHNK CHNK CHNK CHNK CHNK CHNK CHNK CHNK
THUNK!
WHERE'S THE MEETING PARTY?
WAIT, OVER THERE...
WHAT'S THAT?
LOOK OUT!
CRASH
HEATHOBARDS!
AMBUSH!
GASP!
HOLD YOUR GROUND!
BASH!
HIGLAC! WATCH OUT!
WAK!
THERE ARE TOO MANY!
THWAK!
KLOP KLOP KLOP
KLUP KLUP KLUP
FRODA! THE STORES ARE BELOW DECK!
TAKE IT ALL. WE'RE GOING BACK TO CAMP.
AND THE GEATS?
BIND THEM UP AND BRING THEM ALONG...
THEN BURN THEIR SHIP TO THE GROUND.

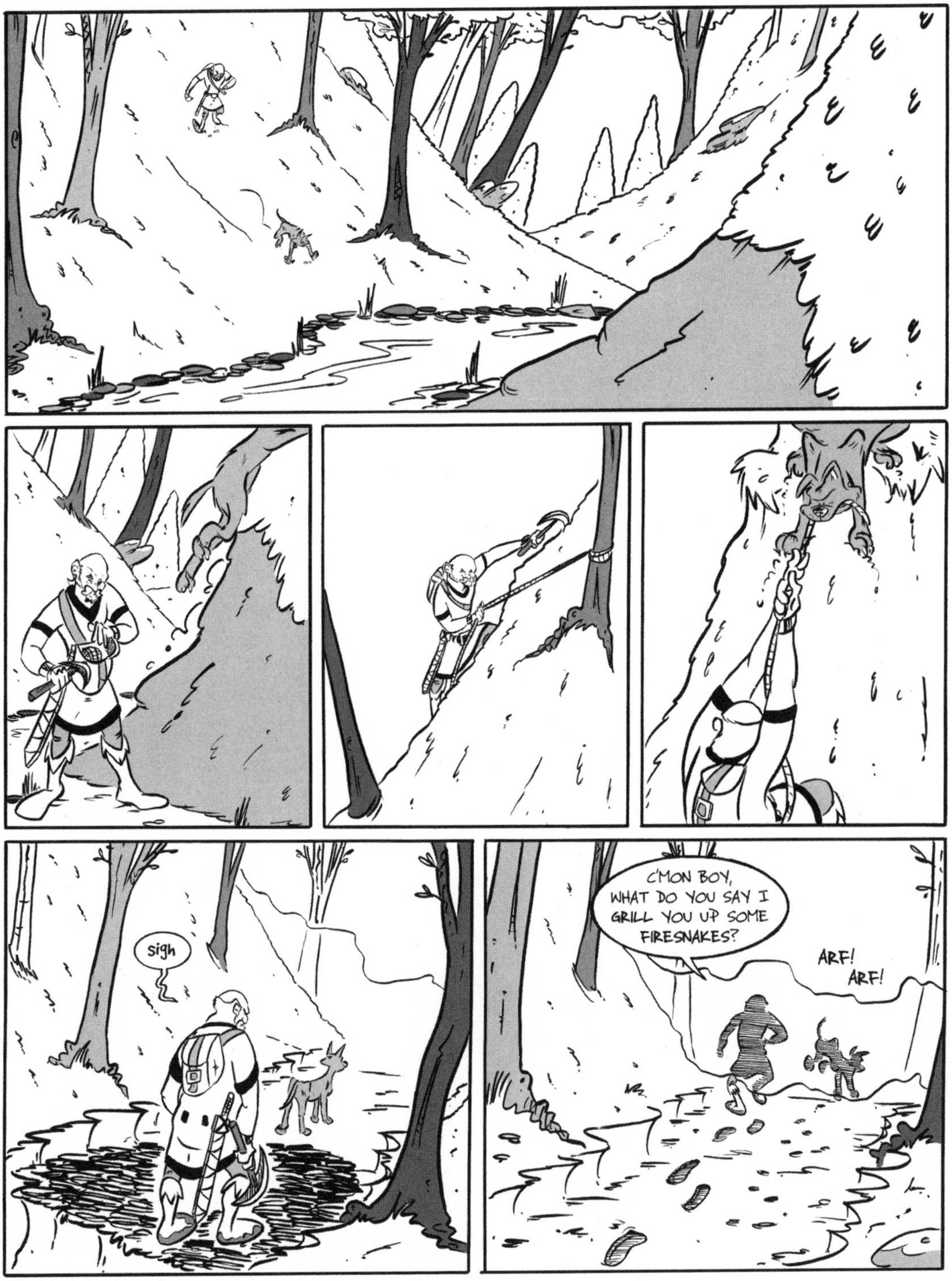
sigh
C'MON BOY, WHAT DO YOU SAY I GRILL YOU UP SOME FIRESNAKES?
ARF! ARF!

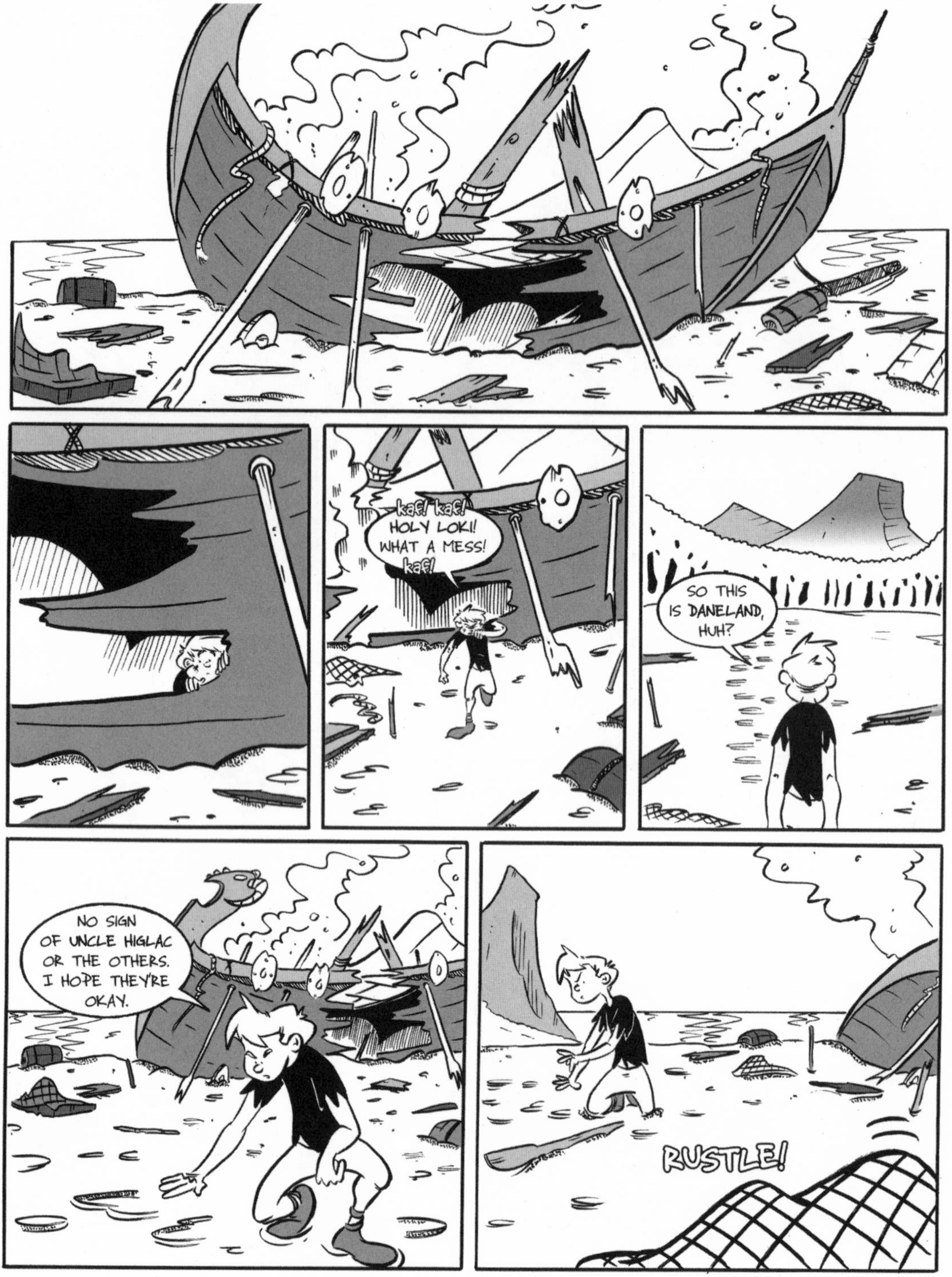
kaf! kaf!
HOLY LOKI! WHAT A MESS!
kaf!
SO THIS IS DANELAND, HUH?
NO SIGN OF UNCLE HIGLAC OR THE OTHERS. I HOPE THEY'RE OKAY.
RUSTLE!

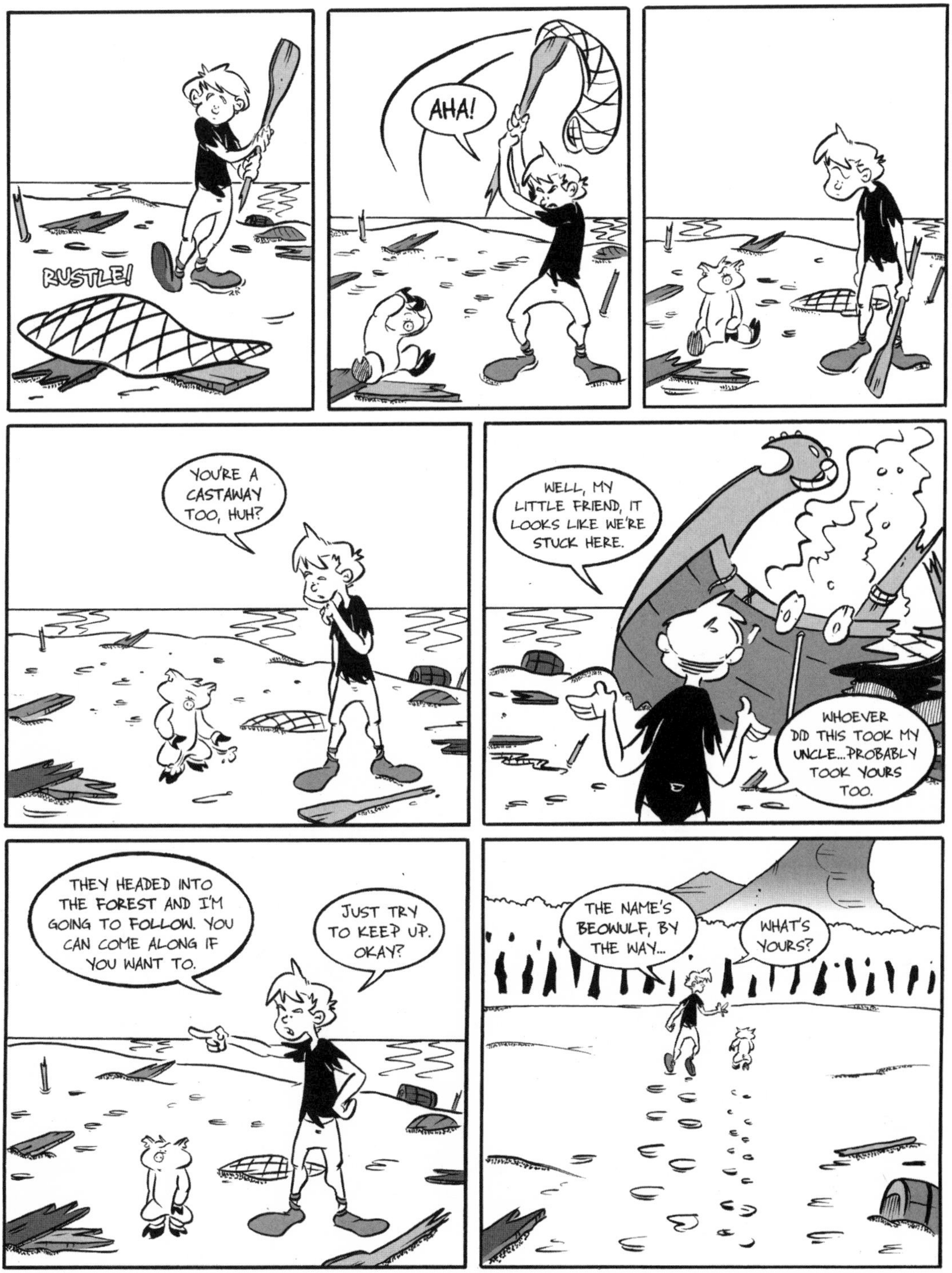
RUSTLE!
AHA!
YOU'RE A CASTAWAY TOO, HUH?
WELL, MY LITTLE FRIEND, IT LOOKS LIKE WE'RE STUCK HERE.
WHOEVER DID THIS TOOK MY UNCLE...PROBABLY TOOK YOURS TOO.
THEY HEADED INTO THE FOREST AND I'M GOING TO FOLLOW. YOU CAN COME ALONG IF YOU WANT TO.
JUST TRY TO KEEP UP. OKAY?
THE NAME'S BEOWULF, BY THE WAY...
WHAT'S YOURS?

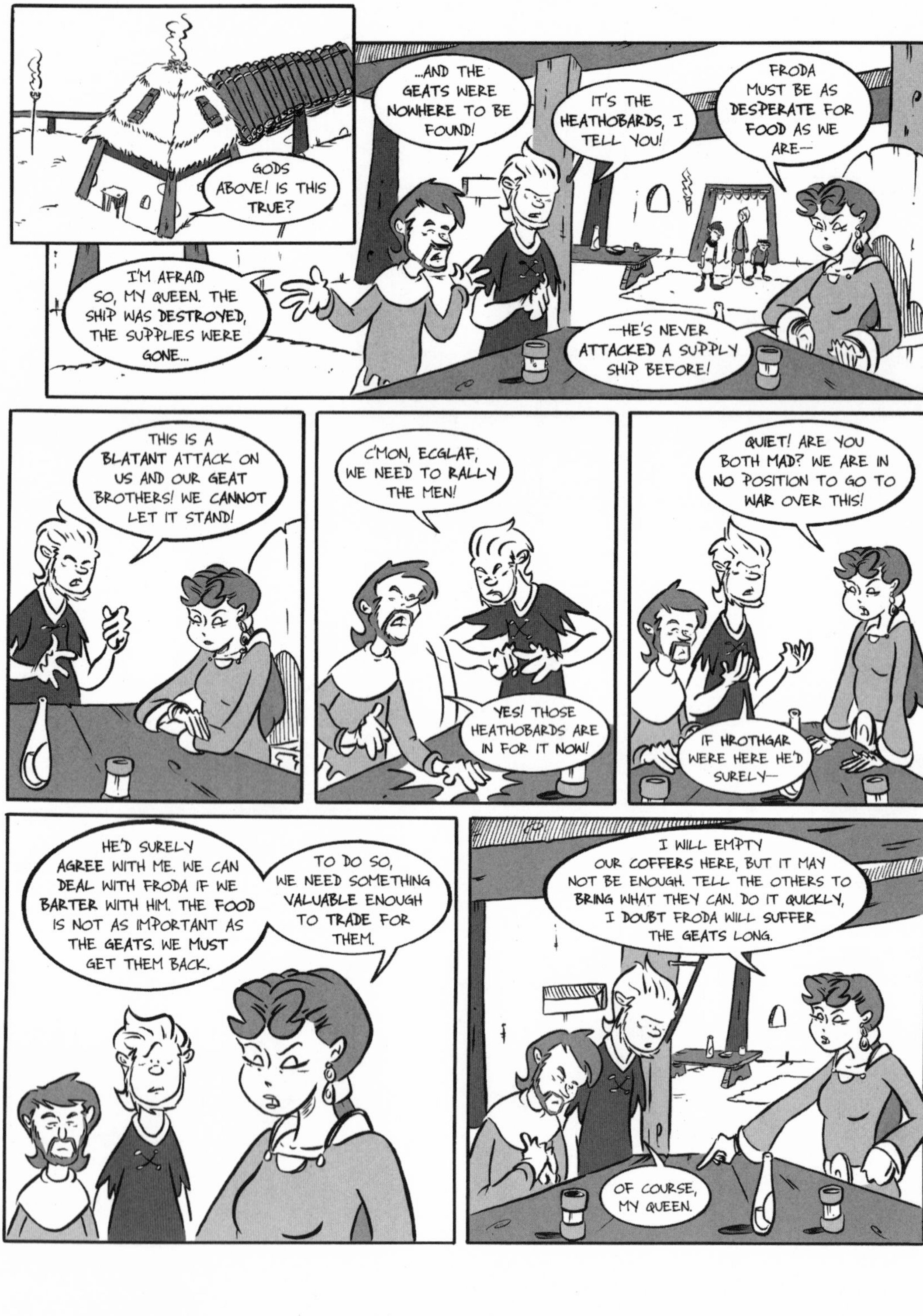
GODS ABOVE! IS THIS TRUE?
I'M AFRAID SO, MY QUEEN. THE SHIP WAS DESTROYED, THE SUPPLIES WERE GONE...
...AND THE GEATS WERE NOWHERE TO BE FOUND!
IT'S THE HEATHOBARDS, I TELL YOU!
FRODA MUST BE AS DESPERATE FOR FOOD AS WE ARE—
—HE'S NEVER ATTACKED A SUPPLY SHIP BEFORE!
THIS IS A BLATANT ATTACK ON US AND OUR GEAT BROTHERS! WE CANNOT LET IT STAND!
C'MON, ECGLAF, WE NEED TO RALLY THE MEN!
YES! THOSE HEATHOBARDS ARE IN FOR IT NOW!
QUIET! ARE YOU BOTH MAD? WE ARE IN NO POSITION TO GO TO WAR OVER THIS!
IF HROTHGAR WERE HERE HE'D SURELY—
HE'D SURELY AGREE WITH ME. WE CAN DEAL WITH FRODA IF WE BARTER WITH HIM. THE FOOD IS NOT AS IMPORTANT AS THE GEATS. WE MUST GET THEM BACK.
TO DO SO, WE NEED SOMETHING VALUABLE ENOUGH TO TRADE FOR THEM.
I WILL EMPTY OUR COFFERS HERE, BUT IT MAY NOT BE ENOUGH. TELL THE OTHERS TO BRING WHAT THEY CAN. DO IT QUICKLY, I DOUBT FRODA WILL SUFFER THE GEATS LONG.
OF COURSE, MY QUEEN.

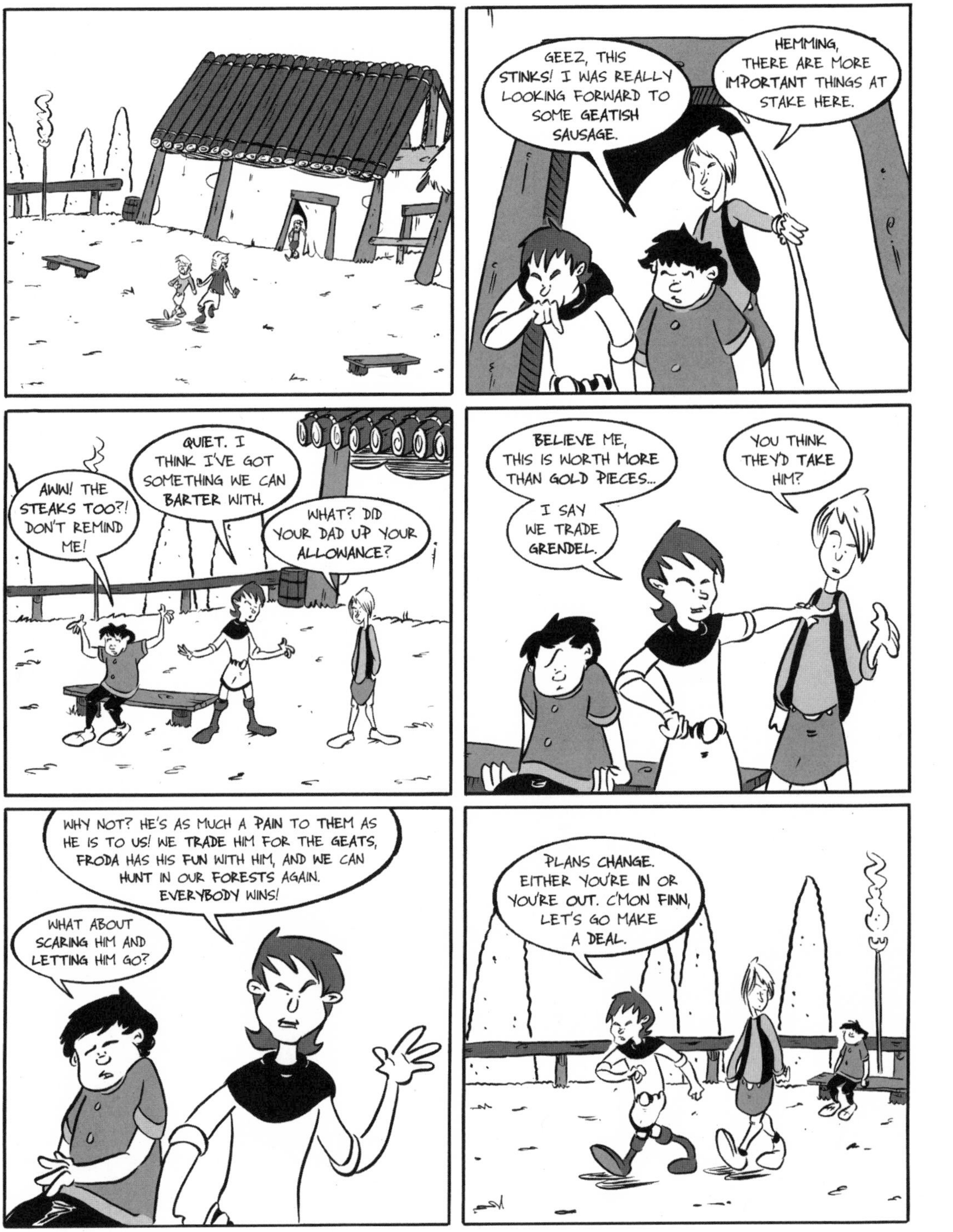
GEEZ, THIS STINKS! I WAS REALLY LOOKING FORWARD TO SOME GEATISH SAUSAGE.
HEMMING, THERE ARE MORE IMPORTANT THINGS AT STAKE HERE.
AWW! THE STEAKS TOO?! DON'T REMIND ME!
QUIET. I THINK I'VE GOT SOMETHING WE CAN BARTER WITH.
WHAT? DID YOUR DAD UP YOUR ALLOWANCE?
BELIEVE ME, THIS IS WORTH MORE THAN GOLD PIECES...
I SAY WE TRADE GRENDEL.
YOU THINK THEY'D TAKE HIM?
WHY NOT? HE'S AS MUCH A PAIN TO THEM AS HE IS TO US! WE TRADE HIM FOR THE GEATS, FRODA HAS HIS FUN WITH HIM, AND WE CAN HUNT IN OUR FORESTS AGAIN. EVERYBODY WINS!
WHAT ABOUT SCARING HIM AND LETTING HIM GO?
PLANS CHANGE. EITHER YOU'RE IN OR YOU'RE OUT. C'MON FINN, LET'S GO MAKE A DEAL.

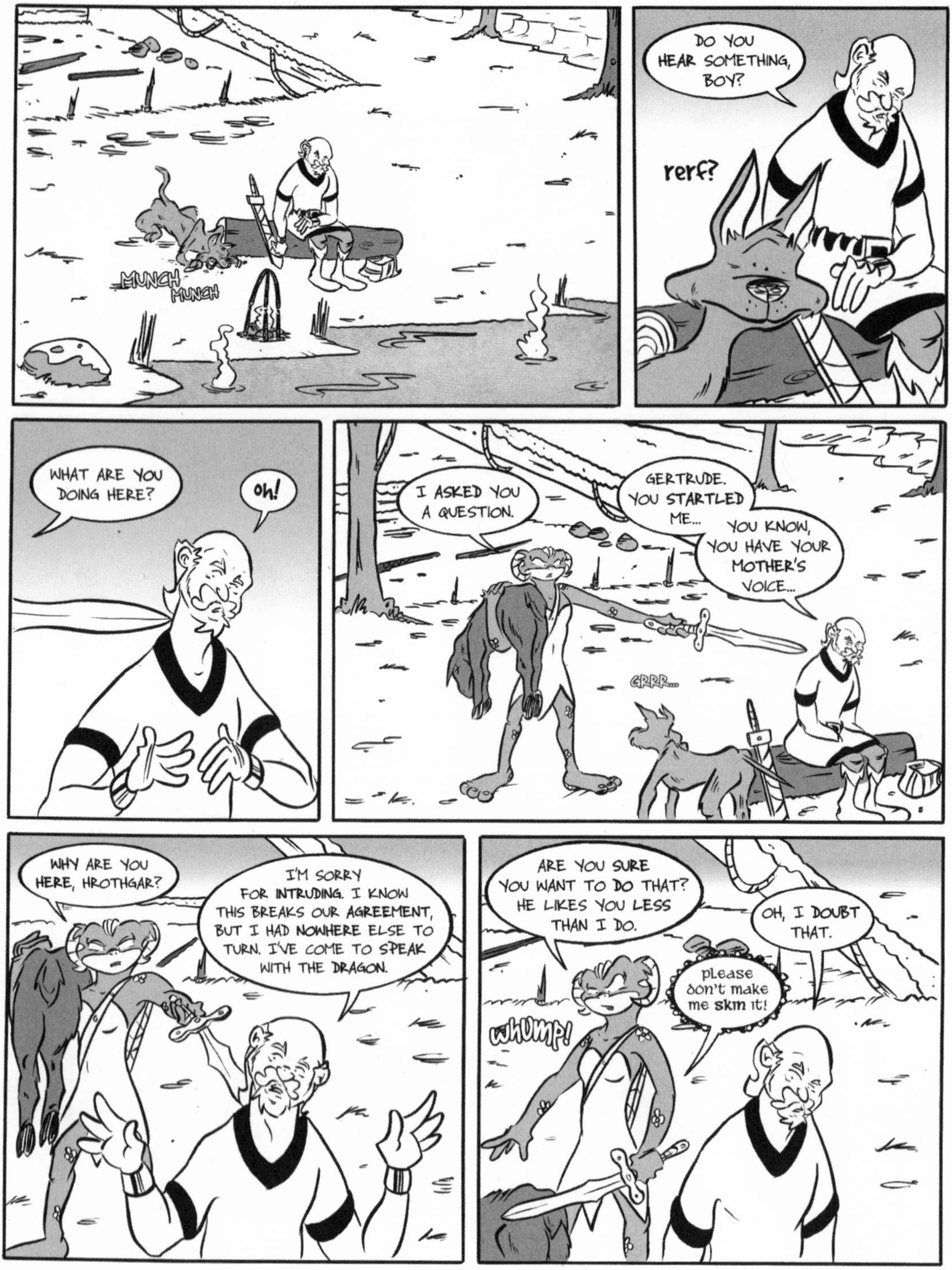
MUNCH MUNCH
DO YOU HEAR SOMETHING, BOY?
rerf?
WHAT ARE YOU DOING HERE?
oh!
I ASKED YOU A QUESTION.
GERTRUDE. YOU STARTLED ME...
YOU KNOW, YOU HAVE YOUR MOTHER'S VOICE...
GRRR...
WHY ARE YOU HERE, HROTHGAR?
I'M SORRY FOR INTRUDING. I KNOW THIS BREAKS OUR AGREEMENT, BUT I HAD NOWHERE ELSE TO TURN. I'VE COME TO SPEAK WITH THE DRAGON.
ARE YOU SURE YOU WANT TO DO THAT? HE LIKES YOU LESS THAN I DO.
OH, I DOUBT THAT.
please don't make me skin it!
WHUMP!

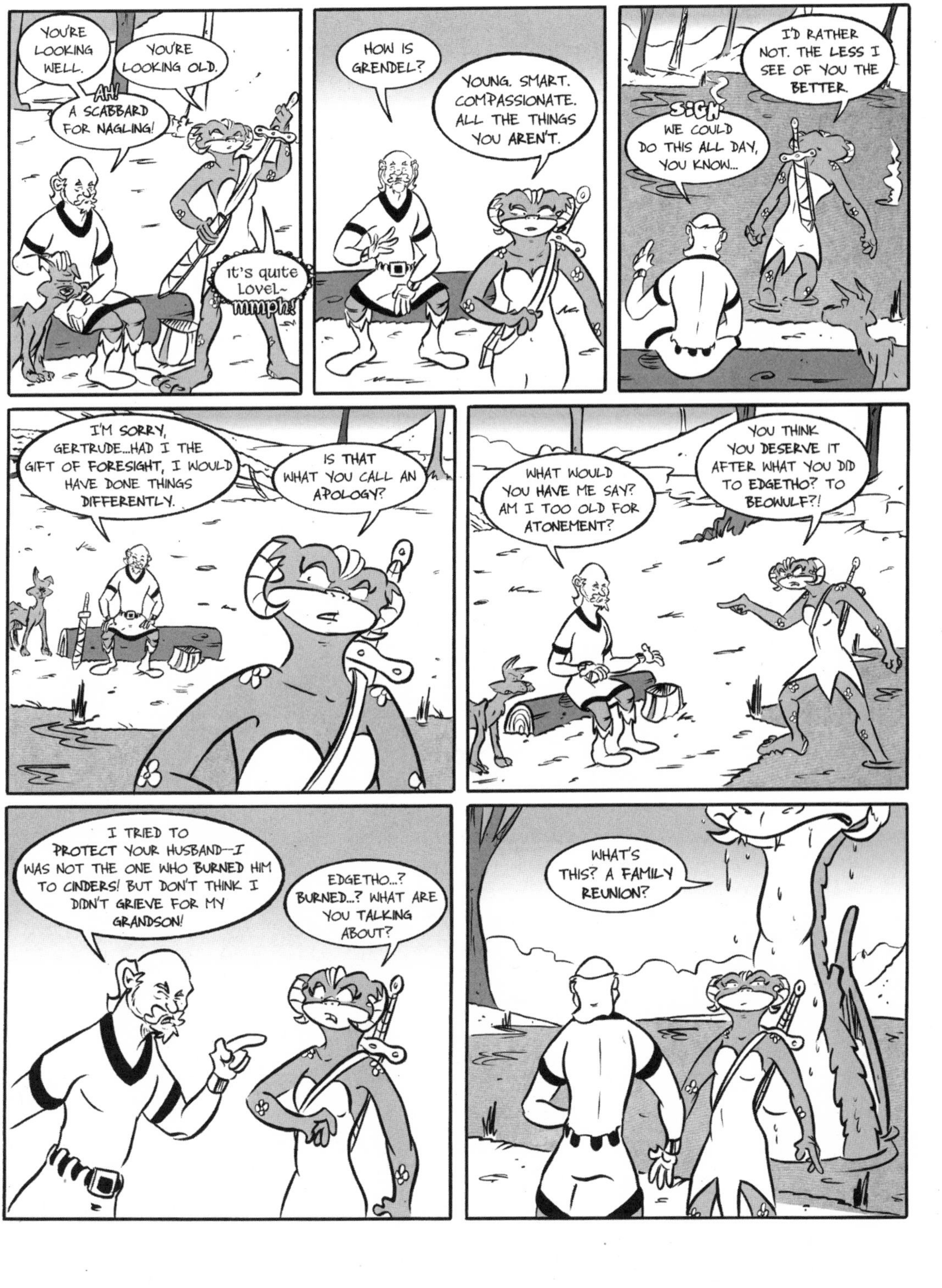
YOU'RE LOOKING WELL.
YOU'RE LOOKING OLD.
AH! A SCABBARD FOR NAGLING!
It's quite Lovel~ mmph!
HOW IS GRENDEL?
YOUNG. SMART. COMPASSIONATE. ALL THE THINGS YOU AREN'T.
I'D RATHER NOT. THE LESS I SEE OF YOU THE BETTER.
SIGH
WE COULD DO THIS ALL DAY, YOU KNOW...
I'M SORRY, GERTRUDE...HAD I THE GIFT OF FORESIGHT, I WOULD HAVE DONE THINGS DIFFERENTLY.
IS THAT WHAT YOU CALL AN APOLOGY?
WHAT WOULD YOU HAVE ME SAY? AM I TOO OLD FOR ATONEMENT?
YOU THINK YOU DESERVE IT AFTER WHAT YOU DID TO EDGETHO? TO BEOWULF?!
I TRIED TO PROTECT YOUR HUSBAND--I WAS NOT THE ONE WHO BURNED HIM TO CINDERS! BUT DON'T THINK I DIDN'T GRIEVE FOR MY GRANDSON!
EDGETHO...? BURNED...? WHAT ARE YOU TALKING ABOUT?
WHAT'S THIS? A FAMILY REUNION?

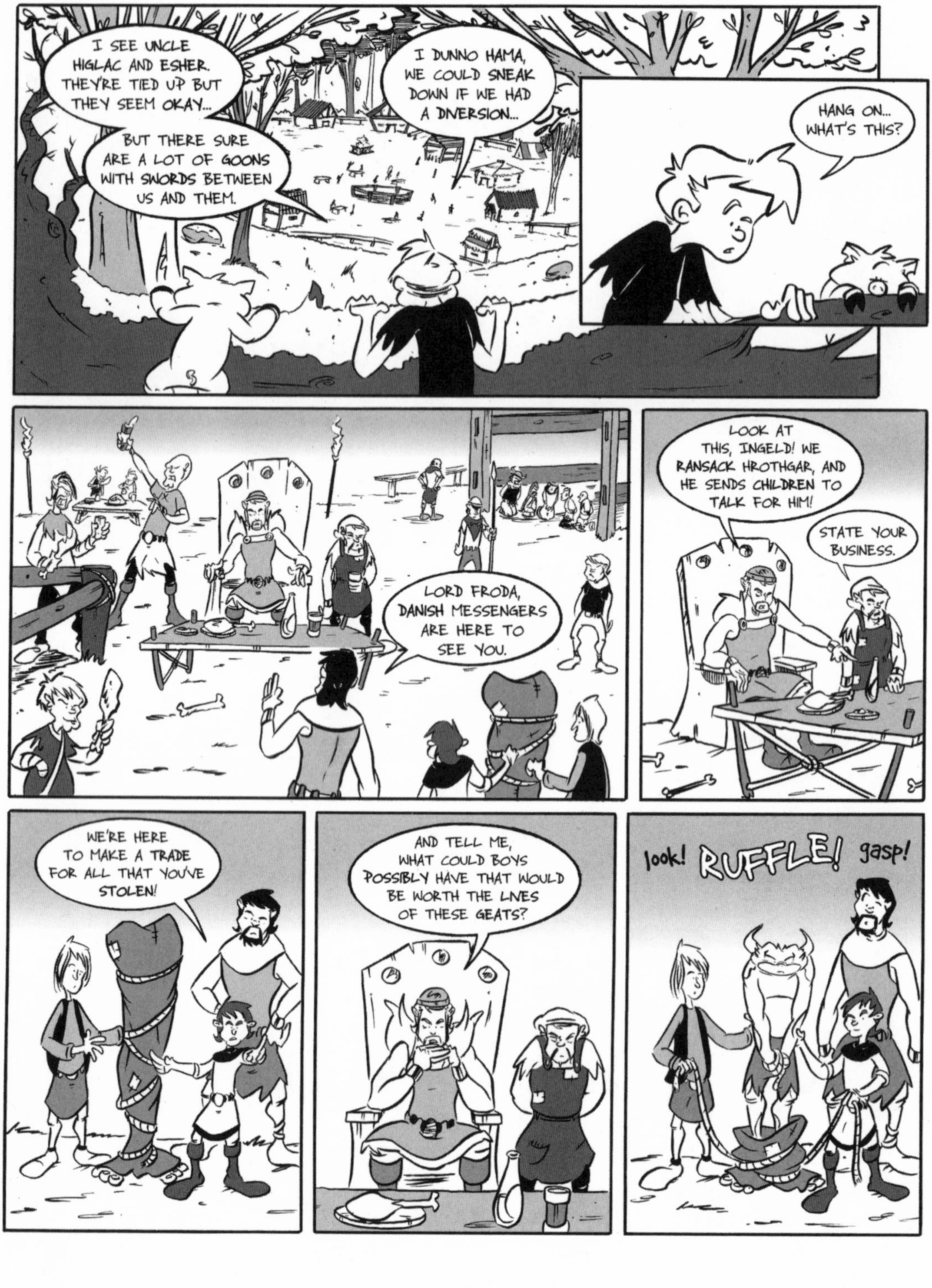
I SEE UNCLE HIGLAC AND ESHER. THEY'RE TIED UP BUT THEY SEEM OKAY...
BUT THERE SURE ARE A LOT OF GOONS WITH SWORDS BETWEEN US AND THEM.
I DUNNO HAMA, WE COULD SNEAK DOWN IF WE HAD A DIVERSION...
HANG ON... WHAT'S THIS?
LORD FRODA, DANISH MESSENGERS ARE HERE TO SEE YOU.
LOOK AT THIS, INGELD! WE RANSACK HROTHGAR, AND HE SENDS CHILDREN TO TALK FOR HIM!
STATE YOUR BUSINESS.
WE'RE HERE TO MAKE A TRADE FOR ALL THAT YOU'VE STOLEN!
AND TELL ME, WHAT COULD BOYS POSSIBLY HAVE THAT WOULD BE WORTH THE LIVES OF THESE GEATS?
look! RUFFLE! gasp!

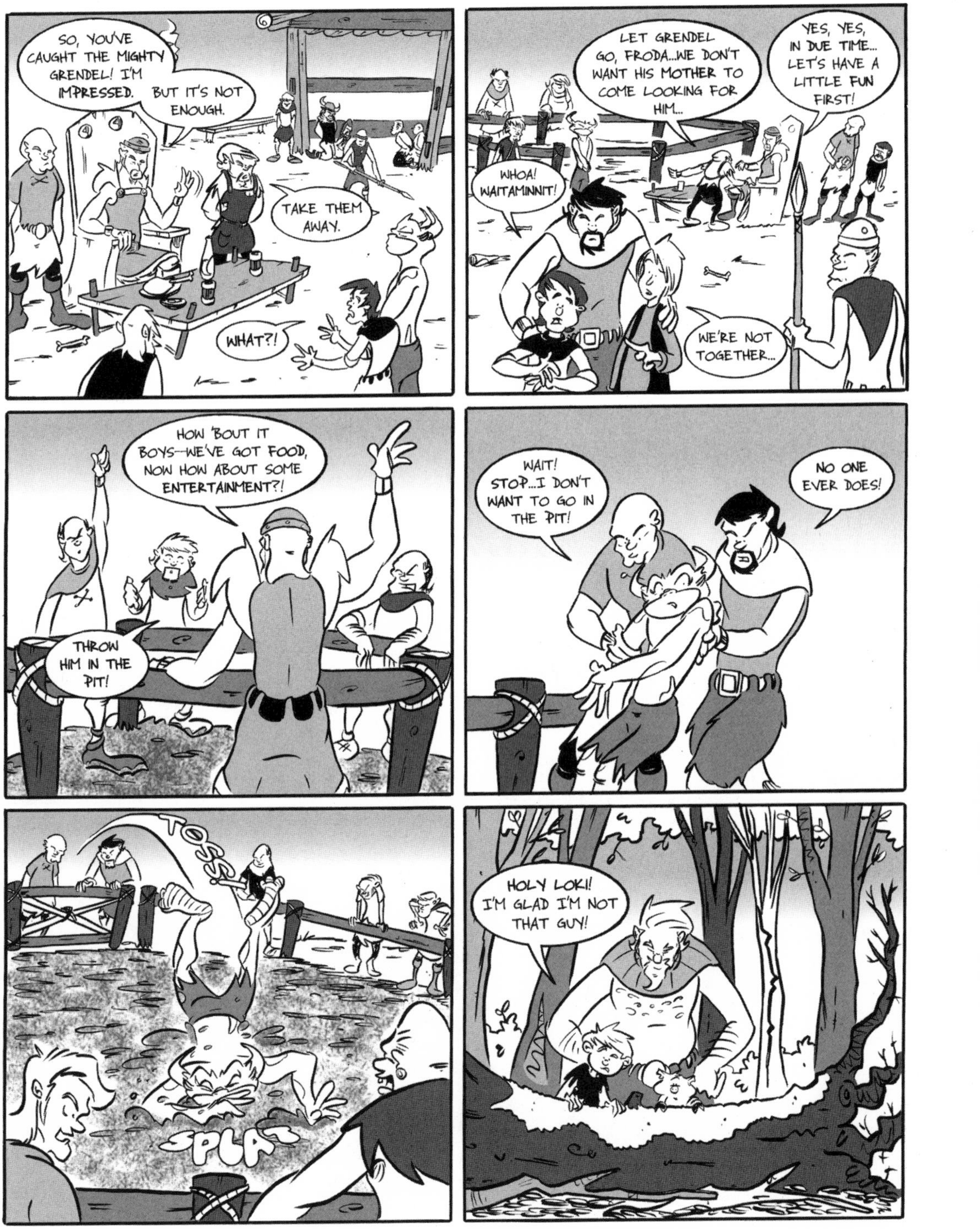
SO, YOU'VE CAUGHT THE MIGHTY GRENDEL! I'M IMPRESSED.
BUT IT'S NOT ENOUGH.
TAKE THEM AWAY.
WHAT?!
LET GRENDEL GO, FRODA...WE DON'T WANT HIS MOTHER TO COME LOOKING FOR HIM...
YES, YES, IN DUE TIME... LET'S HAVE A LITTLE FUN FIRST!
WHOA! WAITAMINNIT!
WE'RE NOT TOGETHER...
HOW 'BOUT IT BOYS--WE'VE GOT FOOD, NOW HOW ABOUT SOME ENTERTAINMENT?!
THROW HIM IN THE PIT!
WAIT! STOP...I DON'T WANT TO GO IN THE PIT!
NO ONE EVER DOES!
TOSS
SPLAT
HOLY LOKI! I'M GLAD I'M NOT THAT GUY!

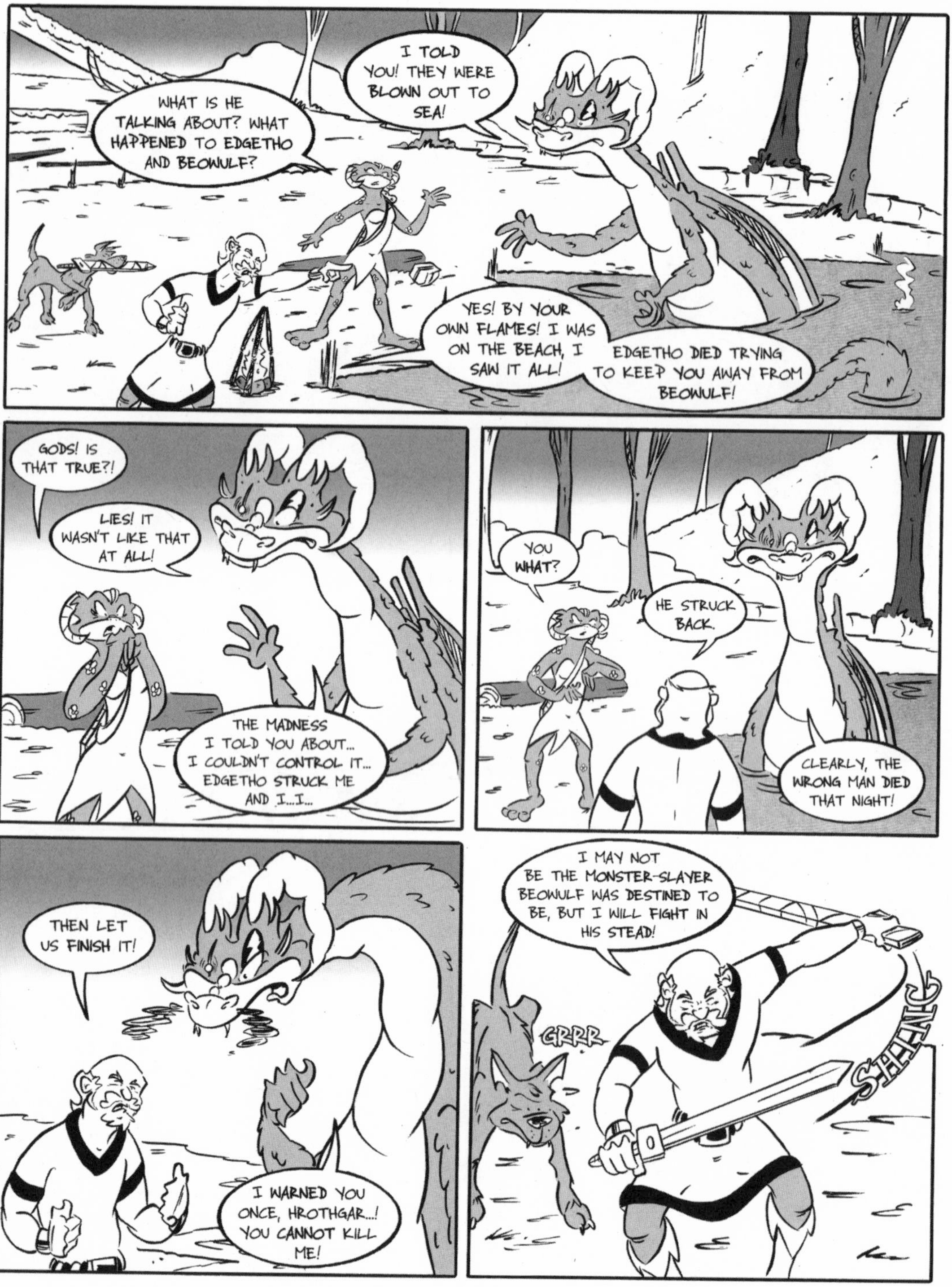
WHAT IS HE TALKING ABOUT? WHAT HAPPENED TO EDGETHO AND BEOWULF?
I TOLD YOU! THEY WERE BLOWN OUT TO SEA!
YES! BY YOUR OWN FLAMES! I WAS ON THE BEACH, I SAW IT ALL!
EDGETHO DIED TRYING TO KEEP YOU AWAY FROM BEOWULF!
GODS! IS THAT TRUE?!
LIES! IT WASN'T LIKE THAT AT ALL!
THE MADNESS I TOLD YOU ABOUT... I COULDN'T CONTROL IT... EDGETHO STRUCK ME AND I...I...
YOU WHAT?
HE STRUCK BACK.
CLEARLY, THE WRONG MAN DIED THAT NIGHT!
THEN LET US FINISH IT!
I WARNED YOU ONCE, HROTHGAR...! YOU CANNOT KILL ME!
I MAY NOT BE THE MONSTER-SLAYER BEOWULF WAS DESTINED TO BE, BUT I WILL FIGHT IN HIS STEAD!
GRRR
SHHNG

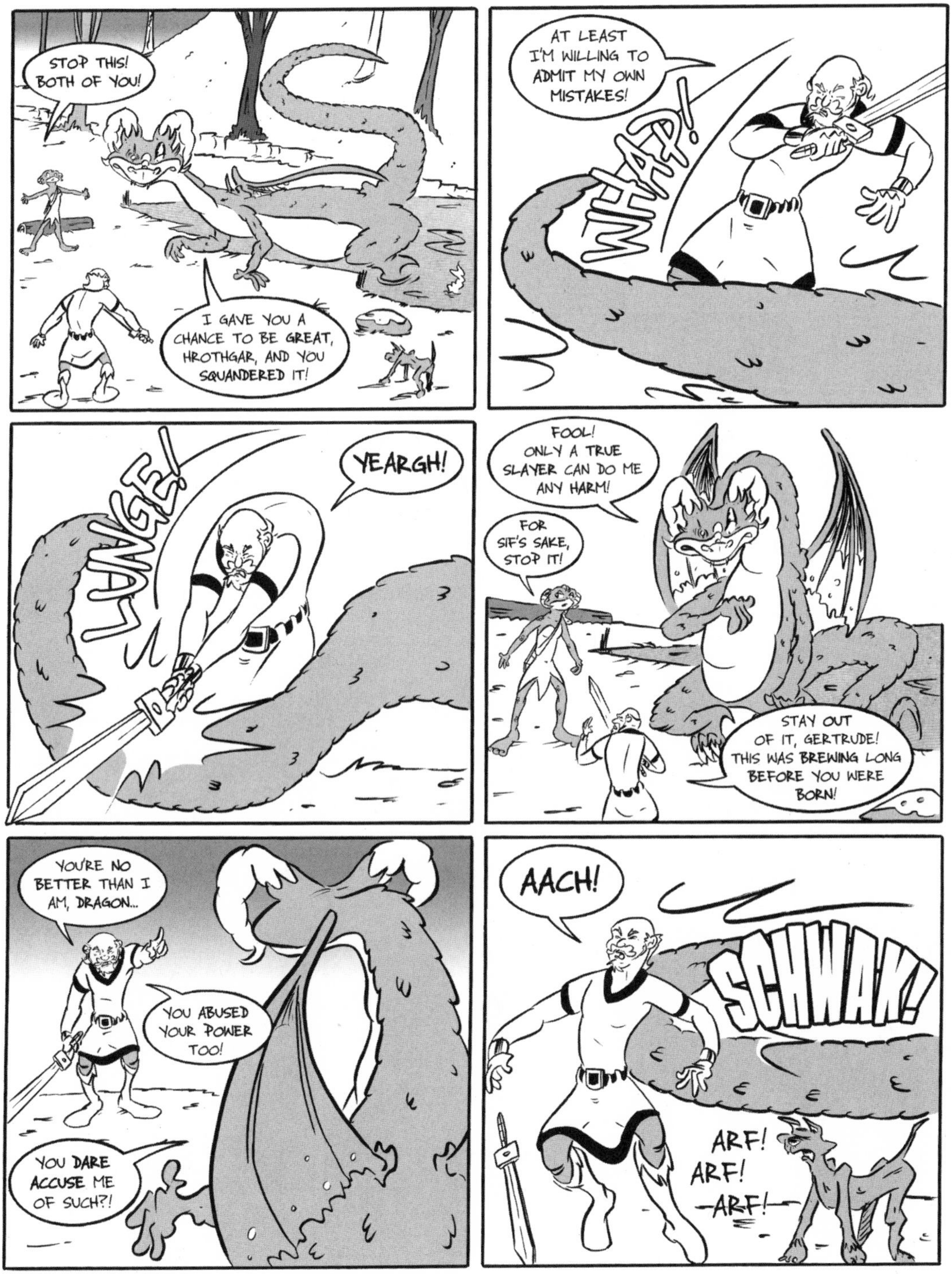
STOP THIS! BOTH OF YOU!
I GAVE YOU A CHANCE TO BE GREAT, HROTHGAR, AND YOU SQUANDERED IT!
AT LEAST I'M WILLING TO ADMIT MY OWN MISTAKES!
WHAP!
LUNGE!
YEARGH!
FOOL! ONLY A TRUE SLAYER CAN DO ME ANY HARM!
FOR SIF'S SAKE, STOP IT!
STAY OUT OF IT, GERTRUDE! THIS WAS BREWING LONG BEFORE YOU WERE BORN!
YOU'RE NO BETTER THAN I AM, DRAGON...
YOU ABUSED YOUR POWER TOO!
YOU DARE ACCUSE ME OF SUCH?!
AACH!
SCHWAK!
ARF! ARF! ARF!

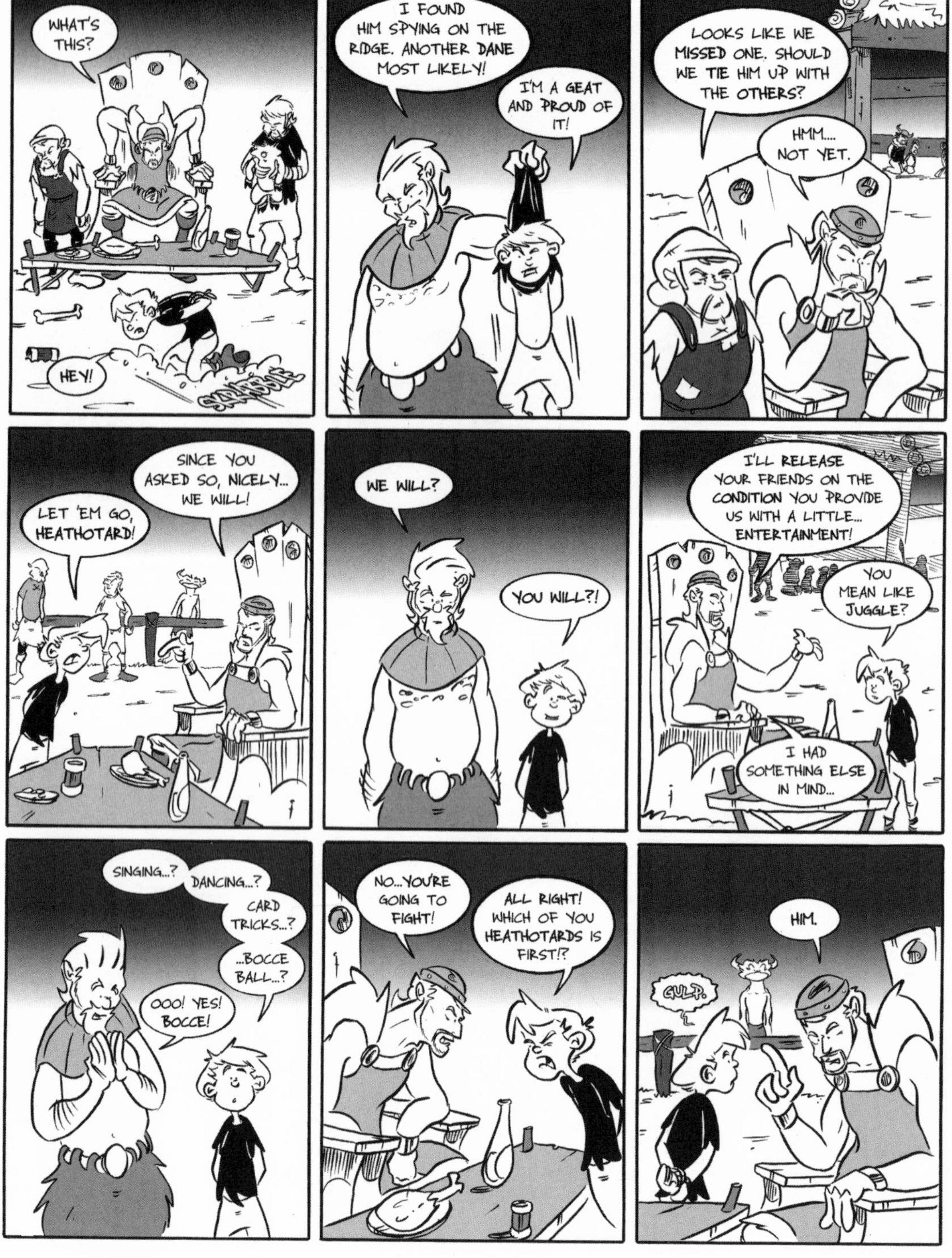
WHAT'S THIS?
HEY!
I FOUND HIM SPYING ON THE RIDGE. ANOTHER DANE MOST LIKELY!
I'M A GEAT AND PROUD OF IT!
LOOKS LIKE WE MISSED ONE. SHOULD WE TIE HIM UP WITH THE OTHERS?
HMM.... NOT YET.
LET 'EM GO, HEATHOTARD!
SINCE YOU ASKED SO, NICELY... WE WILL!
WE WILL?
YOU WILL?!
I'LL RELEASE YOUR FRIENDS ON THE CONDITION YOU PROVIDE US WITH A LITTLE... ENTERTAINMENT!
YOU MEAN LIKE JUGGLE?
I HAD SOMETHING ELSE IN MIND...
SINGING...?
DANCING...?
CARD TRICKS...?
...BOCCE BALL...?
OOO! YES! BOCCE!
NO...YOU'RE GOING TO FIGHT!
ALL RIGHT! WHICH OF YOU HEATHOTARDS IS FIRST!?
GULP.
HIM.

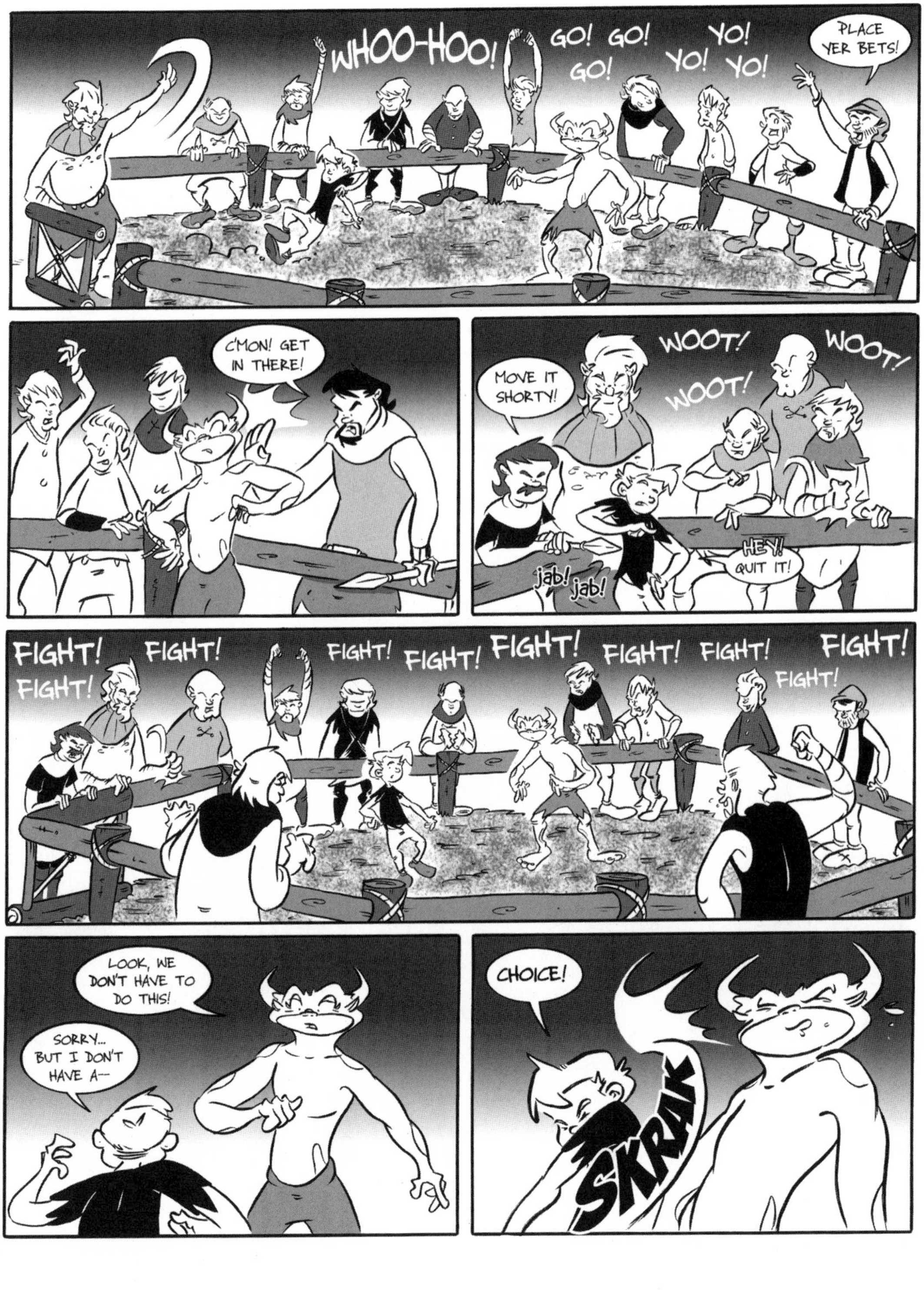
WHOO-HOO!
GO! GO! GO!
YO! YO! YO!
PLACE YER BETS!
C'MON! GET IN THERE!
MOVE IT SHORTY!
WOOT!
WOOT!
WOOT!
jab! jab!
HEY! QUIT IT!
FIGHT! FIGHT!
FIGHT!
FIGHT!
FIGHT!
FIGHT!
FIGHT!
FIGHT!
FIGHT!
FIGHT!
LOOK, WE DON'T HAVE TO DO THIS!
SORRY... BUT I DON'T HAVE A--
CHOICE!
SKRAK

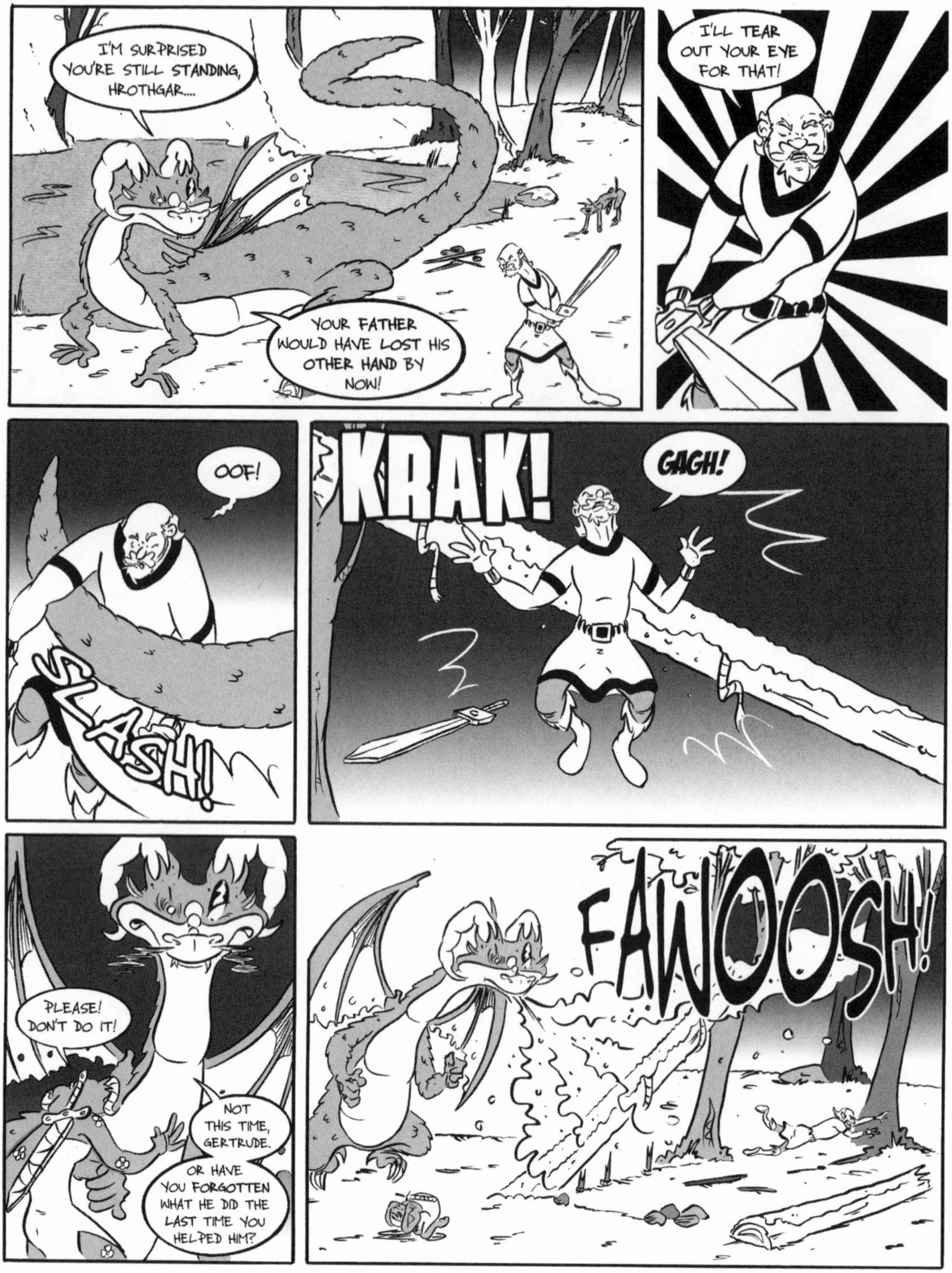
I'M SURPRISED YOU'RE STILL STANDING, HROTHGAR....
YOUR FATHER WOULD HAVE LOST HIS OTHER HAND BY NOW!
I'LL TEAR OUT YOUR EYE FOR THAT!
OOF!
SLASH!
KRAK!
GAGH!
PLEASE! DON'T DO IT!
NOT THIS TIME, GERTRUDE.
OR HAVE YOU FORGOTTEN WHAT HE DID THE LAST TIME YOU HELPED HIM?
FAWOOSH!

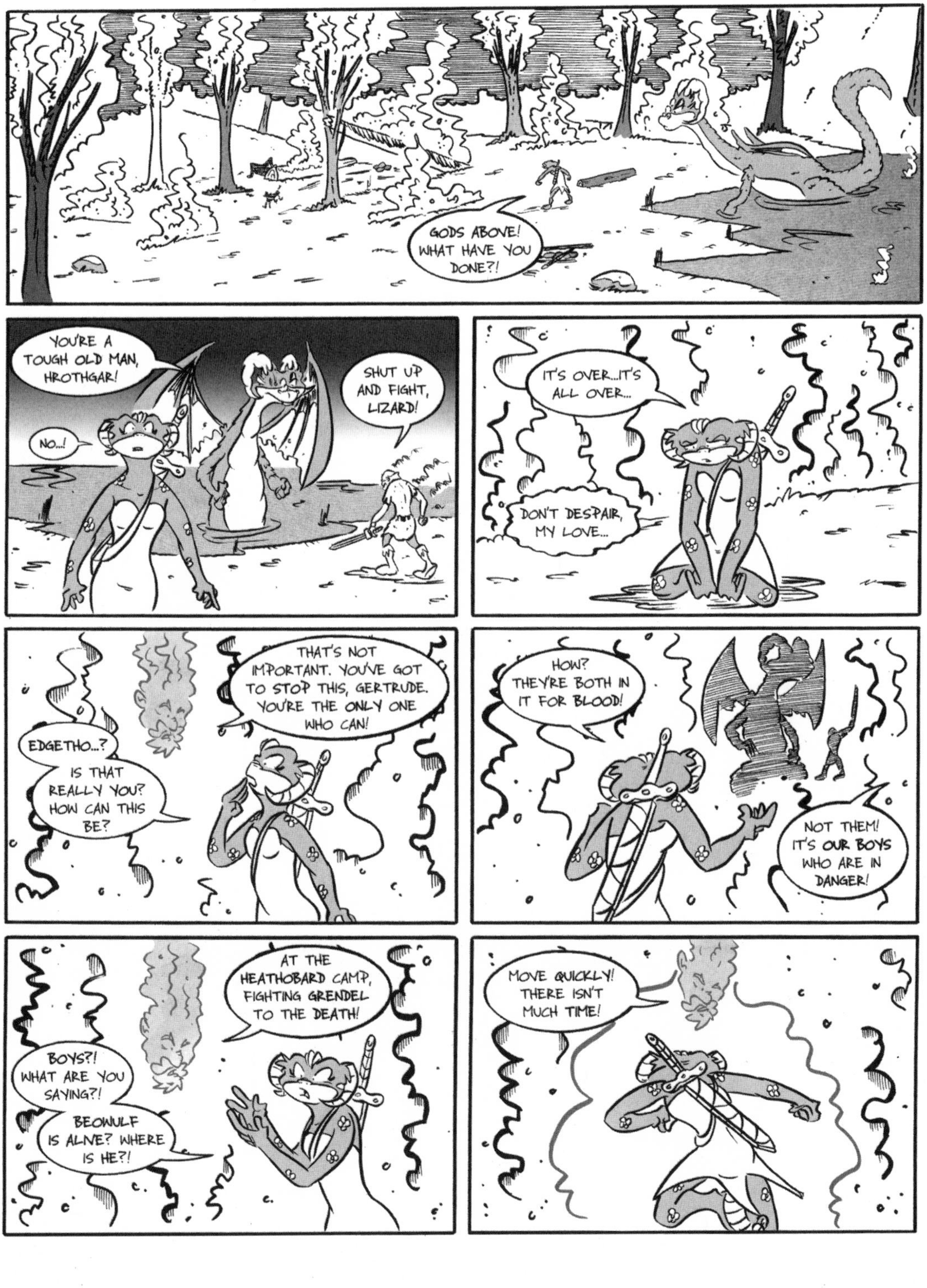
GODS ABOVE! WHAT HAVE YOU DONE?!
YOU'RE A TOUGH OLD MAN, HROTHGAR!
SHUT UP AND FIGHT, LIZARD!
NO...!
IT'S OVER...IT'S ALL OVER...
DON'T DESPAIR, MY LOVE...
EDGETHO...?
IS THAT REALLY YOU? HOW CAN THIS BE?
THAT'S NOT IMPORTANT. YOU'VE GOT TO STOP THIS, GERTRUDE. YOU'RE THE ONLY ONE WHO CAN!
HOW? THEY'RE BOTH IN IT FOR BLOOD!
NOT THEM! IT'S OUR BOYS WHO ARE IN DANGER!
BOYS?! WHAT ARE YOU SAYING?!
BEOWULF IS ALIVE? WHERE IS HE?!
AT THE HEATHOBARD CAMP, FIGHTING GRENDEL TO THE DEATH!
MOVE QUICKLY! THERE ISN'T MUCH TIME!

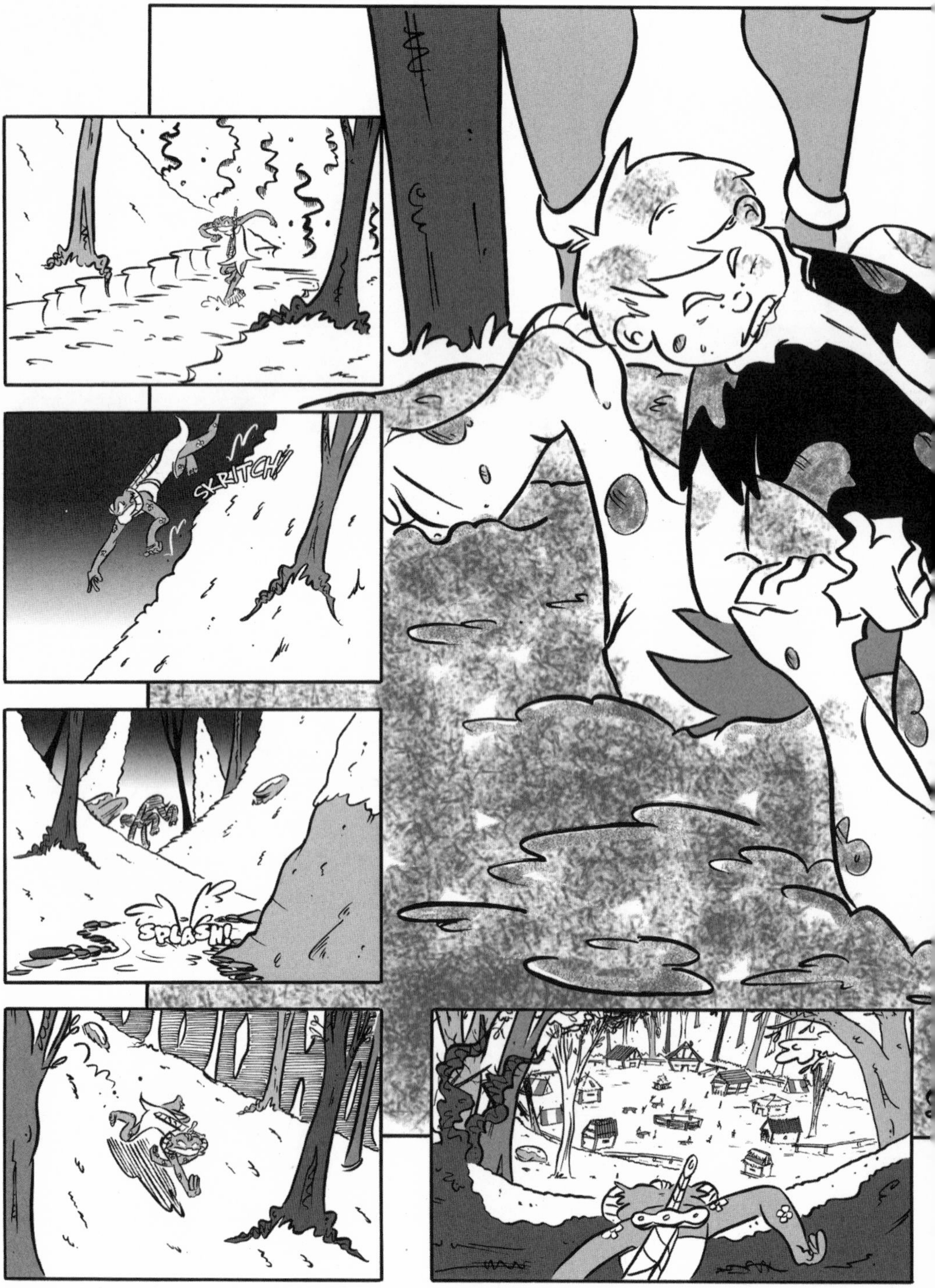
SKRITCH!
SPLASH!

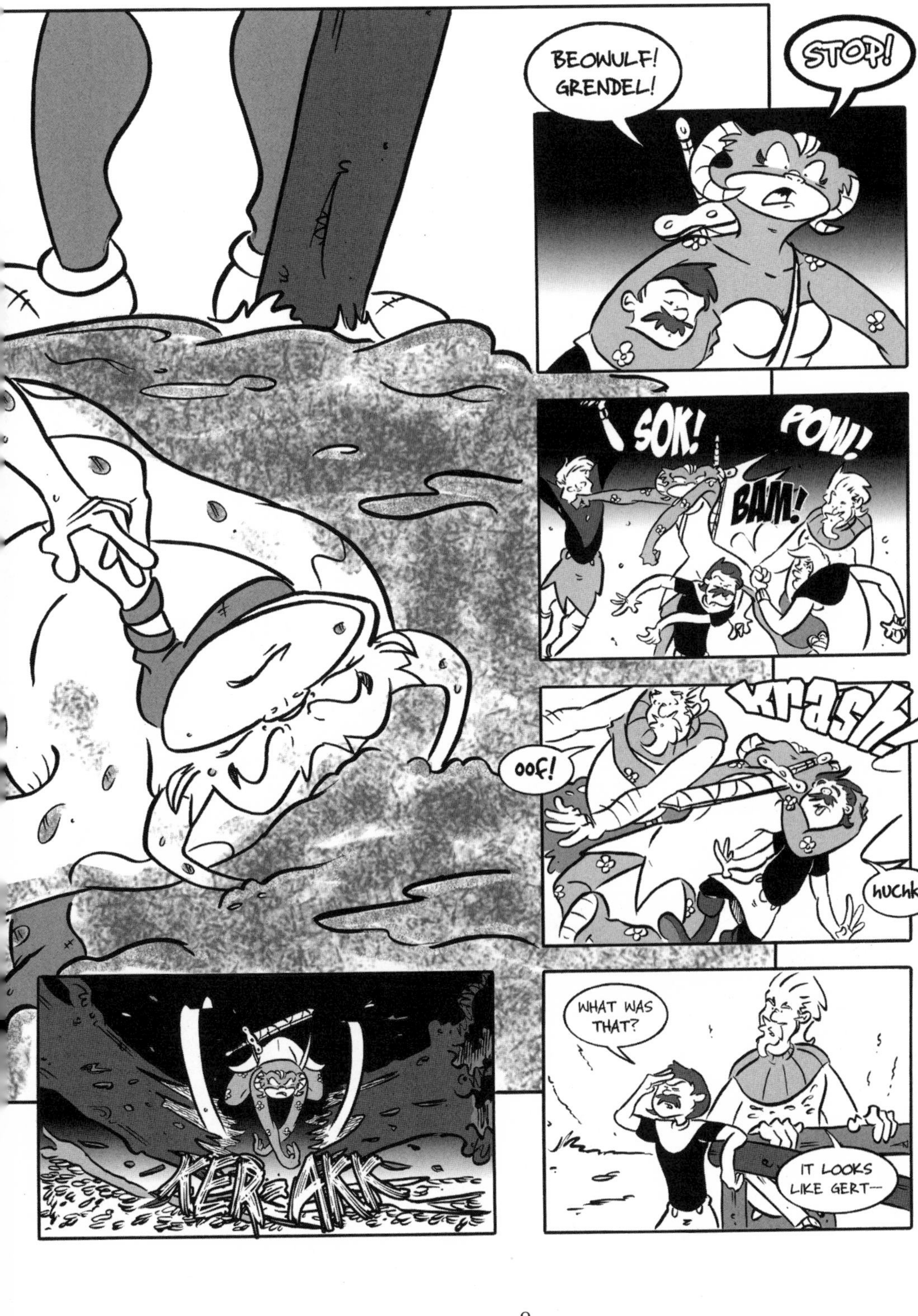
BEOWULF! GRENDEL!
STOP!
SOK!
POW!
BAM!
krash!
oof!
huchk!
KER-AKK
WHAT WAS THAT?
IT LOOKS LIKE GERT--

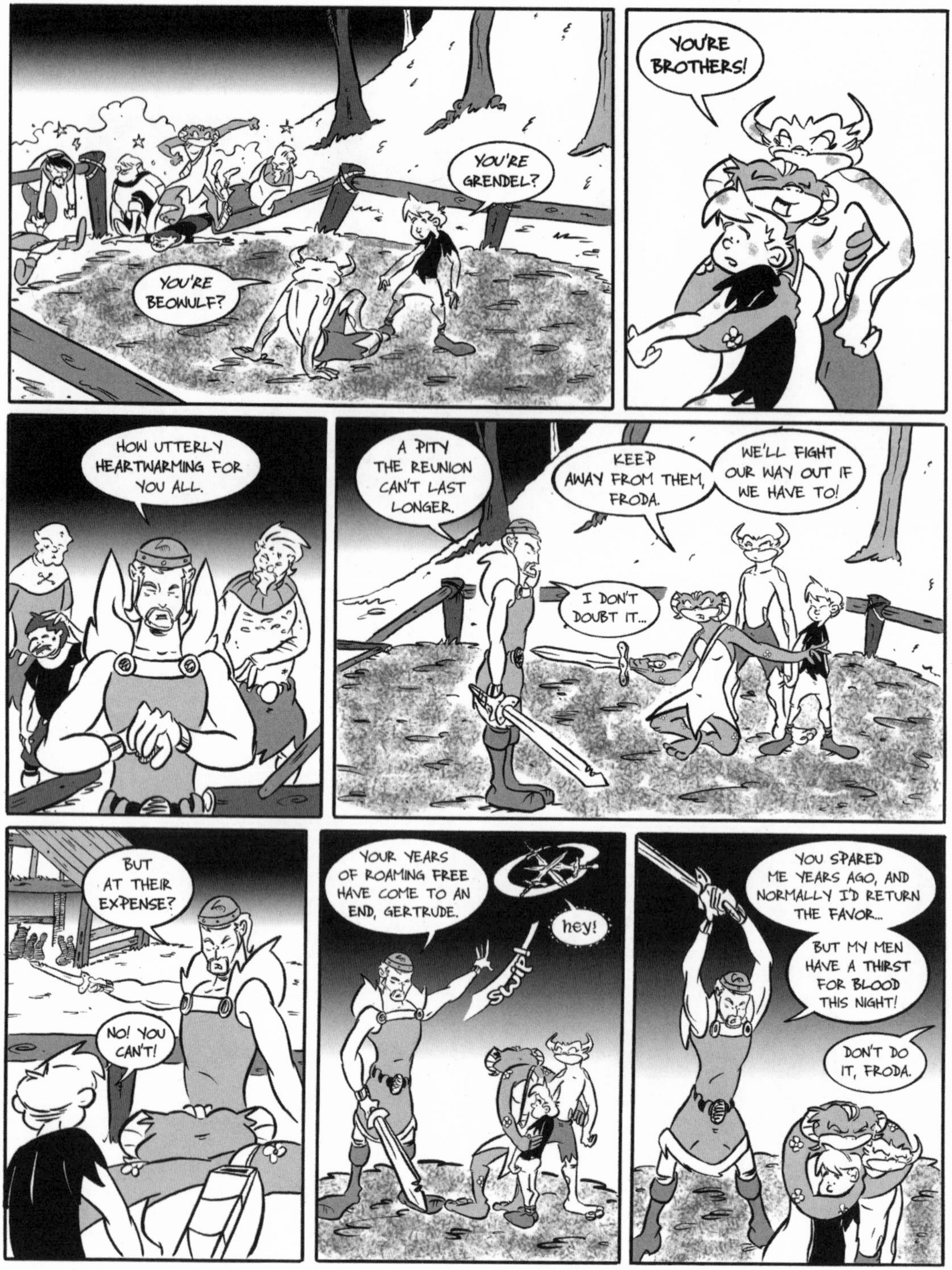

YOU'RE GRENDEL?
YOU'RE BEOWULF?
YOU'RE BROTHERS!
HOW UTTERLY HEARTWARMING FOR YOU ALL.
A PITY THE REUNION CAN'T LAST LONGER.
KEEP AWAY FROM THEM, FRODA.
WE'LL FIGHT OUR WAY OUT IF WE HAVE TO!
I DON'T DOUBT IT...
BUT AT THEIR EXPENSE?
NO! YOU CAN'T!
YOUR YEARS OF ROAMING FREE HAVE COME TO AN END, GERTRUDE.
hey!
SWIP!
YOU SPARED ME YEARS AGO, AND NORMALLY I'D RETURN THE FAVOR...
BUT MY MEN HAVE A THIRST FOR BLOOD THIS NIGHT!
DON'T DO IT, FRODA.

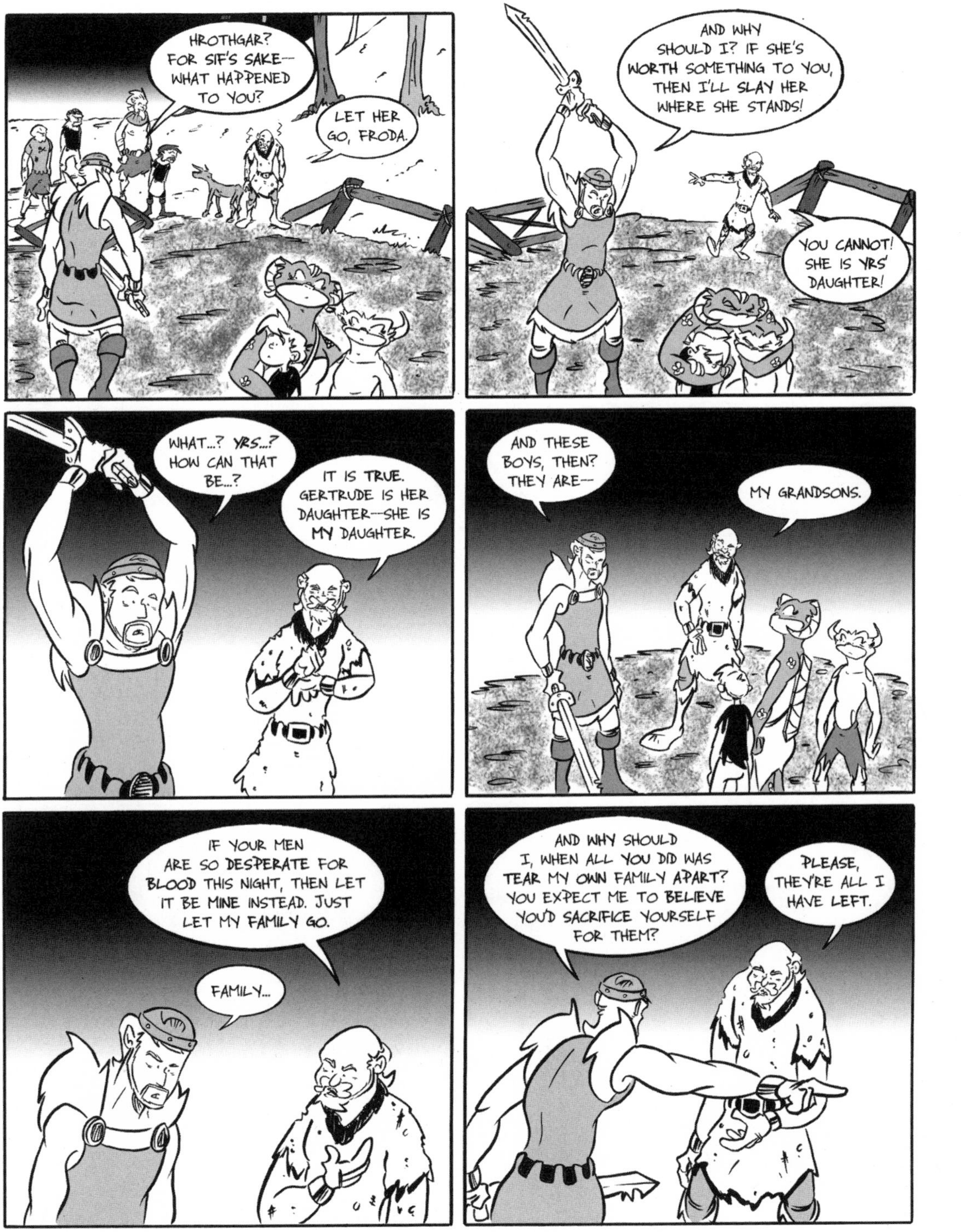
HROTHGAR? FOR SIF'S SAKE--- WHAT HAPPENED TO YOU?
LET HER GO, FRODA.
AND WHY SHOULD I? IF SHE'S WORTH SOMETHING TO YOU, THEN I'LL SLAY HER WHERE SHE STANDS!
YOU CANNOT! SHE IS YRS' DAUGHTER!
WHAT...? YRS...? HOW CAN THAT BE...?
IT IS TRUE. GERTRUDE IS HER DAUGHTER---SHE IS MY DAUGHTER.
AND THESE BOYS, THEN? THEY ARE---
MY GRANDSONS.
IF YOUR MEN ARE SO DESPERATE FOR BLOOD THIS NIGHT, THEN LET IT BE MINE INSTEAD. JUST LET MY FAMILY GO.
FAMILY...
AND WHY SHOULD I, WHEN ALL YOU DID WAS TEAR MY OWN FAMILY APART? YOU EXPECT ME TO BELIEVE YOU'D SACRIFICE YOURSELF FOR THEM?
PLEASE, THEY'RE ALL I HAVE LEFT.

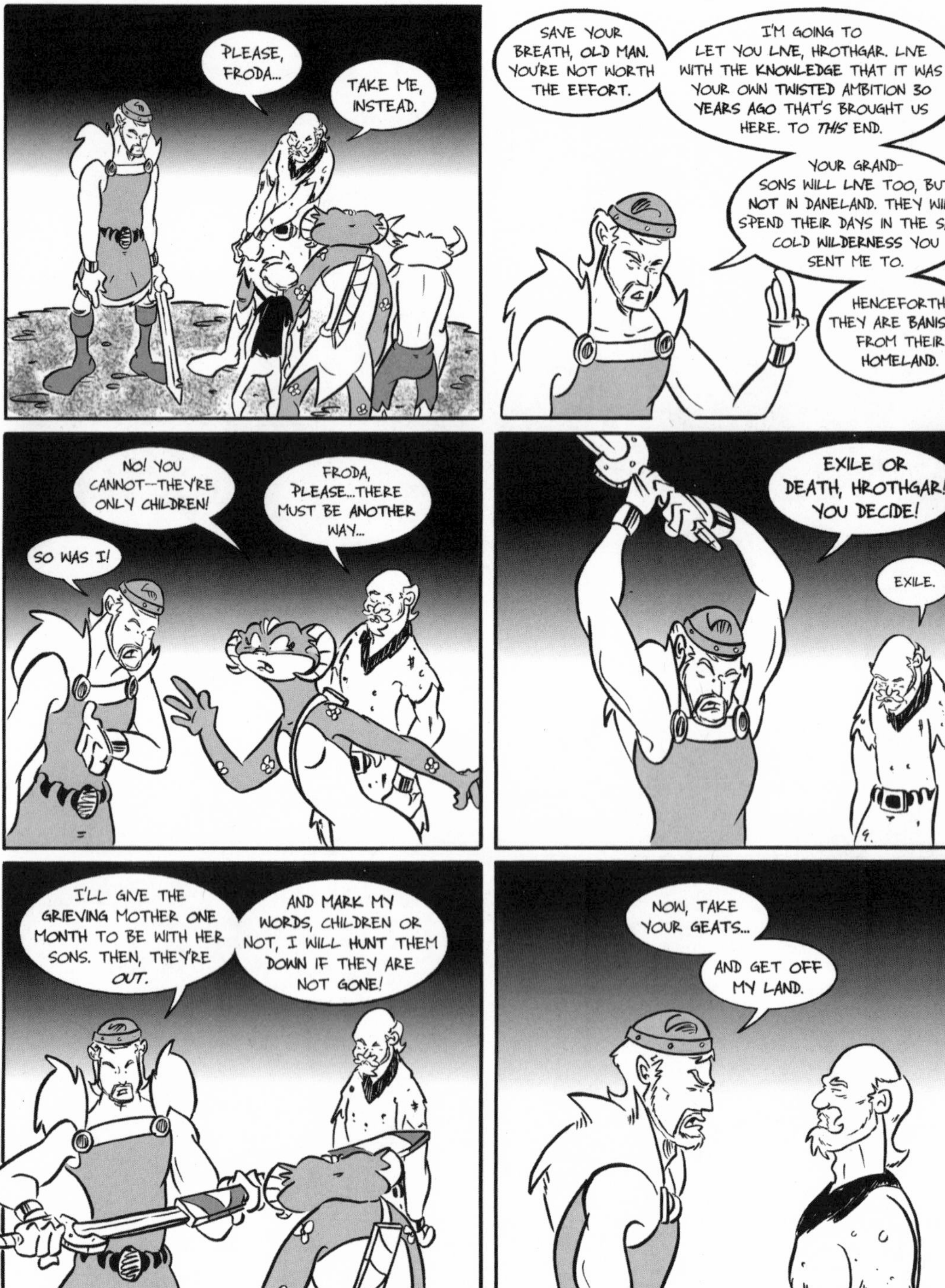
PLEASE, FRODA...
TAKE ME, INSTEAD.
SAVE YOUR BREATH, OLD MAN. YOU'RE NOT WORTH THE EFFORT.
I'M GOING TO LET YOU LIVE, HROTHGAR. LIVE WITH THE KNOWLEDGE THAT IT WAS YOUR OWN TWISTED AMBITION 30 YEARS AGO THAT'S BROUGHT US HERE. TO THIS END.
YOUR GRAND-SONS WILL LIVE TOO, BUT NOT IN DANELAND. THEY WILL SPEND THEIR DAYS IN THE SAME COLD WILDERNESS YOU SENT ME TO.
HENCEFORTH, THEY ARE BANISHED FROM THEIR HOMELAND.
NO! YOU CANNOT--THEY'RE ONLY CHILDREN!
SO WAS I!
FRODA, PLEASE...THERE MUST BE ANOTHER WAY...
EXILE OR DEATH, HROTHGAR! YOU DECIDE!
EXILE.
I'LL GIVE THE GRIEVING MOTHER ONE MONTH TO BE WITH HER SONS. THEN, THEY'RE OUT.
AND MARK MY WORDS, CHILDREN OR NOT, I WILL HUNT THEM DOWN IF THEY ARE NOT GONE!
NOW, TAKE YOUR GEATS...
AND GET OFF MY LAND.

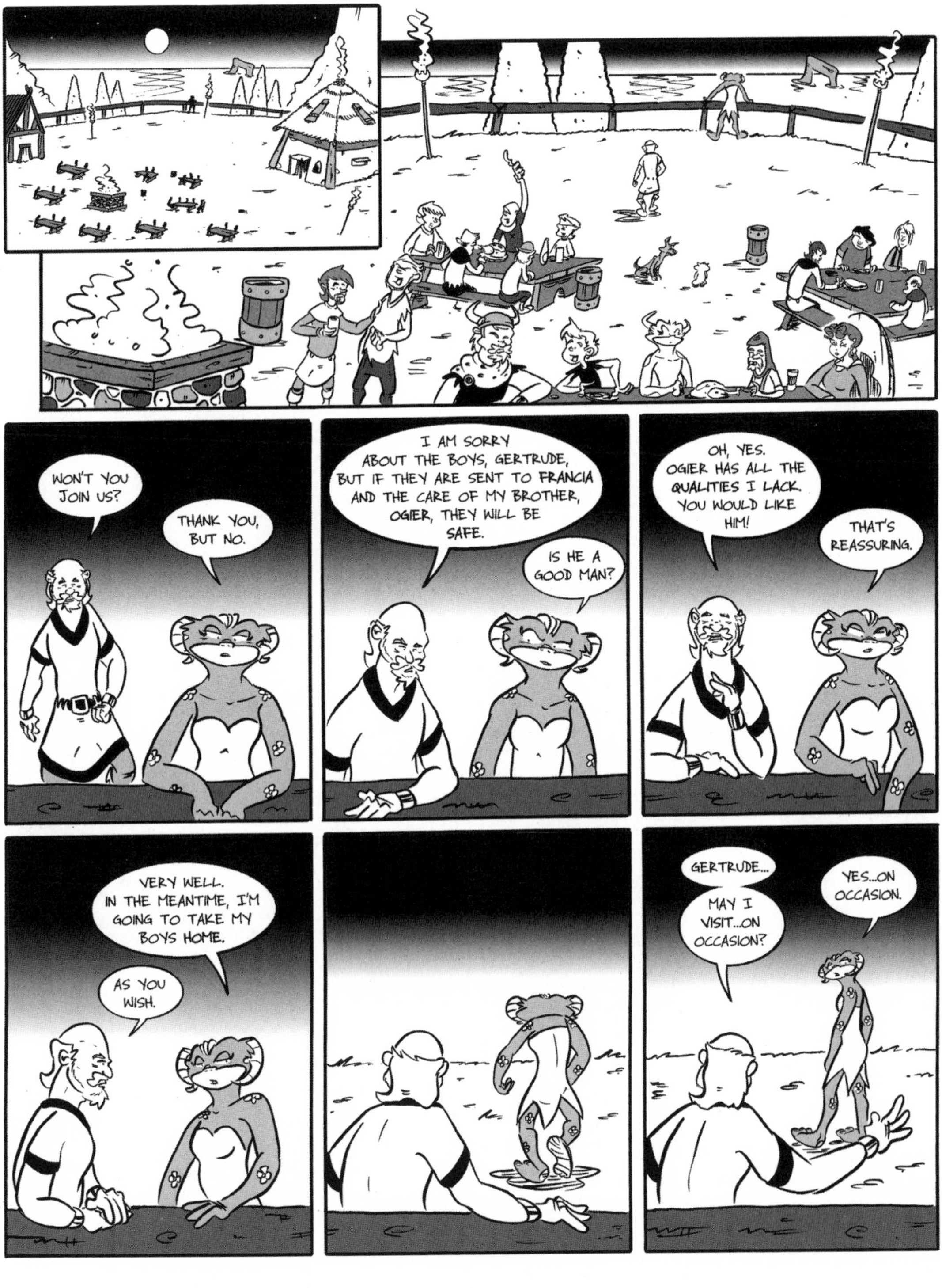
WON'T YOU JOIN US?
THANK YOU, BUT NO.
I AM SORRY ABOUT THE BOYS, GERTRUDE, BUT IF THEY ARE SENT TO FRANCIA AND THE CARE OF MY BROTHER, OGIER, THEY WILL BE SAFE.
IS HE A GOOD MAN?
OH, YES. OGIER HAS ALL THE QUALITIES I LACK. YOU WOULD LIKE HIM!
THAT'S REASSURING.
VERY WELL. IN THE MEANTIME, I'M GOING TO TAKE MY BOYS HOME.
AS YOU WISH.
GERTRUDE...
MAY I VISIT...ON OCCASION?
YES...ON OCCASION.

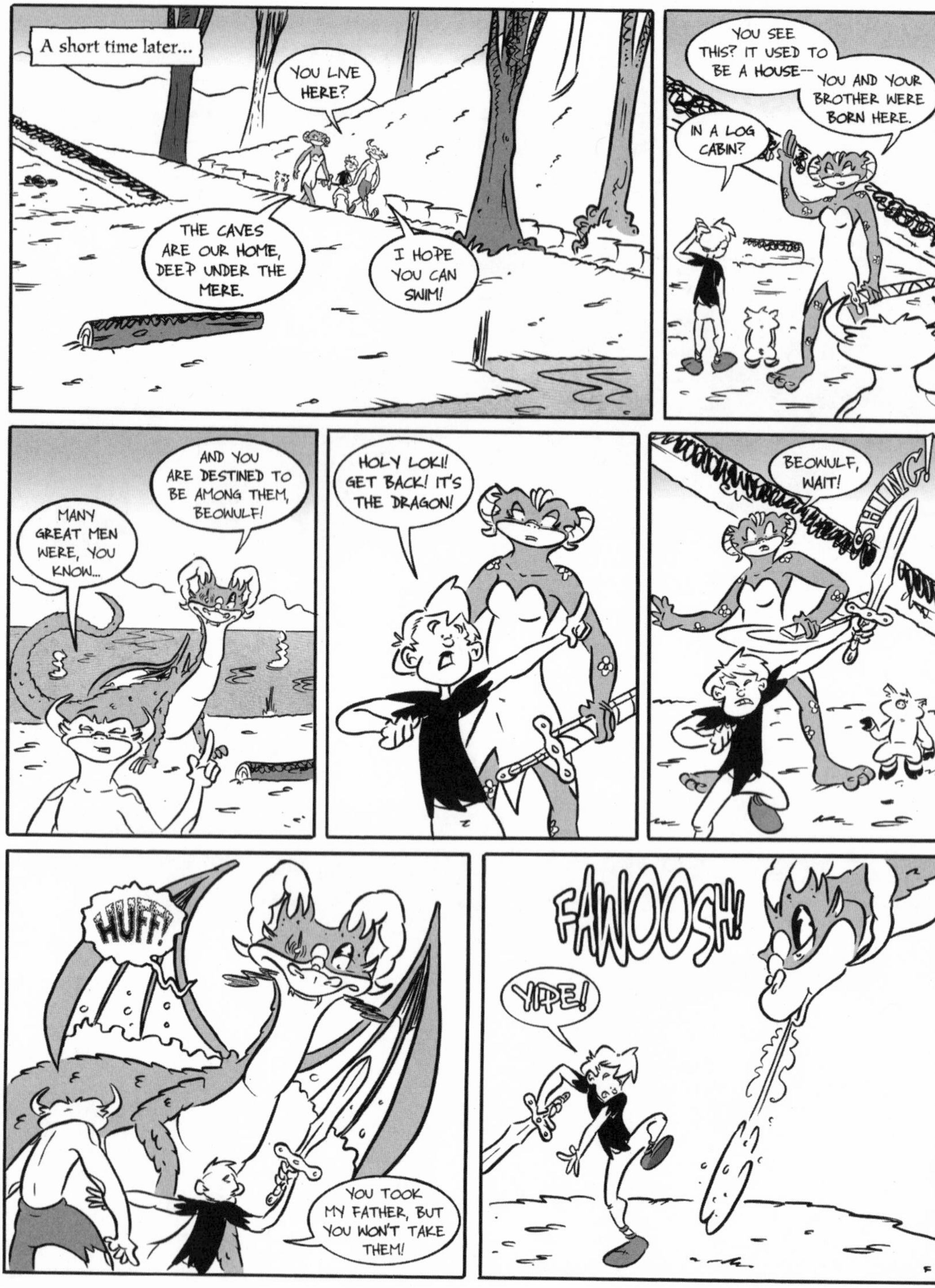
A short time later...
YOU LIVE HERE?
THE CAVES ARE OUR HOME, DEEP UNDER THE MERE.
I HOPE YOU CAN SWIM!
YOU SEE THIS? IT USED TO BE A HOUSE--
YOU AND YOUR BROTHER WERE BORN HERE.
IN A LOG CABIN?
MANY GREAT MEN WERE, YOU KNOW...
AND YOU ARE DESTINED TO BE AMONG THEM, BEOWULF!
HOLY LOKI! GET BACK! IT'S THE DRAGON!
BEOWULF, WAIT!
SHING!
HUFF!
YOU TOOK MY FATHER, BUT YOU WON'T TAKE THEM!
FAWOOSH!
YIPE!

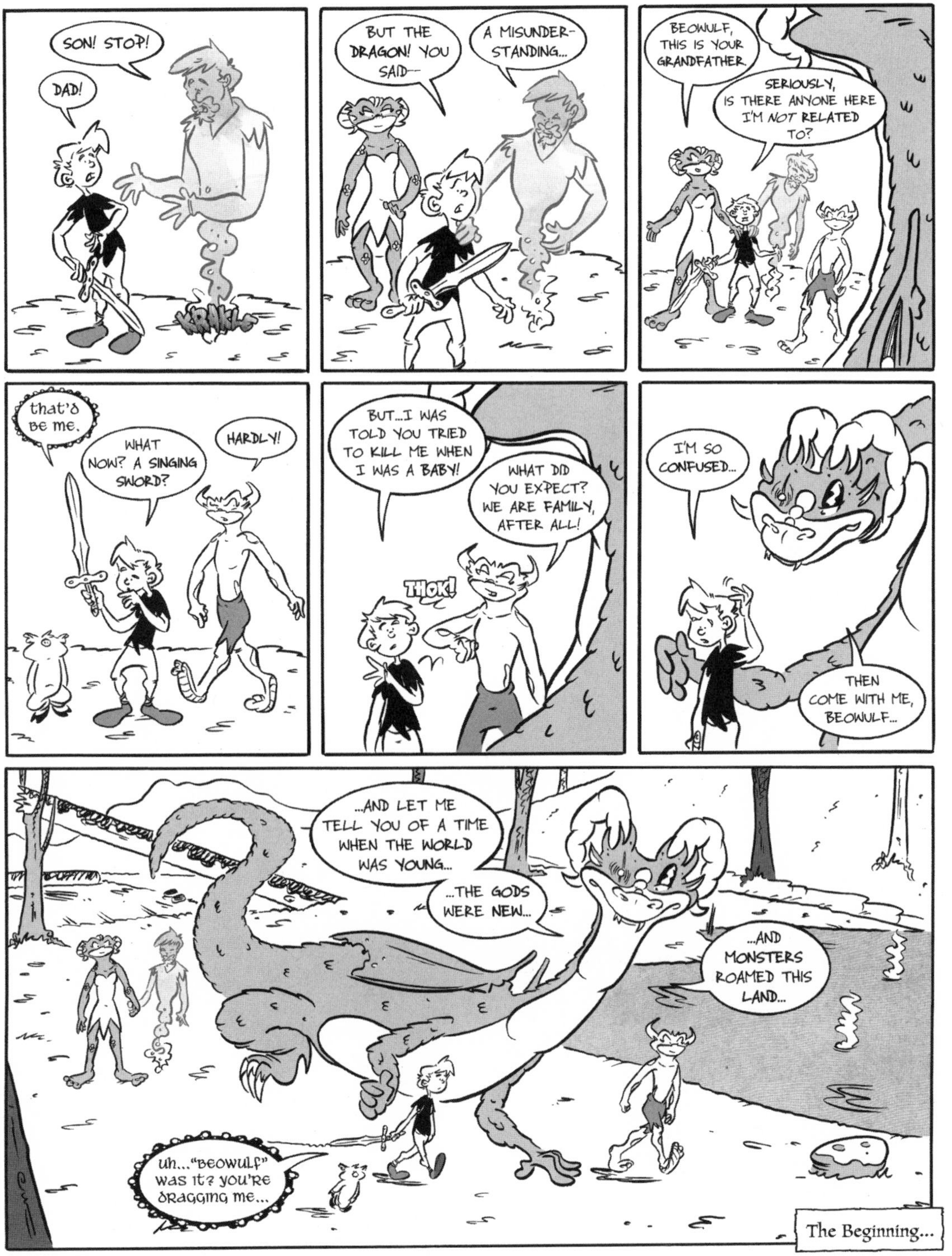
SON! STOP!
DAD!
KRAKLE
BUT THE DRAGON! YOU SAID---
A MISUNDER-STANDING...
BEOWULF, THIS IS YOUR GRANDFATHER.
SERIOUSLY, IS THERE ANYONE HERE I'M NOT RELATED TO?
that'd be me.
WHAT NOW? A SINGING SWORD?
HARDLY!
BUT...I WAS TOLD YOU TRIED TO KILL ME WHEN I WAS A BABY!
WHAT DID YOU EXPECT? WE ARE FAMILY, AFTER ALL!
THOK!
I'M SO CONFUSED...
THEN COME WITH ME, BEOWULF...
...AND LET ME TELL YOU OF A TIME WHEN THE WORLD WAS YOUNG...
...THE GODS WERE NEW...
...AND MONSTERS ROAMED THIS LAND...
uh..."Beowulf" was it? you're dragging me...
The Beginning...

KID BEOWULF WILL RETURN IN...

Kid Beowulf And The Song of Roland

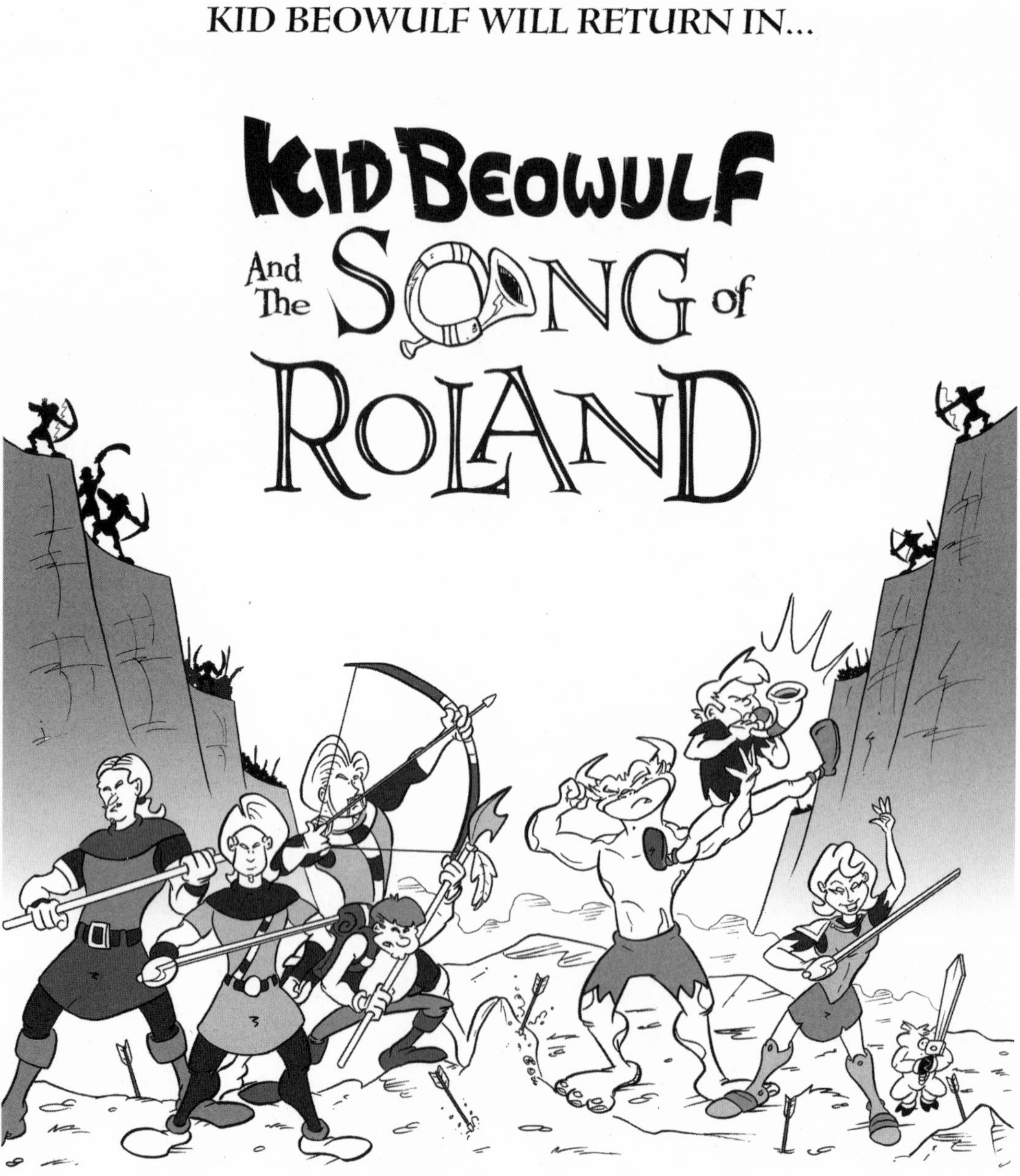